Gla

You're breaking the conditions of your restraining order. Come round here bothering us again, you bastard, and I'll take you back to court.

The bitch. The stinking bitch. Because I never will forgive her for that. For bringing all that dirty washing out in public. And I never will forgive the Law, or trust a court again. Because I thought the Law was there to protect the family and home. But that day they took my kids away from me and awarded them to her and even put restraints on me, their lawful wedded father, I knew the court was solely for the benefit of the adulterers and whores. Because it looks as if a woman can provoke a man to raving madness, or murder, or beyond, by what she does, and go scot-free. But let him only close his knuckles to a fist against her, or phone her up and try to speak to her when she won't talk to him, or lose half a day's pay just to wait and see his own kids coming out of school, and you're in court accused of harassment or molestation or brutality.

Duncan Bush is the author of two collections of poems, *Aquarium* and *Salt*, and a novel, *The Genre of Silence*. His short fiction has been published in *Granta*, *London Magazine* and *Firebird*. He has won the Eric Gregory Award for poetry and two Welsh Arts Council prizes. He lives in Wales.

Glass Shot

DUNCAN BUSH

Mandarin

A Mandarin Paperback

GLASS SHOT

First published in Great Britain 1991
by Martin Secker and Warburg Ltd
This edition published 1993
by Mandarin Paperbacks
an imprint of Reed Consumer Books Ltd
Michelin House, 81 Fulham Road, London SW3 6RB
and Auckland, Melbourne, Singapore and Toronto

Reprinted 1995

Copyright © 1991 Duncan Bush
The author has asserted his moral rights

A CIP catalogue record for this title
is available from the British Library

ISBN 0 7493 1427 3

Printed and bound in Great Britain
by HarperCollins Manufacturing, Glasgow

Acknowledgements

Alimony (Jones/Young) used by kind permission of Supreme Songs Ltd, 1A Waterlow Road, London N19 5JN.

Fun Fun Fun (Brian Wilson/Mike Love), © 1964, Sea of Tunes Pub. Co. Inc., reproduced by kind permission of EMI Music Publishing Ltd, London WC2H 0EA.

Have You Seen Your Mother Baby (Jagger/ Richards) © 1967, used by kind permission of Westminster Music Ltd, Suite 2.07, Plaza 535, King's Road, London SW10 0SZ. International copyright secured. All rights reserved.

Spanish Harlem (Jerry Leiber/Phil Spector) used by kind permission of Carlin Music Corporation, Iron Bridge House, 3 Bridge Approach, Chalk Farm, London NW1 8BD.

These Foolish Things (Eric Maschwitz/Jack Strachey), © 1936, Boosey & Co Ltd, reprinted by kind permission of Boosey & Hawkes Music Publishers Ltd.

Relax (Holly Johnson/Mark O'Toole/Peter Gill), reproduced by kind permission of Perfect Songs Ltd, 42–46 Saint Luke's Mews, London W11 1DG.

Working-Class Hero (John Lennon). © 1970, reproduced by kind permission of Northern Songs, London WC2H 0EA.

C'est faux de dire: Je pense. On devrait dire: On me pense.

(Arthur Rimbaud,
Letter to Georges Izambard,
May 1871)

Glass shot. A shot obtained through a glass plate on which part of the scene has been painted. The painting on the glass is photographed along with the action seen through the clear portion of the glass, providing the illusion of a complete setting. This Special Effect can be used to simulate elaborate locations without the need to construct expensive sets.

(Ephraim Katz,
The International Film Encylopedia,
1982)

One

Christ, they say, is risen.

Me, I'm down. Depressed. Today's Easter Sunday. All day. Right through to midnight. And tomorrow? Easter Monday. Which means another day at home. Which, what with having Good Friday off work too, and yesterday as well, makes it a four-day weekend. Which, aside from not earning an iota of spending money, is a long weekend when you're on your own, just killing the day, awash in the limbo of a sunlit Bank Holiday, watching motor sport on television, eating salted peanuts by the handful, drinking beer.

All this while my wife is probably having a wonderful holiday weekend, making the most of the good weather, off somewhere or other windblown in the car, on day-trips with the kids.

My kids. Though they're not thinking about me at all of course, no more than she is. I'm a forgotten man. I'm not even a random electrical impulse crossing their minds. On a day like this why should I be? They've got the windows down, the sunroof up. And they've got a new life now. With their new Dadda now. Up there in Breconshire, or *Powys* as they call it now.

Because everything changes. Nothing stays the same. The bastards, they won't even leave the names you've always known things by alone.

Like Rutland: that's another case in point. Been Rutland since the Doomsday Book. (The smallest county in England.) All those years. And it's not even a county any more. It's just a part of some conglomerate they call East Midlands.

1

Or take Huntingdonshire. *Huntingdon*: I always thought that was such a lovely, old name, a real old English name, like Arden of Faversham or Westbury on Severn. You know: dogs and deer and yew trees. A lit window in the great house through the mist. But what happened to Huntingdonshire? You tell me. It's a dual-carriageway no-man's-land. It's off the maps. It got absorbed into some other Administrative Rationalisation Scheme, or whatever they damnwell call it. Just like all the other names did, all the beautiful emblazoned names from history.

Because history is all they are now, all those names. You won't see *them* no more. They're about as much use now as a farthing or a sixpence or a two-bob-bit. *Florin*: that's another lovely word you'll never hear again. Gone for ever, like the Maundy penny. Just the word left, floating in amnesia.

Though probably everyone's still got one, somewhere in the house. The two shillings you never got around to spending, before Decimalisation, and now you can't. No longer tender. An old worthless coin tarnishing under the yellow newspaper that lines a drawer. Or in the pocket of some old suit-jacket you haven't taken off its hanger for ten years because you put on too much weight for it, along with the torn half-ticket from some long-dead bus-trip and the grey lint fluff, the eternal, self-engendering bloody fluff.

Or it's in the button-tin. Every household's got a button-tin, where all the odds and ends end up, all the junk that might just come in useful, one day in Eternity. Not just spare buttons but old cotton-reels. A cube of billiard chalk. A card of fuse wire. Brass curtain rings (wedding bands that turn your finger green). Assorted screws. The tail-end of a ball of purple wool, for darning. Half a pair of brown laces. A bone dice (*die* you should say if it's only one). A couple of wooden golf tees. The tiepin you won at a fair. Not to mention various other pieces of tat jewellery, wealth beyond measure, loose pearls no one ever bothered rethreading, a brooch with a ruby as big as a pigeon's egg but not worth a light any more because the pin got snapped. Or, talk about useless riches, all those foreign coins you collected or swapped off someone when you were a kid. There's always one of those hexagonal Chinese ones, with a hole in the middle. I used to have a few of those. I suppose the Old Man must have brought them home from sea. *Polo money*, he used to call it. Not because Marco Polo discovered China, but because of the hole. Because, like he always said (ha fucking ha), it must have been made at the Polo Mint.

Anyway. You know the kind of stuff I mean. Things nobody wants but nobody can bear to throw away.

When I was a kid I used to spend hours sorting through that old button-tin we had at home. You'd have thought it was a treasure-chest. And my kids are the same. Household junk of any kind fascinates them. Mandy used to love picking about in all those bits and bobs. Like a jackdaw. I suppose it's because we're all collectors, at heart.

And why not? Because, let's face it, this is history too: all the different things that over the years end up in this one tin. An old tin which, like I say, probably every household in the country has. And which, if only you knew how to read it, might tell you more about those people's lives than anything else could, more even than the contents of their dustbin. (They always say that's the best way to find out what someone's secrets are, just sift through their weekly rubbish. No man is a hero to his dustman.)

And I can't help wondering if *they've* got a tin like that now. If they've started one. Him and Her. Janet and John. Up there in Powys. An old *Quality Street* toffee-tin, or *Rose's Chocolates*, though any old container with a lid would do.

Somewhere in which they too, and my kids, my fucking kids, flesh of my flesh, sweat of my body, salt of my loins, are already starting one of those little intimate assortments of their life together. Just like the one they left me in the sideboard cupboard here.

And perhaps it's really a thing like this which is the essence or true history of any relationship, or marriage, or family. The real truth of years and lives spent together in the same house. Just a tin of miscellaneous household oddments to a stranger, but a collection peculiar and unique to every family in the land, and with some forgotten story attached to every single item it contains. So that, in the end – if you all just manage to stay together that long, which is one big fucking if – it should be buried with you in the family plot, in the same way that to help him on the journey a Pharaoh would have taken all his jewellery into the Pyramid with him, and corn, and oil.

Though perhaps that's even why she left it here, the cunt.

Because it isn't just the things they take away from you that gnaw you to the bone. It's all the things they leave behind as well.

Let me tell you about him. About Raoul.

He's a teacher. No need to say what a shining precept and in loco parentis he must be to all his youthful charges (including at the moment, of course, mine).

I mean, we're not just talking about adultery here. (In fact, we're not talking about adultery at all. Fuck the adultery. I don't give a shit about the adultery.) We're talking about someone who'll not only desert his own two children but take away another man's as well.

We're talking, in other words, about a minge-rag who'll blight four small children's lives for his own pleasure.

Raoul is not his actual name.

But it's the name I always call him by, because he teaches French. Like calling him her *beau*, or asking if

4

he did the tango too or fucked her with a rose between his teeth.

Not that any sneer I was going to make was going to hurt her the way she'd hurt me, the bitch, the way she'd cut me to the quick. But trying to find some way of goading her at least, of paying her out for that time when all I think she wanted was for me to sit down opposite her long enough so she could explain it, tell me all about *Her Lover*, as she actually had the unbelievable gall to call him to my face, or that other time when she wanted me to stay home from work, lose pay, to spend all day chewing the fat, and the gristle too, about the reason why Our Marriage had gone On The Rocks.

Because I wouldn't ever use his name. I wouldn't give her the satisfaction. The pleasure of hearing her word for him in my mouth. Everything might have been *Gary Gary Gary* to her. (Out loud, for all I know, when he was screwing her. Or like a rosary underneath her breath, besides.) But not to me. Not me.

I wouldn't even look at the photograph of him the bitch wanted to show me. I laughed at her. I couldn't believe it.

Did he sign it? I said. You know, personal? Did he write a dedication on it, just for me?

(Like I should have been a member of his Official Fan Club or some fucking thing.)

I thought you might be interested, she said. I thought we might be able to talk about it. That's all. And I just thought you might want to know what he looks like.

(I mean, can you *imagine* that?)

Fuck you, I said. Fuck the both of you. I hope you scream in hell.

I wouldn't meet him, either. Which was another of her bright ideas. Or actually his, apparently. So we could Talk the Situation Over, Man to Man, I suppose he meant.

I wouldn't, then. And I feel just the same about it now. Not meet in that way, anyway. The so-called Civilised

5

way. Good stiff handshake and, Good Luck, old sport,
all's fair in lust and war, my blessing on you both.

Fuck that.

Like I told her, Listen, I said, don't bother your head
trying to set up dramas like that. Little triangles. I'm not
this guy. I didn't go to Jesus College fucking Cambridge.
Me, I'll settle for being an uncouth. A plain barbarian.

And like they say, Revenge is a dish best served and
eaten cold. An old Sicilian proverb.

And so *Raoul* will do. When it comes down to it, his
real name I don't need to know. What's in a name?

Just say, Raoul, and watch him turn his head and look
at me, Raoul, not understanding, and I'll look back at
him and say, Raoul, this is for you, and put two barrels
of a shotgun to his eye, and that he'll understand.

Like I said, he teaches French. In some school or other.
Up there in Powys.

I suppose he would. I suppose it's chickens coming
home to roost. Because Carol, my wife, did French at
university, that year she was there. That was where I
met her, in point of fact. I was working as a scaffolder on
this new extension they were doing for the Engineering
Block. (That used to be a joke I'd tell people from time
to time: We met At University. Ha fucking ha.)

We met in the student cafeteria. They used to let the
men use the cafeteria at lunchtimes.

We happened to be sitting opposite each other this
day, and we started talking because she had a slug in
her salad. I'm not kidding. She suddenly put down her
knife and fork and looked across at me. Then she looked
back at her plate.

There's a slug in this salad, she said.

I leaned over to look, and it was true, she showed it
to me with the tip of her fork, a tiny grey slug on this
leaf of lettuce.

So what? I said. You vegetarian or something?

6

I could have eaten that, she said.

That's true enough, I said. But if you had it would have been because you didn't know you had. And if you didn't know you had you wouldn't be complaining. So what are you complaining about now?

Look at it like this, I said. It's protein.

Trying to keep things going, you know. I didn't want to blow a chance like that. Because, with chicks, beginnings are always the hard part. Kick-starting the whole thing. But if you can get past that and get a conversation going, crack a corny joke or two, you're halfway up.

Because I'd noticed her before that day, around the place. In those old cut-off jeans she used to wear to show off her legs. And she was always in the cafeteria when I took my break, sitting around smoking and talking with that other girl, the dark-haired one with the green eye makeup, and usually a couple of fellers, except the fellers were sometimes different.

And I'd glanced her over once or twice across the table that lunchtime, to be honest. But I would never have spoken to her first because, well, I'm not saying I would have been too nervous. Me? I've never been nervous of a fucking woman in my life. But it would have been, you know. Uncool. You know what they're like, some of those college girls. I mean, just because you'd have old jeans on and a T-shirt and wear spanners hanging at your belt they'd look at you, some of those chicks, as if to say, My God, a workman. A common fucking workman. What's he doing at a university?

Anyway. Working clothes or not, I never got back on site that day. We sat there all afternoon after that, talking, this and that, drinking about a dozen cups of coffee each. Then I asked her if she fancied a walk, get some air.

It was a lovely day. All the, you know, trees in the park were really out. End of May, it must have been, or June. I shagged her down along by the river. Then again, back in her room.

And that was it.

Jesus, I couldn't get enough of her. I'd never had a student before.

I thought I had it made.

And in the mornings all I had to do, now, was fall out of that little single bed of hers in the hall of residence and stroll over to the site by eight, ready for work. Which was a whole lot better than having to get up at half six and hang around by the lights in Clare Road for the crewbus to show up.

A couple of weeks later, when I did a vanishing act out of that tip of a room in Tudor Road, and moved lock, stock and both bags in with her, I wasn't even paying rent.

I did. I thought I had it made.

But then of course she had to go and blow all that and get herself kicked out. I don't suppose her French was up to much, when it came down to it. In any case, she managed to mess up her first-year exams without too much difficulty. Then fail the re-sits too.

Well, we were out every night of the fucking week. And she never did do much work, as far as I could see. That was her word for it. I must go over to the library and Do Some Work today, she'd say. But she hardly ever did. And what she called work I'd call sitting reading.

The Flesh Is Sad, Alas, and I've Read All the Books: that was another thing she used to say. It was like a standing joke she and that chick Anna had going between them.

But had she? Had she, fuck. I think I read more of her books than she did. She'd hardly read a damn one of them. Let alone in the French.

So I don't know how bright she really was. I suppose she must have known enough to get there in the first place. But then, there's a lot of bright people who never got into a university, and a lot of dullards who did.

Don't give me all this political crap, I used to tell her. The Student Union this, the Student Body that. What the fuck do students know about anything? Most of the people here, I'd jump over their fucking heads. Mentally speaking. It's just I haven't had your chances.

And I proved that when we had that bet and she sent off for that IQ test you could do at home. Of course, she tried to argue later, when the scores came back and I told her how I'd done it, that I'd probably only got that score by cheating. But I said that if you're keeping time and you tell me I've only got sixty seconds left before you blow the whistle and I know I'm not even going to finish the question I'm on, it makes obvious sense to at least make a blind guess at that one and then put down blind guesses for the other questions I haven't quite managed to do or even got to, just ring one of the possible answers from each one, purely on the off-chance of a lucky shot.

You're just cheating yourself, she said. If you hadn't done that, at least you'd really know what your IQ is. But now you'll never know. Okay, you can kid yourself you scored that. But secretly you know it might be a lot less. It probably is, she said.

Yeah, I said. It might be really low. It might be a real cretin's score. Like, about 153.

Which of course was what she'd got. Which was actually a pretty good score. (I think they reckon you have to beat 148 to be bright enough to join Mensa.)

At least I know that's a real score, she said. Without the help of guesses. At least I *know* I scored that many myself.

Listen, I said, this is a fucking intelligence test. What's the intelligent thing to do if you got sixty seconds left? Let it freeze you out of even finishing the answer you're on? Just sit and watch the hand tick round? I had the same exact, timed hour as you did, I said. How I use the time, that's my choice.

It's still cheating, she said. Just because you get a

multiple-choice question doesn't mean you're supposed to have free guesses.

There's a good chance of you scoring nought on them, I said. I agree with that. And I probably did. But if you don't answer at all scoring nought's a cast-iron fucking certainty. So it's not 'cheating', I told her. It's Maximising Your Chances. It's *intelligence*.

Anyway, what the fuck. It was French she did.

And when you come to think of it, it's mostly girls who do. Do French in university. You ever notice that?

I suppose because it's got some kind of snob appeal for them, it's *chic* and all that shit. Let's face it, they're nineteen, twenty years of age and they're romantics. A couple of stages on from Barbie dolls, and now it's French is *style*. And they probably think that doing French will help get them a French boyfriend too, because in the third year they get a chance to spend a term somewhere in France, to polish up their accent and so on. And that's what they all want. A gen-u-ine French lover. Fucking Armand or Michel. Some thin wiry little gink in a Breton fisherman's jersey with the buttons on one shoulder, like that character on the hovercraft when we went to the hypermarket in Calais that time, who kept pulling that crushed packet out of the pocket of his skin-tight stone-washed Levis and taking out a crumpled cigarette and letting it droop down from one corner of his mouth, looking at you quizzical, with a droll face, well, at Carol actually, but carefully enough to include me too, his eyes half shut, almost laughing, all the time as if to say, Look at me, look at me! Because he couldn't even light a cigarette, the twat, without showing off trying to do a Humphrey Bogart, convinced he's a comic, a real card, a regular Fernandel. And knowing that that's exactly what they want, the slags. Someone with *Personality*, they always call it. I.e. some jokester with one of those phoney Sacha Distel accents and a Gauloise-flavoured

French kiss on some balmy Paris night. Some character with a thin brown hairless body like a stripling boy's but with a nice fat dick. That's all they want when they're nineteen or twenty.

I suppose that's all they want at any age.

Anyway, she never got to that third year in France. She never even made it to the second. So she missed out on all that. The romance of France went out the window, along with the grant, the room, the degree, the future job with the United Nations, the ruined châteaus she'd heard that you could buy up for a song, all the other fucking mighthavebeens. She had to settle for me instead, and a rented flat in Riverside, and working mornings in a flower shop, which was all she could get at that time. And then Mandy coming along. And then Darryl. And the four of us trying to manage year in year out on a fitter's wages.

And in the end, the bitch, that wasn't good enough. And that's what I mean about chickens coming home to roost. Even if finally the nearest thing to France and a French lover she could happen on at thirty-one and with two kids in tow was obviously some married man with two kids of his own who *teaches* French. I suppose the bastard at least speaks the language partly.

Me, I work at the Quick-Change Service Centre, on the Newport Road. I'm the guy who fits you a new radiator or battery or exhaust system. Or I change your tyre for you when you limp in on the treadless spare you've had for years under the carpet in the boot.

Mostly I'm in the tyre bay now. It's easy enough work, with all the machinery they've got these days, right up from a hydraulic clamp to strip the old tyres off with. You try doing that all day with tyre levers, like you used to have to. These days the only hint of skill comes when I've got the stripped hub on the machine and I take you to the racks of tyres and offer you the Big Choice,

11

which, let's face it, is the same option wherever you go, whatever you're buying. Cheap or dear. You can have the C55 Radial, with a year's cover on accidents, at £28.12, valve and balancing free. Or you can go for the basic G33 at £22.32, valve and balancing extra. You can have Firestone, Dunlop, Michelin, Pirelli at over £30 a throw. Or you can get our own Quick-Change brand remould at around a score. To me the only diff. is I get a percentage of the extra for every sale of the more expensive tyres. Which I suppose I'm supposed to try to talk you into. But the commission's not that great, and usually I can tell straight off the price of tyre you'll go for anyway, by the state of your car. Still, now and then, when I think it's worth it, I'll go through the various spiels and rigmaroles, price versus reliability et cetera. Your main principle, as the national average small car-owner and general pleb-about-town, is that you want to save money, but don't like to be thought of as a cheapskate who cuts corners on his children's safety. People are definitely more safety-conscious lately. Also, nobody likes anyone, even a garage mechanic, to think they're driving around a car they can't afford the proper upkeep on. (People are very vulnerable about the cars they drive. Because they're all one of two things. They're either proud of their cars or just a little ashamed. In either case, that's how car maintenance, accessory shops, auto magazines, and all the rest of it, get to be what they are. Big bucks.)

So you stand there looking at all those new tyres in the racks and wondering if the extra's really worth it. When you come right down to it, tyres all look pretty much the same to you. (Yeah, to me too, especially when you have to change the bastards fifty times a day.) But it's surprising, if you put your mind to it, how many people you can nudge and shrug towards buying the more expensive type of tyre, even if the doors are hanging off the car. (It's what we at Quick-Change call a Pressure Sale, ha fucking ha.)

12

Anyway, you pays your money and you takes your choice. All I got to do then is bounce the tyre down from the rack, roll it over to the stand, put it under the clamp, and it's on the hub. No time at all. All I got to do now is balance the wheel, another dead cinch job these days. It's all digitalised, and you just read the balance off at a glance on the computer. So you can see at exactly what part of the rim there's an adjustment to be made. And that's all there is to it. It's as simple as that. A child could do it. Even a Quick-Change fitter can do it. That's computerisation for you. That machine cost thirteen grand, by the way. At least, that's what they tell us. But it must be worth it to Quick-Change because it saves so much time on the old way, getting bubbles centred and so on.

But then, that's why they call us Quick-Change, because we're all so slick. Big fucking deal.

Probably you'll have seen the television ads the company runs. This team of handpicked grinning dolts doing a kind of ballet, of mechanics dancing around a motor bay in nice clean new blue overalls and singing:

> *A Quick-Change fitter can change it quicker*
> *A Quick-Change fitter can fit it better.*

Et cetera. These are actors of course. (So-called.) But now, since that ad started appearing the real mechanics, us, actual human beings, have to wear the same message on the back of *our* overalls too. A Quick-Change Fitter Does It Quicker. Some genius must have dreamed it up as the company jingle, and so now it's got to go on everything, like *Barry Island* through a stick of seaside rock. And another thing we have to wear now is this yellow smiley face, on the chest pocket. The Sunshine Boy. The Have A Good Day man, Mister Customer Friendly.

But I tell you one thing, though (and I don't mean two). What's different from the ad is that no one sings in our outfit. No, nor fucking dances either. Not in a normal day. Not unless they're pissing around, in fact, which to tell the truth is a thing you have to do sometimes. Because it might be an easy job to do, but it's such lousy dirty boring repetitive work, taking off old tyres or filthy exhausts all day and fitting new ones, that no matter what rolls up on the forecourt, whether it's a Mini or a Maserati or a Mercedes fucking Benz, believe me, once you've done that on one car you've done it on the lot.

The big, the only, plus is that sometimes of course it'll be cunt in the car. And sometimes, if only on the law of averages, some of them have got to be sharp lookers. Which at least relieves the numbing boredom of a long day helping the driving public. In fact, just as a pickmeup, it's better than an egg in sherry. In fact, most of the time you're there, it's all you think about. No kid. It's what you live and die for.

Take the blonde who came in the other day. (Man, I've been thinking about her ever since.) Thursday, this was. Little MG sports. B-reg. Wire hubs, whitewall tyres, British Racing Green. (I say blonde, but she wasn't what you'd call a light blonde, a Monroe blonde. It was more of a kind of rusty gold. A tawny, almost.) She said she'd had a blowout on the motorway.

I left her by the car and came in to get the pricelist for her from the desk.

Jesus Haitch Christ, Dennis said.

He was standing in the doorway to the other office, staring out across the tyre bay.

Who the fuck is that? he said.

I didn't say a damn thing. I was trying to ignore him.

I'd give a full month's wages for a half an hour with that, he said.

He stood watching her, his eyes shifting.

14

Especially if she left them boots on, he said.

He was a like a man stock-still in some worried trance. Then he looked at me and saw me watching him. A weasel's grin. The little quick, furtive, dark-pupilled, wanker's eyes.

Hey, Yank, he said. Tell her she can squat on my face any time she feels like.

Try getting a new scriptwriter, I told him.

I shrugged and looked around, like I couldn't remember where I'd put down a tool. Because people don't need to know what your private thoughts are in a situation like that. Talk's cheap but cashing it is hard, and it's safer acting as if you hadn't even noticed the girl, or as if to say, Who? Which one? Oh. Her. Yeah, not a bad-looking chick. So what's your problem? (Meaning, Me, I got about as much of that kind of thing as I can manage at the moment.)

The same applies with them too, the girls. I try not to be too talkative or over-friendly, and I make sure I keep my eyes mostly on the job. It's policy.

Take with the blonde. She seemed a little shaken up still, just going back over it, talking a bit too much and too fast, telling me when I hadn't actually asked her how she all of a sudden felt this wobble in the steering, at first she thought it was wind hitting her broadside, then she thought it must be the steering itself, and that, she said, was the only reason she started to slow down and move back into the middle lane. And then the wobble worsened and she started to brake and suddenly, my God, she heard it running on the rim and she said she still didn't realise it was a puncture but she knew from the noise something was wrong so she swerved straight across the slow lane and onto the hard shoulder, And thank God, she said, that lane was empty and I didn't cause a pileup (I suppose she panicked so much she didn't even look in the rear-view mirror before she swung the wheel). And, like she kept saying, What if

15

it had all happened just a little bit quicker than it did? I.e. if she was still in the fast lane doing seventy-five or eighty, like she might have been, and with two full lanes of traffic inside her so there wasn't room to pull across?

I carried on spinning off the wheel-nuts, squatted down.

One in the back tyre's not so bad, I said. Because you don't get the same problems controlling the car. It's when you get a sudden blowout at speed in one of the front wheels you're in trouble. You're not talking about a wobble then. You're trying to stop the whole thing swerving all over the road.

So in a way I was lucky? she said. That it was that tyre and not one of the front ones?

She had a nice, English voice. You know, no accent to speak of.

I suppose you could say that, I said. If you can ever count a puncture as lucky.

(Though lucky was exactly what I already knew this one to be.)

That's some consolation, she said.

She laughed. She still hadn't quite got over it, you could tell. As a mechanic, I see a lot of people like this. People like to drive as if they're going to live for ever. Then something goes wrong even at only fifty, sixty miles an hour and by the time they've nursed the car in here they realise that if things had just gone slightly differently they might have died today out on the motorway. Of pure bad luck, just coming into work.

And it was one of the situations where I could have said more, I could have given her the, you know, odd reassuring smile or two. Used the old eyes. She'd had this shock, and it made her nervous, chatty. Flirtatious, you could almost say. She wanted to talk to someone about it. And anyone would do. And I was the one, I happened to be there.

But with this chick I knew I wanted to play it stone-cold safe and absolutely cast-iron sure.

Because as soon as I saw her step out of that little low green sports job, with that short blonde hair and those long blonde legs, I felt my heart shrink in my chest, and I felt almost sick with it. With wanting. That feeling you get sometimes, like a sudden light quick punch in the pit of your stomach, when out of the blue some girl swings past you on the street in summer, and it's there, it's all there, everything you ever dreamed of before you even saw it. And it's so blatant. So flagrant. It's walking down the street. It's on the town. It's sweet and clean and young and fresh and beautiful, and it's in a summer dress. But you know it's hers. It's all of it hers. It's none of it for you.

So why try anything out there, on a garage forecourt?

Because I knew that in that situation, no matter how conversational she got with me, or let me get with her, no matter how many smiles and shy looks we flashed each other, that would only be my way of passing time. And that would only be her way of getting me, or any other man, to do what she wanted him to, which in this instance was change her offside tyre. It's an instinct they can't resist, women with looks like that. Handling the interested male. They grow up knowing it from fifteen on.

Besides, how can you try on the charm when it's three o'clock on a Thursday afternoon, this is the couple of dozenth car you've serviced today, and your hands and face and fingernails and overalls are filthy with all the shit and grease and rust and oil and general crud, and if that wasn't enough, you're wearing blue uniform overalls cut about as baggy in the waist and as short in the leg as a clown's suit in the circus (plus a smiley face and *Have A Nice Day!* on the chest pocket too). I.e. a real sartorial stunner. Authentic cool. Not even to mention that every time you turn away to pick up a spanner or kneel to loosen the wheel-nuts off, or tighten them, she can't help reading right across your back, in day-glo red, the famous words, *A Quick-Change Fitter Does It Quicker*?

Do you really think you'd have a chance?

Don't make me fucking laugh.

Besides, More haste equals less speed. A saying that's never truer than when you're trying to find the way to get inside a woman. Move too fast, too anxious, and it gets them nervous. You have to slow the whole game down. And, above all, act as if this thing is already destined. Fated.

Which, in fact, the random chance of a puncture on a motorway already made it.

1. Because as soon as she started losing air on that section of the M4 before Junction 29, and all the time she sat parked on the hard shoulder waiting for the AA service van to show up so the guy could jack it up and put on the spare wheel, she was always coming here to pick up a new tyre. Because Quick-Change is the biggest and most obvious, if not the only, firm doing instant services this side of the city.

2. And, when she got to Quick-Change, she was always going to get Stew Boyle to do the work on it for her, since that particular Thursday I was the only one on in the tyre bay, because Danny was off sick.

And so, even on that first meeting, once I'd heard what the problem was and gone in for the pricelist, when I came back out again at least I knew I would act calm. That I didn't need to get flustered or anxious or sick to my stomach again with that winded feeling, that awful sense of the loss of her. (Because that's what that feeling is like. It's like a grief for what you've never had. And are never going to get.)

I knew that I didn't even want or need to keep glancing at those legs criss-crossing criss-crossing as she walked in front of me across the concrete in those white fringed boots. (Let alone stand hungering after her like Dennis, still hovering in the office window, nose near-enough pressed white against the glass.)

No, what slowed my heartbeat down, what kept my look level, and polite, was knowing I didn't have to live off this one occasion, didn't have to feed off what I could take in of her through my eyes this time. That I already had her where I wanted her, since out of all the breakdowns and skids and shattered windscreens and collisions and fatalities that happen on the roads each day, all day, this one puncture had been fated. I.e. that she was as good as in the Book with all the rest.

So she was right about it being a lucky puncture.

(Lucky for some.)

At first I used to be scared for a long time after I saw a girl I had to have as much as that. I'd be shaky, trembly, for days after. And then for days before. But now it only lasts for that minute or so, when it hits me, when I see them for the first time. It's like you lose all your breath. But then I control it, I start breathing deeper and slower, and I just go along with the situation. With what I know I've got to do.

(Which at that particular moment, first things first et cetera, was simply keep spinning off the nuts and finish the job she was paying for.)

I knew that ten minutes later I'd be taking her into the office. (Or, more likely, if Dennis was still in there, I'd fetch the docket-book out to the tyre bay instead.) Clipboard in hand, I'd jot down the price of the job and the Registration Number and get a couple of other details, like Make and Year of car. Then cool, professional, biro poised, as casual as hell, enquire:

Name, miss?

And then:

Address?

*

Sometimes by then I already know something about the girl, some background. You'd be surprised what you can find out about someone just from having their car in your hands for ten minutes.

Okay, I'll say for example. I'm going to be a little while here. Why don't you go into the waiting-room over there and have a seat? Have a look at the magazines or get yourself a cup of coffee from the machine, and I'll call you when I'm finished. Oh, and leave me the keys will you? I need to pull it over a yard or two.

Then I do the job as per normal, drive the car out of the bay and park it for her in the forecourt (all part of the personal service, miss, your smiling idiot Quick-Change fitter here, we only exist to oblige).

It doesn't matter what clues or hard info I pick up. It's all circumstantial, all part of a Life. To me, it's all erotic. And it's all of use. I might get a chance to take a swift glance in the glove compartment. Or sometimes they even leave a handbag on the seat. You can tell a lot about someone from the state of the dashboard ashtray sometimes.

But hard information's obviously even better. For instance, I think I probably already know where the blonde girl works. Because on the back shelf she had these bundles of travel brochures, for Spain and Greece and Portugal and places, and on the passenger seat was a red plastic folder or document wallet with a lot of typed junk inside about various hotels, size of room, number of beds, and so on. On the cover of the folder it said *Asprey Travel*, with the address of their office in St Mary Street. But I'll check that out next week.

Now and then of course, like the boy in the fairy-story, you find out what you'd rather not. Like yesterday, with that dark, Lebanese-looking girl in jeans in that old Cortina with the exhaust outlet dragging on the floor.

I've had to drive here with it like this from Neville

Street, she said. Just hoping I wouldn't pass a copper on the way.

Nice, I thought when I was talking to her. And a nice arse. Not bad at all.

But she turned out to be a real sloven. I mean, when I got in it the car was ankle-deep in sweet-wrappers and cigarette ash and last week's newspapers. You could tell it hadn't been properly hoovered out for years. And then I saw a box of Tampax Supers on the back seat too, which made me shrivel up, or at least any ideas I might have had. It was the final turn-off at the psychological moment. It wasn't just the blood. It was the thought of her having that ridiculous thing pushed up her, tailed with string like a sugar mouse.

And sometimes I just get a bad feeling, for no reason. Something telling me, No, forget this one. Just get the car fixed and get her out of here. This one's a jinx.

So it's only if everything seems okay and things still feel right with me that I take something from the car. Don't get me wrong. I'm not a petty thief. I don't *steal* anthing. All I do is *remove* something that they'll never even notice isn't there. Some tiny part of their everyday life. Something of theirs, that's all. A lipstick-stained butt from the ashtray. Or a whole cigarette from a half-full packet they left on the seat. Which I'll take home and smoke long and slow, inhaling it as if it was a joint and we were sharing it, her and me. I'll take anything I can use and they won't miss. The clippings from their fingernails. One long, gold hair.

From the blonde girl's car I took what I've taken, now and then, from other cars. Two or three Kleenex from a box of them under the dashboard.

Mansize Tissues, the box said. *For That Mansize Job*.

You can say that again, sister, I thought.

Because even those words turned me on. And just the sitting in her car did, in her *seat*.

And now I'm going to have to find her a name. My own,

secret name for her. I thought of *Blondie*. But that's too obvious. Too corny. Makes her sound like that scatty piece in the strip cartoon. And, like I say, her hair's not really that shade of blonde. It's got a kind of tawny, or rust glow in it.

What about *Rusty?*

Yeah. I like that. Why not? And it suits her. It's got that kind of tomboy ring.

Rusty.

I'm going to call her that. And that's her file-name. That's what she'll come under when I start her entry in the Book.

(Like the multiple bigamist said, ha fucking ha, I always like to give them my own name.)

When I come out of the bedroom I put away the magazine. Not that I'd needed to look at it even, as it happens. Sometimes they, you know, blur and swim. But she was sharp and clear today for me. Clear as a bell. Or like they say in bodybuilding, Definition Good. I once read somewhere that this is a power you can lose as you get older, the power to picture, to summon someone up sharp and vivid enough, and put her on Hold. (Which, I suppose though, is why you have mags in the first place. Like the freeze-button on the VCR.)

I make sure I didn't leave that other mag lying around somewhere too. Always clear up after yourself is a good rule. And this is the kind of day Colin will call around, he often does on a dead Sunday afternoon. Sometimes he'll bring a rented tape from the video shop. Because he can't watch that kind of stuff at home, not with his parents living in the house. But then, like I always tell him, What the fuck is a man of his age doing living with his parents in the first place?

Not that I mind him watching the stuff here, or watching it with him, since he'll usually bring a flagon or two or a six-pack. But I like to stay back from it a bit, look amused, like I'm just 'indulging' him. (And some of those videos really are pretty comic, when you think about it. Let's fucking face it, they ain't *On the Waterfront*.)

Anyway, what I'm saying is I don't want him to get the impression I'd pay money to get this kind of tape out of the shop and watch it on my own account, or that I'm into things like this in any shape or form, whether on a video or in a mag. Because let's face it, hard or softcore, all that stuff is is a Private Admission of Failure.

I sit and finish the last of the peanuts and crumple the packet, which balloons and falls short when I try to throw it in the fireplace. There's one more Long Life left.

The racing is on the TV now, or rather the lull before a race, i.e. nilsville. Everything happens so slowly, it all takes so much time, all the bullshit and the buildup and the updates on the changes in the betting and the experts' opinions and the tipsters' tips, and the gees being walked around the paddock. What A Drag. What a mindless drag. All that fucking ritual just to get you involved enough or probably it's bored enough to pick up the phone and get some money on before the off. And then a couple of minutes later it's over, they've run, and all you've done is make Joe Coral richer.

I find the remote control down the side of the chair and switch channels. I can't bear to watch the racing any more. Not now. Though I used to bet like a fiend when I was younger. Many a time I've spent a whole week of afternoons in the betting shop. Just standing there every day staring at the lists of runners. Breathing in all that secondhand cigarette smoke. Adding to it. In those days you couldn't even enjoy watching your money come in fourth or fifth or last in living colour, they didn't have TV in betting shops then. All you got was the audio commentary from the track, all abrupt over the Tannoy and scratchy with static, like when you get the police wavelength on the radio. And even now when I see horse-racing on the television it's not the atmosphere of the course that I start to deepbreathe, nor the green turf or the colours of the jockeys' silks, Glorious Goodwood and The Sport of Khans, et cetera. It's those drab foul-aired sunless stub-littered concrete-floored betting shops of my wasted youth that I go back to. And I have to switch over or switch off. I find the whole thing too fucking depressing to leave on.

The funny thing is that that seedy, worn-down atmosphere was exactly what I loved about it at the time, when I was nineteen, twenty. The sordid semi-tough semi-criminal subproletarian Edge of Things.

That, and the power of names. Or the power I had over names. (Or thought I had.) When I started betting it was really because of this that I got the hook in me, saw myself becoming a Professional Gambler, a real racing man. Because the first time I ever went into a betting shop I won money. I picked a winner. And I thought I must have this gift, this flair. This magic power. Which was going to make the rest of my life easy and me a wealthy man. Because the very first horse I ever bet on, Lars Porsena it was called, came in by a nose. A rank outsider, priced at thirty-three to one. I didn't know a race-horse from a clothes-horse. I'd picked that winner solely on the name, because when I was about twelve or thirteen (I must have been in the third form), there was a teacher, old Cady, who used to read this poem out loud to us in class, *Horatio At The Bridge*, I think it was, about some Roman hero who defended a bridge and saved Rome, and there was this character called Lars Porsena in that poem. (Lars Porsena of Clusium. By the nine gods he swore.) And when this *nag* Lars Porsena, this complete *longshot*, came in first I started to think that absolutely any and every horse whose name I had a feeling for would come home for me too. And when I looked at a list of runners in fact some of the names did seem to be *signalling* to me (Me! Me! Pick me! Bet me!), a signal meant only for me, or that only

I was sensitive or tuned-in enough to pick up anyway. A kind of magic power in me and in the name. In words themselves.

But miracles, as they say, don't strike the same tree twice. Now I don't even remember where my next winner came from, or how much loot I had to spend under that wire grille to whip it home. Probably I got just enough second- and third-place money from time to time to keep the craze alive. That's the way things work when you think you've got a system: you end up having to rely on flukes to prove it. (I suppose that's how mugs get strung along until they're hooked on gambling for life.)

But what depresses me now is not the wasted money. You could say the money was well spent, in a way, since at least I learnt that gambling Is A Vice, and, like they say, you have to pay to learn.

No, what I hate to think of is all those wasted hours I spent studying form, staring at columns of horses' names in the newspaper all morning, even before I went down to the betting shop to pass the afternoon. Not to mention all the other hours I spent compiling my records, for example my own private list of selected horses (Names To Watch, you could call it), their running history, trainer, owner, jockeys, parentage, whatever else I could find out. And then there was that other notebook where I detailed every bet I'd made, kept a running balance, and so on. My trouble is that I never did things by halves. I never have been one for 'hobbies'. But a craze is a craze. And I suppose I've always had a thing about collecting information in that way, keeping logbooks and diaries and statistics and so on (like my wife used to say when she was a student, All the World Exists to End Up in a Book). Probably I should have been an accountant or a tax adviser or, come to that, a fucking bookie. Let's face it, you can spend your time more profitably calculating other people's debts than totting up your own.

So I still hate to think of that wasted time. Because

wasted money's nothing, money's shit, blow one wage-packet and at least you can go out and earn another. But Wasted Time never comes back, nor Opportunity.

And it wasn't only racing I wasted my life on in those days. I mean, when I think now of all the time I must have spent going through a craze on *some* damn thing or other.

Gambling. Snooker. Fishing.

Bodybuilding.

Cycling.

Then it was the drums.

Ever since I was a kid I've been the same. All these fads ever did was cost me big money for all the equipment, and get me fucking nowhere. I always thought I'd end up being famous and making a nice fat living out of being the best there ever was at something on the fringe of things, like betting horses or banging drums. (Instead of which I'm changing tyres and batteries at Quick-Change, and taking home barely a hundred and twenty in a good week.)

Because the terrible thing is, you don't know who you are or what you want to be when you're nineteen or twenty. And when you're thirty-six it makes not a blind bit of difference if you know or not, because by now it's all too fucking late. You've missed the boat.

I switch on through the channels. Something, anything. The Grand Prix is still on ITV, but I'm bored with that by now, seeing the same cars whining round the same three fucking bends. Motor sport's only worth watching in the wet, when at least there's a chance of a pileup or someone spinning off the track.

Other than that, there's only some Open University chemistry course on Two. Or some black-and-white Sixties British so-called comedy on One, with Ian Carmichael playing the usual stupid bastard upper-class Silly Ass. And all those even stupider bastards they always have to play the proles in films like this, the flash harrys and cockney batmen loyal to the death, two-bit bit-part actors all their lives, but it's that kind of film. A part for everybody on the J. Arthur Rank payroll, and the same rogues' gallery of faces every time. In fact: Vintage Pinewood. (Me, I'd rather start learning some chemistry than watch that shit.)

I try Channel Four, but it's a lost hope. Just the usual electronic snow. I don't know why I can't get it here. Tony Barbecue, a mile up the road, gets a perfect picture every time. But all you can get in this part of Grangetown is S4C, Ess Pedwar Eck. Amateur Night. In Welsh, most of the time. (About as much use to me or the average citizen of the capital as an *Echo* in braille.)

I stare at the grey buzzing blizzard.

That's how I feel. Tense with not existing.

I switch back to Three and turn the sound right down so I at least don't have to hear those fucking cars going round. Since I'm on my feet I wander into the kitchen. The fluorescent strip lighting is still on from last night (or the night before that. It's so dim in this kitchen the damn thing's never off). A whole week's dirty washing-up is piled in the sink. Used plates are scattered on the white Formica work-tops, with dried-up fragments of old meals. A half a bottle of yellowed milk turns to cheese or anyway some kind of dairy smegma on the windowsill.

The whole fucking place is running to seed, I think, not for the first time this holiday weekend. The filth just seems to breed in here. The ceaseless filth of life.

Going across to pour the sludge of milk down the sink, I walk (as I always damn well do) through the patch on the floor where I spilt the orange juice the other morning, tottering to the fridge with a whisky headache and craving ice-cold fructose, snipping off the corner of a new box of juice with the kitchen scissors and then dropping the damn thing, half of it glugging out across the floor before I could stoop my head down far enough to right it. I wiped up the mess with a wet cloth, but the stickiness is still there, as if it'll be there for ever, every time I cross the kitchen, the soles of my Pumas doomed to tackily reprint it in an invisible chevron pattern all over the rest of the vinyl tiling.

It's barely 3.30 by the white electric clock on the wall.

I wander back to the kitchen window, sticky soles making their soft, ripping sound, like Velcro, on the grey floor. I stand at the sink and stare out, the fingers of one hand pinching up a handful of skin and flesh at the side of my waist, then moving up to do the same at my right pectoral. At first I wondered if my shirts were shrinking slightly in the machine-wash at the launderette, I thought I might be using a too-hot programme for cottons. But it isn't that. Let's face it, at thirty-six I'm starting to run to seed as well. It's beerfat, pure and simple. I change spare tyres all day, and in the evenings build one of my own.

I gaze down from the first-floor window at brick rear garages, two kids on BMXes, not riding them, just sitting on the saddles. They look bored as I am, too bored mindless even to vandalise anything or throw a wheelie.

Fuck this, I think. 'Bank Holiday'? As far as I'm concerned (and there must be a lot of people like me), a Bank Holiday is bearable only if it rains. If it absolutely pisses down, all day. Then, at least, you don't have to feel *guilty* about being in the house. About being slumped in front of the Idiot Box in the complete fucking absence of anything better to do with your life.

When you're on your own, it's always worse when it's fine weather. But even an ordinary weekend at home is too long, these days.

And Sundays are terrible, always.

I look up, above the garages and the other flats behind, and my eye follows a jet passing down the blue sky. It's very high, probably a 747, from here it's only a minute gleaming arrowhead, but if you were up there onboard it would be packed with people all Going Somewhere, excited, nervous, having their first drinks, heading west, heading right out over green, ragged-coasted Ireland, and all the way to America. The Atlantic Ocean, wrinkly, shining, thirty thousand feet below. They'll next set foot on land in New York or Los Angeles.

One day I'll go to those places too. And to Buffalo, and Butte, Montana, and Memphis, Tennessee. And to all those State Capitals I learnt by heart once, *Topeka, Kansas* and *Boise, Idaho* and *Bismarck, North Dakota*.

I watch that travelling mathematical point catching the sunlight, a vector of silver waste slowly lengthening across a sky as blank and empty as amnesia. I watch it until the jet itself vanishes down behind the parapet of the flats and there is only that pale flight-path, already loosening and drifting in the winds up there at thirty thousand feet, to a more broken trace, like a chalk mark on a rough wall.

(And to *Santa Fe, New Mexico* and *Jefferson City, Missouri* and *Baton Rouge, Louisiana* and *Columbus, Ohio* and *Springfield, Illinois*.)

I mosey into the bathroom. My red-and-white shirt of tablecloth check with the mother-of-pearl buttons, washed by hand this morning, is on a hanger over the bath. I feel it. It's already dry for tonight.

Tonight. On days like this I wait for night with the impatience of a vampire.

In the other room the sun's come around to daze the TV screen. I draw one curtain across to shade it. Never shut out God's daylight, my Old Lady always used to say. But I hate the way sunlight strikes a screen dead. And this is calming, this aquarium dimness, the TV like a lighted tank where faces with voices turned down to nothing mouth like fish.

I decide to give up on the 'Full Bank Holiday Programme of Live Sporting Entertainment' (full details in your *TV Times*). I slip a video from the box and insert it in the slot. The slow whirr takes it in. I press Rewind,

29

the faster whirr, and shake a palmful of salted peanuts from the second bag, waiting for the tape to run back. The film is Martin Sheen in *Badlands*. This is the second time I've watched it this week, and Christ knows how many times I've seen it altogether. But some films you never tire of, and it'll take me nicely up past six o'clock. And then suddenly it's evening.

(My favourite thing in the whole film is when they're on the run and he squats down and shoots the football. For being 'Excess Baggage'. No matter how many times I've seen the film, that always kills me.)

TWO

I hit The Locomotive on the dot of nine. I don't like to cruise in too early (before anyone else I know). If it's a quiet night, you're standing up there at the counter like a spare bar-stool, waiting for someone you can talk to to walk in (trying not to keep on stealing looks at yourself between the urns and flowers in that long mirror behind the bar).

At nine tonight, though, the place is already noisy, crowded. The Bank Holiday crowd who made it back through the traffic, or never went. Either way, tonight they'll be drinking out of both hands. Like there was no tomorrow. Because tomorrow's another day off for most people, and they don't have to get up early for work.

Not that it actually makes any difference if you've got kids, Bank Holiday or not, hangover or not. When you've got kids there's no such thing as sleeping in, they're in the bed with you at half six every morning anyway, seven at the latest, wriggling or fighting, they're an alarm call you can't stop ringing.

Though I don't know why I of all people should happen to think of this. I haven't got the problem any more. Those days are over. My kids are gone, Mandy and little Darryl. They're with their new Dadda now, in a bijou cottage on a ferny hillside up in Powys. Me? There'll be nothing to get met out of bed tomorrow morning but the need to piss.

Okay, Yank?

It's Colin, pushing through the crowd to reach me at the bar. He's holding a half-empty pint glass ahead of him.

With the fiver already in hand to pay, I of course reach

back for Colin's glass too. Which, since this is what he has fought through the crowd just in time to have me do, he drains with an obedient fucking alacrity (as you might put it).

Two pints of light, I tell Phyllis.

Waiting for the beer, I reach back one hand to signal for a cigarette. But Colin doesn't notice, snapping a suddenly wandering light to his own as he gets distracted in the old ocular pursuance of those curve-cleft, tight, W-stitched white Wranglers of the dark-haired girl who just got served before me and is now pushing her way with two drinks through the jostle at the counter, and past Colin. For a second his Colibri still burns that forgotten flame. It's a classic 'double-take', the yokel gawp. Then, before he remembers to light the cigarette (or even that he's got one drooping in his mouth), his eyes flicker to other faces, nervously, to see if anybody *saw*. Which of course no one did, they're all too busy shouting to each other, or were watching her themselves – like that sharp dude spade in the kingfisher-blue Colossal Shirt now is, pink-veined eyes sliding sideways wistful (just for the one, hooded moment) for White Meat: the same downward look of furtive assessment, then the swift look at the chick's eyes, hoping to get your interest returned (and with interest, as they say). Just like Colin did before his look broke, a weak self-conscious fluttering of ginger eyelashes. Because when there's no response from the chick, and you're ignored, the only thing left is to worry if someone saw you make the try.

And it's a source of amazement. It is. People know how much they give themselves away with their eyes. That's why they're always checking whether anyone else has *noticed*. But by the time they do it's too late: somebody already *has*. Click. And has probably already looked away again. So they can't even be sure if they've been rumbled or not. Because these people just haven't got the brain or the cool to control what they're doing *in advance*, and *assume* someone may be watching. Because somewhere somebody is always watching. In This Life you've got to keep your eyes on everyone, eavesdrop with every sense you got. But give nothing away of yourself. Because some people are born to be Readers of a Situation. And others are just Open Books.

Anyway, no one but no one notices Colin. Any more than she did. Though she looked at me right enough. (This was when she was standing at the bar.) She looked me right in the meat of the eye, and held it. But a dwarf like Colin, five foot six or seven in his Cuban heels, everyone ignores. The only fucker who was watching *him* was me. And *I'm* about the only face he didn't check. (Let's face it, some people are always a yard behind the game. But there's not a lot *I* miss.)

I take the change from the woman behind the bar. She's new. Been here a week. Though the joke someone calls out beside me is already old here. As the hills.

Hey, Phyllis! Fillis glass!

Ha fucking ha, I tell him, turning with the drinks. What a wag.

Like I say, some people are struggling from birth just to keep up with the play.

Cheers, Yank, Colin says.

He grasps the beer. A conservative third goes down his throat.

We look around the room.

Then, just to 'do' something (fill the gap of us *standing* there together), he has to smirk and reach out to feel one lapel of my leather waistcoat. Then he fingers the toggle of my hat-string, a black bead. I knock his hand away. (I don't like people toying with my outfit.)

He blinks suddenly and his mouth drops open, stunned. He's agog with recognition. He stands his glass on a cluttered table. He backs away slowly, fearful, against the crowd.

(I should have seen this coming.)

33

Colin.

Okay, Kid Colt, he says. His voice is scared. I'm only gonna say this once. So listen up. And listen good. I want you out of town by sundown.

His body is crouched now, he's watchful. He flexes his fingers like a shaky pianist. Hands hovering tensely over his gun-butts (jean pockets).

Colin, I try again.

A warning he takes no notice of.

His right hand goes for the gun. But he's not fast enough. He barely gets it out of the holster as his face crumples in a grimace. He clutches his shirted belly where it swells out like a filled sail over his belt. He takes his hand away and looks at blood on it. He's aghast. (People are grinning at him now.) He staggers, sways. He gasps his last words.

A gut wound, he says.

He looks at me. Eyes unbelieving, begging.

Do me a favour, Kid, he says. Finish me off. Don't leave me out here with them vultures circling. Don't leave me out here to die slow.

I haven't moved. (People are laughing.) I look at him. I take the matchstick from my mouth and make the crazy sign with one finger at my head. Then I change that finger into a 'gun' and point it at him, thumb cocked. (I haven't laughed.) With a little soft noise in my throat I blow the cunt away.

He shambles back to rejoin me at the bar, smiling modestly. He drains a good half of his beer. I watch his Adam's apple bobbing and the froth shrinking in gulps down the side of the glass. One pale preoccupied blue eye, cold and manic as a gull's, winks once at me over the rim.

Listen, cunt, I tell him quietly. Don't make that mistake again. You ever show me up like that again in public and I'll take you out for good.

His pupils stir. With Colin, sometimes you can count

34

the time it takes a thought to get from cornea to cortex. Or vice versa. (He doesn't dig that something that can be a laugh once, 'impromptu', when there's a few of you clowning about over Sevenoaks Park, isn't necessarily so funny a second time, when there are chicks around.)

After a while he offers me a cigarette. Then he offers the flame of his lighter. But I'm still giving him the freeze. I take a match from my waistcoat pocket instead. (I always keep a few loose in there.) I lift my right knee, sweep the match along the denim where it's tight under the thigh, and bring the light up to my cigarette almost before it flares. I flick the match smoking at the floor. A new record drowns the bar's hubbub.

The Late Great Mister Marvin Gaye, Colin says in a Rosko voice. Ah Heerd it through the Grape Vaarn.

We stand there tapping one toe to it. Smoking, staring around the crowded bar. Colin, short and fat beside me, empties his glass. He's not what you'd call a Nervous Sipper of a drink. (Like Tony Barbecue said to him the other week, watching him gulp them down: Straight back into the fucking barrel.) With the music up this loud you don't have to talk to the bastard. But at least he's someone to stand with so you don't look like you're on your own.

The dark-haired girl is standing over by the jukebox now. She's with another chick and what you might call an attentive group of boys. The old female pairing arrangement: the Wallflower and the Centre of Attention. No competition, I suppose. Or like the shark and the pilot-fish. The one feeding off what sticks in the other's teeth.

I keep looking that way. For the odd white glimpse through the intervening bodies of that high-cleft arse. She stands there with it to the whole bar, putting her weight now on one leg, now the other.

(Women kill me. They know everything.)

I'm waiting for her to look at me again, across the crowded room. (One enchanted evening, You may see

35

a stranger.) Though, when you see the age of the *kids* these girls spend their time being chatted up by, you realise you're another generation. It's not that they're too young for *you*. (Like the man said, Anything with fur on it, you can shoot it if you can get close enough. There's no close season here.) But no matter how brass-bold they'll look you straight back in the eye, let's face it, you're too old for *them*. You can look. They might even like you looking. But they don't want a man of thirty-six. Not right now. Not right ever, as far as they can see. They're into PGA now, Peer Group Approval. An older guy's the last thing on their Christmas list. What these chicks are looking for is hardly even what you'd call Young Love so much as teenage lust. That, plus the big image they make together as a 'couple'. All they want is someone they like being Seen With. Nineteen, twenty at the outside, I suppose that girl would be. And they're such conformists and Slaves to Opinion at that age. (Trendies.) Talk to them and you find they're into Barry Manilow or Buck's Fizz. In fact there'd be nothing in the least bit interesting about chicks like that if you didn't know that what they've got inside their jeans at that age, running just above that stitching at the centre-seam, is the sweetest, tightest, most heartaching thing in all the world. And that's enough. In fact, when you come down to it, that's all there is. That's all there's ever been.

Colin waggles his glass at me. It's empty.

I'll get you another one, he yells.

I shrug Okay.

I stand and look around the bar. *Have You Seen Your Mother Baby, Standing in the Shadow, Have you seen your lover baby, standing in the shadow. I'm glad I opened your (eye, eye, eye) eyes . . .*

SingalongaMick.

But I'm out of all this, tonight. It's like I'm watching it from that underwater restaurant at Butlin's, where you can sit and watch swimming bodies in the pool through thick glass. In fact all that keeps me here is the thought that Rusty is going to walk in here one night.

(She'll be with a girl friend. It'll be Pure Coincidence. This is not a pub she Normally Comes To. She's never been here in her life before, in fact. Neither of them have. They just, you know, Happened to be Passing, and.)

But tonight, the whole place seems *rife* with her not being here. I miss her. In the intervals between records, suddenly, I miss her. And I get a kind of pang every time I think of her or wonder what she's doing instead, and who with, on this Bank Holiday Sunday night.

And yet, ever since she came into the garage on Thursday I've felt we're going to run into each other again, any minute. And I hope it can happen that way. Because there are a lot of girls in the Book, but with Rusty I sense things are going to be different. With her I know something special is going to happen. (Even if it's only going to be the best One-Night Stand anybody ever dreamed of. Because with her, I'd let it go at that. I really would.) (And I can imagine how she's going to be already, her face going from side to side on the pillow with that thrown away look and then that kind of grimace of concentration just as she's about to, and then this long long shudder and she's holding onto me, holding onto me through it, it's never Happened for her with a man before.)

And if I do run into her (in a packed pub like this, or it might be on the street, or, no, in a supermarket) everything ought to be easy now. A dead cinch. All I have to do is wait to catch her eye.

(Hello.

(She's probably buying an individual frozen pizza or one pork chop. I always feel so sorry for people when I see them doing that. People who live alone have so little in their shopping-baskets and spend such a long time choosing it, as if it mattered.)

She looks at this man who has spoken to her, knowing my face but not placing where from.

How's the new tyre lasting?

Now she laughs, remembering, and her face colours. Under this supermarket neon you can't hide a thing. Every eye-fleck, every pore. As clear as air in the Antarctic.

Fine, she says.

She laughs again. She's embarrassed at not recognising me straight off, or perhaps just at being spoken to by a stranger. Either way, I like a girl who's not too insensitive to blush. And I like a girl who blushes for me, because of me, and you see the pupils widen as she tries not to look down, to keep looking back. Old reflexes of fear left in us since we lived in caves. The blood gone to the cheeks instead of to muscles wanting to run. The instinct to be shy of what's stronger.

She puts the styrofoam tray with the one pork chop clingfilmed in it into the wire basket, this single person's shopping-basket with just these few things she's bought in it, and what there is all in the smallest quantity or single portions. And it's as if she was slipping it under her coat. Because although she doesn't understand why, for the first time in her life she's suddenly ashamed to be alone in the world.

We're strolling the same way down the aisle.

The wheel hasn't come off yet?

Not yet.

I must be improving.

Again she has to laugh, high-coloured still as if from this colder, fresher air we're walking in between the refrigerated shelves and the freezer bays. But it's really because she's pleased at this 'chance encounter', even if she doesn't want to admit why yet. And she finds herself responding to this wry, self-mocking tone I've slipped into, and she knows that at least this isn't someone who takes himself – or her – too seriously at the outset. Because (let's face it) she's bored stiff with all those over-intent, too-obvious, Adoring Men, in fact she despises men like that, Lovesick Swains, always begging and pleading with her either to be what she's not and never could be, i.e. 'in love' with them, or sulking at her for the way she is. Which is not in love with anyone. Because the truth is, she's never found a man she can Respect. She's even started wondering lately if being beautiful isn't more of a curse than a blessing. (One thing it *hasn't* made her is popular with other girls. It hasn't even helped her find a man. It's just made her more demanding about men in general.) In fact, she sometimes thinks her beauty is the reason why she's so alone.

(Much later I'll tell her that the only reason I spoke to her was that one pork chop she bought, and the shame-faced way she slipped it into the shopping-basket. And I'll tell her that loneliness is no reason for anyone to feel guilty. And as she looks back at me tears come into her eyes, and she realises that no one else will ever know her at a glance, the way I can.)

But now all she can think about is how 'different' I look now: taller, darker . . . It's easy to look down on someone, even without meaning to, when they're kneeling at your wheel-hub in dirty overalls and with filthy hands, and their only meaning to you is that you're paying them to do this job that keeps the grease out of your own finger-nails.)

I examine my hands. I have big hands, with long fingers. Artistic they're not: every night after work I have to use a pumice-stone on them, or pour sugar into a soaped palm. Though nothing will ever get out all those years of ingrained grease, not if I were to stand at that sud-soiled sink and scrub at them till morning. The first joint of each index-finger will always be a dark pad from spinning oily nuts. And the ball of each thumb is whorled for ever with dark loops, like in a police fingerprint.

And I remember that when I was a kid in school my hands were always covered with ink. These two fingers on my right hand would be blue with it, like an old desk.

(Was I clumsy at writing?) Anyway. What you get on your hands as a kid washes off. Or wears off in playing. But what you do as a man, working in filth day in day out, stays with you. It's in the pores. With these soiled hands they'll bury me.

Still waiting for Colin to bring the beer. I catch sight of myself in the long mirror again. But this time it's that rare sighting: you off-guard. The kind of sullen, half-startled look of someone in an identity parade or one of those early phrenological mugshots of criminal types or idiots. The look you can't *plan* to see. The look your face only has when you surprise it, for that split second when you almost fail to recognise it. Before you do, and change it damn quick into one you'd rather have.

Which is the face I study now, turning my head very slightly from side to side to see the fall of light alter on it. (Self-infatuation? Like the guy said still looking in the mirror when they broke the door down, ha ha, two hours in the toilet just to comb his hair: This is no infatuation. This is the real thing.) To see the dark face and throat above the open-necked V of my pearl-buttoned red-and-white check shirt. The hat-string crossing just under my Adam's apple, and the black moon of the brim rising behind my head. The hair slicked back as if with water.

If ever I went to Hollywood I like to think that there would be a 'new life' for me, that there would be other things that I might do than work in a Quick-Change: if only at first make a small living playing murderous halfbreeds on the run. I have the eyes for it, and the adder cheekbones. And of course the hair. My jet-black dead-straight shiny Maltese hair, my Crowning Glory, as my wife used to call it in the days when she was keen on me, those first few weeks and months when she couldn't get enough of me, her Bit of Rough, her brown-backed Maltese-Irish labourer lover. It was the first thing she ever noticed about me, she said. It was long in those days, of course. Past my nipples, and halfway down my

40

back when I combed it out straight, after I'd washed it. In work I had to knot it up under the safety helmet like a Sikh or something.

I wish I had hair like you, she said, I've always wanted black hair, she said. But your hair, she said. I've never seen hair as black as yours. You've got hair like a Japanese.

Meaning that as a compliment, I know. But I actually didn't like her saying that. Because I always think of Japs as being small and yellowish and polite and bowing from the ankles all the time. I suppose it would have made me happy if, instead of Japanese, she'd said: Apache.

That would have been the perfect thing.

But of course she never did, the bitch. And when you look back on it, she hardly gave me anything of what I really wanted. They never do.

Colin comes back with the two beers. We stand drinking.

There Is A Rose In Spanish Harlem, A rare rose up in Spanish Harlem, It is a special one, It's never seen the sun, It only comesoutwhenthemoonisontherun Andallthestars are shining. It's growing in the street, Da da da da da, Da da da da da, Da da da . . .

I singalong in my dark-brown voice. To dark-brown Ben E. King. (It's all Raves from the Grave in here tonight.)

Colin keeps checking the room. He must have been out in the Bank Holiday sun today, and his pale blue eyes look even lighter in the reddened face. He nudges me and nods.

What about them two over there?

He's looking right across the room at a couple of chicks who've just come in from the other bar. Since nobody's talking to them, they have to talk to each other. But all the time their eyes, casual, unceasing, move elsewhere. One of them has her back half-turned towards us. She's wearing a low-backed round-neck top showing a broad semicircle of pale skin, and freckles or moles so big I can

41

almost count them from here. In the centre of this pale half-circle is a small pink triangle: a V-shaped burn mark left by having worn a top which showed less of her: she's been in the sun too, probably on the beach this afternoon. And it's as if someone's held a hot smoothing-iron there, point-down and smack between the shoulderblades. As she stands there she keeps reaching behind to tuck in one of her bra-straps, which keeps coming out.

The girl with her is tall. In fact she has the stooped shoulders and sheepish look of someone in what you might call permanent prior apology for towering over almost every man she meets. Her face isn't bad. (Whereas the other one looks hard as nails. A real dog.) But you can see she's hung up on being six foot plus. Someone ought to tell her to Think Tall. Dominate. Make the little short guy really know that's all he is. He'll love you for it. He'll crawl to lick the soles of your six-inch high-heeled shoes. (The only rule In This Life being: Let other people make excuses for themselves. Never apologise to anyone for What You Are. Whether by word or deed.)

Me, I'm over six feet two, so tall girls have never bothered me. In fact I like them tall, big strapping girls like athletes, yeah, like those women long-jumpers or high-jumpers in the Olympics, long, muscled gold legs in white calf-socks, and neat, hard little buttocks, in those jazzy satin shorts they wear, like a pair of duck-eggs in a handkerchief, Christ I'd love a girl like that, love her to death. I'd have her wear that outfit all the time at home, those tiny shiny shorts, even the singlet with the track number on it. (Only this one would be *69*, ha ha.) Or if not a number then some words, like advertising or a logo. But instead of *Coke* or *Pepsi* or *British Meat* I'd have her wear one saying *Fuck Me*, yeah, *Fuck Me*, I could just see her in that, that West German girl in the Olympics. Or that other one, the one with the funny run-up, from wherever it was, one of those African countries. I've never had a black girl in my life.

So what about it? he says.

What?

Them two.

I don't even look at them this time. I take the chewed matchstick from my mouth and make as if to spit, like there was a fibre of wood on my tongue-tip.

I'd rather go home and have a good clean wank, I tell him.

Colin doesn't answer. His pale eyes with their light lashes flicker around the bar. Like the two girls themselves, he's Getting Anxious. He knows his time is starting to run out, he's thirty-five years of age, it's nine-thirty on a Bank Holiday Sunday night, and the girl of his dreams is getting snapped up every second by some silver-tongued bastard in some other bar-room. People out there are falling in love this very minute. They're wet fucking without contraceptive or control, they like it so much they don't give a shit. Or they're just walking through the Castle Gardens and holding hands. All this while Colin is forced to stand here drinking ten or twelve pints in a night and waiting for his life to start to happen.

'Girl of his dreams'? It doesn't have to be so big a deal. Just the first fuck in his life he didn't have to pay for would suit Colin fine. Though his dream girl's just what that would be, for Colin, since the only women you ever hear him talk about are the Chinese whores he used to have on leave in Singapore, when he was in the Army, and how there's nothing better than one of those little Chinese girls (as if he had any live thing to make comparison with except his own right hand). There was this one he always talks about called Wei Lee Sung or Suck Yoo Too, and how she used to keep telling him she wanted him to 'stay' with her, move in, so she could have his kid. And I think he actually believed that lying cunt, and he believes it still. He even told me one night how, you never knew about these things, perhaps she

43

did have one, that kid of his she always wanted, and how at this very minute there might be some little ginger half-Chinese kid he didn't even know about running around in Singapore, saying it with that stupid half-drunk smile of the indulgent father already on his face, the silly prat.

And I thought, How dull a man can be, in things like that. And how clever a woman.

Because (let's be honest) they don't even have to be some sewer of a five-bob Chinese whore to sling you a line like that: 'I want to have your baby.' Or for you to swallow it. In fact my own wife said the same to me, or words to that effect. Because the biggest mistake you ever make with a woman is when you get her pregnant, fuck a kid into her on the principle that at that point she'll be 'yours', will have to marry you and be your 'wife' and its 'mother'. You never see how that can work the other way around. Because once she's got your kid inside her the one with the hook in is you. And when the kid is born that barb is lodged in you for life.

And when I think of things like that, of being more or less lured into two kids and a marriage and then, just when I'd started to get used to that, having them taken away from me because their two-titted sow of a mother would rather lie in her own filth than the marriage-bed and, not only *that* (as if that wasn't enough), but just because I raised my hand to her, slapped about a bit out of a rage that, after all, she caused, or because she says I never gave her and the kids, my kids, enough fucking 'stability' in any case (by which she really means I don't make enough a week for her to spend), when I think of all that, even now, I tell you, my throat tightens till I can hardly swallow and I have to start massaging the tendons at the back of my neck in case I get another of those headaches.

Hey, someone says. You going to put that big hat on? Or just wear it slung across your back like that?

The fattish, pink face. A dark mole with shaved hairs in it. I don't know his name. He drinks here.

Really, he says. Great hat.

I look at him.

He drops his eyes to smile at whatever joke he thinks he just made and moves on. A wit. Another one. Another anonymous fucking smiler.

(I'll put it on, I'm not quick enough to tell him. When I come for you I'll put it on special.)

Then he's gone, pushing quickly away through the crowd, glass of tilted beer in hand. (Later I'll tell him. One night soon I'll tell him. And then they'll be picking that glass in pieces from his face.)

I need a piss, Colin says.

He's watching me. He's nervous again, he thinks there might be trouble. (One thing the Army never taught that boy is how to fight.) He puts down his glass and starts to push his way through to the toilets. (Colin, by the way, is one of these 'shy' characters who always go into the cubicle, even to piss.)

But thinking about Colin only makes me feel sorry for myself. I haven't got a family any more. I haven't got a girl. I haven't even got a friend you'd want to call one.

I look across the room. The dark-haired girl has gone.

And I don't even need to finish my drink. I'm going too. I'm getting a headache in all this crush and loudness. And for what? For Colin to come back in a couple of minutes from shaking his dick to try to wheedle me into angling for some crab-ridden pair of slags just on the optimum off-chance of a bout of five-minute, one-off, stand-up sex in a dark street-doorway. (With some previous passing drunkard's piss probably still trickling out of it.) And me, I've seen all that before. I've had enough of that. I've had that all my life.

And less. Because any night of the week in this place you can try them all and not even get that much.

The door to the Gents opens just as I pass it, leaving.

But it's not Colin, thank Christ. (Some greaseball with a cheroot, patting his quiff, backpocketing a comb.)

And then I'm out into the carpark. The air's clean and cool after the swelter and cigarette smoke of the bar, and the keys are out all ready in my hand. I run a '57 Thunderbird, I'm under the limit, and I'm going to drive it with the windows down and play *Born in the USA* on all four speakers, loud, and feel the whole warm night blow through me like it's blowing through the car.

Lake Road East is a long, expensive road with houses on one side only, i.e. facing the lake and Roath Park. One or two of these are probably among the best houses in the city, or were once. Big, old, family houses. (Built in the days when people had big old families, ha ha ha.) (Days when the family stood for something, anyway, more than it does now, and that's no fucking joke, take that from one who knows.)

The bigger houses tend to be opposite the bottom end of the park, towards Penylan Hill. Some of these even have spires or brick turrets. Or even a round tower at one corner, like the rook in a chess-set. Ivy growing on it, little arrow-slots, the lot. I mean, okay, I agree, it's corny building a battlemented tower, complete with flagpole, on a private suburban dwelling. (What you might call thinking your home is your castle.) But let's be honest, who wouldn't mind owning a place that size, private tennis-court et cetera, house set back among its own pines? It's got to have the edge on living in a five-room rented flat above a butcher's. (Go for a walk in the garden there, you have to inch along a sill.) Jesus Christ, if I owned a place like that I'd give the neighbours something more than burglars to think about. I'd put Dobermans and elec-trified fences round the grounds and throw barbecues and swimming parties every night, strictly Invitation Only. I would. I'd run the joint like it was the Hefner mansion.

Of course times change. They're not all private houses these days. A lot of the bigger ones have been bought up and converted to flats or old folk's homes. You can tell these from the zigzag on one side: metal stairs and landings of the fire-escape. They must have to put these in because of safety regulations.

Most of the big private places at the bottom end of the park have nameplates, on big gateposts. As you go north, towards the lake, the houses, or at least the grounds, get smaller, and there are more of these Multiple Occupancies (as they say).

84 is flats.

I pull up opposite, under a plane tree, and kill the lights.

Once upon a time this house would have been like some of those further down the road. A fine family house, lakeside home of some rich bastard or other who made his pile out of coal or iron or shipping one or both around the world. With flowerbeds and stepped rockeries and razored lawns in front, and a wooded driveway of mature cedars and a couple of full-time gardeners and a monkey-puzzle tree. But now, like with a lot of these big old properties the big, Old Money's gone. Number 84 was probably bought out by some speculator landlord or 'developer', some faceless shyster Jew behind a desk, a telephone, a marbled onyx pen-set. And the monkey tree's been cut down, the rockeries levelled, and the whole garden area in front tarmacked for residential parking. And 84, according to the board outside, which I can just read in the streetlight, has been retitled:

Lakeview Apartments. Self-Contained Luxury Flatlets.
Vacancy. Apply for Details
Truscott & Leitman, 170 Cathedral Rd.

(Leitman. See what I mean? There's a yid, for a start.)

I sit in the dark car and look across at the frontage of the building, lit dimly from globes here and there among prostrate evergreens. Behind one of those darkened windows she lives. 'Virginia Hays', she signed herself. And it said 'Ms V J Hays' printed on the cheque. (Lloyd's Bank, an account still at a branch in Esher, Surrey.) (She obviously hasn't bothered to transfer it down here, though she must have lived here a while now: she appears as V. J. Hays even in the 1983 Cardiff Directory.) (I haven't had the one for 1984 yet.)

Rusty.

The green MG is not one of the parked cars in the forecourt, so it doesn't look as if she's home now. (Unless there are garages for residents somewhere behind the building.)

And with a pang of what is already jealousy I wonder where she is at 12.15 on Bank Holiday Sunday night. (In fact it's already fifteen minutes into Monday.) And who with.

(And, as if through a window in which a light goes on, I see into a room. I see her putting her car-keys on a polished table. She looks around the flat.

Tell me where you keep things and I'll make us some coffee.

He takes off his jacket, whirls it into a corner. He throws himself into a low armchair. He looks up at her, arms along the arms of the chair, feet wide apart. White socks, brown tasselled slip-on shoes.

Why not make me instead?

She looks down at him.

Make you? she says.

She laughs.

Or take you apart?

At least I don't have to tell you where things are, he says.

She laughs.

You won't know whether to laugh or cry, she says.

I see her twist her head and look down as her fingers unhook her skirt from its eyelet at the side and then lower the short zip. She lets the skirt drop around her legs. She steps out of the crumpled hoop, one foot and then another, ungainly for just that second in the pointed black high-heeled slingbacks. She crosses the room to him on them. He is now almost lying in the armchair, legs outstretched. He looks up at her.

I want you to take your time with this, he says. I want to make it last and then stretch it out, like chewing-gum. I want you to make me beg for you to finish it.

She drops to her knees between his knees. She looks at him. As matter-of-fact as with her own zip, she starts to take down his.)

I light a cigarette and tilt the rear-view mirror so I can watch myself. I am one red eye glowing in the dark.

It's half past twelve. Lake Road East is silent. Areas of darkness lie between the far-spaced street-lamps. But among the lights the branches of leaf are bursts of new green, new summer. And both ahead of me through the windscreen and behind me in the mirror is this road, these star-blue street-lights, these fluorescent trees. And suddenly I know it's always been like this, and I've always been here.

In the frontage of 84, a few lit windows. But one of those dark ones is hers.

And opposite the house, on my left, is its view, the big uninhabited darkness that is the park and the black lake in the middle of it and the islands in the middle of the lake where the ducks breed and the moorhens, and those far-off lights long and wavery in the water, and all this darkness itself an island in the lit map of the city's streets and arterial roads and roundabouts and junctions, a dark gulf right across this water that is as black as if bottomless, across to the road on the far side which is lit by those taller orange street-lights that make desolate everything they fall on, as if it was always two o'clock in the morning. And I know that all of this too is as it has to be: road, pavement, the bushes and grass verges blanched and exhausted in that dead belt of orange light that follows the road on the far side of the park. And as I look a single car is going along the road. I know it's a car, though I can only see its headlights. They are going so slow because of the distance. Then I can see the changing lights at that utterly empty junction it reaches where, even though there's never any other traffic, you always have to stop and, as alone in that orange glow as if yours was the last car left on earth, wait while a long Red light turns Amber and then Green.

Three

In the dream my wife is wearing this tight blue dress of sequins, it's long, low-cut, a nightclub singer's. The dress has a whitish powder-puff sewn onto it, like a Bunny Girl's. Except that this is fixed not at the back, like a tail, but at the crotch. A dress so tight you can see it crease across her lap like foil, even when she's standing. She shimmers in it like a salmon-skin. She says she can't get the dress off. There are no zips. Her hips are a mermaid's, the only entrance a fish's tiny vent. I rub myself against her, trying to come. When I look down there is a pale dust on my trouser-front, of face-powder from the puff. I know it from childhood, by the smell. I'm in a white room. It's a vast hallway off Heaven. But I know that even when I've been through it all, death and burial and corruption, even when I'm passed through all the angelic ranks and promotions, Cherubim and Seraphim, Dominions and Thrones and Principalities, this want will still be with me. A voice says, Desire Immortal Unto Eternity. And then Seventy Times Seven.

I wake whirring for my wife in a dress of fish-scales. It's dawn. Grey in the room.

The rankness of first-thing sex. Another one-handed catch. And all that silver milt lost in the stream.

I get up at noon. And straight away even a shortened day begins to stretch out in front of me again. It's Easter Monday, for Christ's sake, another fucking holiday. And I remember I'm alone, and I remember why.

Let's keep things brief. I piss, shit, dress, eat a fried-egg sandwich, drink two cups of tea, throw a few things in a shoulder-bag, and drive. What else is there to do with another sunny day when you've got nothing in the diary?

Drive. Out of the summery city westwards on the motorway and into three-lane holiday traffic already all going the same way, hardly any coming at you, it's all on this side of the centre verge, everybody heading for the country, to the 'farm shops' and the garden centres and the Monster Bathrooms and the Texas Homecares and the beaches. Drive, at a steady eighty with my foot down, in the third lane. And every car I overtake is jam-packed with them, whole fucking families of them in there, everyone from babes in arms to their great-grandparents, complete with friends and in-laws. Every now and then I turn my head and look at them as I go past, I've got one hand steering and the other draped along the seat as if I had a girl in here to put it round. (Okay, so it's a pose. You can afford to be suave when you're going past them in a 1957 T-Bird, and even if it isn't hot enough yet to have the soft-top back at least it's bright enough for shades.) Going past, I turn my head and look at them from somewhere way behind my Orbisons, and they don't even notice. They don't even see the car. All these morons do is stare ahead or sideways from the window. They're as flat and blank as playing-cards, and as alike, in fact they're like the townspeople who've already been inhabited by aliens in *Invasion of the Body Snatchers*. And you start to wonder if that really could happen here, affect a whole community like that. And then you realise that it fucking does, it happens every summer Sunday when the sun comes out and each Bank Holiday it fails to rain. No matter where you look, zombies are on the move.

So drive. Passing them all the time, the needle wavering up to eighty-five, west down the blue motorway until the Briton Ferry bridge. Where naturally it all. Slows down. And. Stops.

And starts. Again. In first, wheels barely turning, a

tailback a quarter of a mile ahead to the start of the
bridge, nothing up ahead but car-tops glittering in the
sun, short-sleeved shirts and bare elbows hanging out of
open windows, the odd set of fingers drumming a tune
or just impatience on a car door, snatches of radio, two
kids playing tank commanders from their sun roof. As we
move forward in two lanes of queue I switch the ignition
off and let the T-Bird roll on and on ever so slow in neutral
until it stops eventually through weight or gravity or
friction or whatever the fuck law of matter it is, because
why waste petrol? That's the speed the traffic's going at
with the engine on.

And now it's not moving at all.

I sit looking along the line of car-tops. Then I open the
door, get out and put the soft-top back. (So what if it gets
cool at speed? You got to pay for style.) I stand there in the
middle of the motorway and take my shades off and light
a Marlboro. I watch the tailback lengthen behind me.

Ahead is the long steel bridge, the bottleneck. Above
the parapet I can see the tops of lorries and coaches
across the span, not moving, nothing doing, just waiting
traffic up there, and more waiting back here for it to
start to move before *we* can, before it all gets back to
us, one gearstick after another slipping into first again,
the Domino effect. I look across the riveted, battleship-
grey bridge – that thick grey paint that would have a
dusty glitter of aluminium or mica in it in this sunlight
if you got up close. In rough white painted letters on the
metal, in the centre of a panel right out in the middle of
the span, above the tide-fields and the mudflats and the
River Neath, I read the one word:

Liar.

Not even *Kev Wuz Ere*, or *Free Wales* (Another Hand,
as they say, adds the *With Every Six Gallons*, later), or
CCFC Kill Swans:

Liar.

I stand looking towards it. The only piece of graffiti, what on the Noo York subway they call Public Art, on that whole half-mile of metal bridge.

And there's something about that word. I'd actually noticed it before, now I think about it. But parked bumper to bumper you get time to weigh a thing like that. I mean, what kind of person takes a brush and a pot of white paint all the way out to the middle of the Briton Ferry bridge, climbs out over the side and hangs eighty-odd feet above the river just to daub a single word? And why *that* word? Who was it meant for? For one person in particular? Someone who crosses that bridge every day, and who knows the word is meant for him? (Or her?) (Who was lied to?) (What the fuck was the *lie*?)

Or is it aimed at anyone who sees it? (Because nobody tells the truth *all* the time.) And actually, from that point of view it's very clever, it's like it's saying: I know something about you. Something nobody else knows. Something you don't even know that anybody knows. (And you wonder: *What?*)

You know, you see a thing like that and it makes you fucking think. It really does.

I see the traffic on the bridge begin to move at last, and faster now, perhaps there was an accident up ahead and they've cleared it. I get back in the car, look at the roadmap, and notice a detour up through Briton Ferry at the roundabout before the bridge. Yeah, I'll be quicker that way, today. I'll avoid more of this. Waiting for the cars ahead of me to start to move, I slip a Ry Cooder tape into the slot, mostly for my neighbours' benefit, especially for that girl with her jerk in the Sierra, I winked at her when I got out just now, to annoy him more than anything else, because I hate guys with permed ringlets (like some ponce of an England international footballer), and I hate Sierra drivers, I always have, it's a certain kind of man who drives a car like that or even works for a firm that gives him one.

I turn the key, then turn Ry up a good bit more, above the engine, 'Cause Honey, Me, Ah'm just a Country Boy. I sit there waiting with the soft-top back, smoking no hands, and the shades on now again but right down on my nose so I'm looking over them like Jimmy Dean in *Giant*, tapping one hand on the sill and half-singing with the words, *Alimony, Alimony, Alimony's killing me, Ain't had money in my pocket, not since Nineteen Fifty-Three*. One car after another ahead of me now putting it into first and then getting it out of first and into second, into third, getting out onto the bridge and now I'm moving too, the Man in the '57 T-Bird, still smoking, squinting, one hand guiding the wheel, the other tapping on the outside of the door, just keeping my foot half on the brake in third and listening to Ry, the country blues, that slithery guitar, till on the last stretch, at the roundabout, the car that's been in front of me heads for the bridge and leaves me the space I need to flick the Marlboro away, head for the second exit, and gun the engine just enough to let me hit 'em with a Wheel Squeal.

And drive. Finally getting rid of every car in front of me and all those still tailed back a mile or more behind. They'll all be turning left onto the bridge, then left again, west, west, programmed like migrant lemmings for another bottleneck at Swansea, and then the slow queue out through country lanes to reach the swarming beaches and the Gower.

While I turn right, north, and again north, heading up a valley, then another valley to the hills (or should it be The Sticks), the map's red *A*-road for three or four miles, then a yellow *B*-road (if not worse) for the next fifteen or so, the roadmap open on the seat beside me: this is not my patch. Last time I was up here it all looked different anyway. That was in bitter late December, these tangled woods along the road black then, and snow piebald on the ground in patches and unbroken white up on the hills. But now it looks like pretty countryside (except for those grey pylons): the road, almost empty of traffic, running up through budding trees, the woods like a green haze.

Everything looks different in spring. Not that spring makes you feel any better. Like a Bank Holiday, it only makes things worse.

The road climbs slowly, wooded hills on either side, the odd field of sheep, I slow to look as I pass a pit on the left: a yard full of coaldust and yellow plant, a chained gate, half a dozen sitting men around a fire in an oildrum brazier. A hand-painted sign is propped against the link fence:

NUM Oficial Picket.

The second *f* is corrected in above in a narrowed stroke. And I remember the miners are out on strike, have been for a while now. There's been a lot about it on the TV news.

In a circle playing cards, they stop and look up as I slow, holding it long enough to be a stare. Woollybacks. Up here I don't suppose they've seen a car like this before, except in films.

A mile on I have to slow again for a village, or at least some rows of terraced houses. The front door opening straight onto the pavement, the odd old lady sitting in the doorway in a brought chair, watching things. Kids playing in the street.

Then, right at the head of the valley, is a place I remember, and I know I'm almost at the end of the road. It's only one more dirty-looking, Welsh, played-out little village, don't even ask me to pronounce the fucking name of it. Just another place that grew up around a hole in the ground twenty miles from nowhere, a couple of dozen or so houses, every one complete with outside toilets, and views of half-grassed slagheaps if you take a glance out of the wrong window.

But what I remember from last time is when you take the sharp left out of the place and swing round the corner and across the railway bridge, and suddenly for the first time, right across the next valley, you see the mountains.

And on a clear day like it is again today it's like Wyoming must be or Montana, like a background you'd see in a film. Or some Shangri-la, another mountain land painted on glass. And I slowed the car right down last time to look at it, and I do again now, and it gives me the same lift this time as last. Because it's suddenly like you're not in Wales any more. You're in America.

So drive. Leaving the railway-sidings and the massive coalyard dunes and another chained gate with a half-dozen men who again immediately stop playing cards in front of it to stare me past, the stranger in the two-tone Yankee car.

Then I rattle across a cattle-grid (except that up here you'd have to say it was a sheep-grid). And, on the other side of that, I pass the roadside sign that tells you:

Powys

And there are no pits here of course, no slagheaps. Only those mountains. And the Brecon Beacons National Park. Because what starts here is a Conservation area. It's as if you pass that sign out of West Glamorgan into Powys and the coalfield stops right at the boundary, either because there's no coal in the ground in Powys or they wouldn't let you make the mess it takes to get it out.

So. Drive. And not much further now: just down a long hill to the valley, then a couple of miles going up a valley road, then park and climb. Because as soon as I leave that sign behind, that pit village and those slagheaps, I know I'm fifteen minutes at the outside from another kind of slag: my wife.

I'm sweating like a pig by the time I get to the top. Or what I call the top: a kind of shelf of grass and rock and dry lichen which runs up to the foot of the scree and that rock cliff beneath the actual ridge. What the fuck: it's near enough the top for me. No reason to lug my guts all the way up to the summit of a mountain just Because It's There. I'm no Sherpa Tenzing. Anyway, I don't want to climb too high, too far to be able to see: these binoculars are only twelve by fifties.

I have to sit to get my breath back. This is the same place I was last time, I think. Though I had some trouble finding it again. Everything looked completely altered, and I think today I came up a different track through the woods too. In fact I ended up following what looked like an old cartway, you'd almost say a grassed-over road cut on an angle up the mountain. That brought me out a good way left of where I wanted to be, though at least it was an easier climb than scrambling blind up steep hillside over rocks and through dead bracken like last time, in all that snow, Christ almighty it was cold up here then, I must have been crazy. Climbing all the way up here just to sit and freeze my cock off watching the smoke rise from their chimney for two hours and imagining them down there toasting bread for afternoon tea or roasting chestnuts on that fire with the kids playing on the rug in front of it, and my wife coming in from the kitchen in her apron with her hair tied back and her hands all floury so that she has to rub her nose with the back of her wrist when it itches suddenly, standing in the doorway to ask him how he likes his stuffing done or is it too early for a sherry and he looks up from the glowing fireside and the Christmas book she bought him, and he smiles.

But I suppose if I was crazy then I must be crazy now.

Looking at the map, I think that track probably did use to be a cartway. In the old days there must have been workings on the top. *Quarries*, it says here. And looking up at the mountain you can see where part of the rock wall is recessed as if there'd been more quarrying there too. Limestone, I suppose that cliff would be. Though Christ knows how they got the stone down the mountain, track or no. Carts and ponies, I suppose. Or perhaps they rolled it down on fucking logs like the ancient Britons, up here they probably didn't have the wheel. But whatever way they did it, you can't help thinking, What a bitch of a job. You'd be knackered every morning just from struggling up the mountainside to work. And that's before you've even punched the card and started being paid for getting stone out of the hill. Not that they'd have had time-cards in those days. Nor hardly even clocks. In fact, I expect they've only just now got the wrist-watch in up here, and from what I can see they're all running twenty-five years slow in any case.

I mean, you drive up through these little grimy, run-down hick-town villages, see the old ladies on their way to Chapel, still wearing hats with hatpins in, and you think Jesus fucking Christ, this is another world. This isn't South Wales. It's Nineteen Fifty-Five.

I unsling my gear, bag, binoculars, rifle. Get organised. This is a good lookout point. A stretch of flattish grass behind three outcrop crags. You can watch the mountainside below and the whole valley, north and south, from between these rocks and stay unseen. And from here I've got a perfect overview of the house.

It's a stone cottage with a purplish roof. Those slates look fairly new, and they're a different shade from the older, greyish ones on the outhouse, which are spotted with that yellow lichen. Have they reroofed the place since last time I was here? From this distance, even through the binoculars, I can't tell if they're real slates or those asbestos imitations. (There's a tremendous difference in price between the two.) They look real. Still, I suppose he can afford to spend money on upgrading his property, since he must have bought the whole place for a song, up here, let's face it, it's hardly

Belgravia prices up these valleys, all you've fucking got is views.

At the back of the house is a garden. If you can call it that, since it's just grass and the grass, you'd say, less lawn than walled-off hillside. I suppose they've got that tethered goat to keep it short, and those chickens. (I bet she loves all this, the bitch. Country Life.)

At the front of the house is a rutted track down to that farm I can just see lower down, and then a kind of banked lane that takes you down to the road.

(But I wouldn't have noticed most of this last time, I realise, because of the snow. So I don't know about that roof.)

I can plot it all now, anyway, on my brand-new O.S. walker's map, Beacons National Park (Western Area). 1: 25000. I didn't have one on this big a scale last time. It gives you all the detail you could want, especially when you're overlooking the whole area from this height, it's like you can track anything you want to in a gun-sight and the grid squares are the cross-hairs in it. This map, in fact, not only shows you all these outlying farms and cottages, it even gives you the names of some of them, I suppose the older ones. (Even if they are in fucking Welsh.) I've got my finger on their cottage now. *Clawdd Y Mynach*. I bet she thinks that's really something, having the name of their house on a fucking map like it was some Stately Home. When she first discovered that, the bitch, she must have known she made the right move, assuming she ever doubted it. Because let's face it, I don't suppose the Ordnance Survey is ever going to get around to doing the same for her erstwhile residence, Flat 25A Corporation Road in Grangetown (just above the butcher's).

Checking things off against the map, I even find a dotted line (*footpath*), showing that track I came up and which I still have a good view of, below. And it looks as if anyone else who came up here would probably use that track as well. Which would give me plenty of warning if they did: I'd see them a good half-mile away. Not that I expect anyone comes up as high as I am here. Let's face it, there's nothing up here but rock and grass and scattered sheep-shit. (Or is it rabbits'? Some of those droppings look small enough to be. Perhaps I'll get the chance to pot one off.)

I suppose you do get the odd rambler or rural rubberneck up here from time to time. Or in summer a courting couple from those council-houses down in the valley there, trying to find a quiet spot to do it in. Perhaps that's why the grass looked already flattened here. Or that might be the sheep, sleeping here. Or do sheep sleep standing up, like they say horses do? I dunno. Me, I'm a City Boy, I'm not much interested in sheep unless it comes with mint sauce and new potatoes. (Which is actually a thought. I uncase the rifle and sight one up. It's cropping the grass fifty yards away. Okay, it's hardly Big Game Hunting, but once the echo'd died away no one would ever know.)

Does anybody own these mangy fuckers anyway? Or are they strays? I've never in my life before seen sheep just wandering along the roads like they seem to do round here, bedraggled-looking things with shitted fleeces. Perhaps you can get to own a flock of sheep round here without having a patch of land, or even a lawn, to graze them on. Who knows? Perhaps it's an old Welsh ancestral privilege or commoner's right, so every household keeps a couple and just lets the damn things roam. Or else they're Holy sheep, Untouchables, like Brahma bulls. Nothing would surprise me, I'm not kidding. Not this far up these valleys. Because what you obviously have here is a woollyback society, built on the mighty sheep. Essential not only for Meat and Milk and Wool but for Work, Sport, Health and Recreation (not to mention Sex).

Talking of which, I refocus the house. This house he holds her in for his own pleasure. And which she stays in, for hers. This household they set up together at my expense, taking it out of my marriage, my fucking skull.

Through the binoculars I can see my kids' toys scattered on the grass. And that yellow bike I bought Mandy and that must be Darryl's now, she'd be too big for it at her age. The little stabiliser wheels on either side have been taken off, so he must be able to ride properly. I can remember bringing it in to Mandy that Christmas morning. I'd wrapped up the whole bloody thing in Christmas paper, saddle, wheels, frame, handlebars, I'd even wound wrapping paper round the brake-cables, the whole thing took me ages to do. (It was just a kind of joke of course, since it was fucking obvious it was a bike.)

It's lying on its side on his lawn now, front wheel angled upwards, it's just been let fall there and left. The way kids let go of everything, just drop it, when something new gets their attention.

Jesus Christ, I suddenly think, Jesus Christ all fucking mighty.

And I think of what you have to go through on the off-chance of catching an unscheduled glimpse of your own kids without their mother screaming at you from an upstairs window, not even opening the door to talk to you, just screaming down. You're breaking the conditions of your restraining order. Come round here bothering us again, you bastard, and I'll take you back to court.

The bitch. The stinking bitch. Because I never will forgive her for that. For bringing all that dirty washing out in public. And I never will forgive the Law, or trust a court again. Because I thought the Law was there to protect the family and home. But that day they took my kids away from me and awarded them to her and even put restraints on me, their lawful wedded father, I knew the court was solely for the benefit of the adulterers and whores. Because it looks as if a woman can provoke a man to raving madness, or murder, or beyond, by what she does, and go scot-free. But let him only close his knuckles to a fist against her, or phone her up and try to speak to her when she won't talk to him, or lose half a day's pay just to wait and see his own kids coming out of school, and you're in court accused of harassment or molestation or brutality.

I've got this dull ache. I've had it since I got here. It seems to start between my shoulderblades then go upwards, like I cricked a muscle in my neck climbing up here. You know how you do that sometimes, get a little strain somewhere, and you don't take any notice, you expect it to pass off. Only mine get worse. They go right up the back of my head. And right round to the front sometimes. It's like my whole neck and head's a G-clamp screwed tight on a point that's just behind the eyes. That's when they're really bad. Rubbing doesn't seem to do much good. Sometimes it even seems to make it worse. Perhaps I should just try to relax.

Relax.

I open a can of Heineken and light a cigarette. I let my shoulders slump and sit there. Legs crossed like a fucking Buddha. I let all my breath out and empty my mind, just watching the edge of the paper smouldering down my cigarette. Occasionally swigging from the can.

From time to time I look down at the house. But except for that tiny litter of toys across the grass there's no sign of life down there. (You'd have thought the kids would be out playing in the garden on a day like this.) Someone must be in the house, though, because the car's parked in the drive. It's a blue Volvo estate. It's not a cheap car, a Volvo. And this one looks in fair condition, though I can't tell from here what year it is (I can't keep the glasses steady enough to read the registration).

Not that a Volvo is my kind of car. I see a lot of Volvos in the garage. The best I could say about it is that it's a solid car, not to say fucking stolid. All those crushproof factors. (The Swedes are high on safety.) But of course it all puts up the weight.

And the Estate Model is pure Rural Gentry, natch. It's a snob car. More Country Life. (Not to mention *Homes and Gardens*.) Forget the kids' safety, that's why people buy that kind of car. And that's probably the new Mr and Mrs Cawley to a T. I bet that's exactly how they see themselves, living up here on the old 'estate'. Like in those ads for menthol cigarettes. Parked by a mountain stream, the hatchback open. Brace of springer spaniels in the back and a pair of salmon rods.

I take the second can of Heineken out of my holdall and a big packet of crisps. 'Family size'.

And it's strange how suddenly a little thing like that can still cut you sometimes, when your family's gone and you're opening this bag just for yourself, the way you open everything now, every packet of sausages or tin of beans. Just for yourself. That's why I can't bear cooking now, or even bothering to eat proper food. There was a time when I used to like doing the shopping even, when I'd get home from work on Friday with my wages and we'd all go out as a family to Safeways to get the week's supplies. Darryl was only a baby then. He'd sit in the little kid's seat on the trolley. And we'd always buy him and Mandy a little 'treat', like a Real Cream Cake each because, let's face it, fair's fair, and Mamma and Dadda always had their weekend bottle of Safeways vodka. I used to like doing the cooking sometimes too, especially on a Sunday morning when I'd usually get up before everybody else because you'd never get a minute's peace anyway, what with bouncing kids and the bed a litter of review sections and colour supplements, you could never get Carol to do a damn thing most of the morning, even look up and actually hear what you were saying let alone get a breakfast ready, once she got her nose into the Sunday papers, the so-called 'Qualities', i.e. reading about how the other ten per cent are living. So I'd go downstairs and make everybody breakfast. And I mean Breakfast. Bacon, egg, fried bread, black pudding, beans, tomatoes, fried potatoes if there were any cold from yesterday, mushrooms. Whatever we had in the house that I could find to throw into a frying-pan. Big pot of tea. And that's why, now, I can't bear shopping and don't want to cook. Because when for the first time ever in your life you've got used to doing things for other people, and loving it, it's hard going back to doing those same things for yourself without remembering. All you do is end up crying in the bacon-fat.

There's movement down there, outside the house. I get the binos trained a second too late to see him getting into the Volvo, just his second leg being lifted in and the onside door closing. I still haven't seen his face. And he's on the wrong side of the car for me to see it now.

My wife is kind of ushering Darryl into the nearside back seat. He gets in and she leans in after him, probably fussing around doing up his seat-belt. Mandy is standing in the doorway of the cottage. I can see even from here that she's been crying. She doesn't want to go. My wife shuts Darryl's door and looks at Mandy 'grimly'. She 'points' at the car. She's being 'threatening'. But it all looks so melodramatic from up here. And I can't help thinking, What a way to treat a seven-year-old. I know they can be a pain in the arse sometimes, make you want to strangle them. But she's my daughter. My firstborn. As Darryl is my secondborn. And my wife? She's not that any more. She's somebody else's fucking wife. All she is to me now is their mother.

Finally she marches over and grabs Mandy by one hand and half leads, half pulls her over to the other rear door of the car. Which she opens and 'points' inside again, as if this was a dumb show (i.e. for fucking dummies). As if the poor kid wasn't capable of understanding simple histrionics. Whereas it's obvious to me, a quarter of a mile away, that my daughter is just upset over something and wants to stay at home, perhaps she just doesn't want to go out in the car with that bastard in the driving seat, with my wife's Live-In Lover and her Stand-In Father. Who is staying out of the whole squabble so far (a Wise Move, and keep it that way, cunt. You move a muscle to force either of my kids and I'll come down this hillside in two strides and shorten you a good foot at the neck).

In the binoculars I see my daughter's red face lift and her mouth open in a wail that's silent, like the one on the face of the moon.

And there are tears in my eyes too. Because Mandy has always been my darling favourite, and I can't bear to see what is happening to her. I can't bear to think that she's unhappy, or that since I've gone out of her life she may have become a 'problem child'. (I can't bear to think that she's 'normal' either, that you can break up a family the way my wife did, and just get away with it.) Because Mandy is never far from me. The other night I even woke up thinking one of the kids was in the bed. I think I must have thought my wife was in there with me too, because of course she used to bring them in with us sometimes when they were babies and they'd woken. And I thought I might be smothering it, so I rolled over to the edge and slept on my side. And when I woke up again, in the morning, there was no one there. I was lying in that double bed – which had slept two of us, and three of us, and even the four of us, some nights – alone. And in my mind I knew it was Mandy who had come in the bed with me. And who I rolled away from to keep from harming. And I think perhaps she does come back sometimes. To visit her old Dadda. Even if it's only by thinking about me. (It's true what they say: Thought Crosses Boundaries.) Whereas Darryl's too little, he probably left too young even to remember me. (Like the Jesuits say: Give them a child at seven (not to mention less), and he's theirs for ever.) But I think Mandy does remember. She's old enough to. And she's old enough not to understand why I'm not there.

But now Carol has bundled her into the car too, and is

leaning in after her. Wherever they're going, it's obvious my wife's not going with them. The kids have coats on. They looked dressed-up in fact, in some kind of Sunday Best, as if they were going to visit someone. Whereas Carol is just in jeans and a red T-shirt, it's not one I've seen her in. (After a while you realise everything's different, even the clothes you'd got used to someone wearing.)

For some reason, as I watch through the binoculars, I think of his kids too, Raoul's, and I wonder why they aren't down there. Why they aren't going with him. Why *my* kids have to. Then I remember that they're with their mother too. That he's lost his like I've lost mine.

The only difference being that in his case that's simple justice. After all he's the one who fucked up his own family and marriage, even if only as a coincidental by-product of the process of fucking up mine. In fact, it's a damn sight less than justice, since he couldn't have cared that much about them anyway. He's lucky his wife and kids are all he's lost.

Or lost so far. Because one of these days he'll lose all he's got left. One dark night I'll make him pay for it in blood and snot and teeth. I'll feed him his own balls. Because nobody, But Nobody, does that kind of thing to my kids. Let alone to me.

My wife closes Mandy's door and steps back to wave as the car slides forward and down the track. She watches it out of the gate then turns back to the house. The car vanishes under budding trees, reappears again along the track, and is gone, downward into green woodland.

I focus the house. My wife is at the downstairs window. She has gone straight to the phone. It's the same red as her T-shirt. She stares out at the garden as she talks. She looks at her wrist-watch, shrugs. She turns away, carrying the phone, and moves away from the window.

A few minutes later she comes outside again. She's

carrying a basket in front of her, of washing it must be, and wet and heavy from the stiff-legged way she's walking with it. She carries it to the rotary line at the side of the toy-littered square of grass. Stooping and straightening she begins pegging out kids' clothes on the line, a row of tiny socks and a pair of little blue dungarees, a kid's shirt. Then some blouses of Mandy's, they're much bigger. She takes after me in size.

I've always liked my wife in what she's wearing now, jeans and a shirt or a T-shirt. She's lean as a whippet and she's got the kind of neat arse in jeans that from behind looks like a boy's. Which I love on a woman (provided there's enough in front to let you know she's not). My chest gets tight and sad as I watch her through the binoculars and suddenly, straightening up, she brushes the blonde-streaked hair back from her right eye in a way I remember. And I realise you never know how much people's ordinary gestures go towards their whole identity for you, until you start to miss them, until they're just not there with you any more. And then they make a movement that they're not even thinking about and that you've seen them make a thousand times, although you didn't even know it till this one time. And it lays you open like a knife. Because nothing they actively might want to do to hurt you ever hurts you as quick and as sure as some trivial unconscious habit or expression. That, and remembering the things you did to each other on a bed. Or didn't do, never even thought of doing at the time when you could have, when you were in love, when every time you lay on a bed together you were swimming in each other like the sea. Things you did or could have done that you keep seeing now. It's like some things are burned into you forever with a red-hot iron.

As I watch she straightens and brushes the hair back from her eyebrow again, it's longer than it used to be so it falls over her face more when she bends, and a yellower blonde. And she begins pegging out one of *his* shirts now. Which cuts me too. A light-coloured shirt, probably a small check. It blows aside, arms down, as she pegs it twice at the hem. That's how I'd like to see him. Hanging from his heels. Or like in a Western, when they bring someone in head-down over the saddle of a horse.

And as I watch my wife spin the line to an empty quarter I know it wasn't my two kids that I came up here to see, any more than it was really them that caused all the ugliness and aggravation when we split up, although I always said it was. I didn't mind her having the kids, as long as I could see them when I wanted to. What I minded was anybody else having *her*. What I minded was the thought of somebody at her from the back like a dog, the way she always liked it. I feel myself getting stiff, watching her move about that clothesline, two hundred yards or so away but clear as crystal in the lenses except for the tremor of my hands. Watching her as she pegs out in the sunlight more clothes of the children I might even have conceived with her that way, from behind, dog-style, looking down at her sallow back with the ridge of her spine and every vertebra standing out all the way down to the cleft where she was open and widelegged for me. And I wish I could reach down across all this stone-rubble and bracken, then across a sheep-field and a dry-stone wall, and lift the hem of that red T-shirt and slip my hand in where the column of her backbone rises supple from the waistband of her worn, pale-buttocked Levi jeans.

But I wouldn't even if I could, even if I could get close enough to reach down the binoculars and touch her, on sheer magnification alone. That could come later. Because I wouldn't want to give up her not knowing I'm here. The looking. The watching. The being hidden in this landscape, crouched behind these crags up on this nameless mountainside, with binoculars and all this view of wooded valley and farmhouse and opposite hillside and, as centrepoint and focus of all this, down there in the garden of her slate-roofed cottage, Carol, my wife (and someone else's), in a tight red short-sleeved T-shirt and a pair of jeans so soft and old that when they were stiff and new I might even have felt her up in them, when she was doing the washing-up at the sink, say, coming up behind her and putting my hand between her legs and rubbing the whole edge of my hand backwards along that orange-stitched seaming at the crotch.

I'm kneeling now, right hand inside my belt. But it's hard to do this and keep the glasses trained on her, a telescope on a tripod would be better, steady as this rock I'm leaning on, just me moving behind it or rather this hand inside my jeans, like this, like this, my left arm already aching from holding the glasses and the image wobbling everything whirling about in that circle in a blur of green and purple and red and the white and yellow and blue of the washing, and so I drop my aching arm and close my eyes instead to imagine her like this, like this, kneeling behind the rock so that no one even on the mountainside opposite can see what I'm doing and my back turned from the ridge above me, that long backbone of stone outcrop up there behind me because you never can be certain someone isn't higher than you and looking down on you too, through binoculars even, as you were looking down on her and so you can't relax into it this way, can't roll over on your back and let it spurt into the sun in case there is someone, but you can't save it for later either, not this one, like that time, yes, that night we did it drunk in a dirty telephone kiosk at 2 a.m. because like they say, Man, sometimes when you Gotta Go you Gotta Go, and that was the only place when we came out of that club that wasn't right out on the street so we went into that kiosk and did it standing up, she was hanging round my neck and had her legs crossed round my back and I was blind with sweat, because sometimes you forget about everything and everybody else on earth or caring

70

if there's anybody watching you or not for (*Carol. Carol. Carol.*) that hot second.

Darkening those grey rock cliffs cloud-shadow comes down the mountain and passes over me. Below, I see its dullness spreading onwards, outwards like a stain across the sheep-field, passing over the stone house where my wife is, down one whole side of the valley then up the hillside opposite, dimming the green of budded trees. And abruptly everything is dulled.

How I feel too. As if the sun has gone out of me. There are so many things that seem to matter so much when your bag is tight and full. But once you've shot your load you're just a wrinkled pouch again, and everything in life goes as slack as it has. It's only at times like this that you start to think how fucking boring life is, what little point there is to anything. What's that saying? All animals are sad after sex. St Augustine it was, said that. Or one of those saints. Though how would a saint know about a thing like that? A pope, I can understand. Some of those popes were worse than Capone. But not a saint. Anyway. It's true. And it's even sadder when it's sex just with yourself.

I light a cigarette and crush the second Heineken can. I lie on my back looking up at the mountain ridge behind me. Scree. Stone cliffs. Crags. Clouded sky. I unfold the map again. According to this, beyond that crest of grey rock there's nothing for ten or fifteen miles. Not even a lonely farmhouse or a sheepfold or a pile of stones with *Cairn* in Gothic letters, like there are further south. Just ravens' nests: a couple of stones and twigs raked together on a shelf of rock. Just streams and contour lines and spot heights and a little group of irregular pockmark-like symbols to show rocky ground. Nothing, in fact. All the way over to Llandovery. Just mountains.

I hadn't thought there was wilderness, or at least emptiness, of such extent in this country, where, let's face it, the countryside's usually not much more than the space between dwellings, or worked fields along a motorway. And as I lie there panning those crests through binoculars I wonder if you could live up there if you had to. A man with just a gun, say, and a compass and a knife. A man trained to survive, or for the first time having to learn how to, living off the land, off rabbits and mountain hares, the odd rustled sheep turned on a slow spit, and water from the stream. Living off whatever he could find up there and without anyone knowing he was there because nobody else ever goes there. Like Marty Sheen in *Badlands*.

Except that he of course had Sissie Spacek to run off with and to keep him company up there. And I haven't. I've got nobody. Except my cold screaming wife. Or Rusty.

Rusty.

And I wonder if she would come with me. In some little short, fringed tube of suede, and thong sandals, yeah. I could just go for her in that. My tall, tawny-haired, long-legged squaw, Following Her Man. Following him into the mountains as he climbs, shrewd-footed from rock to rock, following a trail she cannot see high up into his Ancestral Homelands. Into the land of the Thunderbird. He's forgotten her already, his thoughts are ahead of him, on the lie of the land and the scent of the wind and on the pure-white twelve-point buck he's tracked for four hours (and all his lifetime), holding the rifle out crosswise in front of him as he climbs, like Bobby De Niro in *The Deer Hunter*. (Jesus, what a film that was.)

The only problem of course with all this being that round here there ain't no deer.

Not the wild fuckers, anyway. The only deer round here are in the country park at Margam, I remember on the way here seeing the traffic turning off there, all the parked cars in the sun, and that leaping deer sign beside the motorway, a so-called Alert to Motorists, I suppose, just in case one of them managed to jump over or browse through that eight-foot chain-link fence they got all round that park and ran loose on the motorway. Fat chance of that. I bet those deer are tame and stupid as a herd of cows.

Nah. In places this might look like the Rockies or the Ozarks or the Appalachians. But it's not any of those. There's no wild deer or lynxes or bobcats or mountain-lions. And the only wolf now left in all of Wales must be that stuffed one in the case in the Museum I used to take the kids to see, the last wolf left in Wales was hunted down and killed in 1760 or whatever.

(The only lone wolf left round here is me.)

I watch the house again through the binoculars. No movement, just those pale shirts lifting on the rotary line, which the wind turns through a quarter as I watch. And with that freshened wind I feel a spot of rain. Another darkens on the grey rock in front of me, and another, big as coins. I look up at the sky. Purple cloud is coming over the ridge of the mountain. More huge spots of rain fall on my face. The light darkens as you look at it. Any minute now, I realise, the Thunderbird is going to Speak at last. It's going to piss it down.

I look down at the house, the blowing clothes on the line. Fuck it, I think. Call it a day. It's a no-contest deci-sion, since there's no cover for anything bigger than a rat up here. I'm on a soaking to nothing. If I stay all I'm ever going to see happen down at the old homestead will be my wife's face appearing at the window once, watching the rain fall. Knowing her, she probably won't even bother running outside to get the washing in.

I start packing back into the holdall everything that came out of it except the empty beer-cans. (*Heineken: Gets To The Parts That Other Beers Don't Reach*. And, looked at that way, it's true: no matter where you go you'll see one of those crushed cans.)

The rain holds off as I scramble down the mountain-side, skirting huge grey-lichened rocks, keeping out of sight from the cottage. As I come out again onto the old grassy cartway the light darkens again suddenly. The greening tree-tops in the woods below me are intense.

A man. Climbing towards me. Head bowed to the cartway as he comes.

I'd hide. Behind that rock, say. But he may already have seen me first. (It looks suspicious if you just disappear off the mountainside, like the prophet Isaiah.) (Go down to meet him, open-faced.)

A young man with dark hair, wearing a windcheater, hatless.

Shouldering the holdall, I walk down the easy slope towards him. I take him for a walker. Though somewhere I realise his progress is too careful or delicate for that. That his new tan shoes are too light for country like this, even though the ground's dry. That his fawn trousers have a new crease in them.

When we're ten yards from each other I have to kick a stone to warn him, get him to look up. So startled to see me he almost looks scared. (I could have hidden, or come to that just stood there. He would have gone straight past.)

Looks like rain, I say pleasantly.

His face is flushed with wind or the climb. His grin is nervous. That's because of the rifle. But one thing about carrying a gun is this: people eye it and you a bit funny if they suddenly happen to meet you. But at least it gives you a reason to be out here on the mountainside in Powys in a denim jacket and tooled cowboy boots, because, let's face it, I don't exactly look like a walker either (not to mention a local).

I keep walking and don't turn around to look at him again until I'm into the cover of the woods.

Then I suddenly run cold. Through the leaves I can see him halted up there on the track and looking down, over the dry-stone walling, across the sheep-field, to the cottage. And, as I watch from the cover of the trees, he puts both hands on the top of that stone wall and one shoe-toe carefully into some gap in the stonework halfway up, to climb it. Then he seems to think again and removes his toe. He looks along the wall and takes his hands from it. Already it's like it's evening. Then suddenly he's in this lurid patch of false sunlight, as if it's picking out just him and that mountain-ash tree by the wall. He looks up at the sky. It's the colour of the metal of this gun. But there's this uncanny kind of light. He goes a few yards further on, looks at the wall, goes on again, quicker now, he's looking for the easiest place. He puts two hands on the wall again and, careful again not to graze the leather, inserts one toecap in another stirrup in the stones. Before he heaves himself up, though, he looks across at the cottage again. (I know he's looking at the cottage even though I can't see it myself from here, just as I know why he's climbing the wall in the first place. I don't need to take a pair of binoculars out of their case to see a thing as plain as that.) And at that moment he actually takes one hand off the wall again: was that to brush away a fly? Or just quickly to return the wave she must have given him from the back door or an upstairs window? Then he mounts the wall astraddle, swings over his back leg, and slips down on the other side, out of view for me, but now with just an easy field to cross and the go-ahead, the message that the coast is clear, already signalled by my wife, the lousy faithless bitch. Because I'm aghast. I fucking am. I can't believe she'd do a thing so blatant and so prompt.

And the strangest thing of all is that I don't even have the right to say a thing *about* it. It's not even 'my business' any more. It's his problem now, Raoul's. That poor sap she left me for and got remarried to and lives with now, fat lot of good that's doing him. (I could almost start feeling sorry for the cunt.) Because no sooner has he taken her two kids out through the front door than she's back into the house and on that red phone to another man and then, quick, into the bathroom and already fitting in her diaphragm before Lover Boy climbs his wall and crosses a small field and comes in through the back door, coming off the mountain, I suppose, so the people at the farm below don't see him pass the door and start to talk.

But, Jesus Christ. I mean, she's hardly been with him six months. A man with her these days don't seem to last much longer than a pair of tennis shoes.

And it makes you think. It does. It makes you wonder. It makes me even start to wonder if this kind of thing was happening when she was married to me, even before Raoul came on the scene. When I was out at work, sweating off my bollocks down at Guest Keen in the rolling-mill, on shift. (Because suddenly I could see her packing off the kids to school and nursery, or to bed when I was on nights, then sitting down retouching her makeup while she's waiting for the doorbell.) Because (talk about Easy Come Easy Go) a bitch like that is never to be trusted. Because that's what she is, that's all she is. Just look at it. She's little better than a bitch in constant heat.

I take the gun out of its nylon carrying-case, break it, put the slug in it, straighten it and fire the slug into the mud. Then I break it and put another slug in it and straighten it and fire that slug next to the first. I don't know where or on what I would have used the third slug, because suddenly the rain comes down.

And I mean suddenly. The rain comes down just as I'm imagining him getting closer to the cottage, I even see him sprinting the last twenty yards to get out of it and her simultaneously opening the door for him so he won't have to stand waiting there in it, the two of them meeting in that empty door-frame, laughing, him running his hand back through his hair to shake the wet off and his face flushed with the air and their eyes and faces bright with laughing, so that the rain coming down so quick and so heavy like that actually takes that first moment of awkwardness away from them and makes it easier for him to come into another man's house for her and easier for her to have him in.

Because it was as sudden and dense and cold as someone turning a shower full on. And me standing there under it fully clothed, stuffing the rifle back inside the case and zipping it up to try and keep at least that dry, when the rain's already soaked straight through my denim jacket to my back and shoulders by the time I've got the zip up to the top. Grabbing the holdall and carrying the gun sloped under the same arm to leave one hand free, I come down through the wet woods, slipping and floundering on the steep path that's already slick mud. And the woods are green, green as hell, in this rain and this weird light, and loud with the noise of all this rain on all these leaves.

And it's like when all the colours run and merge in the windscreen in the car-wash, because by now I'm crying. I can't fucking help it, crying out of pity for me and for my kids and out of pity for her too, my ex-wife, doing it in the middle of a Bank Holiday afternoon with some local yokel with nothing but a stiff whisky on his breath and something stiffer in between his trouser pockets.

Crying because there must be something wrong with her, it's as if she gives off the smell of sex no matter where she is, even when she's living in an isolated cottage on a mountainside with two small children, men are fighting their way up through the woods and over rocks at half an hour's notice and in glossy shoes to get to her, like mating insects pick up signals or vibrations in the air for miles around.

Crying because I know that nothing will ever come out right for her or for my kids, they're saddled with a mother who's a loser and a slut. Because I come up here on an Easter Monday, a holiday, a Family Day, on the off-chance of seeing how my kids are growing up, and I'm just in time to see her packing them off for the day and whistling in some cock. Crying because I don't know what it is she wants from life. Because she can't even complain now about living in a crummy flat and getting nowhere with her life, about Being Better or Wanting Better than her Surroundings. Because she fucked up my life and my two kids' lives to get away from that. But she's still no better off or happier or more fulfilled, she's got no more class now than when I met her or than that time before we had the kids, when we used to get legless most nights in The Greyhound or The Old Arcade with all those pillbrains and headbangers and refugees from the Sixties, arty university deadbeats like her, who just wanted to be ex-students all their lives, who thought the world owed them a living just because they'd been to college. And I know that nothing will change her now. She'll fuck up everything she ever has.

And I'm crying for me too. Because we loved each other once. And even after we split up, I used to think I still did love her and she loved me, and that we'd always come back to each other in the end, no matter what, as if that was a fate nothing in our lives could change. Because you don't live with someone all those years and fuck a couple of thousand times with her and have two kids with her and see those kids being literally born and give them names and start at least to bring them up together, without still having something going with that person, even if it's only a residue of simple lust, or the habit or the memory of it you haven't burnt off clear, or never will.

And the strangest thing is that her betrayal now, of *him*, is more final even than her betrayal of me was, which he was knowing partner to. Because you can make excuses at the back of your mind for Love or Passion, even if you can't forgive it. But not for cheap sex. And I know I never could trust her after this. Not far enough to let her slip down to the newsagent's two doors away for cigarettes. Not even to go down for them myself. It's true what they say: what you don't know can't hurt you. But what you do know you can never forget. And so even if she wants to leave him and come back to me when this marriage fucks up in the same way ours did, even if she goes down on her bended knees and begs with tears in her tears, I'd turn my back. I would. Because I know what I've just witnessed with my own two eyes. And I'd always know it could be happening again.

Just as it is right now. In a room in that stone cottage. *Now*. This actual minute.

I plunge and slide down through the green torrential woods towards the mountain road, the car.

All I want to do is get in it and drive the fifty miles to a hot bath. But barely a hundred yards down that steep, twisty mountain road from where I was parked, I see another car. It's pulled in on one side, not even tight to the bank and still pointing uphill. Like he'd been too impatient to park, let alone turn it round first to point the way it had to go back (this road peters out in a dead-end further up).

I brake and get out. The rain is dancing hard off the roof of both cars, but already I'm soaked to the bone so what's the difference. His car is a beat-up blue Cortina, with a brown replacement onside front door and bodywork that could do with replacing too, it's so patched with red anti-oxidising paint, mottles big as camouflage. Stuck in the hole where the aerial was is a wire coathanger twisted to shape. The whole fucking thing is just a piece of junk. You wouldn't drive it to the dump, not by daylight. A sticker on the back window says: *Coal Not Dole*. On the back seat are stacks of posters and handbills and sheets with more peel-off stickers on.

I stand looking at this rattletrap. And I wonder if they've ever done it in this car, my ex-wife and her Striking Miner. Perhaps along this same mountain road, this Lover's Lane, with its pull-ins and passing-places on the side. (And I see them. I see him stopping the car and pulling the handbrake back tight on its cable, to the last click of the ratchet because of the hill.

He kills the headlights and turns to her. (I'm in the

back seat, their flat black cutout heads in the frame of
the windscreen, wide as on Cinemascope. If I could be
anything in this world I'd be God, if he existed. Invisible
and everywhere. Seeing everything and never being seen
yourself.) And the wire is in my hands, it's a length of
piano-wire or stripped electrical flex. I throw it over his
head as their merged silhouettes part from that first long
kiss, separate for breath. But it's a breath he never takes,
I pull it tight and twist my wrists and he's threshing and
choking and drowning, he tries to get hold of the wire
but it's into his neck, he kicks one foot clean through
the windscreen like in *The Godfather* when they kill that
stoolie Carlo, one foot uselessly kicking along the bonnet
of the car and his hands trying to grab a greased wire
until the kicking stops and the hands go limp too, not
even a twitch left in him, not a shudder. Just the swollen
red face with the net of veins still standing out in it,
and the flex into his neck so tight you can hardly see
it any more. The way that sapling along the roadside
has swelled its bark over a rusty strand of barbed wire
stapled to it years ago.)

I pick up a mossed rock from the roadside and heave
it at the windscreen. Which, as the rock bounces off and
clatters on the bonnet, shivers white to an opaque craze of
tiny crystals, still in the identical shape of a windscreen,
not losing a fragment. I take up the rock again but then
let it drop on the bonnet. (I'll let him smash the glass
out himself to see his way home.)

I get back in my car, start it, let the handbrake out,
and ease past his, down that narrow road, under the
green trees. The squeak of wipers and the window awash,
awash. (And I keep seeing it, seeing her. In the bedroom
of that cottage. Brushing the long blonde-streaked hair
back from her cheek in that gesture and tucking it out
of the way behind one ear as she looks down, eyes half-
closed. And bows again to take in the glistening arched-
back head of it, mouth working like a kid sucking the

flavour out of a lolly but a current you can drown in till he (*Now. Now. Now.*) comes and she keeps him coming, milks the spurts and swallows it, she swallows it, easy as swallowing your own phlegm when you haven't got a handkerchief, no worse than that.)

By the time I drive past the back of the sign telling you you're now entering Powys the rain has stopped. I drive across the railway bridge and into West Glamorgan, that first village. No county sign coming this way, just meaner, dirtier here. The run-down single street, the vast pub from the boom days huge as some dead customless hotel. The slagheaps still trying to grow a scrubby beard of weeds and clump-grass at the bottom of everybody's garden. A view of National Park mountains out of your front window and coaltips from your back one. You wonder how people can live in a place like this in 1984, under those peaks of waste. Just think of Aberfan, where the slagheap moved one day and swallowed half the village in an avalanche of black wet slurry, all those kids in the school chanting lessons in their little, high, kids' voices swallowed up, all dead, those children, every one of them, I don't suppose they even got all the bodies out, some of them just the ages of my own kids now. Gone, a whole generation in that one place all gone, unless perhaps there was one boy or girl who didn't go to school that day because of a cold or earache, like the little lame boy who couldn't keep up to follow the Pied Piper and all his friends into the mountain, the miracle you always pray will happen for your kids if no one else's. Aberfan. That was years ago. But I still remember that happening. I'd never even heard of Aberfan before, and a place just twenty-five miles up the road. I suppose the only time these places ever reach the news is when there's a disaster or they're out on strike.

I stop at the other end of the village, at the same six men I passed before. There's a sign at the shut gate, though the men are re-seated by the rain in the concrete bus-shelter. You need to talk to someone sometimes, even if it's only to ask the time. Sometimes I think I'm too much on my own, with the same thoughts spinning round. (I've still got that ache in my neck and shoulders, like every muscle there is knotted with cramp.) I get out and walk back to the shelter.

They're sitting on striped picnic chairs around a folding picnic table, playing cards. Two of them still have their shirts off, as if they were caught in rain at the beach. I ask directions for Neath (though I know the way). When the one finishes telling me I nod and say thanks and there's a kind of moment when they don't look down at their cards again yet and I don't walk back to my car.

You got caught in it, one of them says.

You could say that.

I look down at my denim jacket and jeans, black and shiny with wet. Every stitch I'm wearing is stuck cold to me, and my cowboy boots have been pressing out water every step or change of gear or time I brake.

One looks towards the car.

That yours?

No, I found it parked up the road, I tell him. Had the keys in it and everything.

He grins at me. One of his top teeth is edged with the brown of rot. There is a tattoo of a blue butterfly on his naked shoulder. And suddenly I realise that he knows the striking miner who is fucking my wife. I realise they all do.

American, is it? one says.

Yeah.

Me and Butterfly, we're still using the eyes. Like we could get serious about each other any minute.

We playing cards here or not? one says.

They look down at their hands. I watch them bet a round of matchsticks, a few blue match-heads among all the red. The older man wins with a prial of fours.

Where you from? he asks me.

He gathers the matches to him with one hand.

Cardiff way.

Cardiff?

He looks at me as if I'd just said Abilene, Kansas or fucking Tasmania or somewhere.

So what brings you to this part of the world in that Yankee car? he asks me.

I shrug.

Just passing through.

I don't know what to add. I pull the sodden sleeve back from my watch to see the time. I raise my hand in a sort of wave.

So long, someone says.

So long.

I put my hand in my wet jeans pocket, so wet I have to work it in. I've got two pound coins in my palm, some copper and silver change. I put it down on the picnic table, between the circled cards.

Play for that, I tell them. Play for real money at least. Or put it in the collection bucket.

The circled faces look up at me.

And then I'm out of there. I'm on my way back to the car.

Those boys were sat there playing for matches. Matches. Over on the Dow Jones average, on the Nikkei index, on the old FTI, they're yelling down the phone in thousands, millions. Pounds. Yen. Dollars. Belgian Francs. Those guys are where the only game in town is. Man, they're betting with the world.

Just passing through, I think as I drive out past the last drab house in the village. Like the wind, I think. The only way with a no-hope place like this. Like the fucking wind. Invisible. Not stopping anywhere. And leaving not a trace behind.

Four

I've kept the Book a year now, a girl to a double page.

It's a big old-fashioned commercial ledger or accounts-book. I bought it dirt-cheap. They were closing down. The feller in the shop told me there was no demand for a book like that in the Computer Age. They were selling off stock for more or less whatever they could get. Stationery, desk sets, filing cabinets, staplers. I wish now I'd bought two. I've always loved books like that, you know the kind that make you want to keep a diary and write in it every day religiously, like a schoolgirl, with a proper fountain pen, then blot it and close it on a blue silk ribbon.

(Though it *is* a diary of a kind.)

It's a big book with dark-green covers. The spine's bound in thin 'leather-look' material, like a real old notary's register or whatever, with triangles of the same stuff to protect the corners. Shut, the pages have got that patterned edge old-fashioned ledgers have, a scallopy design in green and red and gold (it always reminds me of the featherings of an arrow). The pages are lined in blue, across, and in red, down. So I suppose it's a cashbook, by rights. It's got a little brass lock too. You could probably pick it with a hairpin inside a minute. Actually, you could force it with the same hairpin in less. But like they always say about burglar alarms or nuclear warheads, it's A Deterrent. At least no one can pick it up and open it by chance, just to admire the binding or the marbled end-papers.

They'd blink twice if they did start leafing through, and saw some of the girls.

I say some of the girls only, because the photos, let's face it, are of what they call pretty 'variable' quality. Not to mention being of variably pretty fucking girls. And in a sense, of course, the least interesting photos are those of the girls I have actually been with. That's obvious. All they are is snaps, and they're mostly fully clothed. These vary from, oh, a foggy black-and-white one of me and a girl I went out with for six months when I was twenty-two (me in a Flower Power headband and flares, can you believe it?), to booth pictures of girls I probably only went with a couple of times, to a pretty good colour one, though I say it myself, of my wife in that yellow top and white shorts, it was taken at Barry Island one Sunday, before Mandy was born (or thought of, even). Of course, there are a lot of other girls I've been with who I don't have a photograph of, casual pickups, girls I took home from dances or parties and fucked on the carpet in their front rooms, I was too busy to ask for a snapshot at the time, ha ha.

There might still be one or two I've forgotten completely, not to mention their name. Like 'Bristols' as she appears in the Book, because, well, it was in Bristol and I suppose she had fair tits if nothing else. Sorry about that. You've got to call them something. She might not even have told me her real name. I only remembered her the other month, for some reason she'd completely slipped my mind. It happened when I was working over there for the gas board, with all those other chancers and morris-dancers, converting Clifton to North Sea Gas. (And, in the case of this customer, to a fast fitting with the gas-fitter who only came to fix the fire.)

But I think I've got most of the basic facts on most of them now. Though, let's face it, there are some things you don't get around to asking a saloon-bar pickup on your First and Only date, i.e. ten minutes in the carpark afterwards. So some of these facts are what you'd have to call 'educated guesswork'. Particularly in the *Information* section, which is like the *Playmate Data Sheet* in *Playboy*, though my categories go somewhat 'further', you might say. They're under pretty much the obvious headings. Real Name. Age. Last Known Address. Telephone. Height. Weight. Bust. Waist. Hips. Distinguishing Features. Place of Work. Marital Status. Birthday. Times Fucked. Then a ripoff from *Playboy*: Turn-ons. And Turn-offs. (Though when you've only been with someone once or twice perhaps, obviously you don't get to know what really makes them open up or not.) Finally comes my S.EX. Rating, which stands for Sensual EXcitement or, if you like, PIB, Performance In Bed. This is on a 1 to 100 scale. It used to be on a 1 to 10 scale, but I've had more fun deciding since I've altered it, you're suddenly into a range of much finer distinctions and judgements. I mean 7 out of 10 for something doesn't sound much, but 76 out of 100, say, is a First Class Honours in any university, all you need to get a Pass is 40. (Can you believe that? 40 out of a hundred was all my wife needed to qualify for another whole year of grant cheques. Not that she even managed that, in two attempts. She was more interested in us fucking or in sitting around the college coffee-bar talking about – what were those guys' names? – Lah-di-dah Derrydah and Roll-On Barthes. I got sick of hearing about them. Either that or smoking dope at parties. She would have pulled an easy First in any one of those.)

I use the term Performance 'In Bed', though obviously there've been quite a few I've had in other locations. Outdoors, usually, I suppose. On the way home from a dance. Or on a Sunday walk through the woods. When you're young and you're both living at home with parents, you never seem to have a nice warm place indoors to do it in. (Not that that ever stopped anyone, even in the dead of winter. Human ingenuity and hardiness are infinite in the cause of a swift poke.)

There've been also quite a few who I've only had in one

or other of the cars I've owned over the years. Including (though I'd rather not have remembered this particular one and I'm ashamed to say it, in a way) this girl ('eighteen' she told me she was, but I doubt it) who I picked up one night in Westgate Street. (This was just after my wife had left me. I was a real mess for a couple of weeks, then.) A prostitute she was. Though I didn't actually consummate the transaction, so to speak. Achieve Full Congress. I just drove her down under the railway bridge in East Canal Wharf and had her blow me. At least that way you got a lot less chance of catching something. Cost me a tenner, in advance. (I suppose there's no such thing as COD with whores.)

Anyway, out of honesty I put her in the Book with all the rest. (If a thing's worth doing it's worth doing to the hilt.) But I'm still ashamed of that. Because that really is the only time in my life I've ever paid for it (and that's the truth).

Which is not to say that there aren't one or two others I'm not too proud of now, even if I didn't pay for it. Like (just to go back to the very beginning) fat Janet Parry, the Ugly Dumpling. Who I slid into one misty autumn night because I knew anybody could, in Jubilee Park, not quite in the muddy penalty area but on the unworn grass behind the goalposts, having taken my coat off for her to lie back on. What a gentleman I was then at seventeen, a regular Sir Walter Raleigh. (And her the School Bike, ha fucking ha.)

Janet Parry . . . Who I was so grateful to I walked her home afterwards, down Sloper Road. Next to the bus garages she lived. I probably held her hand too, all the way. Shagbag Parry, they used to call her. But who first showed me what it would be like to live for ever.

I wonder what happened to her. What she's doing now. Probably married some besotted simpleton with a basin-cut and glasses in the end. Some poor former male virgin. Who'd heard rumours about putting your long and stiff into a girl's big and hairy, but never thought it would be anything like this. Who still can't quite believe his luck in finding somebody who'll let him. (For girls like her, who everybody's had the once, somewhere there's always one like that.)

Anyway, I haven't got photos of the early one-offs, like her. Most of the snaps I have got are of 'regular' girls I had later on who I knew well enough to ask for a photo. I wouldn't exactly call them 'girlfriends'. But I never ditched a girl who fucked who I thought I might want to fuck again (that's common sense). And I usually did ask a girl for a photo once I'd been out with her a few times. They probably thought, How sweet: a Sentimentalist. (Like fuck I am.) But I always have saved things in that way, mementoes, letters they may have written, any other stuff. Like I've still got the bill from that place I had a cup of coffee in with that stripper in London (even if I never did get any further than that, 'her boyfriend' et cetera et cetera. I ask you. A fucking *stripper*?). Or that single gold earring Sandra Boardman bought me that day, she said I'd look great with just the one gleaming now and then in my hair, 'Like a gypsy', she said. And I wore it in my left ear because someone said that with gypsies that stood for The Road. But then someone else said that among queers it meant something else, like 'I Suck', probably, or 'I Take It Up the Arse'. So I took it out.

(It's amazing how that hole has never healed, even now I can still squeeze gunge out of the lobe of that ear, years afterwards.)

Aside from these, there are a few photos of Victims. Targets. Hits. (Call them what you will.) I took some of them with the Polaroid. And there are others, portraits or holiday snaps, that they happened to have of themselves around the place. In fact, if I had the choice, I'd always choose one of their own photos rather than use the Polaroid. The ones I took with it have a, I don't know, a kind of 'documentary' look to them. It's hard to explain. Probably it's just the lighting, and using the flash. But some of those Polaroid photos look so . . . empty. Bleak. Like amateur Beaver Shots. Sometimes they remind me of the plates in those textbooks of Forensic Medicine I used to get out of the library. (I've always read up everything I can on that, and on Pathology, and 'Famous Cases' and so on, because you've always got to know the ways your enemies can trap you, it only takes a trace upon a swab to match with yours. But some of the plates can be depressing.)

And so I'd rather have one showing them smiling, say, looking dead into the camera. Not a care in the world but how they look for this photograph, a beach behind them or a fun-fair or, with Buffy, she's in the garden, kneeling by a golden retriever like in a Lassie film, with a tree of that white blossom behind her, big waxy flowers, camellia, are they? Or magnolia? She must be about seventeen. If you concentrate you can almost smell those flowers on that summer afternoon, like she must have.

Yeah, I know. It's taking a big chance to keep evidence like this. But it's a habit with me now. Or more than a habit. Especially with those particular girls. Because whether you've got a photograph to remind you or not you'll always recall something about the others, the 'volunteers', so to speak, even scrubbers you only went with the once because you couldn't face it again or face it sober. But for some reason a girl you have to blindfold is hard to remember, to call up again. She's the one with her eyes masked. But you're the one who has trouble picturing it again.

Anyway, obviously the least interesting photos (*as photos*) are those of girls I have actually been with, slipped the old length to. Like I say, it's Amateur Night. And not just for the photographer, even. Because when you get down to it, very few women have the least clue as to what they're doing in front of a camera, either. Like the man said, A top-class model Makes Love to the Lens. Whereas most women are just hoping they're going to 'Look nice' in this one, i.e. halfway pretty and not too fat. They don't think positive. They don't *project*. Which is why in photographs they never look even as good as they do in real life. For example, my wife looked great in that halter top and shorts that afternoon at Barry Island, I remember I was lying around in the sun and I was getting sticky in my swimming trunks for her (that always happens to me at the beach, after a cold swim in the sea). That's why I took the photograph. But when you look at that photo the colour's all *wrong* somehow. And she's got a shiny nose, and her eyes are squinted up against the sun. And there's some old dears in deck-chairs in the background, I didn't want them in it. Okay, I took the damn photo, so them being there is my fault. But the point I'm making is that, whatever else is in the picture, she herself looks somehow raw and wind-blown and sunburnt pink. Instead of smooth and warm and gold and sexy. Or take Deborah Pugh, who I always thought was the best-looking girl I'd been out with till I met Carol. In the only photo I've got of her she looks terrible. A gross pissball. It was taken at this party we went to. It's the white of her face in the flash and the double-chinned look and the way the light has caught her pupils, a kind of reddish flare, like when you fix a hare in the headlights down some country road. Talk about a glassy smile. In fact she looks like some grinning red-eyed lady vampire. You'd swear the wine she's almost slopping in that glass was blood.

I always wish I had a better one of her . . . And of my wife. I suppose, being sexy in real life is a gift. A lot of people have got that. But looking sexy for a camera's more than that: an art.

Still. At least there's the other photos for that. The professional ones. Ones I've cut out of magazines and so on. Because, okay, the Book started as a register of all the chicks I've actually fucked in my whole life (or my 'hole' life, ha ha ha), and how many fucks in total. I was thinking about that one day, first of all trying to work out how many girls it was, so that I ended up trying to remember them all and list their names, and then how many times I'd fucked each one, so that I could tot up a lifetime number. Things just sort of went on from there. But then after a while it started to expand to include girls I *haven't* fucked but (let's not be too coy about this) would really like to, or (to put it another way) girls, favourite photos of them, I've pulled off to.

This is how the one or two Famous Names, film-stars, get into the Book. Not to mention various 'starlets' and 'model girls', as the caption under their pictures always describes them, though everybody knows that what most of those chicks are is prime-cut high-grade Cunt, their only claim to fame is having that kind of picture taken of them. Most of them are probably high-class (or at least top-price) Call Girls on some Ex-Directory Number if the truth were told, not too many steps up from a Fuck-O-Gram girl. Let's face it, all they're modelling in those pictures is themselves. They'll probably go down with their heart beating like a lark's for anyone who's got a million or been on television. Courtesans they would have been called in one of those novels by Balzac.

With these, I usually don't have much information on file. If any. Sometimes you don't know any more about a girl than what it says under the picture, about 'Curvaceous Terri' or 'Cover Girl Lesley', which are probably professional names in any case, because I've never seen one yet called Ermintrude or Mildred. But I still cut out the caption with the picture. Like I always say, the least bit of information on a girl can be valuable, even if it's only some shit like that. ('Phew, What A Scorcher. Vicki Goes Topless As Brighton Swelters'.)

Sometimes you don't know anything at all about a girl, not even her name. Like with Ramona, which is my code-name for her, she's been one of my favourites, she's got almost a dozen ticks in the box under her photo. (They get a tick in the square if they're the last picture in your head, the one you're holding onto with your eyes closed or propping open to look at on your knee.) She's a model in one of the mail-order catalogues (my wife didn't take them when she went). It was one of the swimwear ads I saw her in first, just flicking through, and I thought, Jesus Christ Almighty. That type of bikini panties with the little knotted bow either side always has turned me on, you'd think all you'd have to do is tug one end of that string, like a tied shoelace, for the whole thing, that whole gorgeous pelvis, that whole beautiful lean brown woman, to be wide open and lubricating gently for you. And the bikini being yellow helps, against that tan, the oiled belly (talk about a heap of fucking wheat). Or that one of her in the underwear section where she's wearing this apricot slip. Satin it is, and you can sense how slithery it is on her. You can't see as much skin as in the other one, it's subtler than that. It's the way one shoulder-strap is just so slightly awry and how she's looking at you, kneeling there and holding her hair up like she's going to let it tumble down onto her shoulders and her mouth half-parted and those eyes, like a tiger's. And your own mouth goes dry just thinking about it, about coming home to something like that every night. Except, you'd never come home. You'd never leave the house. You'd never leave the fucking bed. It makes you eat your heart out when you think that somewhere there must be some guy she's crazy about, who's getting as much as he could want of her.

Because sex is everywhere around you. It's rife. It's bigger than the National Health. Or the Gross National Product, come to that. And sometimes a mail-order catalogue can turn you on more than a porn mag. And as far as the so-called 'Hardcore' stuff goes, that doesn't turn me on at all, never has. Me, I'm a Soft Porn man. With hardcore there's no tease. Hardcore's too upfront, too real, too dirty, the women are too white, too fleshy (somehow you can always see the mark of the bra-strap, or a pimple on their back). And let's face it, usually they're no spring chickens. Usually, in fact, they're rough. I suppose in life they're ordinary everyday whores, streetcorner scrubbers (that must be how they get into those films in the first place). So they're just doing on film the things they all do anyway. They're dulled to it, and you can see it. So what's so special about that? Because those films are strictly From The Gutter, that's where they start out and they never leave it. Me, I like at least a touch of elegance in this. I like to think of a 'nice' girl, a classy-looking girl, doing all these dirty things. I turn on for a girl with clean hair, clean cunt, and long, clean limbs, even if all she is is some anonymous agency model advertising soap or Sunsilk Shampoo or Pretty Polly Stockings.

Like I say, some of my girls are themselves what you might call Name Products. Everybody knows them. You read about them in the papers, they're in films, on television. Which is how, with these, I've managed to piece together quite a lot of information for the Book, even if it's only who they're married to or who else they've presumably fucked over the last few years, i.e. who their boyfriends have been, what other actors or singers they've gone out with or had affairs with. (Because, these international jet-setters, they're worse than a Zulu tribe or royalty, they only ever screw amongst themselves.)

A lot of this kind of info is only scandal, of course, showbiz gossip. You'd have to be a brainless idiot to believe everything they tell you in the papers. So I take a lot of this stuff with a pinch of salt. Let's face it, anything (and I mean anything) they tell you, me, Old Joe Public or John Q. Citizen, is automatically suspect for that reason. Probably it's just free publicity, for example all this Home Lives of the Stars junk. (All publicity is Good Publicity.)

As if they'd ever give away that kind of domestic detail or plain fact if it was true, not when it could be used against them by some lunatic, and the world is full of lunatics. (Look at what happened to John Lennon, and he was living incognito. God, I miss that guy.) No, most of the kind of stuff is just more lies dreamed up for the moron readers of the *Sun* or the *Daily Mail*, like the so-called biographical info on those girls in the soft-porn mags, 'Cheryl Breeds Afghans in her Spare Time', or that guff they sent me about The Big O when I wrote to his Official Fan Club, aged sixteen. Because all these people, the stars and the people who live off the stars, are into one thing and one thing only: multiplying that first million on the public's back. That's why most publicity's a pack of lies.

The public? Like the man said, All those bastards are is mushrooms. Brought up in the dark and fed on crap.

So although I tend to collect anything that's relevant, with any particular girl I only put belief in what I know to be hard fact. Which isn't going to amount to much on someone cut out of a magazine. All they're ever going to be for me, and a couple of million other mugs, is a body with a name under it, which may or may not be a real one. Which is good enough for me, when you come right down to it. As long as the tits and the arse and the legs and the gash are real, that's all I want of them. I don't have to give a shit about what they're doing, or who with, in Malibu or Mayfair.

So when we're talking about hard fact the real thrill's in the girls I've found myself, the ones I've 'discovered' myself, and watched, and researched until I know about them, who they are and what their whole routine is. It's hard to explain this thrill. It's like that scene in the crime film where someone hires an empty garret (there's always one 'conveniently opposite', of course) and spends a month with the binos trained on the diamond merchant's, keeping a book on everything that happens: when the place opens and shuts, the times of the deliveries, every coming and going and exception in a normal day, accurate to the second. (Not to mention the exact times of night the patrol-car goes past or the local copper on the beat.)

I've seen that scene in a dozen films, and it's always been one of my favourites. Like Bob Duvall says in *The Killer Elite*, you got to follow the Six-P Principle: Prior Planning Prevents Piss-Poor Performance. And in fact the planning of the job is a good half of the whole buzz. (It's almost more exciting than the break-in.) Which must be why they keep redoing that scene in just about every heist movie. It's not just a suspense classic. It's more than that. They know that any scene which has a man with a notebook and binoculars or a beam-in microphone or a telephoto lens is a sure-fire certainty with the public. Because that's simple human nature. Everyone wants to be at the eyepiece end of a telescope. Because everyone is curious about another person. Especially some particular other person. Especially if a particular other person's of the other sex. The girl you only have to see once, on a crowded street or pulling away at a traffic light, and it happens, the 'Coupe de Foudre'. Not love at first sight. Love at Last Sight. (Or at least it would be, if you left things there.)

And the more you start finding out about that girl (putting together little bits and pieces, here and there), the Curiouser and Curiouser you become. Until you're hooked. On her and the thought of her and on the whole ritual of finding a way of getting to her. She gets to be an obsession (and nothing's more fun than an obsession). All that waiting and planning, and caution and risk, you start to feel it coursing through you, you're mainlining on it, man.

Which is why when I'm not out Posing in my car I'm happiest lying low in it, parked somewhere On Surveillance. I'm never bored. I take my time. There's never any hurry. I make sure I've got plenty of tapes to play, and cigs and sandwiches. If I think it's going to involve a long wait, I'll bring a couple of cans of pilsner and a Thermos of coffee. I even keep an empty plastic bottle behind the seat to piss in when I need to. Sometimes, on the other hand, if I'm on foot, I'll get a hotdog or a Mars Bar or whatever and a takeaway coffee in one of those styrofoam cups with a lid on, and then I feel like I'm Popeye Doyle in *The French Connection*, where he's hanging around all day in the street in the freezing cold, trying to smell out where Fernando Rey is going to make the big heroin drop. Wow, what a film that is, I must have watched it on video a dozen times or more. Well, Hackman's one of my all-time favourite actors. And that is just about his best film. (That and *Night Moves*.)

Another thing I like about Hackman is that he didn't even decide to become an actor until he was almost thirty-five. (I read that somewhere.) In other words, a year younger than I am now. Which only goes to show. That you can make it in Hollywood at any age, provided you got the Talent. Even at thirty-four or five or six, it's still not necessarily too late.

Though in fact (thinking about *The French Connection* again), okay, if I couldn't ever get to be an actor, get that one Big Break like Hackman did, I wouldn't mind being like Popeye Doyle instead, the character he plays. I mean, we're talking now about a good straight cop, an Irish cop. Okay, so he's a loner and he's tough on suspects. He's tough on everyone, and toughest on himself. We're talking here about the kind of guy, in fact, who's just got too much fucking integrity for the good old NYPD. The one sound apple in the whole rotten stinking barrel of those bastards (all they're in the police force for is fattening second bank accounts from kickbacks and corruption).

And when I actually think of all the 'investigative work' I've done (on various girls), all the experience I've had of Observation and Surveillance and building up a Total Picture of a target, it makes me realise I should have joined the Opposition years ago. Because I would have made a hell of a detective.

Which is certainly more than can be said for any of the Boys In Blue just now, on this constabulary anyway. It's like the joke says, Why is a policeman's helmet shaped like that? Answer: Because that's the shape their heads are, underneath. And it's true, because when have the brains ever rushed to join the police force? Those boys might be alright at pushing miners around on picket-lines for the TV cameras, and waving lorries through to break the strike. When there's enough of them, they're great at that. But when it comes to certain other things where it's not brawn or sheer numbers but the Grey Matter that counts, they've had it, they're outclassed.

Because those dickbrains don't know if they're coming or going. They haven't got a whisper or an echo or a scream to go on yet.

Five

And I used to be a hell. Of a runner once. In school. Run
for. Fucking miles. Now I have to. Stop every couple of
hundred. Yards or so and walk. Next time I'll park and.
Sit and do the. Reconnoitring from the car. It's fucking
easier. I thought the athletic touch, the. Green tracksuit,
the old lemon foam-soled Adidases, might be a good idea.
But it's a long way round. To the Lake Road East side of
the lake. Good couple of miles or more. The whole circuit,
must be. You don't realise. Distances until you try to jog
them.

It's not only short breath. It's a hot day. And I can
feel my face. Start to get red, sweaty. That's not lungs.
It's weight.

Of course in those days, when I could run, I was all
ribs and balls like a gypsy's dog. But let's face it, jogging's a smooth pose only so long as you stay cool-looking
and fresh. A little beaded perspiration's okay, but that's
maximum. Once you start to roll and grimace and sweat
grease, and you feel that vein thicken in your temple,
you're better off walking. Making out like (tracksuit or
not) an easy stroll through the summer air was all you
came out for.

As I come under the birch trees along the path and look
across at the front of the building, it occurs to me, not for
the first time, that Getting In may be a problem. Well, it
always is, till you're in. That's part of the art. But this
isn't like that nurses' hostel, where you could walk in and
out without anyone throwing you a second glance. Okay,
so there was a Porter's Desk, but nobody was ever at it.
They were obviously used to people coming and going,

even (or perhaps, ha ha, I mean especially) men. And it's
not a shared student house, say. Some damp-smelling
decrepit dump in Woodville Road or Mackintosh Place,
owned by a Pakistani Jew, where nobody bothers to lock a
door, not even the one to their own room, let alone the one
out from the filthy common kitchen to the outside toilet
and the rubbish-tip back garden. You know the kind of
joint. Great place for breeding slugs and woodlice. (I've
been in a hundred downstairs flats like that when my
wife was a student, at parties and so on. And in one or
two since where I, er, ha ha, didn't get an invitation.)
The back doors in those old houses never seem to shut
properly anyway, either the door's dropped on the frame
or a floor-tile's lifted, long-term neglect: why should the
landlord worry, as long as the rent gets paid? Like in that
last place, Samantha I called her because she had that
kind of a face, oh so Frightfully Frightfully, as if Daddy
was a QC or a merchant banker. All anyone could have
done about locking that door, short of sawing an inch off
the bottom, was jam it as shut as it'd go, i.e. pull or kick
it tight where it grated against the floor-tiles and at least
that way keep out anything bigger than a cat. I mean, it
was laughable, I actually tried to close that back door
after me when I left and damn well couldn't. Laughable? It was outrageous. Let's face it, a blind burglar
wouldn't see any problem in getting inside a place like
that. (The only reservation there being that no ordinary
housebreaker would want to anyway, or anyone without a sniffer dog, since the only single inanimate and
stealable object worth a score or even a tenner in the
whole run-down dump would be the shared dope stashed
in the teddy or the teapot.)

No, I'm looking now at a different kettle of fish. This
is Lake Road East.

And the more upmarket you go, the tighter, safer, more
security-conscious you get. The point about a student
house or a hostel being that where people have to share

common space, a lounge, kitchen, bathroom et cetera, they get less uptight about their own space too, they're not so territorial. When we were in that flat in Albany Road with those other students, friends of Carol's, people used to wander in and out of each other's rooms without even knocking, or go in and borrow a book or a pen even when the owner wasn't there. It used to get on my nerves sometimes, the way people would take your space for granted. But here, at Number 84, every flat will be separate, it'll have its own private kitchen and bathroom, and they'll come home every day from working in some office or estate agent's and cook for one and eat alone reading last Sunday's colour supplement or watching something on the television while they chew it (I know how it is to live like that, I've done that too). And outside the door of every private flat is just a carpeted corridor or a landing with a door to another flat, and then a staircase and a front door out to where they park the car. And that's as much space as they can bear to share, a staircase and a carpark. And that's why they probably hardly even know the other people in the house enough to say Hello to. Every time they leave their own flat they close the door behind them and listen for the lock to click. Then they listen for the same click to the outside door as well. I expect there's a buzzer button and a talking name-plate in the porch too, so you have to know somebody by name (and they know you) even to get the Open Sesame to the hall. Because these cats don't want a Stranger lurking about the place, an 'interloper'. (I like that word, it's got a good sound to it. As if you've got a long, loping run: a tracking wolf's.) It's not even as if they've got anything of special value in their rooms (and in any case people of that kind always have insurance). It's just that this is the way people *live* in these buildings divided into flats and bedsits, they fight shy of everybody, even their own neighbours. And I can understand that, because I know how it is to live on your own in a flat in a street you don't come from and where you've never even been before you move your stuff in. Nobody scares me, but you can get so Anti-Social that every ring on the doorbell, someone just trying to borrow a cup of sugar, is bad news.

On the other hand, this means that once I *am* in I ought to be home and dry: among people who mind their own business and live their own lives and don't give a monkey's fuck about anybody else's.

: *Once* I'm in.

The thing to do would be to get hold of the keys.

(So I take an afternoon off work one day. Yeah. I go home, have a bath and put on my chocolate suit, with the amethyst shirt and black satin tie. Then I go along to Truscott and Leitman's in Cathedral Road.

I say I'm interested in the vacant flat they're handling at 84 Lake Road East, and ask to view.

He's a pale blond man, with no eyebrows. But he's shrewd (that pale sly light in the eyes). He takes one look and thinks he might just have a High Roller here. He decides to make a rare exception today and take me over to Lakeside to view the property himself. He's not Truscott or Leitman: *those* bastards, they're out playing fucking golf all day with 'clients' or City Councillors and greasing deals. But he's the Senior Manager of this branch, and he looks after the business when they're not there (which is actually most of the time. Let's face it, they wouldn't have a business left without a stooge like this to leave in charge).

He gets through to his secretary.

I'm going to run a client over to Lakeside. Can you bring in the keys for 84 Lake Road East?

He clicks the machine off.

Won't be a minute.

No hurry, I tell him with a smile.

The beige phone on his desk rings.

Excuse me, he says.

The door behind me opens and his secretary comes in.

You know the type. I saw her look me up and down when I came into the outer office. She puts a big bunch of keys on the desk and pivots on one high heel to make her skirt flare as she leaves. Even while he's talking on the phone the manager looks at her legs as she goes out, he can't help it, his eyes just flick there abstractedly and follow her, he does it a hundred times a day and drives home in the car every night still seeing her walk away from him or the way she stands and smooths the creases of sitting from the lap of that tight skirt. But I don't. I just watch him and then examine my nails. I haven't given her a second glance. She can't be sure I've even given her a first.

He talks on the phone, the bunch of keys on the desk between us. The manager's obviously embarrassed by this call, or, at least, by having me present while he takes it. It might be a personal matter or, more probably somebody somewhere has made a fuck-up. Anyway, whatever it is, it's something that needs his immediate and close attention. He clicks the button in and out impatiently at the top of his Parker pen (with the clip like an arrow). He listens, nods, trying to interrupt the hurried monologue at the other end. Finally he manages to blurt.

Could you excuse me just a moment? I've got a client here.

He covers the mouthpiece, to talk to me. His look is hesitant, as if he is about to ask a favour. But that's how he always looks. I realise, behind the slyness he has the weak, blue gaze of Arthur O'Connell playing the perennial bit-part henpecked pharmacist or drunkard doctor, that's why he's where he is and nowhere else. He'll never be more than a competent stand-in for the boys who make the real decisions (i.e. the real money). The man's a Surrogate.

I wonder, Mr Boyle, he says. (Except that of course I would have thought of another name before going in there, Nick Dexter or Anthony Lomas.) I'm afraid something's come up, which is going to keep me tied up here for a while. Would you mind viewing the property on your own?

I look at him, then at the keys. These agents handle the whole building, naturally, and a copy of the key to every door in the place is on this ring. To avoid confusion, they are all tagged. I can see, with the numbers of the separate flats. I shrug as if regretful not to have his company.

I close one eye in a cold wink at his secretary as I go out. Everything you do or say must have the effect of a stone dropped in a windless pool. I can still feel circles moving outwards in her as I come out on the street. The one-pound bunch of keys is in the jacket pocket of my chocolate suit.

Now all I have to do is slip round to the While-U-Wait in Duke Street and get the ones I want copied. *Front Door Bldng, Side Door Bldng, Flat 3 (Miss V.J. Hays)*. While I'm waiting (and if I want to be Real Cool) I can even slip my shoes off one at a time and get them reheeled by the guy on the other machine. Oh, and I'd better get a copy of the key to the vacant flat, the one I'm *supposed* to be going over to view. You never know, I might need to use it as a foxhole.

Or perhaps, yeah, it's actually the flat next door to hers: let's be honest, this is one stroke of luck after another, particularly since these partition walls are so thin. So thin that when I press an inverted tumbler against the wall on my side I can overhear everything that takes place on the other, everything from her brushing her teeth in the morning to the soft whirr of her vibrator at night. (I love to hear that noise and to think of her in there with it, letting her line run out a little, reeling it in tight, playing with herself, bringing herself home like you'd land a big fish. Because whether she knows it or not it tells me how much she really needs 'a man'. E.g. – or rather, i.e. – Me.)

Or I could, yeah, drill a hole through the wall in the

daytime while she's out at work and, yeah, actually watch her doing it. (Why settle for imagination when we're all graced with the gift of sight?) The partition walling is the usual thing in these 'converted', 'flatlet'-type numbers: cheap batten framing faced with plasterboard. I use a small hand-drill so as not to make a sound that could be heard by someone passing in the corridor outside the room. Just the faint squeaking of the handle on its spindle as I turn it, the rasp of the bit into the plasterboard, a fine, pink silent dust of gypsum snowing down on the edge of the carpet near the skirting-board. And then the bit breaks through and I start turning the handle anti-clockwise to withdraw it, just a curl of paper and grey cardboard, a shake more of pink dust, and there's a hole you'd never notice: particularly since the wallpaper in the bedroom is a pattern of peacocks' fans and eyes, the perfect camouflage. I can see this whole wall in the dressing-table mirror which is facing me directly, and even I can't pick out the hole I've got my eye against, a hole no bigger than a knothole in a pine board.

I press my eye to it again and it's like seeing myself in one of those drawings advertising front-door peepholes in magazine small ads, except that this is not the nervous housewife alone at home peering out at the dark-faced stranger in the gloomy porch. This is the other way around. I mean, I can actually for a moment see myself, full-length and from the side, a crudely drawn semi-silhouette in semi-darkness, leaning to a pinhole of light in the black plane that is my side of the bedroom wall: a point of light that widens out on the other side like the beam of a torch, to spotlight a drawn blonde basking in a brassière or what used to be called a low-cut blouse, she's even got the dated hairstyle and curled-up eyelashes and lipsticked mouth of those ads, where everything still happens in the Fifties, they've never bothered to update them, she's even got a rope of pearls around her throat. And of course she isn't Rusty any more, she's blurred and shifted, suddenly she's one of the girls in those old *Detective Magazines* and *True Life Mysteries* I used to find around the house when I was a kid, the Old Man used to bring them home: girls with terrified eyes, tied up or backed into a corner from their shadowy assailant, always in such a way as to show off their colossal, pointed tits, their tiny skirts rucked up around their arses. Just some lurid 'Real Life' or 'True Detective' Sex Crime Scandal hyped up with comic-book pictures, line drawings in black and white. But then, in those days *everything* was in black and white (even Reality itself), most of the films still were, and the television if you had one. Even those photos in that first tit-mag I ever bought were, and the magazines were crummier than now, I mean the girls were obviously amateurs and the whole production had a tacky, undercover feel to it, like the photos had been shot in someone's front room with a Brownie 127. There was none of this glorious Californian cunt, lean-bodied Liberated Women holding it all open for you in the sunshine, tanned right down to the frizzy bush, the very gash. Talking about which, that was another thing you never saw in the old days, tits and arses were as much as you hoped for, and everything was flat and white and had no glisten to it, not like that athletic gleam you get now off arms and thighs, like sun off copper. The girls in those days just sat there pale, protuberant, their tits hanging like big pink-tipped blancmanges. And perhaps that's why the drawings were better than the photos. They were more stylised, with those hard cone-shaped tits, the pulled-up skirt, and the carefully half-torn blouse. They weren't just sitting there, the girls in those drawings, just showing their tits and eyelashes like a bunch of dairy Friesians. There was a lot more going on there than just a pose for a photographer. Those girls knew they were going to get it any minute hot and hard, and lying there like that, it damn well served them right.)

*

Once I'd thought of it, though, I realised that no estate agent in the world would ever do it, just hand over a bunch of keys to a total stranger who'd walked in off the street and who, for all he knew, would go off and burgle every flat in the building.

So what if he accompanies me to the property after all, and shows me round it in the usual way?

(He's pointing out various fittings and fixtures, opening cupboard doors et cetera. Now he's showing me the fitted wardrobe space in the Master Bedroom, the marble washbasin surround in the Luxury Toilet. Okay, so it's a De Luxe Flat. But frankly, by this stage I'm looking polite but unconvinced. He's starting to grin and sweat. He knows he's losing me. It's not 'the money'. Fuck that. The money's the last thing I'm worried about. But to be honest, this place is a *little* smaller than I'd had in mind. And I'm not too sure about the décor, come to that. I'd be prepared to pay a lot more for the right place. Not that it's 'my' money, anyway, frankly speaking. I smile. My company'll be meeting all the bills, American firms are pretty generous with expenses. (They have to be, that's how they keep their top people from being headhunted by a competitor.)

So, to be honest with you, that's the position, I tell him. It's up to me simply to choose whatever place I like the feel of while I'm based over here. But of course, having that kind of range of choice tends to make you choosy.

I shrug.

And of course, I have to entertain important clients sometimes . . .

Nevertheless, I continue to stroll after him, occasionally nodding vaguely at his rigmarole. Which by now, though, is starting to annoy me. He's still trying to swing things with the hard sell, a lot of ducking and bowing and pointing.

When what I really want to do is wander through the rooms alone. I want to savour this empty flat, *smell* it,

106

stiffen gradually to the eroticism of its spaces (or the Erogenousness of its Zones, ha ha): the thought of all the sexual acts that have happened or may yet under these high, corniced ceilings. Because it's like when I suddenly got a whiff of the life of a farm labourer or servant-girl in Eighteen O-Something in that 'National Trust' country house we stopped at once and took the kids in to see, everything just as it had been, the big black-leaded range in the kitchen and the hung rows of copper pans and that old chopping-board with a fresh sprig of parsley someone had put on it for a final touch (but the edge all eaten away by the cleaver a hundred years ago or more). It's as if you're suddenly in touch with Other Lives, like a medium. And there's something, yeah, *erotic* in the thought of all the grunts and moans and little gasps and soft cries these walls, any walls, have witnessed. What I inhale as soon as I walk into this flat, these vacant bedrooms, is not 'new paintwork' or 're-papered walls throughout'. It's the reek of past sex.

Which is why I've always wanted another place, a Second Address, even if it was only an eight by eight by eight rented bedsit garret right under the slates. That wouldn't matter, nor how crummy it was. Because this place would just be for sex. Like in *Last Tango in Paris*, when Brando and Maria Schneider meet by chance when they're viewing that vacant apartment. And they fuck on sight, against the wall in one of the empty rooms. They started out interested in maybe renting the place. But instead they just keep meeting there. Brando doesn't want them to have any identity, any existence for each other, outside those rented rooms. Outside of fucking. They're not even supposed to know each other's name.

(I suppose it's like that with me, in a way. Me and some of my girls. Because although I know their names and a lot of other things about them, they don't know mine and never will. I'm just a visitation out of nowhere, the Answer to the unsaid prayer.)

107

That was a hell of a film, though. It's got a lot of things you don't notice or understand straight off. I mean, I saw it the first time in the university, with my wife, because we both liked Brando. And I couldn't make head or tail as to what it was actually, you know, 'about'. But I've seen it four times since, in difference cinemas, in different towns, and I still don't say I 'understand' it. But I'd drive an hour to see it again this very night if it was showing anywhere. It's One of Those Films. And things from it keep striking you a long time later. Like, what the hell *is* there that's so erotic about an empty room? And meeting an anonymous stranger in it? Or take that bit at the end, where she shoots him: last time I went to see it Tony Barbecue came with me (I'd told him what a fucking great film it was, and so on) and he liked that scene too, he told me, because the very last thing Brando did before he died was take the chewing-gum out of his mouth and stick it under the rail of the balcony. Tony thought that was great. He said that, at the time, that really cracked him up, he thought that was real style, to do that just before you die. And I said that what I liked even better was the shot of the roof-tops opposite just after he did it. Nothing special about them, you might say. Just slate 'mansards', windows, attics, chimneys, typical Paris. Except that in the next shot you see that Brando's fallen on the floor of the balcony. That he's already dead. And it's only when you start to wonder what those roof-tops are even doing in the film at all, that you realise what they are. They're the last thing in his eyes. That's all. The last piece of the world he ever looked at alive. And I still get a lump in my throat and a prickle of tears every time I see that shot.

Probably I even get it again for a minute as I stand by the window in the empty flat. I blink it away, looking out at a tarmac parking space and the park and the lake, some guy in a green tracksuit jogging past among the birch trees. And when I blink again it's all still there.

And I'm still there. And that's the difference, that's what being dead means. (It's like that guy Wittgenstein said: Death's not an event in the world. It's the end of the fucking world.)

Then there's a knock at the door of the flat, and a little old lady comes into the hall. And you'd reckon it was Nigh, the End, at least as far as she's concerned. She can hardly stand up in the door.

She's one of the other tenants, it turns out, a widow, and she's seen the estate agent's car outside and saw us arrive to view. She wants the manager's advice on something, she's got a badly dripping tap, it keeps her awake at night, or perhaps the water-heater isn't working properly. She's been meaning to telephone the office and report the matter but she probably didn't want anyone to think she was 'complaining' or that she was a burden to others. But, since the manager's here now, would he mind taking a look at it for her?

He gives her the freezing smile.

I'm not really a plumber, Miss Hevisham.

He turns towards me.

And I'm afraid I'm with a client.

Let's face it, these bastards never want to do a damn thing except rake in the rent, even for a helpless sick old lady (who, even if she was fit and well, would probably be too much of an Agoraphobe to get down to the phone-box and ring a plumber for herself, and is much too timid to ask a neighbour to do it for her).

Perhaps you should have a look for her, I tell him. Besides, it'll give me a chance to get the feel of the flat, come to a decision.

In other words not only suggesting he doesn't need to worry about me in the least, but implying he damn well ought to go and at least assess the nature of the problem.

And, of course, the last thing he wants to do is offend me. He looks hesitant again.

If you're sure you don't mind, Mr Lomas . . .

I wave my hand, dismissing him almost.

Of course not. Take your time.

He leaves at last, with the old lady, who gives me a grateful smile. I stroll back into the hall and see that the big bunch of keys he put down on the telephone table as we came in is still there. They're all fully tagged and numbered to avoid confusion, and some are actually in duplicate (I notice as I quickly sort through them). Originally they must have had several copies of each key made, three probably: i.e. one for the office, one for the tenant, and one spare. Let's face it, people lose keys all the time, a spare is always worth making. Some of these extra spares have never been used: they're still on the key-ring, together with the office copy, I notice. Even more to the point, there are two identical keys (i.e. both the 'office' copy and the 'spare') to both the *Side Door* to the building and to *Flat 3 (Miss V.J. Hays)*.

I didn't get where I am (as they say) through indecision. I unclip these two keys from the ring, and slip them into my pocket. Let's face it, on any bunch of keys as big as this, no one is going to be absolutely sure exactly *which* doors they still have an extra key for. (Not that the estate agents would ever be likely to need a spare to the Side Door of the building or an occupied flat, in any case.) So, even if there'd only been one copy of the two keys I wanted, I would still have taken them. It might be months, or even years, before those particular office copies were specifically needed and missed. And, by that time, what reason would there be to connect their disappearance with a Mr Nick Lomas, who viewed the property one afternoon in late April or early May? By which time, in any case, Nick Lomas would long ago have concluded his Temporary Business in that area of the city, and moved on.)

Another way of getting in came to me at the Quick-Change the other day.

110

This feller drove in in an Electricity Board van, a transit, Friday, this was. I was in the tyre bay and he, you know, happened to come up to me. He asked what the chances were of getting a new exhaust system fitted while he waited.

Not a hope in hell, so far as I know, I said. We got the three lifts up and in use, and half a dozen cars out in the carpark, waiting.

Anyway, I went to check for him, and came back.

Best we can do for you is first thing tomorrow morning, I told him.

He kind of grinned his teeth and rubbed his stubble, thinking what to do.

Tell you what, he said, I don't want to have to come in on a Saturday morning. Can I just leave the keys with you? Do the exhaust when you like. Then leave the van in the carpark and I'll pick it up before work on Monday morning.

I don't know, I said. It's not up to me.

Because normally we don't let anybody leave a car over till the Monday. (Like Gordon, the manager, says: It's a quid a day or more for weekend parking in the multistorey.) Anyway, since it was the Electricity Board, I went and asked Gordon and he said, What the fuck, I suppose it'll be alright. As long as he knows it's at his own risk. I don't know how many vans and lorries the South Wales Electricity Board have got on the road, he said. But it's a lot of business for Quick-Change. Just make sure he knows it's just this once, though, he said, I don't want them using the place as a parking depot.

It was Gordon saying that about it being at his own risk that probably started me thinking,

(1) About what might happen to the van if it was left there for the weekend: how safe it really was. (2) Then the feller dropping the van keys in my hand kind of kept that thinking going. And then, on the Saturday morning, when it chanced to be me who drove it back to the carpark

to leave it when it had been fixed, I looked in the back of the van and (3) I saw a pair of green overalls rolled up in a bundle and a big blue tool-box on the metal floor.

And the penny dropped.

Because it struck me that having the keys to that light-blue transit van with *South Wales Electricity Board* on the side (plus whatever the fuck that is in the token Welsh underneath) could open more for me than just the van itself.

Because a man working for the Electricity or the Gas Board – or just a man driving one of their vans and wearing a set of their overalls and carrying a tool-box or just a mole-wrench or a screwdriver, so that at least he *looked* as if he worked for them – would be let in through just about any door he chose to knock.

(It's obviously the caretaker of the building who answers. An old man with the kind of thick spectacles that make the eyes big and blurred behind the lenses. The mild, faded, pin-pupilled blue eyes that people who have to wear that type of glasses always have.

Good afternoon. Sorry to trouble you. I work for the Electricity Board. I'm a kind of troubleshooter, if you like. I don't want to worry you but we've got an overload on the line in this area, and we've traced it to this sector.

I look up the front of the building.

What is this place? Private flats?

That's right.

This shouldn't take too long. But I'm going to have to come in and check all the electrical appliances that are run off the mains. And I mean all. Bar none.

I'm polite but firm. Calm, with just a trace of briskness in my voice. A more intelligent person would identify this note as one of urgency, would realise that there's probably nothing to worry about as long as I'm allowed to come in, check the appliances, and make the building safe without delay.

All this old bastard does, though, is blink at me behind

his glasses, then blink past me to the light blue Electricity Board van parked on the tarmac. (The trouble is that I've put him on the spot and he's not sure what to do. He doesn't know where his authority starts and ends.)

I look at him, weighing up the situation. Let's face it, you don't get to be a caretaker by showing quick reactions under pressure or knowing how to cope with the kind of emergency that may be threatening the lives of every tenant at present in the building. It's a light job. Requiring neither brains nor muscle.

In fact (let me be absolutely frank) it's a Soft Number even for an old geezer like this, like with those cripples they employ to work the lifts in big office-buildings (as if you couldn't press a button to the third floor for yourself). Perhaps this guy's a cripple too, yeah, he's got a limp anyway, even just holding the door open he limps suddenly, changing his weight awkwardly from one leg to the other, he's probably another member of the glorious British Legion Corps of Ex-Commandos and Carpark Attendants, it must be an old shrapnel wound in the leg, in a minute he'll start to tell me how it aches like fuck whenever it's due to rain and how he got it at Dunkirk, what a fucking shambles that was. A Race of Lions led by Donkeys, Hitler said, but that was only half right. A race of fucking donkeys led by chimpanzees, more like it.

They've all got easy numbers now of course, these cripples, *Mutilés de Guerre* the French call them in the Métro trains, *War Mutilated* (I remember that from when we went to Paris, Carol and me), they've even got seats reserved for them next to the doors. And, if they're not too badly mutilated, I suppose they run the lifts and apartment blocks over there too, just like here. Not that all these cripples are doing anything at all when you get right down to it, it's like paying a living wage to the models in a dress-shop window: just something to make them feel they're performing a Useful Function for Society. What a joke. What a sick joke. All this while

113

people with all their arms and legs and eyes and grey matter intact are wandering the streets looking for a job, any kind of job, committing suicide even, some of them, when they can't find one, like that case I read about in the *Echo* the other night, a boy of nineteen, in Newport. Depressed, the coroner said. While the balance of his mind was disturbed. At his failure to find work.

Meanwhile, this old dodderer in front of me is on the payroll just for taking out the rubbish once a week or changing the odd fuse.

(I hate the old, there's nothing uglier or more useless than old age, particularly old cunts of this guy's age. You know what it is I hate about that generation? It's this: *That they accepted everything and never asked for more.* Jesus Christ Almighty, it makes you think. To have lived so long and learned so fucking little from it.)

(Like this useless, ugly, half-blind old bastard still blinking dubiously at me through his glasses.)

I don't know about letting you into the flats, he says. I'm only the caretaker. You'll have to ask the tenants themselves. And some of them aren't even in. Like Number Three, I know she isn't in, I saw her go out ten minutes before you came. I couldn't let you into someone's flat without them being here. You'd have to have permission.

What this old bastard really needs at this point is splitting from crown to coccyx with a single axe-stroke, as he stands there blinking on the doorstep. Instead, I'm suddenly cold, authoritative. Crystal-clear.

Look. In words of one. What if I told you there was a bomb in this building and I was a Bomb Disposal Expert?

He blinks, his eyes a troubled blur made huge by the magnifying lenses. He moves his mouth, to murmur something mute and non-committal. I mean, I've tried to spell it out for him, but this old twat still can't make up his mind whether to shut the door in my face or stand aside. (I only hope the landlord knows what kind

114

of a cretin he's got 'looking after' the place, because he won't have a lot of rent coming in when they're digging bodies out of the rubble on the six o'clock news, Mystery Blast Kills Thirteen In City Suburb. Caretaker Held.)

Because that is the potential level of danger we have here, I tell him. We are talking here about an Overload on the line. I don't know if you know what that means. But I do. It's my job to know. I specialise in Overload Emergencies, as a matter of fact. And, in some circumstances, that is precisely like being a bomb disposal expert. Okay, so I didn't scream up in a jeep. I don't wear a red beret. But don't be lulled by that. That's a deliberate choice I made a long time ago, when I was recruited for this job. I decided that the best thing all round was for me to go to work in an ordinary van and workman's overalls, like your everyday Electricity Board fitter. That way everything looks normal, and no one panics. But these situations can be very tricky. Electricity can be more volatile and dangerous than anything there is. At least, when we get in a scenario like this, an Overload. And what we're doing at the moment here is wasting time. Which could mean human lives.

I raise my chin and look directly upwards again, up the sheer face of the building, assessing the number of windows, rooms, floors. Then I look at him again. My voice is clipped, quiet.

Do you understand now, man?

And finally he reacts, to something he recognises in my voice. That's one thing all these Old Retainers and British Legion stalwarts recognise, the Voice of Command. Once you turn on the authority, the old clipped tone, even forty years later. It's all they can do to resist throwing one hand up in a knee-jerk salute. Because they're bred for it. Bred for obedience, instant and unquestioning, and they'll never learn any different. 'Follow orders': that's the only thing they know. (Even though the only thing

115

that this old bastard ever got from following orders is a cripple's limp.)

He steps back, suddenly almost at attention.

You'd better come in, sir, he says.

I enter.

Right. We haven't got much time. First things first. Do you have a master key?

No, he says. But there's a set of duplicate keys. In Case of Emergency.

Do I still have to convince you that an emergency is exactly what this is?

He holds up a big key-ring of Yale keys. They're all fully tagged and numbered to avoid confusion, and, as I quickly sort through them, I notice that some of these duplicates are actually *themselves* in duplicate, originally they probably had not two but three copies of each key made (i.e. one for the tenant, one for the caretaker, and one spare. Let's face it, people are always losing keys, a spare is always worth making). Some of these spare, or third, keys are still on the key-ring. And as long as the caretaker's still got *one* duplicate, he'll never miss a second. (On any bunch of keys as big as this, no one is going to be sure exactly *which* flats they have only the two keys for, and which a third.)

More to the point, I notice there is an extra spare both to the *Side Door* to the building and to *Flat 3 (Miss V.J. Hays)*.)

Entering a woman's room when she's not there can be so intense you don't know what to do or where to start. Whether to strip naked and try and cram yourself into a pair of silky panties from her drawer or watch yourself come in her mirror or just take a shit in her bed.

(I remember reading they did things like that in the Empress's bedroom when they stormed the Winter Palace.)

And I often wonder, is it like that for ordinary burglars,

who break into houses for strictly business reasons, for portable valuables or plain cash? Do they have nights like that too? Nights when they can't stop thinking about bedspreads and tallboys? Trinket-boxes? Nights when they can't stay at home, they're too restless, like werewolves or coyotes in the full of the moon. So that they have to be Out, in the dark, in the dead lunar pallor, creeping to the sharp point of shadow at the corner of each building, sorting through the city on the random lookout for an open fanlight or an unlocked door.

(And, when they find one, pulling the pantie-hose down tight over their heads before they go in, the way bank-robbers do: like massive, bald erections.)

Six

It was the thought that sex is like water. Because (1) it always finds its own level. And (2) is hard to contain, keep in one place, so that in time it will start to seep out, trickle an outlet, anywhere. (Like through limestone.)

It was this that made me realise that, with Rusty, I couldn't make my move too soon. Or, to put it the other way, that I could easily delay too long. A chick like that isn't going to stay a 'bachelor girl' all her life, let alone an unescorted virgin. Assuming (big assumption) that she's either of those two things now.

I understood this plain as day that Friday lunchtime I followed her from Asprey's.

I'd taken the day off work to see her, by which I mean watch her, find out more about her, her daytime life. On odd nights, from the car or the big black park, I'd been watching the window of her flat, dark or lighted, for a week or two. But so far I hadn't even found out if she had a boyfriend.

I don't know what I wanted or expected to happen, that lunchtime. It's better that way anyway, to hang loose and just see what turns out. (As long as you understand that there are times when you've got to *do* something, commit yourself, try and make things happen – if only because up to now things have been drifting, and you with them. Because the watching, the following, can begin to seem and end in itself. So you've got to be Ready. Like they say, the readiness is all.) (Otherwise you can start to live things so much in your head that they stay there, happen there, and nowhere else.)

So around twelve I get in position in this bookshop.

Bowes and Bowes. For what I wanted, this was the perfect place. Almost directly opposite Asprey Travel. A couple of those rotating stands of paperbacks in the window, for me to watch behind. And, of course, you can stand browsing in a bookshop for ever and no one blinks an eyeball.

And it's lucky I'm there early. Because she comes out of Asprey's on the stroke of half twelve. (I thought she'd probably go to lunch at one, but I suppose if you work in a travel agent's at this time of the year, when people are booking their holidays, dreaming of getting to look like some of that suntanned cunt on the covers of the brochures, or simply of fucking it blind in their hotel room, I suppose you have to stay open right through lunchtime and the staff take their hour off one or two at a time, in rota. It's the same at Quick-Change. In point of fact, after one is a more than normally busy time for us, most days. I suppose for a lot of people the lunch-hour is the only time they have to get things done, whether it's getting a new battery or booking two weeks on the Costa Plenty.)

She is with this other girl, who must work there too. They come out of the double glass doors to the shop. They're carrying handbags, but it's a warm day and neither is wearing a coat. They stand talking on the pavement outside Asprey's, as if they have to go in different directions. But then, it looks as if they're both going left, down St Mary Street. They start walking together in the sunlight, the other girl talking forty-two to the dozen, Rusty just listening, smiling, it's probably gossip about someone they work with, garrulous girl-talk: So I said, What? And she said, He Did. And I said, Ooo. He Never. Rusty smiling and kind of sauntering, swinging each foot ahead of her, keeping pace with the other girl as if she's actually used to walking faster.

And she looks so clean and fresh, so cool and summery in those low-heeled white shoes, with Oh my Christ those long beautiful sheer brown legs alternating under the sway of her white skirt. And I'm heartsick again, just seeing her.

And I realise too that now there's no way out of this.

Because you know how it is. Sometimes you see a girl the second time, or maybe just in different clothes, and you're disappointed. Suddenly you find you've changed your mind, and you wonder what you ever saw in her. But with Rusty, it's the same now as it was the first time. Watching her from that bookshop, across St Mary Street, I get the same, empty feeling of sickness in the bottom of my stomach, like I had that afternoon in the garage when she opened the door of that little MG sports car and swung those fringed boots out onto the oil-stained concrete, and I felt my guts drop, sudden, like when you take a humpback bridge too fast.

I take a long breath. Empty it out. Control your breathing and you control the world. I remind myself that there's no hurry. They're not walking fast.

I slot back the book I'd been looking at, *The Fall*, by Albert Camus. I read another one of his once, *The Outsider*, it was one of Carol's (though she was supposed to have read it in French, of course). It was pretty good. It's about this guy who meets this girl. And they start going out together. And he's fucking her. And then he kills this Arab on a beach. It's like it's a very hot day, and in the end the heat gets to him. I always liked Camus because I read somewhere he'd played in goal for Algiers or some team like that. I suppose that's because I used to play in goal myself. They say that to be a goalkeeper you've got to be tall and a bit crazy. But really what it is is this. It comes down to two things. You've got to be an indvidualist. And you've got to have guts. When you're between those two posts, there's nowhere you can hide. You've got to stand or fall on your own game.

As I leave the bookshop an orange double-decker bus slows to wait in the traffic, between me and the two girls. I cross behind it to reach their pavement before the queueing cars get the green light.

And their tops and chromework are suddenly aglitter all down the street as the sun comes out again from cloud. (Sometimes in life there are these instants, like in films.)

The two girls walk slowly ahead among a lunchtime crowd. I'm on the Sunny Side now, fifty yards behind her at a forced stroll, in my sharpest chocolate suit (you can't say Nigger Brown even in a tailor's these days) with two-tone brogues, pale lemon shirt, no tie. I did put on a tie at first but then I took it off, I didn't want to look overdressed. Because you can look sharp without being stuffy. And let's face it, as I catch myself sidelong full-length in Hector Powe's window: I do. I fucking do. Suave, you might say, but not Smooth. 'Interesting'. I've always been one for the well-dressed but tieless look. Like an all-night gambler or a gigolo coming home at dawn. (You know what I mean, he may have started out wearing a tie the night before but now he's torn it off and thrown it in a fountain or gambled it away or left it somewhere, probably still tied to a bedpost in some Rich Bitch's flat.)

Now twenty yards behind her, sharp, casual, I follow without appearing to that sunlit blonde head, that cream blouse (through which shines now and again a bra's paler backstrap), and that confident stride, as easy as a gymnast's.

I follow. While beneath that swaying skirt I glimpse and glimpse again at will that subtle muscle in her calves, first one calf then the other.

And I'm abject with heartache. Because it's, you know, like when you're seventeen, say. And you keep on seeing girls in dances or clubs, or standing at bus-stops, or coming out of offices at five o'clock, the kind of girls you never know a single thing about and never see again, but who you eat your heart out for all day and night just on the seeing them that once. Because at that age, seventeen, all you want is to be In Love with a girl like that. But at that age you can never get one like that. And even when you do get girls, later, you always know you're settling for less than you imagined would be yours. Because there are so many beautiful girls in the world, everywhere you look, on posters and in magazines, on television and even in real life, even in a city the size of Cardiff (because they don't all live in London or Los Angeles. There's beautiful girls any place you go). But somehow, you always seem to get the slags and scrubbers, the ones who come to the party or the dance because they're 'spare' already, and once you've shafted them then they're spare again, they're always spare. Because that's how it is when you're that age, or twenty even, or, let's face it, thirty fucking six. You never seem to get the girls you dreamed of getting.

And that's why you have to take what you can and run. Not wait around for Luck or Fate or True, True Love. Fuck that. You wait for things to happen to you, you'll eat your heart out all your life. Best thing of all is be a rock-star or a tennis-player or a film-actor. That way you can get to slip it into probably any girl you see. Like Leonard Cohen said: The girls I wanted when I was sixteen, I've got them now. I advise everyone to become rich and famous.

But what you don't get given you like that, you've got to take, in This World. Which is the only one you'll ever see, and only the once you'll see it. Let's face it, Life isn't a dress rehearsal. It's the real thing. And sex is everywhere in it. These days you can't blink without seeing it.

It's like I was saying to Tony Barbecue the other night in The Locomotive.

We were watching the fight on the big video screen and they kept showing adverts after almost every round and Tony was complaining about it and saying how they

122

don't even *allow* adverts in Russia. (So what the fuck do that prove? I said. They don't allow adverts on the BBC.) Anyway, Tony, who's a bit of a, you know, Communist, 'Marxist' is what he says he is, carried on about Advertising and the Consumer Society and how the whole show ran on making people 'buy' things they didn't 'need', et cetera.

Give us a break, Tone, I said.

(I mean, I'd heard all this before, at just about every student party I'd ever been to. And, anyway, nobody has to convince me that people are as dull as blocks. But to listen to Tony talk you'd think citizens were being forced out of their homes at gunpoint and marched into the supermarkets and car salesrooms and department stores to buy things they'd rather not have and couldn't afford.)

Listen, I said. If people are stupid enough to believe anything as moronic as some of these adverts, they deserve everything they fucking get. In fact, they should be whipped and chained.

But they did deserve everything they got, Tony said. That was the fucking point. They deserved *more* than they got. They deserved every fucking thing there was in life to have. Because everything there was was made by work, by ordinary working people. And everything that everybody saw on television, all those symbols of the good life, Martinis and after-dinner mints and washing machines, were made out of human sweat. And, what's more, they were a promise of utopia, a utopia that was within the grasp of man, because man made the wealth for all but only distributed it to some, and what any society makes its citizens hunger after it ought to be capable of providing for them, for all of them. But how you could say that in a country with a conservative four million on the dole and, on top of that, a bastard government hell-bent on closing down its coal-mines?

I don't know about Martinis made out of human sweat,

I said. But it's not a drink I like at the best of times. Me, I'm more into that chick on the roller-skates in the Martini ads. Sashaying through the traffic with a tray. The way that tiny little skater's skirt of hers blows back for just a second. You seen that one? She can bring me a personal bottle of that stuff any time.

Of course, he rose to it.

You're trouble is you're a fucking sexist, he said. To the fucking bone.

A sexist? I said. Me?

It's not me who's a sexist, I said. It's the whole fucking system.

Listen, I said. You're on about the system selling you what you don't want. My point is, whatever it *is* they're selling you, whether it's booze or smokes or low-fat fucking margarine, what are they *using* to make the sale? Eh? What are they selling it *with*? I'll tell you. Cunt, I said. They're selling it with cunt.

Except, I said, I think it's actually the other way around. Sex is the thing they're *really* selling you. Only they keep on *promoting* it with booze and margarine and so on, different products, so it doesn't get too obvious. It's like John Lennon said, I said: Keep you doped with religion and sex and TV, And you think you're so clever and classless and free, But you're still fucking peasants as far as I can see.

That's what I said.

So don't talk to me about the Man in the Street, I told him. I don't give a flying fuck for the man in the street. The street's where those bastards belong. Listen, I said: It's like with everything else in life. You get two options. Take what you're given. Which means Fuck-All. Or take all you can get. It's up to everyone to get what they can out of this life. It's a free fucking country.

Tony laughed.

Living on credit don't mean free, he said. That's what I've been fucking trying to make you understand.

124

(But he's alright, Tony. Get him off Politics and the Distribution of Wealth, and he's as good as gold.)

Tony Barbecue's not his real name, of course. It's Barbaggioni, Barbazone, or something, he did tell me once. But Tony Barbecue's what they call him. And when they give you a nickname it's kind of an honour, in a way. It's to show that you're a Character. That you're One of the, you know, Crowd, Like they call Colin 'Baz' and me 'Yank' or sometimes 'Cowboy'.

Or what was that Gerry Richards called me when I dropped in for a pint last week? 'Crazy Horse'. (Except, an honour wasn't exactly what that was. He was taking the piss. Because I'd got slewed in there the other night and there was a bit of trouble. In fact I would have bottled that headcase if his mates hadn't grabbed him round the arms and dragged him out.)

Jesus Christ, look out, he said. It's Crazy Horse.

(In front of everybody, this was. Soon as I walked up to the fucking bar.)

Hide that firewater, he said. Crazy Horse one heap bad Injun. Him go loco in The Locomotive. I see it many time.

I had to grin it off. But what I should have done is given him a brisk head-butt instead. Just to take the pleasure out of the joke for him and out of him repeating it to anybody else. There's something about that Gerry Richards I've never liked. You never know quite how to take the things he says. He's a smart little bastard. A Cutie. Or thinks he is.

Anyway, fuck him. I don't want to think about Gerry Richards. I don't need Negative Tension on a day like this. (Breathe in. Roll the head until the shoulders loosen.)

There's a panic for a second when I can't see the girls ahead, until I realise I've caught up till I'm practically abreast of them, we're walking in threesome almost. Before they notice me I have to stop, quick, and kneel and tie a lace I've just undone, and take a long breath in and let it out, and out, and out (concentrating on a crack in the paving). Then I stand again what is now twenty or thirty yards behind them, and follow them from there, along St Mary Street and now turning towards Working Street.

And we're all nice and easy again in the sunshine, me relaxed, taking in the air and the scene in general, and even starting to think Christ, I wish I had one of these office jobs and could do this every day, take a pleasant midday constitutional around the city centre to observe the passing cunt during its lunch-hour, all this nice young suntanned cunt strolling on view in summer prints and shoulder-straps. (There's not much chance of that when you work at Quick-Change. It's a pint and a pasty in your overalls in The Butcher's Arms. Or brought sandwiches and a cardboard cup of coffee in the tyre store.)

But one thing is this: watching her today, following her, I realise that I'm pleased with Rusty. Proud of her almost. Proud that this is how she actually spends her lunch-hour, going for a stroll with a girlfriend. Because I'm glad she's sensible in things like that, she's not flighty, she's got her head screwed on. She's not a bimbo. Because let's face it, she could be out with a crowd of fellers from the office instead, playing one off against the other and both ends against the middle, the way you always see with sharp-looking girls, they surround themselves with men in groups because they like to multiply the attention and, besides, that way they feel safe from any particular one man.

So at least she's not a 'flirt'. I can tell that, even though I can't see her face. I can tell she's not from watching the faces of the men coming along the pavement towards her, they're on their lunch-hour too, glorified office-boys mostly, that's all they are, clerks, or ginks in shoe-shops, wearing to work the only fucking suits they got (though ask them what they do for a living and

126

they'll tell you *Junior Executive* or *Assistant Manager* or *Trainee Hotshot*). You know the type I mean. I watch them coming along the pavement and the change in their faces when they see her for the first time, I notice how their walk alters or shifts direction slightly so as to pass closer to her, and how their eyes flick down her legs and body quicker than a lizard's tongue, and then back to her face. And then they stare at her, watching her eyes as they're coming closer to her now. They're not looking at the girl she's with, nobody takes any fucking notice of her whatsoever, it's Rusty they look at, eyes sly about doing it or frank, but either way all hoping to make her look back at them, that much if nothing else, trying to get at least a flicker of Eye Contact, some acknowledgement from her of their actual fucking existence on the street. Because they're no-hopers, every one of them. The poor pathetic bastards, this must be how they spend every lunch-hour, every working day of all their working lives. Wandering up and down Queen Street or St Mary Street like white mice in a wheel, just hoping to get some twenty-year-old, gorgeous, long-limbed chick like Rusty to look them in the eye once. Once. Once and for ever.

But she won't, this girl. Not even 'won't'. *Doesn't*.

Because she doesn't even try to avoid the stares, or look downwards in that phoney 'modest' way some girls have, as if they're 'shy', or else they flick their eyes away from you in that cold, superior way some bitches have, they *want* you to look at them just so they can do that, it's their way of putting you and all men down. I hate that, I really do hate that, the way some cunts think they can dismiss you with a glance. It always makes me want to walk over and smash them in the nose, just let them see if they can still flash that look from behind some pieces of floating bone and a pair of black eyes bigger than a panda's.

No. Rusty doesn't play that game, getting men to look so she can cut them dead. I can't see her face. (Like I say, I'm twenty yards behind her.) But I can still tell that she doesn't *notice* these men who stare at her. Not doesn't 'deign' to notice. Just doesn't *see* them. And, to me, that's Style. To me that's Class. Because obviously a girl like that has to get used to being stared at. But at least she's not interested in turning heads along a pavement.

Turn they do, though. Turn they fucking do.

Like this clown now. This young ginger guy with his tie-knot 'loosened' and his jacket 'thrown' over one shoulder (and one finger hooked into the tab). A real Playboy of the pavements, obviously. Mister Debonair himself. Talk about uncool. I mean, even as she goes past him he's staring at her. Holding the stare so long, so open-fucking-*mouthed*, he's almost walking sideways by the time they're level. Then he actually *turns*. He actually half-pivots on one heel to watch her *legs* as she walks on, or as if he's going to follow her as well.

I quicken pace and change tack slightly as he stares after her. As if by accident I catch him across the chest with the best part of my suddenly hurrying six foot two, knocking him a yard aside in passing. He staggers and almost sits down on the pavement outside Allder's.

You want to look where you're going, son, I call back to his shocked white face.

(Then I feel almost sorry for him, he can't weigh more than ten or eleven stone. The impact must have knocked the little fucker sick.)

The two girls cross the street, towards the grimy sills and tall windows of the Central Library. Are they going to the open-air café on the Hayes Island?

I used to go there with my wife sometimes when we'd done the Saturday shopping in Fine Fare, and we'd sit at one of the tables under the plane trees and have a cup of tea and a sandwich and the kids would have an orange-ade and a rock cake, half of which they'd end up throwing to the pigeons waddling round your feet, I always said it was a waste of money, buy them one cake between the pair of them instead of one apiece, maybe that way they'll actually get to eat what I paid for. If you want to feed the bloody birds, I'd say, bring old bread in a bag, don't give them cake. You don't cut sandwiches to feed the ducks in Roath Park Lake, do you? But she'd always say, O, leave them be, Mandy likes the pigeons, don't you, Mandy? Look at the colours in that one there, the purple and that lovely green. She was soft about things like that. Women always are. They don't have to go out and work to get the money in the first place, that's why. It just gets magically put into their hand each Friday night.

But she always liked it here on the Hayes Island, Carol. The French connection again. Like she said once, This is the life. Pavement society. Rickety iron tables under the trees, and the pigeons, and the down-and-outs. A real whiff of Paris.

And she laughed. And I looked towards the railings of the underground toilets and sniffed the air in deep, like on some azure fucking headland, and let my breath out slow again, with satisfaction.

Ah, I said. Is that what it is? I thought it was the pisser.

Because it was a sweltering summer day, I remember. And you could smell that mix of urine and Dettol you get there sometimes from the toilets when it's hot, I suppose, or the wind's in the right quarter. And it's always worse around the steps down to the Women's, it seems to me. I don't know why that should be. Does a woman's smell ranker than a man's? It might. There's no reason why not. (Let's face it, they're not all Sugar and Spice.)

On the subject of toilets, I remember Carol telling me some of the things scrawled on the walls in the Women's in the College Bar. Really filthy things. Which actually doesn't surprise me in the least, not any more. It probably would have, once. It might even have at the time she told me, to think of not just 'women' but *educated* ones writing things like that on a toilet wall. But it wouldn't fucking surprise me now. I can believe anything of them now. Because anyone who's been around the bitches long enough, let alone been married to one, knows better than to think that any of them is as innocent as they like to make out.

I've lost her. I was somewhere else for a second there. And now I've lost her. I'm standing on the pavement under the trees and looking around me, desperate as a spare groom at a fucking wedding.

And then I see her. Her head among other heads, of people sitting in the outdoor café. Her hair bright in the sunlight where it's slanting on her through the trees, blonde fire like half-cropped grass. *Jesus Christ*, I think, or even whisper. Because even the sun picks her out, *her* out of a crowd, that diagonal yellow ray falling down on her head and shoulders through the leaves and branches like on an angel in a picture or on Bambi hiding in the forest. And it turns my stomach over again, that faint feeling of sickness again, to think how natural she is and how everything loves her for it, even the light of the world.

Then I see that the other girl isn't with her. That a Moustache is in the frame instead.

A black moustache, emphatic as a jay's. Beneath it a red bow-tie, a white shirtfront. In a snazzy, snobbish cream-coloured, slightly creased linen jacket.

He is sitting opposite her at the metal table. He's smiling, talking. Smiling too much. Talking too much. I watch as he lights a cigarette with accomplishment. (Oh, he's one smooth bastard, this boy, I can tell, a positive magician with that Ronson. You can bet he's a real wow with the office tea-ladies: the fleshily handsome not-yet-middle-aged face, the gallant successful sideburns and that semi-Zapata moustache he's not quite young enough to wear.)

130

It's one of those faces you recognise immediately. A case of hatred at first sight. That of a man who for a couple of pins you'd kill and gut.

Her face I can't see. She's sitting with her back to me.

I stand under the eaves of the café kiosk and light a cigarette to give myself something to do with my hands or, come to that, my entire fucking life. And as soon as I do it, even if not exactly cupping the match with my hands, I feel like the lurking gumshoe in some French detective film, hangdog and awkward and obvious.

So instead (sometimes my own sheer, unthinking nerve amazes me) I thread a way between metal chairs and tables and sit on an empty chair immediately behind hers. So now we're sitting back to back, at separate tables, but a yard apart (if that).

I share the table with some old bastard whose hand shakes so much he's already spilled the top inch of his tea into his saucer. Probably a dipso. That always was the trouble with this place, all the bums and poor who use it, you can always tell the really poor, one glance into their faces is enough. Summer or winter they look pinched, and cold, and wan, they've had it and they know it, something's perished in them. It's a look that's unmistakable.

Not like Moustache, behind me, with that senatorial red dickie and the woven Irish lawn. He's going for a different look entirely.

She didn't want to bother with a solicitor, I hear him saying (the loud, educated, Llantrisant Road via west-of-Carmarthen voice). So she said she'd do the conveyancing herself. At this point she thought she had him over a barrel, in so far as they'd agreed a price. I could have told her differently, of course, if she'd asked me. If she'd asked me, in fact, I would have had to. But she didn't ask me . . .

I hear in that chuckle, without having to turn to see it,

his coy shrug and spread quoi-faire hands. 'Chuckle' is what you'd have to call it. One of those laughs that's like a nudge. It says, No flies on me. (Confidentially, you're dealing with a smart fox here.)

I can't quite hear what she says (murmurs) in reply.

Anyway, he says. Shall we adjourn?

(I realise he's been waiting for her here, but they're not staying.) She scrapes her chair back and I have a rush of fear that she'll touch my chairback with hers, turn, apologise, and see me. Even recognise me. (I'm not ready for that. Not here. Not now.)

Then there's the heeled click of her shoes on the flag-stones as they leave. I turn my head to see her sway her hips narrowly, deftly between two chairs occupied back to back. (And again my heart, my poor heart, tightens at this girl. Everything she does is somehow modest but as stylised as a dance, even moving among crowded tables.) I turn my head away as she turns back, to wait for him to join her. And the smile she gives him cuts me.

Just as they move off together, of course the man from the kiosk has to come to swab the tea-pooled tabletop and ask me for my order. So I have to mumble how *I just forgot something*, sorry, standing to leave as soon as he gets there as if I'd been trying to get a free sit-down, or didn't have the price of a cup of fucking tea on me. Things like that annoy me. They really do. Jesus Christ, if all they were doing was meeting here before going on somewhere else, why the fuck sit down at all?

The reason, I realise, being that they don't have any agreed plans for this lunch-hour in the first place. As I follow them away from the Hayes Island I can see they don't know where they're heading yet. They don't even care perhaps? *He* don't, anyway. He don't care in the least. Why should he? The bastard's strolling through the city in the sunlight, under the budded plane trees, among the shitting pigeons, with a girl like Rusty. And that's enough.

More than enough. And I envy him. Envy him the envy he knows he gets from every other man who looks at them 'together'. Envy him that fine, full feeling of existence that must be flooding through him as he walks along with her in public on a public street, walks and talks and laughs and gesticulates with his hands, the old consummate relaxed urbanity on show, the practised ease, although that don't fool me for a minute, that don't fool me for a millisecond, I know how hyped-up he really is, he's running upon pure adrenalin, the suave smooth-talking bastard. He's up there like he was on rocket fuel.

I follow. Them, the slim brown legs, the swing of her white pleated skirt as she walks beside him, nodding at what he's saying, looking across at him from time to time, her arms now crossed in front of her in a kind of thoughtful or attentive way, listening to his bullshit. Bullshit which keeps on coming, coming. (He's a real patter-merchant, this boy, he's hardly stopped working his big mouth since they started walking.)

But Silence is Strength, I know. A strength you can use to make other people talk, get garrulous. Like she's doing. All she does is listen, walking alongside him. But let's face it, he's the nervous one. (She's got him on a short lead, and you can bet she knows it.)

And I see a hope in her silence, in that reserve she has. I can sense an independence. She may be 'listening' to this popinjay, she may even turn her head to him from time to time in 'interest'. But she's not fooled by his spiel. He may be glib and witty and assured as hell, saying something now to make her laugh as (what a prince) he reaches ahead to pull open the door they've arrived at, for her to precede him (into Bernie's Bistro, *Seafoods, Steaks*, façade of bogus rough-plastering, a pair of carriage lamps, brief dim interior). But the point is, she's not buying all this easy phoney gallantry any more than she believes the line he's feeding her. She knows full well that behind the charming manner, the silver tongue, the dextrous handling of a fucking wrap, there's only one thing scratching, scratching, like a rat bricked in a wall. And that's the burning itch to Get Into Her Body.

And that's why she's so self-contained, so calm, so (what's the word?) Serene.

All this is in the Body Language too (like in that article I read). Take the way her arms were folded in front of her as they were walking along. That's a Defensive or Protective Posture, she's 'hiding' something from him, she's 'nursing' a secret in there, something she hasn't told this guy about and never will. (Something she probably hasn't told anyone in fact, not even the girl she was with earlier, who is probably her Best Friend at work. It's something she may only just have discovered herself, today even, just now, in the last ten minutes since she met this character at the Hayes Island. Something she hadn't realised or quite put together before. But she's realised it now, and it's given her a new strength, the quiet strength to wait, to be patient, and the stength, if ever and whenever she has to, to give a playboy like this a straight, N.O.: No.

Because what she knows now is that there's no use giving it away just to be 'going out' with some professioned poser, just to be on the 'social scene'. What she knows now is that she has to wait for Mister Right. And Mister Right's a funny guy. You don't know who he is or what he looks like. In fact he's an act of faith. And it's only now, perhaps for the first time, that she begins to get a sense of him being out there (like they used to tell us Jesus is everywhere in the world, in every twig and flower, and you know it even if you can't see him). For the first time she begins to think that if she don't play things straight and honest with herself she won't be worthy of him. And perhaps she even has an instinct that he isn't far away. But in any case, she'll wait, she knows that now. (Because your cherry is the one fruit you can keep without it going rotten.) And she senses he's the One, the only one who can open up her mind and help her discover her body to herself, there's that roar like a waterfall slowly crashing endlessly inside her that only he can still and silence, the man she was conceived and born and fated all her life to fuck and get fucked by, even if she didn't, couldn't, know that till the moment when it happened to her for the first time, when he knew what she wanted better than she did or could ever admit to and he was so gentle and firm with her until she Oh my God felt the bigness of him in her.)

For a few seconds I watch from the corner opposite Bernie's Bistro. Then I quickly cross the road: to get in close, in case they find a table by the front window. In films they always show you a guy with his coat-collar turned up watching a house from the far pavement. (He usually stands just under the street-lamp too, to make sure you don't miss him.) But of course you've got much less chance of being spotted if you stand on the *near* side of the street instead, in the very lee of the front wall. It's a question of angles and fields of vision or, put at its most basic, fucking simple common sense.

I stand by the door and study the chalk-scrawled menu, an old classroom blackboard, propped at an angle on the step. *Baked Shark Mexican style. Entrecôte Steak & Green Pepper Sauce. Sea Bass with Lemon. Quiche Loraine*, the dummies, I hope their cooking's better than they spell. *Assorted Salads. Pâté de Maison. Pick Your Own Lobster. Special Today Oysters*. Moustache will probably go for a plate of those, the cunt, maybe even try a wink of 'complicity' at her or of 'innuendo' anyway, just before he throws his head back (showing all his upper fillings) and lets one slither down his throat. I hope it's off or got that poisonous hair in it. Though, me, I don't see how anyone can eat those things, aphrodisiac or not. I tried one of my wife's once, when we went out for a meal

135

on her birthday that time and she ordered them. That was the first time I ever tasted an oyster, and the last. It was like swallowing your own snot cold. No, worse. Swallowing someone else's.

I hover there, like I'm trying to make my mind up from the menu. (You never know who might be watching.)

Not, come to think of it, that there's anything to stop me actually going in, or even ordering something. He won't remember my face. He don't even know he's ever seen me. At the Hayes Island he was sitting facing me, or at least my back, when I sat down but, of course, his eyes were full of her. And she had her back to me.

But the truth is, I don't like going into restaurants at the best of times, and least of all alone. Unlike my snob of a wife, who loves that kind of thing, linen napkins on the table and avocado spoons and fingerbowls. (You pig, I said to her that time, you've eaten all the fingers, ha ha ha.) The bitch actually used her fork in a different way when we ate out or in company, the point of the tines *up* instead of down, as if this was the paragon of style and elegance. But me, I'm never sure if I'm doing the right thing. I'm not saying I get *nervous* when I eat in public. Don't get me wrong. It's just I hate all that snobbery you get in these pseudo-French places. Not that anyone cares what a fucking waiter thinks. Let's be honest, all they've got to do is be clean, servile and able to balance a tray. They might act like they know everything, but they're hired help when you get down to it. (If they had any brains they'd own a restaurant themselves, not have to make up their lousy wages by currying tips and swabbing tables in someone else's.)

A young waiter in a white jacket comes out onto the step. He carries a round tin tray. He begins collecting glasses from under the Cinzano parasols of the two pavement tables.

And the Right Move, the surprise move, comes to me

out of nowhere, just like that, a variation on some half-remembered or even half-invented incident in some old black-and-white romantic film, I don't know which one or even who the actors are (I've seen so many of those films on TV now that I can watch them with my eyes shut).

The guy, the hero, is in the foyer of some nightclub, while inside the girl (she's probably the singer in the joint) is getting chummy drinking cocktails with the owner, who you know is a crook and a slimy bastard because he's got that thin moustache, like the banker or saloon-owner who runs the whole town in a Western. (So okay, this guy with Rusty, his is more Virile-Mex than Banker-Smooth. Fashions in facial hair change. But a slimeball's still a slimeball, and identifiable on sight.)

So I ask the waiter if he noticed the girl in white who just went in.

Yes, sir, he says.

(I bet you did, I think. I fucking bet you noticed her.)

Fair hair, he says. She was with a gentleman.

That's right, I tell him. Un monsieur. Okay. Have you got a pad?

Pad?

I make a squiggle in the air above my palm.

Paper. For writing on.

This I got, he says. Is all.

He shows a book, mostly stubs, of perforated blank sheets, lined and columned, *Total* at the bottom. (The cheapskate, I think. Bringing her to a place where they don't even have the name of the establishment heading the bill they sting you with.)

I take the pad and remove the blue biro from the breast pocket of his white jacket. I tear off the top sheet at the perforation and write on the blank back:

Remember. There is no such thing as a Free Lunch.

I reread this, and add:

Particularly for the man who is buying it. (One way or another he will want his money back.)

I read it again, wondering if I should sign it *From a Friend* (or, putting my quid in once and for all, *An Admirer*)?

The waiter has now filled his tray with empty glasses from the outside tables. He waits. I give him back his order pad and slip the biro back into his breast pocket. I leave the note unsigned. He watches me fold it carefully, twice. In the film the hero would probably have taken the rose from his own lapel to send in with it, but, like they say, times and fashions change, who wears buttonholes now? (And anyway, the last thing women want from men these days is courtliness, 'romance'. Treat them like dirt and they'll follow you for ever, send them orchids and they'll walk all over you.)

Okay, listen, I tell him.

There are some coins (pounds and silver) scattered on his tray: tips, I suppose, or change. I throw another pound coin among them, and hold up the note.

I want you to give this to the lady in white. The lady with fair hair. The one who is with the monsieur with the moustache. You understand?

He picks up my coin. He looks at it, turns it in his fingers as if he might never have seen one before. Black, glittery Franco-Italian eyes, with yellowish whites. He reaches towards me and tucks the coin into the breast pocket of my chocolate brown suit.

There's your pound, he says, and here's one of mine.

He takes another pound from the tray and tucks this one into my pocket too. He takes the folded note from my fingers and stuffs this into the same pocket, then straightens it like a tiny handkerchief.

You give it to her instead, he says.

He smiles, winks, then pushes backwards through the door, turning inwards deftly halfway through, the full tray of glasses balanced in one hand. All I can do is

stand on the step and watch the door decelerate on its
hydraulic arm, slowly closing on a glimpse of dim interior,
some kind of potted tree, a foyer with a pay-phone on
the wall.

I push the door open hard again, an instant before it
fits to the jamb. I go in and I am just in time to catch
his glance as he backs with the tray thrugh a pair of
white swing-doors into a white-tiled kitchen. He winks
at me again as he turns in through the doors and (short
of following him in there), all I can do is laugh and show
him a middle finger. By which time he's gone and there
are only those two swing-doors swinging, and swinging
again, the left door on a longer arc than the right and
every time just missing it at mid-swing. (Though, as I
see from a lifted face among the room of crowded tables,
mouth open and a loaded fork stopped halfway to it, one
of the diners at least caught the message. So I have to
laugh again and shrug.)

I look for 'someone', a face among the faces. (Not here
yet.) Then at my watch. (I'm 'early' anyway.) I don't see
Rusty and Moustache, until I go towards a bar area
where people are waiting for a table to become vacant.
They sit on high stools at the short counter. He's pointing
to something in a menu. (Her legs are crossed.)

The Head Waiter or some other menial comes up to
me. Black tux, frogged shirt.

Good afternoon, sir.

Good afternoon. Do you have a table for two?

Have you booked, sir?

(Indecisive, I reconsider my watch, the room.)

No. But I'm early anyway. My friend isn't here yet.
Look, no problem. I'll have a drink at the bar just while
I'm waiting. Yeah.

I go across to the bar. (I'm on a high of recklessness.)
I'm standing five yards from Rusty and Moustache, if that.
But I don't glance at them. They're what you might call
'engrossed' in that menu they're so touchingly 'sharing',

139

anyway. And I know if I don't look directly at them, they
won't see me. (I feel hard, invincible, invisible.) Nobody
sees me now, not unless I want them to, no more than
they notice *Moon River* oozing out of the wallpaper, the
way it always is in these places. No more than anyone in
the dining-room out there can overhear what I'm saying
to the barman now.

I'd like a beer.

Only bottled beer, he says. Or halves of lager.

Halves of lager?

I look at him in his white uniform. Young, ferret-
chinned. The raspberry rash around his mouth, the
faint, beginner's moustache.

You mean you don't serve pints?

No sir.

But I don't drink halves. This *is* a bar, isn't it?

Yes sir.

Okay. So this is what you do. Give us half of lager.
Twice.

And for him I hold up two fingers instead of one.

I lean at the counter and watch him fill two half-pint
glasses at the tap, as Rusty and Moustache leave their
stools and go past behind me. (I'm not even a Profile
or a Nape to them: just a head. A back. A brownish
suit.) I give the barman a rolled five, turn to the room.
Rusty and Moustache are near the door. They're standing
with a waiter, who Moustache seems to know. And of
course wants everyone to know he knows, Rusty especially, it's the usual story, the old Regular Customer and
Big Spender routine. As if having a waiter know you is a
big deal (or maybe it makes you a democrat or at least a
proper gentleman to swap familiar backchat with one).

The three of them are looking into a lighted glass tank.
But it hasn't got tropical fish in it but slow, blue things,
stirring like big insects. Yes, Moustache has taken her
over to Pick Out her Own and he's looking on proud and
paternal like he was buying her a puppy. She's smiling

too as she bends level to the tank to look in, she puts a
finger on the glass to point and the waiter bends to look in
as well, and Moustache bends, then nods. Yep, that's the
one. And then they all smile, what a touching fucking
scene. And in a minute now the waiter's going to take
that slow blue speckled live thing out and break its claws
to fit it in the pan, and drop it into freshly boiling water.
(My wife told me once exactly what they do with lobsters,
she was full of information like that, about whales or
wildlife or what they're doing to the Tropical Rainforest
or how they get astrakhan, which is the fur of a lamb
killed within three days of birth, it's only when they're
that young that lamb's-fur has those knobbly curls in it.
And that's why you should never wear astrakhan, she
said. And you should never order lobster in a restaurant,
because it isn't just the same as eating meat, killing
an animal as quickly and humanely as you can to feed
yourself. The awful thing, she said, is how they cook it
for you in the pot still living, that's why it's pink, she
said. Wouldn't you turn pink if they did that to you? And
Yes, I said, I suppose I would. But don't tell me about it.
I've never tasted lobster in my life, and I'm never likely
to wear astrakhan. And, anyway, you, I said, you're full
of shit. How can you spend so much time talking about
lobsters and three-day-old lambs and Tropical fucking
Hardwoods, I said, then march down Queen Street with
a banner in support of Free Abortion on tap?)

I look back to the counter as the barman puts the
change in front of me and turns away. It's now I see
that Rusty has left her handbag on the stool in front of
the bar.

I look at the back of the barman's neck. He is slicing
a lemon.

I look at Rusty and the waiter and Moustache, all still
looking at those doomed lobsters moving claw and feeler
in their bubbly lighted tank.

And I'm suddenly so invincible, so calm, that I have

time to take a mouthful from one of the half pints of lager, time to take out a cigarette and put it in my mouth and time to light it, before I slide from my stool and go to the other end of the short counter for an ashtray and slip the cream leather handbag up under my jacket, holding it in place under my left arm.

Invisibility is a strange thing. It's like a magic cloak I somehow forget I've got, and it's not until I absolutely and utterly need it that I find it's there. Like when I used to shoplift. Because the first thing I learnt was that if you start worrying if anyone is watching or can see you all you do is *attract* their look, they home in on your anxiety. You have to ignore everyone, blank them out in your mind, and act as if you were alone. Then you can just simply put away out of sight whatever it is you're stealing, in a pocket or a bag, and no one will ever see you steal it, even if they're looking at you at that very moment. It's not the quickness of the hand deceiving the eye. It's the total unconcern. And that's a power. One that I've tried to develop. Which is why no one has ever caught me, for shoplifting, or worse. When it matters, it's as if I can stop my heartbeat and go transparent. Like when that girl's flatmate came back and went into that other room and stood there in the doorway with her back to me and screamed and screamed and I walked across the lit room behind her and through the door she had just opened, into the hall of the flat, and then into the corridor and away through the outer door that she'd just closed and locked and put the safety-chain up on as well.

I go back to my stool, put the ashtray on the counter, flick into it ash that has barely had time to form, glance at my watch and go towards the foyer. I raise a lightly clenched fist enquiringly to my right ear as I go past the head waiter, and follow his obligingly pointing arm towards the pay-phone on the wall, which, as I come out from the dining area, a man in a short-sleeved red shirt is conveniently using so that (letting a moment's irritation at this fact publicly cross my face and glancing purse-lipped at my watch again) I pause in indecision, obviously not sure whether to wait until this telephone is free or look for a call-box outside. I go to the door with its *Exit* sign, pull it open, and emerge into the brilliant street, an afternoon as bright, sudden and dislocating as if I'd just come from the darkness of a cinema.

And as my foot touches the pavement there's an instant of panic, because I realise my invisibility was only good as long as I was in that dim, crowded room of diners, was moving silently beyond the hubbub of their conversation and their cigarette smoke like a fish past weed.

Out here in the sunlit street, and on the sunlit side of it, my shadow is suddenly black, dense and irregular, a foreshortened splash across the pavement startling as an inkblot or a spattering of blood. Out here, with this handbag clutched under my armpit, I'm a Fugitive (and as obvious as the one blue-burnt brick in the wall that my eye inexplicably picks out).

I button my jacket and walk swiftly, trying not to hurry. But I can feel how my heartbeat has restarted and I'm conscious of the size of my own too-gradually-diminishing back, thrown up to sight and wobbling away on a rail like one of those hinged targets marksmen use.

(She will be getting back to her seat precisely now. She looks for the handbag. She is only puzzled at first. They look along the counter for it, on the floor. She looks at the barman. She speaks to him and he turns from the lemon he is endlessly slicing. He is puzzled too. Then they all look simultaneously towards the two glasses of beer at the other end of the short counter and at the cigarette I realise I no longer carry in my fingers and which I must have left in the just-borrowed ashtray, uncoiling greyish smoke. Then the head waiter comes and the waiter with a tray who I spoke to outside. They all speak excitedly. The young lady is clearly distressed. The head waiter clenches a fist beside his ear and points towards the foyer, where they move as one and with increasing sense of mishap, just as the man in the red shirt is hanging up the receiver after his call. He turns in surprise, but the waiter, the head waiter and the barman are already pointing to the door out to the street and hurrying past the telephone. But everything is speeding up and slipping away from them faster now, like a weighted rope snapping off the coil and running out. They throw open the door and crowd out through it and into the street. There is a second of dazzlement before their eyes adjust and they can look along the pavement, precisely as I reach the corner.

I am not actually running. But it is with a visible shudder, as if still expecting a rifle shot behind me and a bullet exactly midway between the shoulderblades, that I turn into Queen Street with my stark black shadow now ahead of me, vacating the bright, abruptly vacant pavement of Charles Street. I am gone from their sight almost in the instant of their eyes' habituation to the sunlight out of doors, so that I leave behind only a glimpse – or even an after-image – lingering against the empty perspective of the paving-stones, like in the last frame of a cartoon-strip or a photograph taken a split second too late: one lagging trouser-leg in full stride, and (in the act of springing out of sight behind the brickwork corner, to overtake – and then in turn be overtaken by – its hurrying partner) one flexed foot shod in two-tone tan and white, a lifted heel.)

Seven

By the time I turn a second corner, I know I'm lost among the lunchtime crowds, I'm safe, I'm In The Mainstream now, I've got the Freedom of the City. Because if you've got a minute's start it's easier to vanish in a city than a jungle. And you leave less trace of the vanishing. No scent, no broken twig or slashed palm-frond, no footprint in the mud starting to fill with water as your pursuer looks at it. Only a perspective of a busy street, the traffic, the crowded pavements, the countless exits. Only the prints of two fingers and a thumb on a beer-glass, and perhaps a saliva sample on a Marlboro cigarette still smouldering quietly in an ashtray. (And for a simple everyday handbag snatch no one will even take the time to notice evidence like that.)

I turn off into the entrance to British Home Stores. Through the plate-glass box of the window-display, I can see back down the pavement I've just come along. I watch for a minute or so, searching faces, and in that mingled crowd which is endlessly approaching or going away, no one is following me or what I'm gripping under my left armpit.

It's a big handbag, it feels bulky there and makes my arm hang a little awkwardly, as if it should be in a sling. I readjust it, go on through the shop, and leave by one of the rear doors. (You never know. Caution costs fuck-all, and it can save your skin.)

I have to keep shifting the handbag, which tends to slip down. (Carrying it there reminds me of a gun-and-holster set I had as a kid, sometimes I used to wear it buckled diagonally across my chest like a gangster instead of

round my waist like a cowboy, so that the holster was
under my left armpit where the bag is now. I used to
zip up my windcheater and walk around like Eliot Ness,
thinking nobody knew I was carrying a gun.

It was a Hopalong Cassidy gun. I can see it now. It
was silver and had white handles with a steer's head
and horns embossed on them. There wasn't a kid in
Grangetown who'd ever seen a gun like that. It was
Yankee, of course. The Old Man brought it back from
Japan for me, he was still at sea in those days. (Well,
he's been at sea most of his fucking life, if you ask me,
and still is.) He brought that gun for me, and for the Old
Lady, I remember, a kind of dressing-gown or belted robe
of green silky stuff with a big yellow and silver winged
dragon on the back (embroidered thick the dragon was,
like that wire look you get on a blazer badge). I suppose
it was real Japanese silk, that gown. Probably a genuine
kimono. The Old Lady never liked it, though. I don't
think she ever put it on. Where am I supposed to wear
a thing like this? she said to him. You gonna get me a
part in *The Mikado*? She laid it on a chair. I suppose it
had to be green, she said. Like I always say, the Irish
got no taste. No taste in anything. But it wasn't the
colour she didn't like. What it was, I think, was that
she thought the dragon was unlucky, because it had
wings. Like she would never wear a thing with birds
on it either, or have birds in the house. And that was
why she wouldn't give me that gown years later, when I
wanted to cut it down and make it into a shirt or jacket
for me. Because I don't know whether the Irish are short
on taste, but the Maltese are long on superstition.

I wonder what happened to that gown or, come to that,
my Hopalong Cassidy gun. I could have given it to Darryl,
whatever my wife (or Ex Wife, I should call her) would
have to say about it (she'd probably come out with the
usual shit about not letting them have guns or anything
'military' as toys). It must have got broken or stolen or

given away. (It's amazing how things pass through your hands and vanish. You can't ever seem to hold on to a damn thing.)

Darryl would love a gun like that. I bet you couldn't get one half as good these days, for love or money. Though why the Old Man had to sail all the way to Yokohama to buy a Hopalong Cassidy gun (probably made like my Estwing axe in Rockford, Illinois) beats me. But I suppose it's the same as the Japs being mad on chewing-gum and golf and baseball. That's what happens when you lose a war, you gain a whole new civilisation.

Whatever happened to Hopalong Cassidy? He'd seem pretty old-hat now, I suppose, after Eastwood and Terence Hill. Come to think of it, he seemed pretty old-hat at the time. One of a previous generation, like Tom Mix and Will Rogers, the last Gentlemen Cowboys. William Boyd it was, who used to play Hopalong, he was silver-haired when I was a kid. He must have snuffed it years ago, I suppose. Gone to the Great Ghost-Town in the Sky.)

I halt and stare into a butcher's window. Pinkish pork-chops and bloody beef ranged on the slab, a couple of cock pheasants hanging from an S-hook by their necks. The dark shot-silk green of their heads is the green of that dressing-gown my father brought back for my mother from Japan, and she never wore. Next to them, from another hook, a long hare hangs head-down. His eye is blood.

I'm trying to think where I want to be heading.

(I get these blank spots sometimes, when I forget things. Or rather, I start remembering things and lose track of what I'm doing. Memory is a weird thing.)

Seeing where I am, I realise my footsteps have brought me in a circle, or rather three and a half sides of a square, so that I've been walking back towards the Hayes Island again.

147

(It's just a kind of fadeout, I suppose. I get it sometimes, when I need to. And not only then but when I'm working in the tyre bay, say, or just driving. Sometimes I'll get to a place and I can't remember driving the last five miles. Or the cassette will click off in the tape machine, and it's as if that little noise wakes me up and I don't even know what it is I've been playing, I haven't heard a note, though all this time I must have been watching the road ahead and braking, changing through the gears and so on. Perhaps I'm even driving better, safer, this way, because it's all being done on pure instinct. I don't know. But anyway, it's like I've been on Daydream Automatic. Perhaps it happens to me like this because I never dream at night. Yeah, okay, I know: everybody dreams. Everybody dreams every single night of their lives, they've run tests on the movement of your eyelids and so on. What I mean is, I don't *remember* my dreams hardly ever. And if you don't remember your dreams, you might just as well not have had them. What the fuck. I know one thing: I'd rather have a nice wet daydream than a nightmare.)

I push the handbag up more, under my jacket. And cross the pedestrian area to the Island itself. I skirt chairs, metal tables, customers (bums and businessmen alike) grouped in dappled afternoon sun. I do a quick trot down the worn stone steps between the railings, passing from the bright lunchtime into the cool of the *Gentlemen*, so cool and dim it's more like underwater here than underground.

White glazed brickwork. Black streaked-marble stalls to stand and piss at. The cavelike trickle of green Victorian plumbing. Mahogany doors. That faint, tidal whiff of Lavernock beach and seaweeded rocks and the old rusty sewage pipe. And overhead, a gridded skylight ceiling of thick pale-greenish glass crossed by foot-soles and dim shadows, all the city's numberless destinations.

Finding an empty cubicle along the row, I go in and shut the door and shoot the brass bolt home. I lower the cracked mahogany seat and sit on it. And here I *know* I'm safe. Inviolate. (If not exactly in violets. Ha. Ha. Ha.)

This was why Instinct brought me here: the peace and security of sitting in a locked toilet. And many's the time, I suppose, over the years, that I've sat underground here in one cubicle or other of the Hayes Island bogs after a good stiff walk and felt a good stiff shit at last ease out of me and slide into the water, looking around the cell as I'm doing now, in perfect Calm and Contentment, beneath the pavements and the crossing feet, myself the still, quietly voiding centre of the hurrying world. Sometimes there can be an almost mystic peace in a toilet, not to mention in having a good shit there. And in fact as far as that goes (like I had occasion to say to Tony Barbecue only the other day, after I'd had to walk rather purposefully from Glossop Terrace to The Locomotive so I could have one) the only thing I know to beat it is a lovely fuck.

The handbag is like a small satchel in design. Good leather. Solid, hardwearing, serviceable. Space and Style for the modern Working Miss. Mushroom, they call it, this greyish beige.

I turn the bag in my hands. Feel it. Weigh it. I don't even want to *open* it for a minute or two. Every stitch and fold and wrinkle in the leather itself is already intimate and erotic, like the creases in the insteps of her white fringed boots would be, or the paler, worn rucking that radiates at the lap of her skintight jeans, creasing from how she sits. I lift the handbag to my nostrils and sniff deeply, it's almost odourless except for the smell of leather itself, though there's the faintest sweetish trace of cosmetics too. For smell boots or jeans would be better, to breathe in from a tall, heeled boot the sweat-darkened inside, that faint pong from cramped toes and crinkled arches. Or jeans, yes, even better, best of all, to put your nose delicately just there where the double-stitching runs back under her.

And already I know it'll be harder to 'hand back' this

149

handbag of hers than it ever was to steal it. Without even having unbuckled the flap and seen what's inside, already I want to keep it, put it in the Museum, even if this would be ahead of the event instead of afterwards, a 'promise' rather than a Memento. Because although I don't always remember or have time, I try never to leave without a Souvenir of some kind (some harder fact than memory). A lock of hair. A bra. A scarf I used. There's even a diaphragm in its little hinged case, like a compact or a clam-shell, she actually asked if she could put it in, that girl, Blue Eyes I called her, she didn't mind anything, she said, as long as she didn't get pregnant, she was very calm and self-possessed and trying to be sensible about it and to keep talking, so I said, Yeah, Okay, only she had to let me watch her put it in, and she was embarrassed by that, she said she'd never even let her boyfriend watch that, she always went to the bathroom to do that, and as soon as it came out she knew she shouldn't have said it, about her boyfriend, she was trying to keep things chatty, but Careless Talk Costs Lives, and that night I told her to take it out again and put it back in the case and she wasn't embarrassed by anything now and it looked like one half of some old busted tennis-ball as she was washing it at the sink and she asked me why I wanted it and I said, I just do. Don't worry. You won't be needing it now for a while.

When I open the handbag what stuns me is the amount of cash Rusty was carrying, First, there's a red leather purse with ten ten-pound notes and a few quid in change (perhaps another tenner's worth). And that's only the sterling. There's also a kind of document wallet with *Thomas Cook Traveller's Service* on it. It feels thick, substantial in my hand. And when I open it I see it's lined with money too. In pesetas. Spanish banknotes. A neat-edged little tablet of stiff, clean, never-used, never even fucking folded, Spanish spending-money, direct from the mint or at least from the Exchange Counter at Cook's.

Boy, this bag's a mugger's dream. I don't even know what all this is worth. I tot up the peseta notes to a figure which sounds a lot. But I don't know what the exchange rate is. And I suppose Spain has one of these Mickey Mouse economies, the peseta's probably no better than the lira. (To convert from pounds just think of a number, divide by three, and add six noughts.)

I put the purse and the money side by side on the speckled terrazzo floor.

I lift the flap of the handbag and inhale again a faint clean feminine cosmetic smell: of the perfumes or deodorants she has carried in it, nothing special or unusual or even expensive, probably, just the usual brand-names sold in millions, in every corner chemist or highstreet Boots. But to me, now, in now as deep as a horse into a nosebag, it's a smell addictive as wintergreen in a changing-room or mentholatum rub or tar on just-tarred streets, it's as personal as the scent from the pouch of her panties, or, come to that, the real Fur Sandwich itself (because, like the man said, If you want your steak that rare then you should get it but don't forget to ask the waitress).

I take out of the front compartment of the bag a pair of goggles. Swimming-goggles. They have faint blue lenses. (I have to lengthen the barred black-rubber strap before I can put them on.)

There is also, in a clear plastic bag, a one-piece swimming costume: black, with a green flash at the hip, a white mesh inset at the crotch (unstained). I hold it up, no more than a scrap of material you could compress in one hand to squeeze out dry and then stuff into a sandwich bag for carrying, the whole garment no bigger or heavier or damper than a dewy rose, a rose smelling of chlorinated turquoise water from the Empire Pool and, if not of her, then at least of cleanness and athleticism and beaded skin and splashed laughter. (I see her crouched in a racing dive then swimming up under that wavering blue surface like a seal, the Lycra costume as slick and black on her as sealskin.)

Through these goggles, everything is now the same tint as that chlorinated water. And everything I take out of this stolen handbag gives me the same pang, in the sense it gives of her Unknown Life, mysterious to me as a seal's below the polar ice.

Everything I touch she has touched. I look at this plastic hairbrush and think of her fingers handling it. I weigh in my palm this hard green Cape apple, and think how probably she brings an apple to work every day for her teeth, to eat in the afternoon coffee-break instead of the sugared cakes or doughnuts the others have and which one of the girls goes out to buy from Eynon's. (I feel the juicy crunch of it and the flow of saliva starts under my own tongue.) I take out the yellow plastic comb, and there is a single chestnut-brown hair caught in the teeth. (It is enough to conjure with.) And then I find her mirror. A small oblong hand-mirror bordered with imitation tortoiseshell.

I'm stiff, whirring. So that already I know that before I leave this cubicle under the street I will have to bequeath her likewise a specimen of my Scent, a Trace of me hot on the surface of her mirror's face, barely a smear, the smallest smudge, like a sample on a slide. Unidentifiable except under a microscope. So small she'll never know it's there. But there. There every time she checks her face. In a kind of (what is it called?) Deposit on Account. (On account of what? On account of how this is just the first instalment, ha ha ha.)

I was right: ripping the bag off in the first place was the piece of cake. Easy as pissing the bed. The hard part will be giving the damn thing back, and I don't mean just the giving it up, the relinquishing it, I mean the getting it back to her. Because with this handbag of Rusty's, I know that the only thing I *can* keep is the last damn thing I want, i.e. the cash that's in it. In fact, any money that's in there I *have* to take, like a common thief. I don't have any choice. (All I can do is find some way to make it up to her, such as buy her something out of it, say, some things she can wear for me, yes, something in blue for example, swimming-pool blue, she's got the kind of skin and colouring for that, yeah, a slithery little satin thing to start with, some nice little backless number open right down to the cleft.)

But everything *except* the money has got to go back. I've worked this much out already.

The whole point being this: that once I've had my own set of keys cut from hers I've got to have the handbag found again, and handed in. Because from start to finish the whole thing has got to look like your ordinary everyday impromptu Snatch And Run, and nothing more. The last thing I want is for the police to guess that the least thing on my mind was how much cash she was carrying, and to start advising her to change her locks. Taking the money is the necessary motive, or the pretext if you like.

To put it another way, the police will think it's the crime. But really it's the alibi.

So I've got to manage this. Otherwise I lose all the advantage I had to take so many fucking chances to gain.

First things first, though. Because before I do anything else I've got to go down to the While-U-Wait in Duke Street and get the copies cut, turn that advantage to hard, metal fact.

What I've got is this. One key-ring with two Yale-type doorkeys on it: these must be her house keys. Plus three other keys on an old *Mobil* fob, the blue word and the red flying horse sealed in clear plastic so old it's scratched and worn opaque. One of these must be for the MG, but I don't know about the other two. One might be for the garage. The other, who knows? Petrol tank and boot? (I don't know if there's a separate key for these on an MG

153

or whether the ignition key fits the lot.) (Anyway, I get one each of these cut too. You got the right key, you can find the right lock.)

Then I just put the originals back in the bag with the rest of her stuff. So now everything's there, except the cash (Spanish as well as English, because it's obvious any petty thief would have that too).

I also do a slightly crazy, impulse thing, I try that green Cape apple. It's so hard and green the imprint of my teeth is perfect top and bottom of the bite, and chewing it has the explosive crunching of an apple bitten into in a film. (You ever notice that? They probably amplify a horse snaffling a carrot or something, to get that noise. It must be to show that American apples are crisper than any other. Or what great teeth American actors have. Despite all the root-canal work and the cappings they can still bite through stones.)

I put the apple back in the bag too. That big white bite out of it will go brown. But it's another signature or message, if you like, or really just a joke. Everything else is as it was, more or less. The keys. The diary. The swimsuit and goggles. An electricity bill that probably came this morning. The comb. The Hermesetas. The Mum Rollette. The biros. The Shell petrol stamps (you'd have to be a pretty petty thief to steal the first instalment on a Free Glass). The receipt from Chelsea Girl (I wonder what she bought?). The zodiac goodluck charm (a small gold crab, that means her birthday must be in September, is it, or October?). The broken watchstrap. And the emptied purse. I also leave the Thomas Cook wallet and the return airline ticket that was in it, in the pocket opposite the Spanish money. The tickets are *Cardiff – Alicante – Cardiff*, Flight Number AO 2904, leaving Friday 11th of May (in almost a week's time), and coming back Saturday the 19th. I wouldn't want to spoil this holiday she seems to have planned – or perhaps it's business, yes, probably some trip in connection with her job at Asprey's. Anyway, a trip to Spain is something she must have been looking forward to, and I don't like to cause her an unhappiness I can avoid. (I mean it, I don't even like fucking taking the money she's just changed for the trip. Really I don't. It's hers, I know she had to work for it. But, like I say, the money I have to take. There's no way out of that. I can keep it for her, pay it back to her, buy her things out of it. But the money explains the whole thing.)

But the money is all I take. Except for a small handkerchief she'll never even think to miss. It has a sprig of lavender embroidered on it in one corner.

It's like they say, it's easy to kill someone. The hard part's knowing what to do with the body. It's the same problem with a handbag. I'm walking around the streets for twenty fucking minutes with the bag under my jacket, looking for the right, the safe place to leave it.

In the end I go into Conti's and get a cup of coffee, and drink it and get up and go. Minus handbag.

It's a nice clean place, Conti's, good cup of coffee, waitress service, not the cheapest place you can find of course, but at least that means you don't get the drunks and deadbeats in there. It's more a place where middle-class middle-aged women go when they're having a shopping day in town or getting a perm-job.

Basically, then, I'm assuming that whoever next sits at the table I leave it under will call the waitress, even if the waitress doesn't find it first. (Sometimes you have to put your faith, ha fucking ha, in people's honesty.) And that there should be no further problems from there on in. There's an electricity bill with her name and address on it inside. Even the police, for Christ's sake, should be able to work it out from there. (Nothing missing but the money, you say? Obviously panicked. Clearly an amateur. Be more careful next time please, Miss Hays.)

Nothing's certain, of course. But that's the story. And once I've got up from that little tiled table and left the handbag on the floor, that's it. Things have a life. No point wondering about what else might 'happen' to it, what more 'adventures' it might have. Though it reminds me of that story you used to have to write in school, you know the one, where you have to follow some ordinary everyday object through all its amazing exploits and encounters. *A Day in the Life of a Postage Stamp* was a favourite one, or *A Day in the Life of a Pound Note*. (Huh. That dates me. The Pound Note. Just one more part of life that's gone for ever, like the Florin and the Farthing and the Great Auk and the Irish Elk and a lot of other things you'll never see again. I suppose the teacher gives you a different title for that story now. Like I say, everything changes so fucking fast, these days. Even the little things like *words*. That's why you've got to grab what's rushing past you while you can. Because once a thing is gone it's not just gone for good. It's like it was never even there.)

Eight

(On her first full day in Spain the manager of the hotel asks her out for a meal the following evening. They are standing in the foyer. She is on her way to the beach.

My chef here is very good, he says. But sometimes even I have to take a change. And there is this wonderful restaurant I know. Quite small. Very good seafood. He laughs. I know it's good. My brother runs it.

She laughs with him. It is hard to say No when you are staying in this hotel at a special rate. In your own mind you are here purely for a 'holiday' (with pay). But this man is now asking out not you but a representative of your company. Because that way he knows you cannot refuse. (This is what you have to pay for a cheap week in the sun.)

He has a moustache. He is dark, tall for a Spaniard, attractive. Only, you know that the sense of his own darkness, tallness, attractiveness is continually at the front of his mind, like Height, Colour of Eyes and Occupation in the front of his passport.

She smiles, however.

Thank you. That might be nice.

He is one of those men who insist your looks entitle you to be treated like a celebrity. Barely ironic flourishes and bows, an effusive gallantry sweeping the path in front of you. And with every smile, the lightly oiled charm of a poor man's Cary Grant.

When they arrive at the restaurant he disappears just for a moment. Then not only his brother but the whole family, plus employees, seem to crowd out of the kitchens after him, to look at her and shake the hotel manager's hand in congratulation. It is as if the couple have announced that they were married secretly two days before. And in fact the manager wears the look of modest complacency of a man who now has nothing left to wish. At least with him, she realises, there will be no problem. Simply to be seen with her will be enough.

When they are seated with the menus the brother himself waits attentively for her to choose. He is shorter than the manager, tougher looking. You can see the white singlet through his shirt.

I think the lobster, she says.

This allows the manager's brother a small smile of triumph, as if that item in the menu is a trap yet another customer has fallen into.

You must please come and choose, he says.

He reaches out one hand, imperious and reverent as Nureyev, for hers. He escorts her personally into the kitchen where aquariums stir with giant insects and live fish. A ghostly, undulating ray lifts, showing its pale underside, the tiny cupid's-bow of a mouth.

After the meal the manager suggests they have coffee and brandy at a pavement café a little way down the street.

She has brought a wrap in case the evening turns cool. As they leave the restaurant, he manipulates it with glittering ease to present it for her shoulders, the way a matador advances with the cape. She stands for him to place it on her. For a just-appreciable moment his palms linger on her upper arms, resting there as if in encouragement.

Palms grow at intervals along the kerb, each in the space of a left-out flagstone. They are floodlit, shabby. They clash like metal venetian blinds in a windy hotel room.

A friend of mine may be here later, the manager says.

He is a photographer. He is working on next year's brochure. I told him about you. He wants to meet you.

The photographer, it turns out, is already there. He is unshaven and wears a white singlet under his unbuttoned shirt. Gingery hair sprouts over the singlet's neck. He is sitting alone at a table, under a slow fan. Somehow you know that helicopter rotor-blades whirl in his head, he cannot hear what the marine is shouting, he is photographing burning bodies. He does not stand when they join him.

Have a cognac, he says. I'm getting through a bottle of it here.

He looks around, two fingers raised as in the peace sign for more glasses. The waiter is not there. The light inside the café is a bluish neon. The photographer shrugs and lights a Marlboro. He stares at her with a curious, appraising interest, as if he might be trying to remember where they've met before. But he doesn't ask. He and the manager talk about the brochure. As he talks the photographer watches the lit cigarette smouldering in the red ashtray, transforming itself intact into a column of grey ash.

I'm trying to stop smoking, he says. But I keep lighting the damn things without thinking.

A young waiter comes. The photographer asks for two more glasses. They order coffee as well.

They sit in silence until the waiter has set the coffees in front of them. The photographer looks at her and then looks at the manager and shrugs, as if there is nothing more to say except to ask her.

No problem, he says. She's perfect.

She laughs and colours and asks him exactly what it is they want her to do.

The photographer shrugs. You got some suntan oil?
Yes.

Did you bring a bikini?
Yes.
Just put them on.
She laughs again and shakes her head. She is flattered and scared.
I don't know about this, she says. I really don't.

She stretches full-length amid a choppy sea of footprints on the narrow, dusty beach. She puts her head back to show her throat, and lifts one knee. The photographer crawls about her on his elbows like a troop in combat training, taking her from the lowest angles, the long blue bay behind her.

She stands on the slatted wooden pallet under the beach shower. She throws her face up joyfully as if to the vivifying downpour of tepid water barely trickling from the perforations of the metal sprinkler. It is like the rose of a galvanised watering-can.

She catches and catches a borrowed beach-ball. The pleased, embarrassed owner throws it a dozen times before the trajectory lets her catch it in the way the photographer wants.
Okay, he says.

She lies on the trodden beach again with the strings of her pale-blue bikini-top undone. She cradles the fabric to her breasts with both breast-offering hands. The photographer puts his head on one side for a moment, critical of something in the shot.
What about this? she says.
She lowers her breasts, still wet from the beach shower, bare to the sand. She lolls them so the dry grains stick, lifts them.
Okay. Okay. Okay. Okay. Okay. Okay.
Quickly, kneeling, crouching, prone, he takes her, takes

her, takes her. He shoots a whole roll of film, and then another, from all positions around her. There is only the clicking and the whirr of the drive advancing film while she lies there, moving her limbs this way and that, smiling, changing the position of her head.

Okay, he says. He throws her the green silk beach gown she came down from the hotel in.

A thick growl of disappointment and ribald comment comes from the thickening male crowd that has gathered to watch in a crescent about her. The beach is otherwise almost deserted. She pulls the gown on and knots the fringed belt tightly at her wrist. A spatter of applause and obscene speculation breaks out as, barefoot, laughing in embarrassment and riffling sand out of her hair, she follows the photographer up the sandy concrete steps towards the tower-block hotel.

The photographer waits on the little balcony of her room while she dries herself and changes into white slacks and a mustard shirt. She comes out and hangs the scraps of pale blue bikini on the white rail of the balcony, to dry. He watches her as she stands there for a moment and closes her eyes to the sun, full on her uplifted face.

Another couple of rolls of film should do us, he says. We'll shoot those after lunch.

Mmm, she says, sun-absorbed.

His eye follows a jet crossing the blue sky, a vector of silver waste heading west, across the brown and green interior of Spain and then out over mid-Atlantic. The land will fall away. The ocean will be wrinkled, shiny, miles below. That plane will next touch ground in Florida or the Bahamas – another dusty, glittering landscape of heat-wobble and aridity. The thirst for the mirage, he thinks. The migration of nations. Smoking or non-smoking, aisle or window, fully booked. The boredom people flee from, as their grandparents fled poverty and death.

He stares down from the fifth floor at the long curve of brownish beach, the scrub dunes, the empty blue pool in front of the hotel. (From here it would be a high, impossible outward dive, down, over the parterre, the tables and the Martini parasols, to where the squares of tiling waver in the chlorinated turquoise depths.)

He looks away, right, towards more of the gleaming jerrybuilt blocks that have sprung up like oil wells all along the bay. He leans his weight against the rail of the balcony experimentally. It holds.

She sits under the silver thatch of the patio bar. She is lifting a glass of cold beer from the counter and chatting with a young bronze American. The photographer comes in again. The mustard shirt is knotted up under her breasts, but he cannot see her belly. He repositions them so he can, backs away.

Okay. Okay. Okay. Just smile at him. Okay.

The photographer comes back and slides his seat onto the high stool at the bar. He looks at the back of the camera and, pointing the lens anywhere, click click click, at sea, sand, sky, wastes the remainder of the roll of film in the buzz of the machine-drive. He looks at the back of the camera again.

Last one, he says. One of the brain behind it all.

He looks at her, grimacing. He points the camera at his temple like a gun. He presses the trigger.

They sit at a warped table of silvered boards beneath a sunshade. The beach around them is blank with heat. The photographer raises his beer-glass to his mouth. It is empty. He frowns, swigs instead from the brown bottle and stares balefully out to sea.

The young bronze American wanders out from the bar. He carries a bottle. He arrives at their table vaguely, eventually, as if by chance. He grins at her, hangs there a moment.

162

Mind if I join you guys?

The photographer stares out to sea.

The bronze American lifts his arms, yawns, stretches his body in the sun, as if he has just got up. He sits, blinks coldly for a moment.

Too much beer, he says.

He is wearing faded denim cutoffs and a faded olive singlet. It says *US Army* in a faded stencil over the heart. He reaches for the photographer's camera. Gold hairs glitter on his dusky forearms as he inspects it. He turns his mouth down in a grimace that is finally one of respectful approval.

Nikon, he says. Not bad.

The photographer reaches and takes the camera from him.

Handmade by robots for robots, he says.

The bronze American glances at her ironically and shrugs. Then he stares at the bay shrewdly for a while.

What I like about this place is the pace of things, he says. Know what I mean? Real slow.

She asks, How long are you here for?

He squints along the beach for a little while, as if assessing this.

Two, three days, he says. Maybe a week. I might try to get down to Torremolinos some time.

They allow the sectors of their separate views to occupy them. Overhead a light plane drones. A gust blows dry grains of sand against their bare legs and feet. The photographer drains the beer in the brown bottle and stands.

I got some things to do, he says.

He slings the camera on his shoulder and trudges off. The sand is as soft and loose under the feet as the sand of nightmares. He leans forward as he walks, as if climbing a dune.

Yeah, the bronze American says. It's okay here.

He scratches a dusky, gold-fuzzed thigh under the fraying hem of his jean shorts. He glances towards the

hotel. The toiling photographer has reached the sandy
steps. He climbs them and is gone.

Hey, the American says. You feel like a swim?

His face is expectant, encouraging. She notices again
the leather thong, shiny with wear, that hangs a black,
holed pebble round his neck. Under the worn, clean
clothes his body would be clean and simple as that pebble
from swimming already that morning, with a faint taste
of salt. She turns her face to look out across the stunned,
dust-coloured sand and thinks of the blue water pouring
clear off their shoulders, their splashed white laughter.

He is standing, to encourage her.

She smiles up at him.

Thanks. Not just now.

The photographer is in his room, sitting between the
opened doors out to the little balcony. He is in a singlet
and white Y-fronts, bare feet up on the rail outside, pale
legs crossed in the sun.

What happened to Tom Mix? he says.

He wanted to go for a swim.

Why didn't you go too?

I didn't feel like it.

You didn't feel like what?

She looks at him.

It.

She pulls a cane chair towards the sunny doorway. He
waves a bottle at her.

Drink?

What is it?

Spanish brandy. Matured in oaken casks for twelve
long days.

She fetches the thick tumbler from the glass shelf
under the bathroom mirror. She looks at herself there.

I ought to wash my hair, she says, holding out the glass
for him to pour. The sea and the salt in the wind make it
go like candyfloss.

He half-fills the tumbler.

Do you want me to put some clothes on? he says.

I've seen bare legs before, she says.

(He cannot tell her what he has seen. He cannot tell anyone what he has seen.)

But have you seen a man in underpants before? he says. Swimming trunks is one thing. Even nakedness is one thing. But a man sitting around in his underpants? That's intimacy.

He sights the colour of his brandy against the sun.

Of course, the final intimacy comes later, when I get you to wash them out. Then you'll have to marry me.

You're probably married.

He tastes the brandy.

I'll divorce her. I'll divorce them both.

She laughs.

Out at sea the afternoon grows white. A heat haze covers the horizon, so you cannot separate sea from sky. He cannot tell what he has seen.

He pulls on a pair of white slacks and a shirt, takes the bottle, and they go down again onto the beach. The haze has thickened into a luminous fog. For a while they walk slowly, barefoot, along the tideline, away from the hotel. Then they sit on the slope of trodden sand and stare out into the pearly brightness where, far out, the sea vanishes. The slight tide is turning, and waves lap the shore as if only from memory. The long beach is almost deserted. It is still the beginning of the season. Then a motor boat crosses and recrosses in front of them, steering huge circles out in the bay and pulling a waterskier in the huger circles of his swathe. The waves of their passage break repeatedly, more strongly, on the sand. Then the engine cuts and the waterskier sinks to his shoulders in the water, the trapeze gone slack in his hand. Laughter and shouts drift in on the lifting haze as the boat taxis back to pick him up. Then they are gone, the white boat droning back towards the southern arm of the bay, the harbour and the raw hotels.

The photographer takes a swig of the brandy. He feels its reckless heartburn bite and clear. He holds the bottle out to her.

No thanks.

He grimaces and swigs again. He has never found a woman who will drink all the way down a bottle with him.

Sun is now on the beach again. She undoes the top two buttons of the mustard shirt and pulls it off over her head. Under it she is wearing the pale-blue bikini bra. All it is is two glossy pouches and a pair of strings knotted against the brown back. She lies back and closes her eyes to the sun. The photographer watches his fingers slowly filter sand.

I'd like to take some more photographs of you, he says.

Mmm?

I'd like to take some more photographs of you.

You just did.

Real ones. Not just bikini shots for some travel brochure.

Mmm.

Her mouth smiles.

He stares at the white bay, sun on the blue water again further out. Only suffering is really photogenic. He looks at her. Shifting closer he reaches out his clenched hand, lets a fistful of the pale dry sand trickle onto her brown belly, into her navel's sunken rose.

My Christ, he says. You're like a heap of wheat.

She brushes off the sand with one hand, mouth smiling, eyes still closed. Then she sits up.

What time is it?

I don't know, he says. Three? Four? (He knows it is later.)

She sits, knees drawn up, the bottoms of her white

trousers rolled back to the calves. She watches the bay.

I think I'll get back to the hotel, she says. I have to wash my hair.

She draws a comb of fingers loosely back through it.

He watches identical small waves come up and fail on the shore.

I read somewhere that the Mediterranean takes a long time to replace itself out of the Atlantic, he says. Years, he says. He drinks from the bottle. The same old water coming in on the same old shore. I suppose you couldn't even float your name off in an empty bottle. It would just keep washing back to the same beach.

She gets to her feet, spanking sand from her seat.

You coming back?

He swings from the bottle. It is almost empty.

I'll stroll back later, he says. He looks at the bottle. Always finish what you started.

Okay. See you.

He watches her walk away, down the tideline, towards the sun's light. He notices how the gleam dulls for a moment under each bare footsole where it presses on the wet sand. He never has a camera when he needs it. But then, all a photograph is is one way of forgetting. He can never tell anyone the half of what he has seen.

She is sitting at a metal table on a café terrace. It is evening. A beer, half-poured from the brown bottle, stands untouched in front of her. The thin Spanish boy sits at another table, tense over his Coke. He came up to her near the harbour, said something in Spanish and tried to take her hand. Now he has followed her all the way here. He has the eyes of a sick dog, which keep turning nervously, lingeringly towards her. He is afraid someone else – an older boy perhaps – will come up and sit down on the empty chair pushed under the table opposite hers.

That one leaning in the doorway to the café interior, for instance. For the last ten minutes he has been gazing across the terrace at her with a magnanimous expression, his head thrown back stiffly, like a dancer's.

Or that other one, who has passed several times now, drifting to and fro in the two-way currents of the evening promenade beyond the terrace. Every time he goes past, his eyes catch hers, as insistently and infallibly as they would find themselves in a shop window. There he is again. A tall dark, beautiful youth, in dazzling white like a cricketer. He carries his cigarettes and matches in one hand – since his trouser pockets are so tight. In the other hand, like a small rosary, is a string of the worry-beads they all carry here, which he keeps flipping back contemptuously about his fingers, a ruthless look of vanity on his face.

He stares across at her again. The bluish tint of her sunglasses is just deep enough to hide any gaze he might interpret as invitation.

The evening crowd mingles about him, beyond the café's pillared trellises, where grey shaggy vine-trunks twist up out of a margin of dry soil and cigarette stubs. It is the evening ritual, this strolling frieze of the young sleek-headed local males, the glamorous foreign couples with hotel rooms, the migrant vagrants who sleep on a beach or at a campsite, brown-legged and dressed in scraps of faded clothing. They pass her and each other endlessly: a ritual compulsive as a neurosis, to see and be seen.

At eleven o'clock she goes to the café the hotel manager took her to after their meal the other night. She drinks the same drink, gin and bitter lemon. It may even be out of the same glass. It has a faceted stem, which she rotates constantly in her fingers as she sits there. She chooses a different seat, however: on a high stool at the bar, though the table under the slow fan is unoccupied.

The same waiter serves her the first drink.

An Australian in a T-shirt leans on the counter along-side her and throws several remarks at her. She looks at him once and then ignores him. After a while the Australian grins and swaggers away.

On her second drink the waiter pauses. He swabs the ring of liquid made where he puts the glass in front of her and she picks it up.

Your friends, he says. They are coming in tonight?

She looks at him.

No, she says.

His name is Francisco. Sitting at a wiped table in the closed café, she waits while he and the other waiters wash the glasses, invert every second chair onto its neighbour and then sweep the floor between them all. She feels the other waiters look at her from time to time and then, perhaps sardonically at each other. And once she sees – peering in at her through the closed glass door, blank and wan as a moon – the mournful face of the thin Spanish boy who has been following her.

At last Francisco comes from the kitchen. He has a jacket in one hand.

Let's go, he says. It is finished.

His fingers press the small of her back gently as he ushers her ahead of him into the night, the warm night, through the door whose turned sign now reads *Open*.

The thin Spanish boy hangs in a doorway opposite. He is with another boy now. When he sees her emerge with Francisco, he throws up his hands and protests to his companion, a petulant look on his face. She tells Francisco that this boy has been following her, and about the other boy at the other café, whose face she smacked, in front of everybody.

Why are so many Spanish men like that? she says.

Francisco laughs.

They are men?

But why are they like it?

He shrugs.

This is a small village, he says. But now lots of girls

come here. English girls or American girls, or Dutch or Swedish. Many of them come here for the whole summer, or just to stay as long as they can. They sleep in a tent, or on the beach in a sleeping bag. It is very cheap. But still, soon they have no money left. So they want to find a rich man. But the rich men have girlfriends already.

Francisco laughs.

So, he says, these girls who sleep in tents let the Spanish boys take them out sometimes, so they can eat. They don't want anything else, only to eat. So they take the Spanish boys for a ride, as you say. At the end of the evening they say, Thank you very much for the meal, and goodnight.

He laughs again and takes a Marlboro cigarette out of the packet.

But if you are a Spanish boy and you have told all your friends you are taking out an English girl tonight, how can you tell them she has used you: You have paid for the meal, and now she is gone. So you have to tell a little lie, otherwise you are a fool in front of your friends.

Francisco puts thumbs to his temples, points his forefingers upward.

It is like having horns, to be so stupid. You understand? So the Spanish boy has to pretend he has slept with you, to save his face, and everybody knows the English girls are easy anyway. The Swedish girls are the best. But the English girls are easiest. So it goes on. One boy tells another, and he tells someone else.

He laughs.

This way the English girls are getting easier every year.

He shakes his head.

What a terrible thing, he says, to believe everybody else's lie and think that only your own is not the truth.

When they have walked a little way down the street Francisco looks back. Then, somewhere within the jacket he is still carrying in one hand, he pretends with amazement to find a bottle of red wine. He holds it up.

It must be a miracle, he says.

They laugh.

I live here, he says.

Three dustbins wait outside the door off the street. They are so full the lids are askew. He finds a key. They go into a hallway where a single bare lightbulb burns. He lays a finger on his lips for silence and they begin climbing the concrete stairs. When they reach the top he smiles, patting his heart to show what a climb it has been.

It is a room made angular by the slope of the roof. There are four bunks; a pair on each side, against the walls. The bedclothes are unmade.

This is it, he says. It is a slum.

He draws an old armchair forward for her, into the space between the pairs of bunks. In one corner of the room is a sink and an old Belling stove. He rinses out two tumblers and stands them on the table. He strips the leadfoil from the neck of the wine-bottle, twists in a corkscrew and draws the cork out with a squeak. Looking at the sordid room she hears the wine gulp into the first glass.

Who lives here with you?

Some friends. They work in a restaurant. The Lanzarote restaurant. Do you know it? They work in the kitchens.

He looks at his watch.

They will be home soon, he tells her. They finish late.

It is almost one and the bottle is almost empty when Francisco's room-mates arrive. Francisco gets to his feet and introduces them to her: Fernando and Carlos. Fernando, a big, heavy man, nods politely. Carlos, though, smiles intently at her. He is slim and dark and dressed in tight, black clothes, like a Spanish dancer.

The older one, Fernando, sits on one of the bottom bunks. He takes out a packet of cigarettes. It is a cheap, Spanish brand. He puts one in his mouth and then remembers to offer the packet, with silent courtesy, to the girl. She smiles and shakes her head.

I don't smoke, she says.

Carlos laughs.

And he don't speak English, he tells her.

Fernando lights his cigarette and sits there silently, hands hanging between his knees and staring at the floor between his feet. From time to time he inhales deeply on the cigarette.

She finishes the inch of red wine in her glass.

It's late, she tells Francisco. I'd better let you all get some sleep.

But Carlos is already making coffee, filling the saucepan at the sink.

You must have some, he tells her. To make you sober after all this wine you have been drinking.

He picks up the bottle and swigs a mouthful from it. He swishes it about his mouth and swallows it. Then he raises one eyebrow at the label and, laughing, says something to Francisco in Spanish.

It's not the one we prefer to drink, he translates to her. But free, it is cheap enough for Francisco to afford.

They laugh and Francisco sits down on the other bottom bunk and lights a cigarette.

Hey, old man, Carlos says to Fernando. Do you want coffee?

When it is made they sit and sip it black from white cups, in silence. Fernando lights another cigarette. He sits staring down at it in his big hands.

The old man is tired, Carlos says, and winks at the girl. Then he says it in Spanish.

Fernando says something placidly. He bows his head to the cigarette again, under the smiles of their gazes.

Fernando is the cook, Francisco says. He is the only one

there. He has been working since eleven this morning.

Fernando inhales deeply again on the cigarette, and examines it interestedly between his fingers.

He cannot smoke in work, Francisco says. Because of the food. So every night when he comes home he just sits there for half an hour and smokes like a train.

Head bowed, Fernando's eyelids flicker sideways nervously, politely enduring being the topic of their unknown conversation. Or perhaps he is embarrassed at her being there? Either way, he stays silent and never once looks at her. But every time she turns towards Carlos, who never stops talking, she finds his eyes, intent and shining and somehow triumphant, on her face.

She sips some more of the coffee. Then she looks at Francisco and stands.

See you soon, Carlos calls as they are leaving.

Fernando raises his head, smiles awkwardly in farewell and moves one of his feet. Then, furrowing his brow, he stares with immense concentration at his newlit cigarette.

Goodbye, she says.

Francisco precedes her down the concrete stairs. A man and woman are shouting in one of the rooms on the third floor. Then it is silent as they reach the drab hallway. Somewhere else a bed creaks and creaks.

She sits at a table on the hotel patio with the photographer. Being with a man keeps other men away. And he makes her laugh.

The photographer is drinking beer tonight. He is going to stay sober, he says.

He has been telling her about the time he lived in Sweden. He lived with three American soldiers who were on the run from the Army. He was young then. They all had soft blond beards and let their hair grow long. It was summer. They lived in a shack on the banks of a small lake. You could fish and go out in the boat. If you had a strong heart you could even swim, he said. But even in summer the water was so cold it made you gasp.

He sits there in silence, smiling, thinking back. After a while she realises he is not chuckling at these memories but crying, his shoulders shaking gently and one hand delicately pinching the bridge of his nose as if to cut the flow of tears. There is nothing she can say. She sits there looking at him quietly until he stops crying.

Damn, he says.

He wipes his eyes, snuffles, and blinking fiercely stares out, beyond the apron of light about the lit blue pool, to the black water.

Damn, he says.

She looks at him quietly. He offers no more explanation than if he had been slicing onions. But when a waiter goes past he calls to order brandy.

She watches him drink the first and pour the second.

Let's go and dance, she says.

Masturbation is the only exercise I ever take, he says.

She stands. She looks at him.

Well, she says. You're still going to dance.

Now he stands too. He salutes her and the lit hotel and the second brandy, drinks it back not quite in one.

Yeah, he says. Out of our skins, man. Out of our fucking skins.

The hotel disco is the first of the new season. There is one every night from tonight. The photographer stumbles slightly as they go onto the dancefloor. It is like a helicopter landing pad. It is early. They are one of the few couples dancing. Most of the dancers are girls. They are tanned, and please themselves. They come in pairs to dance all night, shimmying and shrugging out of laughing lusts for men, like snakeskin. In Saigon it was different. In Saigon, a GI once told him, there were more prostitutes than bicycles. And every street was full of bicycles. He spins to face her. He stands at the centre of the floor. The other men just ring the space and watch the

174

girls dance, solitary, impassive, their cigarettes glowing like red eyes.

He dances wildly, strenuously in the pure gloom of ultraviolet. She is a glowing shirt. He is a pair of incandescent whites. Dancing opposite her, envy bronzes his face like the sun.

With Frankie Goes to Hollywood he yells along.

Relax, don't do it, When you want to get through it, Relax, don't do it, When you want to come . . .

When it ends they stand there, already sweating, as the casual couples desert each other and the dancers thin. In the momentary quandary of intervals they look at each other. He puts his hands lightly on her hipbones, just below the waistband of her lemon slacks. He looks at her. After a moment she takes one of his hands and leads him out through the ring of men that still surrounds the dancefloor as if it was a contest.

I Heard It through the Grapevine, the late great Marvin Gaye, starts as they go out through the swing-doors into the harsh light of the hotel foyer where a youth lingers at a table with a cashbox for non-residents. A windless gust of refrigerated air makes their shirts cool and stick. They wander out from the hotel into the warm night again, along the quay wall. On cue, a dull moon rises yellow from behind the town. It is dipped, like a headlight.

She still holds his hand. They walk alongside masts and white prows with aluminium rails.

I don't know how to put this, she says. I like you. You know that. But I'm not Available.

Awkwardly she laughs at the awkward word.

Sure, he says.

He laughs. He stares at the black bay. He detaches his hand from hers and takes out a cigarette and puts it between his lips, then he takes it out and flicks it unlit into the glittery black water at his feet, where a wash of scum and orange-peel sways lightly, slapping at the harbour wall.

Look, she says. This suddenly all seems to be happening at once, but I have to go soon. I meant to tell you before. I'm meeting someone.

Sure, he says. I understand.

He laughs. He takes another cigarette. He puts it between his lips, staring away into the black bay.

No problem.

It is almost midnight when Francisco finishes at the closed café. The *Open* sign again admits them to the night. They walk through the town for a long time, a directionless circuit through streets gradually becoming empty of other people. When, for the third time, they pass a still-open café, they go in for coffee. It is served in white cups, beside a glass of water misted with cold. They stay there talking for a while. Then they pay and walk further and sit again on a stone bench under palm trees along the promenade. They talk. At one point they get up and look at the illuminated map of the town that stands opposite them. There is a row of red buttons to press, which light up the various places of interest on the map. Through the little round holes you can see the tiny bulbs behind the board. The *You Are Here* bulb does not work.

As he looks at the map he cannot think of anywhere to take her now. The little bushy, railinged park behind them is locked at night. And the big, open park behind the town is where the men go, the men who like men.

It is because he is not from this town. In the town he grew up in he would know where to take her. If you walk from the little square with the café for ten minutes in any direction you come to the fields and the olive groves. Fields which, beyond their little walls, are as intimate to you as to the sheep in them. You have known them, all of them, since boyhood. Even the walls you know, and the places to get over the walls, because a stone is out or it is lower there. Probably it was like that here too once, before the hotels stretched this far along the coast, and the shuttered villas no one lives in nine months of the year.

Here there is only the long beach, the long shadow at its extremities, away from the town's lights. But after dark foreign couples knot like jellyfish along the dark beach. And then sometimes there are the police, picking you out on the grey sand with torches dramatic and abrupt as flashbulbs.

There is his room. But his room is full of snores. And there is hers, in the hotel, but she doesn't mention her room. And he is afraid to.

Then a faint wind is stirring uneasily off the sea. On the still-dark pavement a sheet of newspaper lifts and slides. He looks up beyond the silhouettes of buildings and the tattered heads of palms, and nudges her to look as well. They have been talking all night, till the sky is blue.

Along the promenade a cleaner with a metal pushcart sweeps last night's gutter into spaced piles. The day has not begun. They are the only three people up.

The couple walk until the streets give way to a waste-ground of future building-plots in front of the beach. She says goodbye to Francisco at the bottom of the steps down to the sand, the somnolent sea.

Don't come any further, she says. You've got to work later. Go home and sleep for a few hours.

Waving once, she flounders away over cold, loose sand to the flatness and firmness of the sand at the water-line. She starts running along the slow curve of the tide towards the stepped hotels west of the town.

On the horizon east the cloud gleams between its layers: first light. From the white rail of his fifth-floor balcony the photographer contemplates the dawn like suicide. He has not been to bed, let alone to sleep. Below the mindless machinery of the immense grey bay casting its trivial tide against the greyish beach, a tiny figure runs on, unpursued. He identifies her for certain, focused as in a telescope or gunsight in his Nikon, with 300mm, f4 telephoto lens attached.

Friday is Francisco's afternoon off. They meet at a corner. The street is hot and blown with shallow drifts of sand after the wind. It is a wind from Africa, he tells her.

They go into a café to drink a cup of coffee. The place is crowded with holidaymakers and the tables are too close together. Perhaps it is because of this that they seem to converse so quietly, almost furtively. Speaking or listening, each leaning forward concentratedly, straightbacked and with shoulders hunched. Francisco's fingers play continually, nervously, with a sugar shaker, from time to time pouring a little from the nozzle into the cold dregs in his glass cup. They both watch the little poured heap sink, slowly saturate with brownness.

She is sixty now, my mother, Francisco is telling her.

Then a waitress comes and collects their two cups with a clatter and empties the ashtray peremptorily into a zinc bucket. Francisco speaks to her in Spanish, his head thrown back. He watches the waitress flounce away between the tables.

She thinks we have to hire the tables, Francisco says. He laughs. Two coffees is good only for half an hour or so.

The tip of her index-finger takes up stray grains of white sugar from one of the table's tiles and carries them up to the tip of her tongue. Sweet or sour? This way they have less taste than a snowflake.

What do you want to do this afternoon? she asks him. It's your afternoon off. You choose.

He shrugs evasively.

I've got my swimsuit, she says. Do you want to go to a beach?

His eyes are so dark with pupil that he is ashamed to look at her.

No, he says.

*

They climb the concrete stairs. There are no windows directly onto the stairwell, only closed green doors, so that lower down, even in the afternoon, it is cool as stone. There is only the dazzling rectangle of light they are mounting towards, in the roof's slope. As they climb the last flight to his door, she sees that a mesh of wire squares is sealed in the skylight's glass. Reaching the landing they stand in its sudden direct shaft of stale heat, sweating, while he fits the key. A fly buzzes. The room, too, is sweltering, a windless gust of warm air that makes their clothes cling.

This room is an oven, he says. Except in the winter. Then it's a refrigerator.

He throws open a door onto a tiny railinged balcony, actually the top landing of a fire-escape. They stand on the diamonded metal grid, looking out towards the dry hills, a section of the bay. He points out landmarks across the roofscape of the town.

Side by side they stare over the roofs, leaning on the green chipped rail, faces into the breeze, sweat at least cooling on their bodies. He shakes out his shoulder-length black hair and feels it streaming back from his face, his closed eyes, like a drowned man's in a current. They are suddenly only profiles, like the figures on playing cards. They cannot meet each other's eyes.

Below, in the backstreet, a red car tries to reverse into too small a space. They lean over, grateful to have it to watch. With a sudden irritated vehemence of tyres the car drives on elsewhere, around the corner. They laugh. Still they do not look at each other. His mouth is dry. Taking her hand for the first time in his life, he leads her in off the metal landing. It has a slight vibrancy to their feet as they step from it, like a diving-board's.

His body is beige and almost hairless. His nipples are brown. One or two single long hairs grow near them. As he turns away slightly and sits on the edge of the bed, even his buttocks, she sees, are the same sallowness as his back. With a deft, hurried modesty he slips off his distorted white Y-fronts.

His dark eyes keep hers on his as he lifts his feet back onto the bed and settles full-length beside her. So that it is only her hand, trailing lightly across his body as if in water, that dares to go to the bony saddle of his hipbones, the coarse black hair there. A muscle in him works. He closes his eyes for a moment as if to pray or curse, then stares up at the bottom of the bunk above. She looks at the stringy clot of silvery fluid on her inner arm, above the wrist. Smiling, she looks again at him. His eyes seem hot, or hurt. They stare up at the bunk. He laughs clumsily.

Sorry, he says. Must be too long without.

It doesn't matter, she says.

Frowning, he touches fingertips distastefully to the sticky pool sunk in the hair below his belly. Then he watches as she raises her forearm towards her face, the paler-tanned veined inner side towards her. The bracelets slip down from her wrist. She sniffs his flung gout delicately, deeply. Then, watching him watching her do it, her mouth closes over it, as if sucking a wound clean. She looks at him over her lifted arm as if making a pledge of eyes over a glass's rim. A muscle in her throat works as she swallows it.

The sheetless blanket is rough beneath them. The orange curtain stirs, lifting at the open door to the balcony of the fire-escape. It fills like a sail for a moment, then falls back into its old folds like a swirled skirt.

Your friends are working at the restaurant? she says.

Yes.

He wants to say also, in a joke, that is why they have come here this afternoon. But she knows this. And he is not confident enough now for a joke. He stares at the webbing of the bunk above, creases of a stuffed-in sheet.

All day yesterday, she says, I lay on the beach and thought of getting brown for you.

Eyes hot, he stares up at the webbing.

I might as well ask you now, he says.

Ask me what?

His naked shoulders crease into a shrug.

Why me?

She smiles.

I don't know really. Why not you? You're not like the rest.

She shrugs.

And perhaps you remind me of someone.

Who?

She laughs.

Nobody. A guy whose name I never even knew, she says.

She laughs again, a hurt laugh.

Someone who changed a tyre on my car once.

She is silent. They lie there.

Her hand begins to move lightly, constantly over his shoulders and neck. At last it moves down, without urgency, over his chest and nipples. His sunk belly trembles with the intentness of held breath. He closes his eyes and lies submitting to the thin metal clashing of the bracelets as her hand rouses him again. The framework of the bed creaks suddenly as she kneels and swings one thigh across, bestriding him at the waist. He opens his eyes to her blinding brown body. Her lighter breasts hang tapered to his hands between the pillars of her arms. She sits back gently, reaching one hand back to introduce him into her with expertise. Her face comes lower over his, frowning now, eyes closed in staggered concentration. With terrible slowness she rides him, awestruck, to ejaculation in her.

*

She lowers herself as if tired into his arms, her face against his neck, they lie there. Gradually he shrinks in her, then flops out like a fish spilled on a slab. They both laugh.

He wakes in the light room. He turns to look at her. Heads turned inwards, they gaze at each other across the striped, slipless pillow.

Was I asleep a long time?

Not long. About half an hour.

How you are beautiful.

You're beautiful too.

She raises a hand to his face to touch his nose, his cheek. Then she strokes back his hair from one eyebrow.

Your hair, she says. I've never seen hair so black. You've got hair like an Apache.

They gaze at each other across the striped pillow. Her hand slides across his ribs. Her voice is hoarse when she speaks.

This time, she says. I want to do it for you, only for you. I want to fuck you with my hand. So I can watch it. So I can see you come.

He closes his eyes and lies there, hearing her hand move expertly on him in a thin clashing of the bracelets at her wrist.

She wipes him with a tiny linen handkerchief.

This is too small, she says. I never knew a man could come so much.

She continues to wipe him, folding and refolding the handkerchief several times.

I love the smell of your come, she says. I'm going to get this soaked with it, she says. I'm never going to wash this handkerchief.

He laughs, not sure if she is being serious. Propped on one elbow, he watches as she leans over him once more. A last milky drop is squeezing out of the reddened cupid's-bow of those two tiny lips. She wipes it away delicately with the handkerchief.

I mean it, she says. When I go home this is what I want to remember you by.

She raises the crumpled handkerchief to her nose again. He watches as she closes her eyes to inhale with satisfaction, as if taking a first deep breath on a headland. He notices that embroidered in one corner of the handkerchief is a tiny sprig of lavender.)

Nine

Like I said: nothing good ever happens on a Sunday. Not
to me. Ever since I was a kid I've hated Sundays. Then
it used to be that smell of cabbage-water through the
house, and all the windows in the kitchen steamed up
with the cooking. That was for dinner. And for tea it was
that plaster Virgin the Old Lady had in the front room.
We hardly ever went in that room, except at Christmas
or if we had visitors or on Sunday nights for tea. No
wonder. Who the hell would want to go more than once
a week into a room like that, joyless as a tomb with
that smell of lavender polish and the air always still a
little chill because the fire would only just have been lit,
not to mention that you were scared to move because of
all those cheap knicknacks and gewgaws cluttering just
about every level surface you could balance one on. And
then all those things from their wedding, behind locked
doors on the glass shelves of the cabinet, that spray of
imitation orange-flowers she must have worn on the day
or that gilt ring with the white dove on it, the Dove of
Peace it must have been (not that it was a marriage which
saw much of that). Even some of the wedding presents
were still there, like that so-called cut-glass jam-dish,
or the cakestand, things that never actually got 'taken
out' or 'used' in case they got broken, the Old Lady even
dusted those things as if the older they got the more
delicate and priceless they became, whereas of course
they were just bestware for people who never have the
best of anything, junk from a Woolworths or Longstaf's
bazaar, Petty Bourgeois is what my wife calls that but
I'd rather say petty poor because only the poor make one

room into a permanent showcase of a lifetime's second-rate and cut-price tat.

The centrepiece, you could almost say altarpiece, of the whole room of course, right smack over the fireplace, was that picture of Jay Cee (Our Ell and Ess) just after Final Takeoff as he's flying upwards, arms stretched out (well, they'd have to be, he's still nailed to the Cross). You see him from above in that picture, so it's like he and you are looking down the upright of the Cross, looking a long way down, back at the Sea of Galilee I suppose it is, there's a wooden fishing-boat on it as I remember it, a long long way below. And from that point of view it's a very clever picture, was it Salvador Dali who painted it? (Avida Dollars, as my wife said once, that was his name in anagram, some French poet made that crack about him. T. S. Eliot was another one. His anagram was Toilets. And what was the other one? Oh yeah, Proust was Stupor, and according to my wife, who had to study him, that was about how he was. So many pages, she said, and so little happening. But I was home ill one day, and I picked up that book and started reading and I thought it was pretty good. It was about a kid waking up and not knowing where he was. That happens to me. In fact sometimes I think I must have been like that most of my life, not only as a kid.)

Yes, it's a very clever picture from the point of view of perspective and so on. When you're older you can appreciate it, how the artist is trying something different at least, trying to see an old subject from a new angle (to coin a phrase). But when I was a kid that picture scared me. It gave me a funny feeling in my stomach, like going up in a lift. I never have liked heights and I used to get that feeling looking at that picture. Vertigo it's called. (Like in that film with James Stewart in, it was on the box the other week. Shit, I meant to watch that. I always did like Jimmy Shtooart. I must have gone out that night.)

But it wasn't only the height Jesus is looking down

from, and you with him. It was the fact you knew he'd already Kicked It. And I suppose I must have wondered if you really did that when you died, or at least your soul did: floated up into space and just kind of hung around there like a severed astronaut, for ever, looking down past your feet, a long long way below to where you used to live during your days on earth.

And so I never liked that picture. And I never liked that room. It was half a museum and half a shrine, full of those trinkets from the past you couldn't touch or scary things like a crucified Jesus levitating five miles high or the eyes of that blue painted Virgin, because my mother told me once that wherever you went and whatever you did, even in the dark, Our Lady would be Watching You. And then the Old Man used to say, Stop filling the boy up with your Maltese nonsense, your Maltese Catholic superstitious nonsense, Our Father This, Our Lady That, Our Son Who Art, there's no help there. He'll do more for himself by learning how to stand up on his own two feet, like I had to, than going on his bloody knees to Rome.

Because he used to get bitter with her sometimes, although he was a Catholic himself, I suppose, at least by upbringing. Though even as a kid you knew better than to mention the priest to him. He wouldn't let a priest come into the house, not when he was in it anyway. And you can understand why, if you're married to a not so much devout, I'd say, as frightened Catholic like my mother. Because in a marriage like that you have to take Church and priest to bed with you as well. I never will forget what my Old Man said that time when my mother wouldn't give him any money to go out one night, and they were arguing. Will you deny me this? he kept saying. Will you deny me this? Who put it in your purse in the first place? I'm not denying you, she said. I've never denied you a thing, she said, holding the purse away from him. But it's my last pound note and you're not having that. Never denied me a thing? the Old Man said, and suddenly he could hardly speak in his bitterness and fury. Jesus Wept, woman, how can you say a thing like that when you been denying me in my own bed for fifteen years? For fifteen bloody years, he said, and his voice choked on it.

I suppose I couldn't have been more than seven or eight then, and I had no idea what he meant, what he'd been denied or why she should have been denying him it, let alone that it was the Church itself behind it all. Because like the Holy Pope said to the girls when he opened the new brothel, Now remember that there's only two methods allowed by my Infallible Decree. The Rhythm one is one, so look for the red days on the calendar. And the other one is not to let them put it in at all. Now God bless you all, and good luck in this new venture.

But there's a lot you don't understand when you're a kid. Like that other time when I came home from school or came in early from playing and the house was all quiet. (Was I older then, or younger than that other time?) And I must have gone upstairs to look for them, and they were in their bedroom, the door was wide open, and my mother had one shoe on and blood trickling out of her nose where he'd belted her one and he was hunched over her on the bed in his shirt-tails, hunched over her like he was trying to cover or protect her almost, and I didn't know what it was he was trying to do to her but I knew enough to know from the look on his face and the look on hers and the way he was moving that protect her wasn't it. And they didn't see me, and I knew enough too to know I had to creep downstairs before they did or we would all be struck dumb like that, me looking at them and them at me for ever. And I sat by the fire and waited. And it's as if I can still hear that fire hissing, hissing, it must be poor coal or wet from the yard, and I can see myself as I was and must have been, looking into the fire and sitting so far forward that when I come away one leg is burnt red all down one side from the heat because I'm wearing short trousers and the sock has fallen down on that leg. I might be five or six, I can't be more than seven or eight. Sitting there not even noticing that my leg is being burned, just staring into the fire and waiting for them to come down, finish whatever it is they are doing up there, it's like they are fighting on that bed in a kind of terrible silence, and I can still hear the bed. Then it stops, and I hear the floorboards. Then I hear the stairs. And then my father comes into the room, his braces are still down, he stands there looking at me, and hitches them up onto his shoulders. And then my mother comes to the top of the stairs, I can't see her from where I am, and screams down at him in a voice I don't even believe for a moment is hers. If it's born, she says, it'll be born in your sin. Do you hear me? Do you hear me? My father doesn't look back up the stairs. He does up the top button of his trousers. According to you, he calls over his shoulder, we're all born that way anyhow. So where's the difference there?

I am staring at something on the television screen, a preview of some panel game. (I like that actress in one of the teams.) And there are tears in my eyes suddenly and running down my cheek, tears for that boy who didn't understand, because what you can't understand you can't speak of, ever.

(I see him sitting by the fire in that dim kitchen, as if I'm outside of myself again, and looking back. And I'm touched by his long short trousers and the imbecile's haircut, with the sides and back shaved blue, I'm crying for the innocence of that haircut and for the boy who is gone, that boy in the one photo of me gone brown and yellow, faded from being left in the sun once, and the sun strong in the photo itself, as it must have been strong on that day in June or August in the Fifties, perhaps that's why my face is creased up or I'm frowning, frowning against the sunlight as if I'm about to start crying, in those little chaps my mother made me out of that Rexine left over from re-covering the chairs, and the holster and the braided cowboy hat and holding that silver Hopalong Cassidy gun, all Gone things, all disappeared, like that reddened mark all down the one side of my bare leg. It was only painful when I noticed it and took my leg away, and it took a long time to fade pale again, but it did, and now I don't even know which leg it was. Everything like that passes. Except some things don't, like this scar on my jaw where I fell trying to climb onto a roof and cut myself on the edge of the rusty corrugated iron, I was lucky I suppose I didn't cut my throat or get tetanus. It must have been a deep cut, because it's still there, that one, angled like a little white arrow or one of those French accents, a circumflex, in the black stubble. That's another thing they'll bury me with. I suppose every kid gets cuts, and most cuts fade, you can't even remember doing them or see where you did. But some things stay for ever.)

The doorbell jars me. I get up and go into the bathroom first and rinse my face in cold water and blow my nose. In the mirror my eyes are sad and bleary from crying, bloodshot as a black's.

And I wonder whether to just ignore the ring or at least stand behind a curtain in the front window, try and see who it is as they walk away. (The only problem with this being there's this gravel-covered flat roof overhanging the butcher's window and the other shop-windows in this block. Which means you can't even see the edge of the pavement from the first floor, let alone your own door. So unless a caller happens to cross to the other side of the road in leaving, you don't even get to see who the fuck it is or decide if you want to be in for them or not.)

189

Of course, if I was being logical I'd ignore the damn bell every time on principle, or better still disconnect the fucker (save on batteries). Because the number of people in the world I positively welcome on my doorstep can be counted on the fingers of about one hand, excluding thumbs. (I'm not sure that shouldn't actually read thumbs, excluding fingers.) On the other hand, there's an awful lot of people I don't need to see again or don't care one way or the other if I don't.

But, like I say. This is a Sunday afternoon. You'll go for anything on a Sunday afternoon. You'll even watch a British film. (Why else do you think they put them on then?)

So, even though the odds are bound to be that it'll turn out to be somebody you don't want to see, you end up answering the fucking doorbell anyway, on the remote longshot it might, just might, be somebody you *do*.

I clatter down the uncarpeted wooden stairs to the street door, where a pinkish smudge is trying to peer in through the bubbled glass for signs of life. I know from the flattened peak of a yellow golf-cap that it's Gordon, manager at Quick-Change. (Which should tell me Something is Wrong. Somehow it doesn't, though. Not that there's any choice but open the door to him now, anyway.)

Hello, Stewart, he says.

Gordon, I say.

I stand looking at him. Nobody at Quick-Change calls me 'Stewart'. Nobody anywhere calls me Stewart. It's always Yank, or Stew. (Or Stoo.) The only place that Stewart exists is on things like my birth certificate or insurance cards.

Can I come in a minute?

He looks awkward.

Pull the door to after you, I tell him.

I go back up the stairs in front of him, and go into the lounge.

Okay, I say. What's your problem?

(Although I half know already that this fucking problem's going to be mine.)

What happened to you Friday?

Friday?

(I have to think.)

(Friday is the day I followed Rusty.)

(Friday is the day I took off, is what he means.)

Friday, I say. Oh yeah. I had a recurrence of that back trouble. I must have strained it lifting something Thursday afternoon.

I clamp a hand to the small of my back and grimace. (It's better now, but I still, you know, get A Twinge from time to time.)

You get a doctor's note?

No, I didn't bother. You should have seen the queue.

Gordon looks round the room, like he's in despair.

Christ All bleeding Mighty, Yank. I've told you and told you about just taking days off like that, whenever you feel like.

I didn't exactly just take the day off, I tell him. I just told you. I had back trouble. I could hardly walk across the room with it.

Gordon lifts his hands and sighs. (He's a 'reasonable man' harassed and defeated by attitudes out of his own control.)

So what's the big problem? I say.

Look, Yank, he says. This is nothing to do with me really. I'm just paid to see the cars get fixed. I don't make Company Policy, and I don't hire and fire.

What the fuck you talking about?

Area said you've already had two Official Warnings. About 'unexplained absenteeism'. Is that right?

Well, yeah. But I can't help it if I'm off sick, can I?

But you don't have a doctor's note. You never fucking do.

It usually clears up in a day or two. I know already

what the bastard's going to say: Just stay at home and take it easy for a day or two, he'll say. See how you feel.

Like I say, this has got nothing to do with me, Gordon says.

(In spite of this, he's already starting to plead.)

But let's face it, you didn't give us no notice you were going to take a day off. You didn't even bother to phone in to say you wouldn't be in. Nothing. It might not have mattered on a normal day. But we were short-handed on Friday because Cliff was off too with a broken bone in his foot. I don't know how he done it. And of course Danny's still on the sick. And it would have to be one of those days when they were queuing out into the street for service. So I had to phone Area to see if they could lend me somebody from one of the other depots, for the day.

How come you're short? they said. (It was Oliver, you know what he's like.) I only got three men on the bays, I told him. Who's off? he said. Swambo and Andrews and Boyle, I said. (I mean, I didn't have no choice.) Boyle? he said. What's wrong with him this time?

Oliver said that? The little bastard.

I don't know, Mr Oliver, Gordon says. You don't know? he said. Why don't you know? Has he phoned in? Well, no, I said, not yet. Not to my knowledge anyway. Though I been out on the bays myself most of the morning being as we're so short. He might not have been able to get through. (I mean, what else could I tell him?) Not get through? he said. Not get through? What do you mean, not get through? There's supposed to be somebody available to answer that phone every minute of the day. Well, yes, there is, I said. Only it's been one of those days today. Look, he said, let me get this dead straight and crystal-clear. Just for my own satisfaction. Has he rung in or not? Yes or no? Well, not to my knowledge he hasn't, I said. Not so far, anyway. (I mean, I done what I could for you, Yank. But you didn't leave me much of a leg to stand on.) Boyle he said. Hasn't he had a couple of formal warnings about absenteeism already? I don't know, I said. I don't know nothing about that. I've got an idea he has, he said. But I'll check on that. He's a good worker when he is in, I told him. No problem there. He knows the job inside out. He's one of the best mechanics I got on the bays. When he *is* in? he said. When he *is* in? Take a look outside the bays sometimes, Gordon. Turn the television on from time to time and watch the news. There's four million unemployed out there. Even according to the Government. Some of *them* are good mechanics. Some of them are probably wonderful bloody mechanics. They want to work six days a week. They want to work twelve-hour shifts. They're just dying to get the chance to do it. Listen, he said, and get this straight. There's no future for us in employing a man who only comes in to work on the days he feels like it. As if it was a hobby. We got a business to run. Anyway, he said, I'll check on whether he's had a warning or not. I got a feeling he was issued one only the other week.

Gordon pauses, swallows. His eyes implore me. (Somehow he's telling me the whole thing too fucking fast.)

I tried to phone you, he says. It must have been a dozen times over the day. I couldn't get an answer.

In the afternoon, was this? I must have been at the doctor's.

I tried all day, he says.

He shrugs.

Anyway, he says, I didn't hear no more about it till about ten to five that afternoon. (I'd forgotten about it, to be honest, and I thought Area probably had as well.) Then Alec Horner rung me. (Like I say, it was about ten to five.) Boyle in yet? he said. (You know what he's like on the phone sometimes. Like he's not so much busy as on a bonus to get it said in as few words and generally make it as unpleasant as he can.) I had to tell him, No. (At that point I didn't have no option.) He phoned in? he said. No, I said, not yet. Not yet? he said. He laughed. Waiting for the cheap rate, is he? After six, when no one's there? Alright, he said, he knows the score. For simplicity's sake, let's leave out all the reminders about Poor Timekeeping. Let's keep to Repeated Absenteeism. He's had two formal warnings already on this, he said. And I don't have to give anyone a third. He's entitled to one week's notice from receipt of severance. I'll draft a letter of dismissal now, he said, and get it off tonight, First Class. He'll get it Monday.

The lump bobs nervously in Gordon's throat.

So I thought at least I'd better come round and let you know, he says. Before you, you know, open the letter. In the morning. I thought you'd rather someone tell you straight out. Face to face.

Face to face we stand there. Gordon's eyes look hot and anxious, as they usually do. They're that green of stewed rhubarb, or the pale snot you blow and blow into a handkerchief when you're starting to get rid of a bad cold.

Noble of you, Gordon, I say. Real noble. Warms my fucking heart.

I grab the collars of his denim jacket with both hands and bunch them up under his chin, forcing him back against the wall.

What could I do? he says.

His eyes now are scared wide.

Yank, he says. All I am is the Manager. All I do is give out jobs on the cars as they come in.

I flinch, as always, from the sour gust of his breath. (And it's one of those situations where suddenly it's like you're in a film. 'One man holds another against the wall.' Only, I don't know what to do next. The obvious thing is butt him swiftly in the face or bring the old knee up hard into the groin. Or both.) (Except they actually don't show anybody doing things like this on screen. Even in a roughhouse fight, both fucking combatants are punching clean as Marvin Hagler.) (But the other way, believe you me, is how it's done in life, because you're using both your hands already to keep him still enough for you to do it.)

But as we stand there, me taking the breath of his rotten gums in my face, I realise you can't fight everyone. Or (what's the saying?) beat the bearer for the news. Let's face it, Gordon can't even stick up for himself, let alone for someone else. If in doubt, Smile, and Watch the Birdie: that's his rule of life. (Which is why they made him 'Manager' to start with.) He ought to have it up above his desk in pokerwork. (Or what I scrawled up for a joke once on that sign outside his door, so it read not just 'Gordon Cox', but 'Gordon Sux Cox'.)

I slacken my grip on his jacket. I've got the wrong man to the wall. (The one I want wears dark suits, and ties with a diagonal stripe: I don't know what you'd call them, Mock Regimental, I suppose, or Pseudo Public School. He has a bland, blond salesman's face, like a shorter, pudgier Jack Nicklaus. He drives a BMW, and is too friendly when he gets out of it in the yard and comes into the office. But then, like Gordon says, talk to him on the phone and he's brisk, brusque, sometimes barely civil. It's like dealing with two different people. But talking like the Harassed Hotshot and hiring and firing long-distance on the telephone is obviously where he really lives.)

I let my hands drop.

Alright, Gordon. 'Thanks'. Now go on. Fuck off. Before I change my mind.

I stare at American Football on Channel Four. The quarterback backpedalling, the flat, spun throw, the tackle piled up on the Astroturf, smacked hands, remote crowd jubilation.

The door clicks to at the foot of the stairs as Gordon leaves.

Hands on hips I stare at the screen.

The game flickers on in surges and stoppages, the dark blue team have the ball, then the maroon and white team have it. But it's further away from me, this game, than the three thousand miles it's been brought, than the seven days ago it was filmed.

When this scrimmage on the Two-Yard Line was taking place, I was a Quick-Change fitter. I had a job, the money coming in each week. Not a lot of money, compared to what some people make. Certainly not as much as this numbskull hunk of a pro footballer (diving over the scrimmage for an easy touchdown) earns, even if he is thick as two short planks, and black, that makes no difference any more, he's a rich man, they're all rich men, they're probably all on a couple of hundred thou a year, these top pro footballers, and like Jim Brown of the Cleveland Browns said in that TV interview, Black Power don't interest me, I'm Into Green Power, Man. (And he made the money sign.) Jim Brown. Didn't do too bad, did he, for a footballer with a dodgy knee? All things considering. Ending up in films, then having a big affair with Raquel Welch. Who most men would give an arm or a leg just to spend a night with. A single night.

That started when they co-starred in *100 Rifles*. (It came on the TV a month or so ago, but I saw it in the cinema when it first came out. I've seen all her films, just about.) I remember there was all that gossip in the papers at the time, How Raquel had 'Met Her Match' at last, blah, blah, the usual pre-release hype. Not saying he was Dark Meat, of course, acting too polite to mention that or even 'notice' it. But always showing you a picture of a big buck nigger so there could be no mistake, just in case you didn't know who Jim Brown was. Just to get the old imagination ticking.

And when I saw the film I remember thinking that in every clinch or close-up they did together onscreen, there's a moment when all 'this' is suddenly For Real. There's got to be one day on location, one scene in the film, where it happens. Where after warming themselves up during the shooting they go back to his luxury caravan, or hers, to 'discuss the script' (like hell they did) and to finish what they started lubricating over on the set. Because, let's face it, a dodgy knee's no handicap if you're already a millionaire football hero and a film-star, and you're big enough and black enough in bed.

Like these boneheads playing in this game I'm watching. Black or white. They've all got open-plan houses in leafy suburbs and drive Lincoln Continentals and go out with models. They can break a leg tomorrow and retire from football on the insurance money and go straight into TV or even politics, you don't need brains for either of those careers, let's be honest about it, not in America, and not here either. All you got to do is carve the opening or get the lucky break and then stay a little sharper than the muppet-minds who watch your programmes or who vote for you. And that's not hard, not when you think of them out there, the Silent Majority, the Floating Voter, the Moronic Millions. Scratch them and they're little better than the handpicked idiots they bus in by the coachload for a studio audience, goggling at the TV lights and pointing themselves out in the monitors and creaming themselves in their seats for all the so-called stars (*Wogan!* or *Lulu!!!*), bred for devotion and applause on cue, the cretins, just like these clowns here on the screen between plays, the 'crowd scenes' or 'stadium atmosphere': grown men waving like kids do when they see a camera's on them, holding up their home-made banners for the *Minnesota Vikings* or the *Redskins* or *Go, Joe, Go*, forty or fifty thousand of them paying big bucks to fill this stadium just so they can cheer their team and make its players heroes. Which public displays of public stupidity is what pays all these guys a hero's wages.

(Me, even in the street I live in, in my own home city, I'm anonymous. I got a car I can't afford to run, and which probably cost me my marriage to maintain. I've got to work in lousy jobs and live with dirt and grease engrained in my hands. And they're a workman's hands, a nobody's. They're not famous hands. They're not Horovitz's hands, they're not Joe Thiesman's hands (as he throws a looping cross-screen downfield pass), oh no, that guy's an All-American quarterback, a Hall of Famer, what he can do is run a bit and dodge a bit and throw a football sixty yards. Me, all I am is a mechanic. A Rude Mechanical, as my wife used to describe me. The only thing these hands were ever any good for is for stripping tyres and spinning nuts.)

The caption shows the Vikings now leading the Redskins 22–7 (they must have just made another touchdown) and I suddenly catch one of those brief and deliberately almost 'accidental' glimpses the director from time to time allows you, lets you see: an intercut second of the cheerleaders, they wear tiny satin shorts and white boots and leap into the air whenever their boys score. (Whatever team you support, you can spend a long time waiting for a touchdown just to see those chicks take off.) Part faithful girlfriend on the touchline, part ecstatic groupie, they're the team's Biggest Fans, and you can't help wondering if the scorer later gets to chalk his name up with his pick of them. (Or if they're like those sorority chicks who get drunk one night and take on the whole Home team.) Though I don't suppose that kind of stuff really happens here, this is a Pro league and those girls are on the payroll too. They're just employees like the team. That's only what you're *meant* to think, wonder at, just more bait for the audience to bay at. The college-girl enthusiasm, that sexy co-ed innocence, those leaps of joy: just something for the suckers in the stands to fantasise over. (Just think of all those nice young, brown-limbed clean-haired American English majors giving head in the team bus all the way home afterwards.)

(Though somebody or other somewhere must be getting head off each and every one of them.)

(Almost everybody is getting head off somebody.)

(And somebody *some*where must be getting head off almost *everybody*.)

I don't want to think about these things. I get up and go into the bedroom.

For the next ten minutes I push iron, just to get all this mess out of my system, purge it off. I feel strong and savage, and I like to taste my savagery, feel my strength. But what pushing iron does is calm that feeling. Give it purpose. Give it concentration. When you're pushing iron properly everything else falls away, sometimes your mind is just like a point of light in a darkening universe, like that one star that comes out over the roofs at evening. I'd almost forgotten that feeling because I haven't touched the weights for a long time until just recently. That was my bitch of a wife again, she never took my using the weights seriously, she used to raise one eyebrow at it like I was a freak, Schwarzenegger she used to call me, for a joke.

That big muppet, I said. Anabolics, that's all he is.

Anna Bollocks? she said.

She laughed.

Actually, she said, these bodybuilders always seem to me a little small down there. Can't they work on that as well? Isn't that a muscle?

(She had a coarse mouth sometimes, Carol.) I tried to explain it to her.

Look, I said, It's not just Mister Universe types who work with weights. Athletes do. Ben Johnson does. Daley Thompson.

Well, she said, if you get a build like Daley Thompson, I suppose I can live with that.

If you like, I'll wear a curly wig as well, I said.

(Of course she ignored that.)

But there's nothing uglier to me, she said, than one of these muscle-brain bodybuilders with gigantic shoulders and pin heads and every vein and sinew standing out. If anything's obscene, she said, that is. It makes me shudder.

It all depends how you use the weights, I tried to tell her. Press big, slow weights, you get big, slow muscles. You press little weights a lot, and very fast, and you get little muscles but fast ones. That's what an athlete does.

I shrugged.

Me, I said, I just use these to keep in trim.

But I always knew she thought it was ridiculous. (Shagging was about the only exercise she was ever interested in taking.) She was one of these people who never seem to put on weight.

Anyway, so I got out of the habit. I left the weights and bars in the cupboard under the stairs. I even tried to sell them once, I put a postcard in the newsagent's window (*Set of Professional Weights, Stands, etc. As New, £30 o.n.o.*), because I had a lot of work to get done on the T-Bird and I could have used £30 at that time. But I never even got an enquiry, and they stayed under the stairs, and I forgot about them. It's really only this last week or so I've started to work out with them again. Because, aside from anything else, I realise I've got to get in better condition if I'm going to pull a girl like Rusty. Let's face it, I've put on a few pounds of flab over the last year or two. I've let my body go downhill a bit. And she's a girl who looks after herself, probably eats the right food and doesn't smoke and swims to keep in shape. I mean I expect she'll come back from Spain and she'll be long and hard and brown and gorgeous with all that sea and sun and you can't expect a chick like that to have respect for a man whose stomach wall is getting slack.

Don't get me wrong: it's not exactly as if my gut is hanging out over the waistband. I mean, I still look pretty good in clothes. (When you're as tall as me you can carry a few pounds extra and it doesn't notice.) And if I remember to keep my gut pulled in I can still get away with wearing just a T-shirt and a pair of jeans. I haven't got the tits yet. But let's put it this way: when I take the T-shirt off I can't expect a woman not to see that I could lose a little weight.

I lie on my back exhausted and blink away sweat, staring up at the styrofoam tiles of the ceiling, the 50-kilo weight back on the stand above my chest. My arms are weak and shrieking from finishing off with ten quick upward presses. My shirt, clean on this morning, is sticking to me all over. I should have put on that old, rank sweatshirt I usually wear. But there's nothing wrong with sweating, I like sweat, I believe it's good for you, not just physically but mentally.

And I'm starting to get back into all this, I realise: fitness. I need to start a new programme.

1) No animal fats. 2) Less bread. 3) Less beer. (That's the hard part.) 4) Twenty press-ups every morning. 5) Grapefruit juice before every meal (to help cut the fat). 6) Twenty sit-ups before going out at night . . . It all helps harden you up. And you can really become obsessive about fitness sometimes, like a boxer in a training camp sweating rounds away to make the weight. And driving yourself that way, flogging yourself to the point where you can feel clothes sticking to you and sweat trickle down your body, helps heighten sexuality too. It puts your Power Centre back where you want it: back into your scrotum and away from your head.

I go back into the other room. Mopping my chest dry under my shirt, I watch a few more plays. Suddenly it seems to be a close game now, the Redskins must have pulled back fourteen points. The crowds are excited, the commentators are excited. The play is frantic.

But I still can't get involved like I usually do. Even if there's only one point in it and two minutes left on the clock, and the Redskins carrying the ball. Like I say, this result, whatever it is, is a big Foregone Conclusion. It's seven days' worth of sporting history (with the emphasis on history). Nothing can change the result of last weekend's game. Any more than I can go back to a time before last Friday when I had a job to go to and I hadn't taken that day off. (Life isn't like in the Superman film, where he puts the world in a reverse spin to save Lois Lane. You can't change what's happened, go back and make things come out different.)

But, there again, if I hadn't taken Friday off work, I wouldn't now have the keys to Rusty's flat.

And there's a fate in that. A kind of tightening.

I go into the bathroom and do deep breathing, in front of the washbasin mirror. It's this breathing, and the work with weights beforehand, which help me to stay calm. Because I'm cold and clear and relaxed now. All I have to do in life is stand there, breathing deep and watching myself in the bathroom mirror. Because a destiny is working out through me. I'm its beneficiary. And to be that I have to be its instrument.

From the other room heightened excitement and incredulity as the lead changes hands yet again or is extended for a last time. (I don't know who's scored.) And I ignore the commentary team, I switch off from their words inside, as if it was a foreign language I can choose not to concentrate enough to hear, and I am already far away from their hype. It's not even week-old hype, week-old passion, a seven-day-old classified result in the NFL. It's like the million years or whatever it takes light to reach us from the nearest star.

(And as I stand there, deep-breathing and looking into my own eyes, I know that it is going to happen again, as it does sometimes, though I never know when, and I have stopped being scared of it by now. That I'm going to go into a trance in which I come out of my own body and float above myself somewhere. I'm high up there, but safe, I know I'm safe because I'm on a filament, it's not something visibly and so obviously thick enough and strong enough like the cable to a spacesuit or the cord you're born with, it's more like uncooked glair of egg or a spider's silk (which is, though, I remember reading somewhere, the strongest tensile substance known to human science). The difference with this filament is that you can't see it, all there is is this kind of bobbling tug that you feel in it to tell you when you're at your limit, when you've floated taut. It's the end of your tether. And it's the only thing that's holding you but you can't quite make it out. It must be transparent in air, the way a nylon fishing line goes invisible in water.)

Ten

Next morning is Monday morning, I'm up bright and early, it's the start of another glorious working week and yet another lovely sunny day, bringing joy to the heart and the postman whistling down the street and a letter on Company notepaper posted at 17.30 Friday sacking me with one week's notice from the job I've supposedly just got up for and am going in to do. 'Dear Mr Boyle' et cetera. 'Despite previous warnings' et cetera. 'No option but to terminate your' et fucking cetera. 'Yours faithfully, A. M. Horner, Area Manager.'

Go fuck yourself with a blowtorch, I scrawl across the back of the letter. Then add three more words: *Live in fear*.

I put the letter in a new manila envelope, address it to the Quick-Change Area Office in Monmouth and drop it in a postbox as I pass, no stamp, let those bastards pay double postage on receipt.

Fuck them, is what I say. What I say is: Fuck them all.

When I roll in to work at noon Gordon is in the warehouse, checking spare parts off on a clipboard. A Manager's job is never done. I go across and take him aside for a minute, between metal shelves of parts. His stewed, green eyes are darting intently from one to the other of mine. (They teach you that in karate classes, watch your opponent's eyes, you'll see his hand move there first. But I suppose it's instinct, when you're scared.)

Relax, I tell him. I got no argument with you.

To reassure him, I put my hands away, in the back

pockets of my jeans, and hang my head, coy, embarrassed, likeable. (Marty Sheen out of Jimmy Dean.)

I got the Dear John this morning, I tell him. No sweat. I just wanted to say I'm sorry about yesterday.

It's alright. Forget it.

I mean, I know it wasn't your fault I got the bullet. I flew off the handle. And I appreciate you coming round to tell me like that.

He nods unhappily. We look at each other.

Right, I say. I just wanted to tell you that.

I turn to go back to the bay, but Gordon stops me. Now it's him looking awkward.

Yank. Do you mind kind of staying by the phone this morning?

'Staying by the phone?'

Yeah. You know, just handle any calls?

What about the tyre bay?

He makes a lame joke of it.

I thought we might give you an easy week of it this week, Yank.

Suits me.

I've hardly been ten minutes at the reception desk before it strikes me what Gordon was actually saying to me.

He's standing under this old Cortina up on the lift. I have to duck my head to join him, and talk to him stooping. The others never raise the cars high enough for me. Gordon is passing a caged bulb along the underside of the chassis.

Look at the state of this, he says. The whole thing's held together with chewing-gum and chicken wire.

He tugs in more extension cable and hooks the bulb to the back axle and pokes upwards with a screwdriver. There is nothing blacker or filthier than the underside of an old car, that inches-thick caked paste of crud and engine oil. (Though there is nothing cleaner or brighter or smoother than the silver of a moving part among it all.)

How can you put a bracket on this? he says. It's rusted to fuck. I don't think it'll even take a screw.

Squinting up, he realises I want something. He looks at me.

What's the problem?

This 'answering the phone' business. Am I off the tools, or what?

He shrugs some apology or other. He unhooks the lit bulb and I follow him out from under the car. He hits the button and the Cortina is lowered slowly, with that inevitable slowness and immense, compressing force that have always reminded me of the spiked walls that close in on the hero at the end of every episode in those old Flash Gordon serials. (I can always hold Gordon Cox's head on the concrete apron under the lift, too, if I have to, and get the straight truth out of him that way.)

It must just be the policy, I think, he says.

'The policy'? The fucking 'policy'? What does that mean?

With, you know, dismissed men.

He grins, uneasy with the term. (Me, I'm uneasy about it too. I'm one of them. I'm a man who's been dismissed.)

It's nothing personal against you.

Now I laugh.

Oh, you mean in case of 'sabotage'? In case some disgruntled Dismissed Man like me starts loosening a wheelnut here or there? Instead of tightening it?

Gordon watches me with his stewed eyes and constipated man's smile.

I don't know, he said. I only know what they told me.

I don't bother to unbutton my overalls down the front. I just rip them open to the waist, step out of them in shirt and jeans, bundle them up and walk across and drop them in a drum of waste rags, if Quick-Change want them back someone can rescue them from the bin, they can get them washed and pressed and smelling of lavender all ready for whatever gink they take on in my place, good luck to him, I only hope he's grateful for the chance to join the famous Quick-Change team (as seen dancing on national television). I only hope he's proud to wear on the pocket over his left tit, if not his heart, that imbecilic smiley face.

I better get back to the phone, I tell Gordon. Just what I always wanted: a nice clean desk job.

But it's a long day in work today, despite not starting till twelve.

It's three now, and the novelty of lying around on a bench in the waiting area while everybody else is up to their wrists in exhausts and oily gunge has long worn thin. (It's true what they say: Idleness is harder work than being busy. And looking as if you're busy when you're not is the hardest work of all.) For a while I was mooning around in the yard out there, talking to the boys, trying to make A Joke out of the situation. But I noticed it was nearly always me doing the talking. I don't know whether this was just because we had a lot of work coming in this afternoon. Or perhaps it's not a thing those bastards can find it in their hearts to joke about. They probably resent me getting paid the same as them for sitting on my arse and watching them do their work, and now mine too.

But I don't know if it's that. Really it's as if a man gets the bullet and suddenly he's Bad Luck, people's eyes slide off you when you look at them. It was like I'd left already.

Anyway, I gave up on the subject, and came in. Fuck them too.

Thursday I'll be gone.

Thursday I'll get paid the two weeks' wages (this week plus the week in hand), this week's up to and including Friday. Though they won't see hide nor hair of me on Friday, like the man said, Take the money and beat it.

Not that you can beat it that far on two weeks' worth of a fitter's wages, not these fucking days.

But what the fuck. There's other jobs. It's a fate, just go with it. These things are for the best. They got to be. And there's a meaning in them all if only you could see it.

Who knows? Perhaps a new life's starting for me.

I open the afternoon paper I just bought at the corner. And, it's not a thing I normally do. (I'm not kidding, I almost never do. I mean. I don't *believe* in all this astrology shit.) But I look up my 'stars' in the paper. Part boredom, part curiosity, really. Just to, you know, see.

Scorpio: The vitality and energy flowing through your sign continues at a torrential rate leaving you in a position to get exactly what you want. Be assertive and positively aggressive in those ideals and principles that reflect your interest, for you have an overall charm that will cover up any signs of naked ambition.

(You don't have to believe it. But I suppose things could be worse.)

Out of an old habit I look for my wife's star sign too. She's Pisces. Often she'd read out my forecast and hers, if she happened to see them when she had the paper, I don't think she believed any of it either. But I suppose everyone's a little bit superstitious. (Better that, at least, than being religious.) Her day sounds pretty ordinary:

Electrical faults or gadgets that are on the blink could turn this into a frustrating day, but instead of losing your cool, leave things to the experts. A breakdown in your home will lend to the overall angst, but things will only get worse if you allow them to.

Not to say downright banal.

My kids' predictions I don't look at. I never have. Horoscopes are for anxious people, people with problems on their minds, people looking for a Sign, or a way out of things, and kids don't lead that kind of life (or damn well shouldn't).

But I wonder what sign of the zodiac Rusty is. (To see which it might be, I read through them all.)

Aries: There may be rumblings in the deep, dark recesses of your subconscious mind, which need dealing with out in the open. A man may be at the centre of any conflicts or problems you currently have.

Or what about Leo?

Hostilities may break out in your emotional world if you allow others to provoke you. Don't fall into the trap of getting involved over someone or something that isn't worth it. By keeping a low profile and playing a dark horse you'll create an air of mystery and your impact will be far greater.

Which, could be telling her (a) not to waste her time in trying to prolong things with anyone (any man) she meets in Spain (whatever happens when she's there). And (b) to bring the goods home again, and see what turns out then.

Leo sounds possible, at least. (As I say, I don't really believe in all this anyway. But sometimes it's interesting to see if a forecast turns out to be true.)

Actually, though, the reason I bought the *Echo* was for the Jobs, first, and then the Cars For Sale. I want to get some idea of what secondhand prices are like at the moment. I've been wondering what I might get for the T-Bird. I don't want to sell the car but I'm going to need the money. And there's no way I can even afford to run it now, not now I'm out of work, the damn thing costs more to keep going than I do.

The trouble is it's not a 1957 T-Bird market, these days. Not with petrol at 189.9 a gallon. A car like that, it's like running a private seaplane to your average turkey, all he dreams of is an A-Reg Toyota Corolla or Nissan Sunny, Nimbus Grey or Strato Silver, low mileage, One Owner guaranteed, does forty to the gallon and a pair of furry dice or a bouncy skeleton in the back window. That's where *his* fucking head is at, in something under three years old and made by Japs. Whereas when you're talking about a T-Bird you're talking about a car for the Aficionado. One for the Cognoscenti. And probably the only chance I've got of getting rid of a car like mine is by private arrangement or through that dealer in Bristol who specialises in Yankee cars (I've seen his ad in *Exchange and Mart*). I could ring first and sound him out.

Of course, I've got a bit of rust under the sill of the doors. Couple of other things. The car's not perfect. But if he talks a fair price I could probably do worse than unload it there. That would be a nice last drive over in it too, across the Severn Bridge, okay it may not be the Golden Gate but it can't be that far short of it in span.

I always like driving across the Severn Bridge, over the mile or so of estuary sea all that way below. And Bristol's not a bad town.

I suppose I could go over this weekend or Friday or, come to that, Thursday afternoon, once I've picked up my final windowed envelope from here, the Lead Handshake, and that's me and Quick-Change finished. (And to tell the truth, I won't be sorry to go, all things told. Because I've had enough of this place now. Four years you work here and, snap! they sack you just like that. Your workmates aren't even interested, they're all right, Jack, so Fuck you.) (They don't pass a hat round. Nothing.) (In fact you get the impression they can't even be bothered to be friendly any more. They're glad you're going and just wish you'd gone.) (Not that any one of them, nor all of them together come to that, would have the guts to fucking say so to my face.)

But I could. I could go Thursday. Why not? I could make a day of it. Drive over. Sell the car. Have a few drinks and a meal out of the proceeds. And come back on the coach. That would be something to do, something to look forward to. (Look on it as a trip. A day out in a different place.)

I wander across the waiting area and switch on the TV, an old reconditioned set installed on a high shelf in one corner. It was meant to be for the customers, though usually no one thinks to put it on for them. And that's no disservice I realise, switching round the channels. (Midweek daytime television? Jesus Christ, talk about a Lowest Common Denominator, they're better off as they are, killing the waiting time by smoking cigarettes or staring at their feet like in the supplementary benefits office. Talking of which: I suppose this is what unemployment's really going to be like. Afternoons spent half-watching *Playschool* or the Open University or women's programmes on the box.)

I finally come up with an afternoon film, some kids' adventure yarn. (The schools must still be on holiday.) I've seen this one before, of course. (And so have you.) Doug McClure's in it, the usual role as ageing juvenile lead. I've missed the beginning and the credits, but it looks like some remake of *Journey to the Centre of the Earth* or *The Land That Time Forgot*.

Anyway, you know the type. What does it matter what it's called? They turn these things out of a mould. I suppose they're okay for kids or people in traction or agoraphobes, who've got nothing better to do on a lovely sunny afternoon than watch TV.

Me, I know already that the only thing that will induce me to keep watching this film is the odd, tantalising glimpse they keep giving you of the gorgeous cave-girl. There's always a gorgeous cave-girl in these Lost World-type films, a bit-part for some raven-haired gold-thighed starlet in some skimpy little off-the-navel number, like that fur bikini Raquel wore in *One Million B.C.* It was some outfit, that. (More bare skin than bearskin.) It made her famous overnight, just from the posters.

The girl in this hokum today, though, is still as unknown as when she made the film. One of those untamed, lissom, jewel-eyed pieces who you can't help watching every second she's on screen, but who you know you'll never see again. (They never seem to make it to a second film, those girls. Their screen début's their swansong. I suppose Hollywood just eats it up alive, cunt like that.)

And it always makes me sad, in a way, to see a girl like her and to think of the hopes she must have started out with, coming all the way to Hollywood with her heart hectic for stardom, and ending up like all the rest, taking it into every aperture she's got and on the scrapheap by the time she's twenty-two, probably the only paying openings left for her a job as a cocktail waitress or a full-time call-girl. (Nobody gives a fuck how fresh and wholehearted and shining-eyed and clear-skinned she was when she came out to California, probably the only man she'd ever let sleep with her before – or even see or touch her tits – was her boyfriend back in Omaha, Nebraska, and him she'd known since they were kids on neighbouring farms. The plan was they'd get married when they finished college, and that was all she wanted, be his wife. Except she never finished college. Some whiz-kid young producer happened to see her in some student musical and wheedled her Out West with promises.

And probably it was seeing all those other would-be starlets there that first made her realise just how competitive she had to be, made her understand that great looks and perfect limbs would never be enough. (Not even talent was enough.) What counted here was who you knew and how well they knew you. And that was when she started taking dick, first it was the whiz-kid young producer then, when that affair finished, all the famous faces and important men he introduced her to at parties, because it didn't take her long to understand that if she didn't let them slam it into her another would-be actress soon would. Not realising that the only reputation she was getting out here so far was not for acting on

212

her feet but working on her back and belly, and that far from advancing her career, this would actually count against her, not for moral reasons (because let's face it, the studio bosses and movie-brats and ageing stars and Jew producers and all the other who can give you your first real break have the morality of dingos). But because of the simple fact that she had nothing new or special left to give them any more. Which is why, in Hollywood, the Big Men don't do favours for chicks who are ravers. (Why should they, when they know they've got you going down on them in any case, just on a wild hope that they might?)

(And, who knows, that's probably how it really happened to her, once she'd got her first part as a cave-girl in this film. (To her and thousands like her.) It was a 'springboard' to sweet f.a. So that out of all those hopes and dreams, she probably ended up as just another piece of prime hole, like all the other one-line hat-check girls and beach-movie bimbos.)

I light another cigarette and stare up at the screen. In this film she's still innocent, at least.

And by now, of course, she's fallen innocently and devotedly in love with Doug McClure. He's the leader of the exploring party who have somehow stumbled through the mirror into this strange world of prehistoric throwbacks. She wears a leather thong round one ankle. Her eyes flash. Her brown thigh glistens as she crouches in the light from burning brands. She is showing them a way out of the volcano, a secret path, known only to her tribe. (Everyone has to inch out along inch-wide crumbling paths over precipices and across airy rock bridges over boiling magma.) She is saving them all because of her unquestioning love for him. All she wants to be allowed to do is serve him, follow him. (She's never seen a man with such pale skin, he's like a god to her, she literally worships him.) And such fidelity, such *fucking*, she offers him (if he could only see it!). She's the most glorious-looking piece of cunt you could ever hope to find. And for him (and *only* him!) she's on a plate. (And he's too dumb or deaf or blind to even notice her.)

And suddenly I don't want to watch this stuff any more. It's not that I believe in this shit for a moment, or even begin to get involved in it: I mean, it's just a third-rate piece of junk with stilted dinosaurs and even woodener actors.

It's the thought that *somebody* (I don't mean Doug McClure, I mean a real person) has had her (this real girl) offer him that in real life. Somebody somewhere knows what it's like to be able to do Anything You Like to her (and know that she'll not only take it from him, she'll be quivering for more). Because every girl meets one man in her life. The man she can't refuse a thing to. (Just as every man meets one girl.)

And my problem is I can always imagine, *see*, too much. Because, like I say, everyone you see, everyone you pass in the street, is fucking or getting fucked by someone else. All over the world, and at this very minute. (This very second.) *Now*. So many people fucking, and so often, that the mind can't really take it in. Because they say there's a new baby born somewhere every second. (At the very instant when you think of it happening, it *is*.) And that's only the actual *births*. That's just the fucks that *take*, are *fertile*, and go to *term*.

So, on the same principle, you only have to think of the babies that must be being *conceived* every second too.

But then (and this is the really staggering statistic) just think of all those ones that *aren't* being conceived: all those fucks *without* result or issue, but which are happening every second, every *fraction* of a second. (Because, just on the law of averages it's obvious there must be a hell of a lot more of these than of the fertile, successful births.) (I mean we must be talking numbers in astronomy.) (Like I say, the mind can't take it in.) Because, okay, at any given time one half of the world

214

is light and one half dark. But day or night, all over the world, it's *happening, and there's never a moment when it isn't.* (This very second.) It might be nine o'clock at night in some bamboo hut in China or two in the afternoon on some island in the South Seas, and it's happening there. It's spurting. *Now.*

While in Los Angeles this girl with a thong around her ankle and in a chamois loincloth (she's probably a woman in her thirties now, but still a knockout, still a dish) is getting humped at dawn (it might even be her legal husband), there's just enough light to see her by, the long black hair spread on the pillow, eyes closed, as she feels him sliding and sliding tight in her, she moans, her teeth gleam. Come on, come on, I want you to come inside me. As at last he does so, gasping it out into her. Now.

(Or *now*.)

(Or *now*.)

I get up from the bench, go to the set and switch it off. It's a hot day, and there's only one customer waiting inside, who half looks up from his paper. Another, who's just come to stand in the doorway from the tyre bay, neither in nor out, stares at me. The first one looks back at his paper p.d.q.

You weren't even fucking watching it, I tell him.

I stand there rubbing my neck. I'm getting it again, this ache. The sun hits me as soon as I walk outside, out of the shade, even if it's sweltering in there too. If God is anywhere, he is a fly on the wall in that bedroom in Los Angeles. And in every other room or tent or mud hut or igloo or parked car or common field that people, a man and a woman, are doing it in, all over the world and at every moment, all those simultaneous acts reflected in a different facet of that composite eye.

(Sometimes, in a split second of imagination, a kind of *vision*, I can see a thing exactly as it's happening, somewhere else. But God is the ability to watch so many things at once.)

215

The sun and shade are sharp across the white concrete yard. A shadow: the fact even the sun can't see round corners.

Across the street a young mother bends to her squalling baby. Jeans with white high-heels, and the backside of a heifer. I can see the outline of her panties through the too-tight denim of that packed-in seat. VPL. Visible Panty Line. That always turns me off. Though I suppose it might turn others on, some men are into that. Dennis, for one. I wonder what colour *her* knickers are, is one of his big sayings. (Give him a pair of X-ray eyes and he'd be happy.) (Reminds me of that joke when I was a kid: Why are all the girls wearing lead knickers? Answer: Because Superman's around. Or, what's the latest one? If Superman's so clever, why does he wear his underpants outside his trousers?)

I suppose when you're a kid the word 'knickers' is enough to make a thing a joke. In fact, the only reason for the joke is *saying* knickers. When you're a kid words intrigue you (the way the things themselves do later, I suppose). If you're old enough to know what the words mean, at least. But you don't always. Like that joke about the 'Fuck Bird'. I don't even remember how it goes, now. Those bigger boys told it to me, and I wrinkled up my nose at it because I didn't get it, I didn't know what it meant, and David Tucker, it was, said Go on home and ask your mother what it means, she'll tell you. And I did. And she turned red, and I thought she was going to hit me, but she turned away, doing things in the sink so I wouldn't see her face. And I knew then that the word meant something bad. Although I must have known that anyway, from the way the bigger boys were laughing. I suppose I thought if I asked her what the joke meant I'd know what it was that was bad. But the joke was only to get me to say 'fuck' to my mother, and that was all that was bad about it too.

I'm glad she's dead. It's a terrible thing to say. But

I'm glad she is. I'm glad she won't ever find out now about me and those things I do. Because the dead don't see a thing. The dead don't judge you. I know that now. It's only the living who do that. Like it's not the dead who haunt you, who follow you or float above you like ghosts. It's the living, those who know about you, those who can tell what they know. That's what *haunting* means. A kind of *hunting*. Coming back and hunting you with what they know. And that's what those girls were sinful of. The sin of knowledge. That was what they they had to be cleansed of. Not the sin in the body, that was nothing, barely a tablespoonful. But what was in the mind. In the memory.

Out in the street cars glitter. It's the sun that's giving me this headache. Not the heat: the light. The sky is empty, a mild pale blue, but the light out of it is as hot as if reflected off copper or stainless steel.

It's another of those days when you can see, high up, one of those brief lines projecting itself, so white, so straight, so sure of where it's going, lengthening as you watch: a plane crossing above the earth. Then, next time you look for it, it's gone.

In five days' time Rusty will fly back to me. (And suddenly I see the man on that beach outside the hotel. He's a young lawyer, French, one of those Frenchmen who look well-dressed if not the Height of Fashion even in swimming-trunks, and it's not the solid gold Rolex Oyster Perpetual he doesn't need to take off to go swimming. It's the olive-green all-over tan: what costs the real money is the way he lives. Only under the banded Benetton shorts is he paler. There he's a dirty whitish colour, he's wrinkled and still shrunken from the water. He drips onto the dry hot sand, black hairs running in rivulets down his chest and his dark fuzzed thighs and shins. He rubs his face and hair with a towel, looks at her again from under it, and then sits with his back to her and his face to the sun, eyes closed, letting the sun dry him.

217

Every day this week he's looked across at her, once. She never looks back, but she's always alone and he knows that most men would have made a move by now. But he's too suave and sure of himself to do anything as obvious as try to pick up a strange girl on a beach. (Because he knows that's the secret, with a woman. Make a play, and she might buy it. On the other hand she might not. But get her wondering why you *haven't* made a play so far, or if you ever will, and she's a pushover.)

Anyway, if he's here tomorrow he'll say *Bonjour*, or *Ça va?* and see if and how things go on from there. No one can call that harassment.

(And it's mathematics again, the sheer number of it all. It's figures out of astronomy. Because for every instant or millisecond that it's actually *happening* in the world, in a hundred or a thousand other places (in that identical single millisecond) the *idea* of it is coming into someone's thoughts, and being dwelt on there. Because this is not a passing or occasional or random thought. (The opposite.)

Because the world is just one seething, crawling hive of people with their minds on sex.)

Eleven

Take the money and run, that's what they say. Meaning, In That Order. And it's good advice, because money's what you need most when you're running. And if I'd only sold the bastard car Friday or Saturday like I said I would, at least I would have had the money I got for it to take to run with.

But then, on the Friday morning I started to change my mind. You know how it is. Procrastination is the Thief of, et cetera. Leave it till next week, I thought. Leave it till after Saturday (the 19th) when, according to that air ticket in her bag, Rusty will be back from Alicante. Mainly because, well, okay, why not admit it, mentioning you just sold a 1957 T-Bird for a damn good price isn't the same thing as saying offhand, Yeah, that one there, the white one with the blue top. That one's mine.

Because sometimes just the sight of it is enough. Like with that girl at Sully Island, Val her name was, last summer this was, no, it was the summer before. It was a hot Sunday, and I was just cruising round, really, I'd been down the beach at Lavernock, but there was no action down there, no one I knew, so I drove on to Sully. The tide was right out, so I thought I might walk across to the island. I pulled into the carpark and there they were, the three of them, sitting on the low wall outside the toilets eating icecreams. I went past in second over the stones and potholes, looking at them looking at me, or rather at what I was sitting in, except for the one at the end, the dark one, who was the one my eye picked out because she was slim and brown not fat and sunburnt like

219

her slaggy friends, and she wasn't coy and brazen like the others at having a man in a sports car give them the once over, she was more, what's the word?: intent. She was looking at me almost as if she was trying to remember my face from somewhere, or thought she recognised me.

And it's hard to explain this, because a lot of women, and men too, can't help staring after a car like mine and at the guy who's driving it. But the way she was looking at me was more than that. It was like we read each other for life in the same glance.

And I knew all I had to do was park somewhere in that carpark and let the rest happen. Because happen it would. And it's a weird feeling, a feeling like that, there's no experience like it, because your mouth goes dry and you're so nervous your heart seems to be fluttering in your chest somewhere, no bigger than a bird's or butterfly's, it's like the way you get before a break-in. But at the same time you know that if you just stay calm, and don't rush things, it'll all come to you. Because somehow you know just from the way she looked at you that it's the same for her.

And so I parked and went over into the shack to buy some cigarettes, although of course I had some in the car. And, as I knew it would, everything worked out like this was in a film and we'd rehearsed the scene a half a dozen times to get the timing right. Because when I came out of the shack with the cigarettes, her two friends were coming in again for something, more to eat, by the look of them, and she was on her own, still sitting on the wall. So I went across to the litter bin outside the toilets to drop in the cellophane off the cigarettes like any model citizen, and then I looked at her and she looked at me, and I pushed the shades up on top of my head, girls like to see your eyes, and I said Hi. And she kind of smiled and swung her feet. Then she looked across at the T-Bird. What make of car is that? she said, and as soon as she opened her mouth you could tell she was common as dirt. A Thunderbird, I said. She was still looking at it. That's a nice name for a car, she said, though you could see the name didn't mean any more to her than if I'd told her it had a V8 engine, an 8 foot 6 wheelbase, a compression ratio of 8.4 to 1, and ran to 200 horsepower at 4,600 rpm. All she saw was a big white open car, a muscle car, the tail sticking out a long way behind the little family saloons and Jap hatchbacks it was parked between. Yankee, is it? she said. Yeah, I said. You fancy coming for a spin in it? A spin. A fucking spin. You'd have thought I was Kenneth More playing Douglas Bader the legless air ace chatting up his nurse. She sat there on the wall looking at the car, in those lime-green shorts and the salmon top, colours that really showed up her tan well, that was the first thing I'd noticed about her. And I knew she would.

And when I parked again at the end of that lane in the wood it was all shady and quiet, but with the sun kind of twinkling through the branches of the trees as we sat there in the car and smoked two of the cigarettes I'd bought. And we got out and I took her just inside that hot, empty field, and my heartbeat was thick in my chest now.

It was obvious she was a married woman, of course. I remember I tried all the Mullens in the phonebook afterwards, because she wouldn't give me her phone number, but that was the name she'd told me, Val Mullen, or Mullin it might have been. But I never traced her. I tried for a week to get hold of her again. I rang them all. But she couldn't have had a phone, or perhaps she gave me a false name even, or just a false surname, I wouldn't put it past her, fancy being the husband of a bitch like that. What am I talking about? I am, or was.

But I'll never forget that afternoon, slamming it into her on the edge of that big field in the hot sun, her brown legs up over my shoulders and her brown eyes watching me, she didn't shut her eyes like other girls, she watched

221

me all the way through, Come on, Come on, she kept saying, her crotch was the only part of her white, white and bushy black. Come on, she kept saying, and then I rolled off her with sore knees and the pattern of the stubble and the grass-stalks printed in them, Christ, she said, and we lay on our backs, and I can remember the vertigo of lying there staring up at those big white clouds toppling over on us in a blue sky. And if only getting your end away could always be as easy and quick and good as that.

Let's be honest, probably she was one of those who'll do a turn for anybody in a sports car, from a TR7 upwards. It's a sure thing that any chick who lets herself get picked up and driven down a tractor track into a wood like that is expecting everything she gets. I'm not arguing with that.

What I'm talking about is the way I knew it from the second that our glances locked. That I could pull her. That it was going to happen. Just like that. Because it wasn't just the car. It was more than that. I only knew her for that one afternoon. But it was as if we'd both lived our lives out accidentally until now, just for that second when purely on the off-chance I drove into that gravel carpark down at Sully and saw her, saw her see me, and then something must have happened in our heads, crossed between us, crossed and held (like when those guys on the trapeze catch in midair), so that now all we had to do was go somewhere else out of sight and get down and do it in a field so that after that Sunday doing it was what we could remember rather than that the chance had been there and we'd missed it.

It was the way things worked out for once, for that one afternoon, the way you always fantasise they will. As I say, like in a film. And that's not just the car. Kismet is what they call that.

And I've sometimes felt that, with Rusty, things might turn out that way anyway, even without me making them happen. Which doesn't mean I think she'll turn out to be as big a pushover (or, not to mince words, as big a slag) as that Val (if even that was her real name). Far from it. But it doesn't mean I hope she's a virgin, either. This is 1984. I don't mind a girl having a little bit of experience (enough at least for her to know what's what and what it's there for). What I am saying is that I know (even just from what I know about her now) that Rusty isn't some scrubber who'll drop her drawers for a complete jerk just because he's driving a Yankee roadster, or, come to that, a Roller. I wouldn't impugn her like that. No way.

But on the other hand, everybody has to have an image, and everybody wants to look as sharp as poss. And so I thought keeping the T-bird for a little longer wouldn't exactly be a raging handicap. I mean, I could just see myself swishing up outside that flat of hers in Lakeside and waiting with one elbow draped out over the door, not even needing to punch the horn to let her know I'm there because she and the whole damn street can hear me, Springsteen or The Beach Boys belting out 200 watts per channel, *And we're gonna have fun fun fun till Daddy takes the T-Bird awayeee (Fun fun fun till Daddy takes the T-Bird awayeee) Till Daddy takes the T-Bird away (Ooeee, oo oo oo ooeee)*, it's another hot day, I'm in white chinos, black T-shirt, shades. (And I just wait, listening to the music, one hand tapping on the steering wheel, I look up at her window as she runs to it and smiles and gives me a big wave, then she has a last look in the mirror and now she's almost running down the stairs she's so excited that I'm finally here, she doesn't bother trying to act cool and ladylike no more, not with me, her heart's beating and she's smiling like an idiot just going out to meet me through the hall.)

Anyway, what I'm saying is, in the end I didn't get round to selling it.

Which, as it turned out, was only my first mistake. Because if I'd driven it over to Bristol this Saturday, at least I would have had the money. (I don't really know what the car is worth now, to a dealer, what with the work and refitting I've done on it over the last few years. But I know I'd rather have even a couple of thousand less than I could get for it by private sale, than have a useless car sat in a garage because it's so noticeable I don't dare drive it out of there and show it on the roads, not to mention the useless set of keys to it in a trouser pocket where I might instead have had a thick wad of those nice big crisp brown tens of folding-money.)

And another thing: if I'd gone to Bristol that day, I wouldn't have bastard well been there when the doorbell rang. (Though I don't suppose that would have made any difference. They would only have camped in a car across the street till I got home again. They don't give up, these characters, not once they've tracked you down that far.)

But then, look at it another way: if I *had* gone over, sold the car, hadn't been there when they came, in the end things might have fallen out differently and worse when I got back. Because like they say, it would have been a Whole New Scenario. And things might not have worked out as lucky as they have done. Because you never know. There's no point talking If This, if That, if only the Other. Everything's iffy. It always is. But once a thing like this has happened, you've got to grab out of it whatever luck you can while you're on your way out running, and just hope it's enough to bring you more.

I'm actually standing looking in the mirror when they ring.

I was just about to go out and do some shopping, you know, odds and ends, usual thing, I'm out of cigs and there's nothing in for the weekend but empty beer-cans. I've got my denim jacket on, I'm ready to go, in fact I've almost gone, and would have been. Except I feel like wearing a bandanna, and I don't know which one.

I like the red and white spotted one, only last time I wore it Tony Barbecue said I looked like a gypsy in it. He probably thought that was a compliment (knowing him), but who the hell wants to be taken for a gyppo? So I wasn't sure about that one. Maybe red with white spots is a bit corny. So I find the green one, only that wants washing, it's got come all over it because I didn't have a fucking tissue to hand. Which in effect leaves the black satiny one. Which I'm actually putting on when I hear the doorbell ring. I've just wound it once round my neck and I actually go down the stairs tying it to answer the door.

I remember all this. It's not as if it's important, it's just details, but I suppose it's like somebody asking you what you were doing when Kennedy got shot. Everybody is supposed to know exactly where they were and what they were doing then. (Though I don't. I was just a kid.)

As soon as I open the door, of course, I know I shouldn't have. I should have been deaf. Or I should have left five minutes ago (as I would have if it hadn't been for this fucking bandanna). I should have been gone. Out of the building. Out of the fucking country. On that Columbia probe to Mars or Jupiter or wherever the fuck it's headed, travelling outwards into space for ever.

You could have picked these two for what they were out of the crowd at Ninian Park. They always come in pairs, like the bollocks they are.

Mr Boyle? the one says. Mr Stewart Boyle?

That's right.

I look from one to the other. I suppose I have always known that one day they would have to come. But I have never expected them. Not this day. Not any day. And, looking back on those few seconds, at least the fact of not expecting them helped me stay calm, appear untroubled, helpful. Which must have put them off their guard. (It's anticipation, fear working away inside you that frays you,

puts a glitter in your pupils, makes you give yourself
away at times like this.)

He flashes me a card in a wallet and tells me their
names. He's a DI something or other, Crouch I think.
(I forget the other one's name. You're trying to think
too fast to take much in at a time like that.)

He says, We'd like to have a word with you.

I nod, pleasant.

What about?

He says, If we could just step inside, sir?

I remember that they've got to do it this way, unless
they've got a warrant. You've got to invite them inside.

Sure.

I show them the stairs up and, Mister Politeness himself, press back against the wall to let them go ahead
of me.

After you, sir, he says, and doesn't move.

He looks at me as if he's trying to tell me he's a bit
too long in the tooth to fall for that one, me slamming
the door on their backs and scarpering. (He can't know
he's going to fall harder and heavier for something else
in about fifteen seconds' time.)

I turn and go ahead up those narrow stairs, and they
come up after me, the three of us in single file. And
I think it must be my calmness, my whole behaviour
on the doorstep, that makes them confident enough to
follow right behind me. But as soon as I start going back
up those stairs I know I haven't got a clue what I'm going
to do next but that every tread I take is taking me up into
a jail cell.

When I reach the landing I turn and lift my knee and
kick the front one quick and hard in the face with the
back edge of my heel. He falls back against the other
holding his nose and mouth, they do this little drunken
dance, both trying not to fall back down the tight stair-
way. I gather my weight again and jump down on them
feet first, like a long-jumper, thirteen stone something

of motion in gravity. We all go down the flight together, bumping down the treads, them under me, and the back one thumps into the door he's only just closed at the bottom. I hope it breaks his bastard neck. I get up first and kick the first one's face twice to move it out of the way so I can pull open the door and get out onto the pavement and slam the door behind me on his moaning. There's an old lady looking at the meat in the butcher's window on the ground floor, a couple of people shopping further along, I don't run, don't draw attention, I act normal. I just walk, walk, one foot and then another, till I reach the corner of the block. Then I go back along the lane behind the shops and then start running. Halfway down it one of the latched garden doors leading off the lane is ajar, I go through into someone's back and shut the door behind me. Two lovely coloured butterflies flirt up off a plant and flutter by. But no one sees me, there's no one in the yard, no one in the back windows of the house I'm looking at or in those on either side. I go around the side of the house and into its front garden, a square of concrete on which a tarpaulined motor bike is stood. I come out on the pavement in Ferry Road. No one. Only some kids doing wheelies further along. I cross the street, go down the lane opposite and skirt along the waste ground behind the houses, it's safer this way, the long way round, past the car stripped to its axles and along the council fencing. This is the last fields of the city, scruffy leasehold grazing bordered by the Ely. Across the flats of wet greyish mud, I notice that the tide is coming in: the river's running backwards.

I have a sudden fright, like lightning passing down me and bolting me to the ground. But it's alright, thank fuck, the garage keys and the car-keys are in the top pocket of my Wrangler jacket, and those other keys, and my wages too, sweet fucking Christ, my wages. Clutching the car-keys tight in my hand as if to keep them even safer, I have to climb a barbed wire fence and cross a waste ground of eggshells and old ashes to reach the garage. There's nobody around. Just the backs of council-houses.

I unlock the hasp and bar holding the corrugated iron doors shut. I open the lefthand one, go in and pull it to after me. Daylight comes in thin under the corrugations of the roof and through cracks. My eyes are used to the dark by the time I switch the dim yellow bulb on.

And I'm still breathing hard now, sweating. But I'm here. I don't think anybody saw me coming. And I must have got here before those two bastards would even have managed to stand up together straight enough at the bottom of those narrow stairs to get the door open, and that just so they could fall on their knees again and crawl outside to spit their blood and teeth out on the pavement. I must have felt like a ton of rocks falling on the one. And then we all bumped down those stairs so fast, with the other one at the bottom. But it's as if I didn't feel a thing, myself. It's like breaking that stack of roof-tiles in karate or heading a football: it's only when you hold back, do it halfheartedly, that you get hurt. But go for it with everything you've got and at least it won't be you that comes off worse.

It's only when I lean against the car to get my breath back that I feel a soreness at my right hip, I must have banged it against the edge of the stair as we went down together. I'll have a bad bruise there tomorrow. But that's nothing, what's a bruise? It's always like that when you're pumped up. You don't feel a thing till afterwards.

Not that I'm not still pumped up now. In fact it's the being pumped up, and the having got here and having the car-keys sweaty in my hand, that almost makes me get into the T-Bird and start it up and burst out of this lockup in a squeal of tyres like Burt Reynolds in a red-neck movie (not even bothering to swing the doors out first).

But then I start to think I'd better use my head instead of my adrenal gland.

The first thing to consider is that I'm safe in this garage, for a while at least. Let's face it, hardly anybody even knows I keep the car here, being as it's a couple of streets away from where I actually live. (The reason for that is, it was the only one I could hire around here big enough to drive the damn car fully into and have a yard of space to work on it in too, because of course you need a garage for a car like this, you can't leave a collector's car out at the kerbside overnight, not with the kids round here. They'd slash your tyres for practice, just to try their Stanleys out. They'd be chiselling the eagle off your bonnet for a badge.)

The second point, though, like I say, is that a car like mine is more of a limitation than an asset in a situation like this, where I need to slip out of the city quietly. Driving an auto like this is hardly Incognito Motoring.

And this is where for a moment I actually and for the first time start to hate this useless fucking machine, which has cost me thousands and thousands over the years. Because I realise I should already have sold it by this time today and recouped all that expense, just like I'd said I would. So that by now I would have had the money in my pocket to go out and buy another car instead, the kind of anonymous dull car all these anonymous dull bastards set their hearts on, a car you pass in thousands and don't notice. Let's be honest, as far as getting out of this place is concerned, a T-Bird at the moment is about as much use to me as a dog sledge or a horse and buggy. There's not a trainee cop or *Echo* reader in South Wales who won't know all about it by tonight, Man Evades Arrest, Flees Scene in Showpiece Car.

A third thing, though, is this. Where the fuck would I flee to anyway?

Look on the plus side of things. What I do have is my wages. Two weeks' money, almost three hundred pounds. It's still in the buttoned-down righthand breast pocket of my denim jacket, the jacket I'd just had time to put on before the doorbell rang. (And at least there's an omen there that things might actually be with me. Anyway, that they could be a damn sight worse. I could still be running across the gardens in my socks.)

The money will get me away from this place, even if the car won't. And I can always use the garage as a hideout, at least for tonight.

I take out the money and count it again, note by note. They're not stiff, new notes. They're old, they're used. That's Quick-Change for you. Life is a retread tyre. But they'll buy the same as new.

Not quite three hundred pounds is not a lot of money. It's not a lot of money when you've been working in a place four years, and when they cash you in that's all the green stuff you've got to show for it, except you can't even call it Green Stuff any more, or Lettuce, not since the one-pound coin came in. (And a five-pound note is blue. The Blue Stuff just doesn't ring as good.) (It's true what I say: every day they're taking more and more away from us so we can't recognise ourselves in things any more.)

I push the righthand door a few inches ajar and look towards the council houses, the ash lane that runs here from between the middle pair. Still. No one. (Still no one.) From the back of the garage I can see out the other way, across the fields, through a crack in the boarding I nailed up as shutters on the window. Nothing. Just a heat waver in the air across towards those piebald ponies, and those thorn bushes white with may. It's been so hot lately, I can't remember when it rained last.

Skewbald, actually, my wife said, that time. *What?* I said. The brown patched ones are *skewbalds*, she said. I laughed. 'Actually', I told her, I never actually went to an actual riding school like you. Jodhpurs and martingales and all that. Actually, we used to have to catch the fuckers and then get on and try to ride them bareback. And she said, What a deprived, urchin childhood. How you must have suffered. And put her left fist under her chin and pretended to bow a gypsy violin for me in sympathy, laughing at me, and something snapped in me and I slapped her hard. Nobody takes the piss out of me, I told her. Or my childhood. She was holding her face. You bastard, she screamed. I was only teasing you. *Nobody teases me either*, I said, and I threw my coat on and went out, to keep myself angry, because I knew I'd got myself worked up in a rage for nothing again.

(Except that nothing I ever lost my rag over with that bitch turned out to be for nothing. Not a fucking thing.)

I'm still thinking about my wife as I unlock the door of the T-Bird so I can sit inside and sort things through. (I've been pacing and wheeling like a madman in the yard of space between the bumper and the corrugated iron door.) I'm wondering if I should pay Him and Her a visit. Janet and John. Up there in Powys. It's off the beaten track. And barely an hour and a half's drive away. if I could get a car to get there.

But then as soon as I take the car-keys out again, I see the extra keys I clipped onto the ring last week, the three keys I had cut. They're gleaming, brass, new.

Of course.

And suddenly I'm so calm I'm almost high. I can feel my heart beating, but it isn't nerves. It's solid certainty. Because sometimes you understand how everything's fated, and then life is simple. It's like how I've always wondered if one day life would unravel and remake itself. If one day everything that had gone wrong would suddenly, magically, unexpectedly click together like a Rubik cube when it comes right again, with the six sides back in place, just like it was when it was new.

But now this has happened. And it isn't luck or chance or happenstance. I know that now.

And I don't need my own car any more, nor this garage as a hideout. (I think of her flat, her space, her rooms. The intimacy of ordinary cupboards and bathroom cabinets and smooth-sliding drawers.)

All I have to do now is wait till dark. Then get to the locks these three keys fit. Get to what they open or start.

Twelve

'The A-Team' one has written on it with it a fingertip, and circled, in the grey dust (the metal back so filthy only those fresher letters show the blue paint underneath). Another, two lorries back, has 'Scab' in savage red (like a finger was licked clean to do it).

And they keep passing me, passing me. I know it takes a lot of coal to keep a steelworks going. But there must be over a hundred of these cowboys running this shuttle. They've been passing me a full five minutes now, taking up the whole damn middle lane.

And you realise how low you are in a little sports car like this, particularly when you're boxed in with these six-axle juggernauts going past you hell for leather in a convoy, turn your head and you're barely at the height of their hub, have a rush of blood and suddenly try to pull out between them, and those big double wheels spinning past would run over this little MG (like the next lorry, and the next) without a driver even noticing it, no more than whoever it was ran down that fox I think it was I passed back there, or what was left of it, a bloody rag at the side of the road it looked like, with a bit of reddish fur on it.

Because not a fucking lot is going to stop these boys, I've seen them roaring out of the dock gates through the pickets on the TV news. One of these days some miner's going to not get out of the way in time and go down under the front wheels and come out as a tyreprint at the other end.

They're empty now, which is why they're so fast. They've tipped at Llanwern and now they're heading back to Port Talbot for reloading. Another load of coal, another fistful of folding money. And these boys are on Special Rates. They say they're wheeling the dough back home in wheelbarrows. No wonder they're in a hurry.

Me, I daren't go over sixty, not with all these police about. As soon as I see an exit I'll get off this fucking stretch of motorway and wait till the road's clearer. I'm not a nervous driver. But coinciding with this convoy is bad news. It's not just the motor-cycle outriders and the escort cars with the blue lights turning on the top. There's something fucking *scary* about so many lorries travelling so close together and going so damn fast. They're even armoured, all those metal grilles fitted over the windscreens and side windows. (I suppose because of pickets throwing stones or heaving the odd housebrick or concrete lintel down off a bridge.) It's like that film of the German motorised divisions taking Poland. It's like we're in a state of war.

A blue sign tells me there's an exit coming up.

I'm going to pull off and take five minutes out and park, wait till these bastards have gone past. What's so scary is the thought that all you have to do is jerk the steering to go under one of them (you could drive a car this size straight in between the wheels). And once you get the idea in your head, it's like you almost *want* to do it. Don't get me wrong, I'm no suicidal. I'd take out the rest of the population of the fucking world first. You better believe it. But it's the same being scared of heights, like when I worked for Bechtel on those big container towers: if you start to think about it you can get frozen with fear. It's really a kind of tension, and it's almost as if throwing yourself off the top is the only way to put that tension at an end. As if you'd do it for the release, the experience of falling. Just for that one second of unwinged flight before you hit the deck and burst.

I pull off the motorway and park in the first lay-by after the slip-road, by the rusting perimeter fence of a school field. Outskirts steel-town suburb. Grim, pink-grimed Port Talbot. I can still see the high backs of the lorries still passing, passing, and stretching ahead up the long hill-curve of the motorway.

It's only when I switch the engine off, in the silence and stillness, that I realise I'm trembling.

I can remember Mandy when she was little trying to pick a picture off the page of her story book. She was sitting on my knee. She must have been about fifteen months or so. It was a picture of a little cartoon racoon in a red car. She kept making little racing car noises, which was a thing she'd just started doing. You know, making the noise things make. And she tried to pick it off the page, scratching at it with her fingernails.

It's only a picture, I told her. It's not real. You can't pick it up and hold it. It's just to look at.

And my wife said how she'd started doing the same thing with pictures of food in one of her magazines, I think it was one of those luscious photos, you know, with everything glistening in it, probably of a strawberry flan or something, and Mandy trying to pick it up so she could eat it. And then she got cross, my wife said, and tried to rip the magazine. It's a stage they go through, my wife said. They think they can have everything they see. They don't understand that some things are only pictures.

And that was how it was with Rusty in the end.

I don't know why I should think of that little racoon now. Mandy was sitting on my knee and she kept scrabbling at it with those chubby fingers, I think she wanted to hold him, like one of her cuddly toys or bed-pets, kids always like animals like that, racoons or pandas, cartoon animals with stripy faces and big round eyes.

But it had never happened to me like that before, because the others I didn't care about. Just so long as I worked them up enough so they got wet, that was enough to prove to me they liked it, that I was doing them a favour, even if they'd never admit it. Women are such hypocrites. They'd rather die than admit in public that they might have liked it. But I knew. The body doesn't lie.

But, with Rusty, I knew from the beginning that at least the one thing I had now was time. Time to let things happen properly, *in* their own time. With the others, time was the one thing you didn't have and so it was the one thing you always had on your mind, you always wondered if somebody else might come in suddenly, a flatmate or whatever, or if you'd been spotted going in and some do-gooding bastard of a busybody had dialled 999. And so you never knew how much time you had. It was like a clock was in your head (or just a second sweep). Going round and round. And so everything was rushed somehow, days like that. And that was why you were always under pressure, it was like you were on a time-and-motion study, or on one of those television shows where you've got to assemble things from parts to beat the clock, or in a bad dream where you're in water to the thigh and you're trying to escape and you don't know if you're wading or running. And it was because of that pressure that on occasions things went wrong. Badly wrong. I never meant to, but sometimes you can hardly stop yourself. You don't realise how much tension and rage there is in you when that ticking in your head is all you hear.

But with Rusty, time, like I say, was no object. The only object was her. Her and me: the couple we were going to become.

Because I knew at least I was going to be safer in her flat than in any other place I might have thought of going. And the way I saw it, I might even stay a week or so, if things worked out between us. I had to let things outside blow over anyway, give the local police a chance to find some other poor bastard to chase and harry, some international dope smuggler or a shoplifting miner on the run.

Not that they'd ever actually forget about me, of course. Not now, I knew now that they'd never stop looking. Because I don't know, I'll probably never know, how much they might have had in hard fact or suspicion when they came to my door. (We'd like a word with you, he said. What about? I said. But I never did find out.) But either way, they've got a lot more now, of both. Because by now they'll have been through my place with a fine tooth-comb. With the finest tooth-comb they can find. They'll have found the Book, the mementoes, inside the first five minutes. (It makes me shudder even to think of it. As if now someone else has seen those things they must be true.) It struck me afterwards that they might even have found my green bandanna with the 'traces' on it. Assuming, that is, that one of them has enough of a nose for detective work to sniff it once and then the wit to have it tested for a match.

But I also knew that no matter who they were looking for, and for no matter what crime, after a day or two the trail would cool on them, and they'd start working on the principle that I'd got away, was hiding out in Glasgow or The Smoke. So, once that initial heat was off, I thought I'd have a better chance to make an actual getaway.

I say *I*. But what I actually thought was: *we*. Not me, my getaway. But *us*. *Ours*.

Because I thought that if only Rusty spent that week with me, twenty-four hours a day together with me, in her flat, she'd end up on my side. She'd start to learn to be aware of what and who I am, of just how much there is to know and understand about me. That she'd start to learn respect. And that gradually she'd realise she was in love with me. That she'd never met a man like me before. That every other man she'd met had been an old man or a boy.

It wasn't even as if all I had going for me in this

was myself. Because I remember reading in the Sunday papers once (it must have been in the old days when we used to take *The Observer*) about how that happens with air hostesses in these airport sieges. It's an established fact. They spend a couple of days cooped up in the plane on the runway, with a load of passengers and a couple of terrorist gunmen, and next thing you know one of them ends up falling for one of the gunmen and taking up his cause. She writes to him, she visits him in prison afterwards, she even wants to get married to the guy, for Christ's sake, though by now he's probably doing thirty years and no chance of parole. Which actually happened with that one girl they mentioned in the paper. Her parents got all kinds of counsellors and psychiatrists and hypnotists and fuck knows what to get her to change her mind, but the only thing she dreamed of was a prison wedding so she could hitch herself for life to some stubbled desperado who'd spent three days holding a Kalashnikov against her head. (And this is probably some ripe juicy Dutch or Nordic blonde who's going to put a lock on all of that and throw away the key till he gets out. She might as well have become a nun, a fucking bride of Christ, for all the marriage she was ever going to know.)

Anyway, my theory is that it's the strength of conviction in these terrorists that makes these girls go ape for them. Women can't resist a man who knows exactly what he wants and where he's going, even if it's only some fanatic greaseball Arab in a yashmak. *The Stockholm Syndrome*, they call that effect, it's in the medical dictionaries now. They call it that because it was after a siege on a plane grounded at Stockholm airport that they first noticed it among the female crew. Though I suppose it's been proved since again and again, all over the world: how hostages, particularly when they're young unmarried women, come to love their captors.

It's like that jingle the Old Man used to come out with

now and then: *A dog, a woman and a walnut tree. The harder you treat them, the better they'll be.*

(Or was it: *Beat* them? No, it couldn't have been. I mean, you'd beat a dog or a woman, that makes sense. But who'd beat a walnut tree? What'd be the point?

Unless: to get the nuts down?

Yeah. Nuts. That must be it.)

Anyway, I think that was my big mistake with Rusty. In trying to treat her With Consideration. In trying not to scare her too much, by showing her how I was, you know, not a crazy, but 'sensitive', 'intelligent'. In actually trying to get her to 'like' me.

Because that's always the big mistake, with a woman. Once you start trying to please them, they know they can treat you like dirt.

And now I think of it, I've probably made that mistake all my life, with women I liked. And all they ever did was make a cunt out of me for it, make me eat shit. Like with my bitch of a wife that last time, when instead of just belting her again so she stayed belted, I ended up on my knees afterwards, feeling guilty like some henpecked husband or a mournful-looking cocker spaniel, trying to tell her how sorry I was and I'd never do it again, I'd never lift a hand or close a fist to her again, so help me God. And that point, natch, was where I lost all the advantage, and she knew it. Whereas if I'd just spat once on the carpet, spun on my heel and put my sharpest shirt on, gone down to The Locomotive or The Bristol Packet and started buying some slag port-and-lemons, she'd have followed me down there if she'd had to crawl it on her hands and knees. She'd have come in the saloon bar after me and hauled me out of there, black eye and swollen lip and all. She wouldn't have been able to drag me back home quick enough to give me a really dirty fuck, just to remind me. Because there's never been a hotter turn-on than jealousy. Or a bigger turn-off than devotion: all the cunts see that as is a chance to hoodwink you.

And this is why women don't want Mister Nice, no matter what they say. (Except as someone to fall back on, someone to use. Mister Safety Net.) All the nice girls love a bastard. And the bigger the bastard, the more they go for you. They love you for treating them like shit because, let's face it, all anybody loves in someone else is the other person being Free. Free enough to take it or leave it. Freedom and Inner Certainty: they're the only things anyone respects, we're all on heat for them, they're more important than looks or even dough. And we're all the same in that. What we love is the hand that holds the whip.

Yeah. And that's what it must be even with those air hostesses. Because, when you think about it, those girls are probably pretty mercenary little bitches to start out with. It's obvious. They only take a job like that in the first place for the glamour. So that they get free flights to all the exotic places, have a two-day stopover and hang out with the pilots and meet foreign businessmen and young executives and male models on location. (The cunts probably imagine themselves lying around on all that tropical white sand chopping coconuts in half and eating Bounty bars.) Hey, I'm Cindy, Fly Me. Except they don't really want to fly, those girls, what they're there for is to *climb*, get somewhere socially. And the only way they can do that is through sex. They even have that club, the Mile-High Club they call it, I read about it in the *News of the World*. It has a very exclusive international membership, it said, mostly airline pilots and hostesses and businessmen, or people like top sportsmen and stars who do a lot of flying. Well, it would have to be exclusive, who else would ever get the chance to qualify to join by fucking in a toilet five thousand feet or more up in the air?

(Though I tell you what'll stop all this International Jet Set screwing around, if it just gets going, which they say it will: this AIDS.)

But what I'm saying is this: when even some snobby money-hungry hostess can end up falling hook line and sinker for some unshaven Palestinian whose entire nation hasn't even got a pot to piss in let alone a bed to put it under, it only underlines what I'm saying.

Because why they go for these guys is dead simple. It's because these guys are fanatics. These guys are absolutely single-minded. And in a situation like that, on an airliner, they're the ones with guns. They're in control. And women worship power.

So perhaps I should have used my own power more.

Perhaps I paid her too much attention, even. That might have been a mistake, trying to 'talk' to her, you know, get a 'conversation' going. Because it was nearly always me doing the talking. In fact for the first hour or so I might just as well have gagged her too, for all she said. She just sat there, propped against the headboard, watching me, her eyes moving whenever I did, following me everywhere. I tried to act natural, pleasant. But she didn't say a word.

You don't mind me smoking, I hope? I said.

Do you want one? I said. I'll hold it for you.

Have you got an ashtray here? I said.

I got up from the chair and went out into the kitchen and came back with the saucer.

I couldn't find one anywhere, I said. So I've been using this. I didn't think you'd mind.

I lit a cigarette. Then I got up again and opened the top light of the window an inch or two. I stayed back against the wall to make sure no one saw me.

Let the smoke out, I said.

I gave her a smile.

I know it can bother you if you're a non-smoker.

I sat down again in the armchair.

Me, I've smoked since I was a kid, I said. Off and on. You know. And a smoky room bothers me too, to tell you the truth. So I know what non-smokers mean. There's nothing worse than a smoky room, I always think. Particularly in a pub. You know, you walk in through the door and start inhaling everybody else's cigarette smoke. Like a friend of mine said once, 'Christ, what a fug,' he said. 'Why even light your own?'

(Actually, it wasn't a friend. I was just being modest.)

It's a silly habit, I said. When you think about it. Putting a paper tube in your mouth and lighting it.

Hey, I said. Have you ever heard that Bob Newhart record? *Nutty Walt*? About Sir Walter Raleigh? How he discovered tobacco? It's a scream.

I squashed the cigarette out in the saucer.

He discovered the potato too, didn't he? Sir Walter Raleigh?

I looked at her with a puzzled look, smile of uncertain factual memory. (No point playing a bighead knowall.)

I think he did. Was that on the same trip, I wonder?

Those dark eyes glittered at me with this kind of ceaseless quality. It wasn't what you'd call a fixed or steady look like a stare. It was more as if it was swarming, like an anthill. Like someone slightly absent because they're thinking under pressure. She never took her eyes off me, but she watched me like someone thinking of something else all the time, and thinking fast.

They must have been two pretty important discoveries, I said. When you think about it. Potatoes and tobacco. You know, for that time.

I suppose they still are, I said. Important. When you think about it. There's a lot of money made out of spuds and tobacco. Two great staples of the British way of life.

She watched me light another cigarette and cross my legs, settling back a little more in the chair, those eyes swarming like ants on my every movement. I watched the ash burn back after a deep drag, in a faint rustle of smouldering paper.

Though I think a lot less people smoke these days, I

said. And even those who do, smoke less. Which must have hit the tobacco companies. Though I don't suppose old W.D. and H.O. Wills are on the brink of going under. Not just yet.

I examined the cigarette again.

You ever smoke? I said.

Me, I said. I been smoking too long to give up now. I don't even bother trying to cut down on it any more, I said. I don't expect to live for ever.

I examined the cigarette again.

But it's a stupid habit, I said.

(I pronounced it *stoo*pid, it just kind of slipped out that way, because my voice was getting a kind of drawl now I was feeling more relaxed.)

Still, I said. At least it didn't stunt my growth.

You're tall too, I said. You know, for a girl. How tall are you? Five nine? Five ten?

Those ceaseless, jewelled eyes watched me. She shifted a little on the bed, and frowned, as if her wrists might be hurting.

Is it too tight? I said.

She watched me, those dark eyes aswarm with glitters. Then she made what looked like a kind of nod. Which, even though she still hadn't spoken yet, was still a kind of word, or at least a way of saying Yes. And that was the first thing she'd said since her key went into the lock at just after four o'clock that afternoon and she came in through the door and just dropped that fat holdall with the flight tags on it, as if she couldn't wait to put it down after lugging it up the stairs. (I could hear it swishing against the wall as she came up and I was waiting beside the door, after I'd been waiting all day for her minute by minute, my heart shrinking tight in my chest every single time I heard a door closing downstairs or a noise out in the corridor in case it was her, and once the phone rang in the room and nearly scared me out of my skin, literally, like the cat in the cartoon, until I realised what it was, and sat and watched it ring and ring with my heart beating with fright, I never knew a phone could ring so long and loud. And so all day I was nervous like that, and I kept going hot and cold and fevery at the thought of her, you'd have thought I was a teenage boy out on his first date ever and wondering if she's going to turn up for him at all.) But as she dropped the bag, and sighed, and flexed her shoulder, I pushed the door not quite shut gently behind her so it didn't touch the jamb and make a noise. Then I went the two paces quickly up to her and put my hand over her mouth and held her round the waist from behind, and felt her squirm and fight against me and heard her try to yell and scream under my hand, and I held her tighter to me and I was whispering into her ear all the time, It's alright, I don't want to hurt you, and I did feel gentle with her, just holding her, because I know how to break a trained soldier's neck from that position let alone a surprised girl's, but I was just holding her, like with a kid in a fit or a tantrum, for its own good, its own protection, the tighter the better, and I was whispering all the time to her, It's alright, I don't want to hurt you, Just keep still, Calm Down, until she stopped trying to squirm and fight and scream and she just kind of leaned back against me, trembling, waiting, so I almost thought she'd fainted. And I was whispering in her ear and I was so close I could smell her hair, like we were dancing.

I sit with the road atlas from the MG's glove compartment, and look at where the fuck I am (just off the blue motorway, outskirts of Port Talbot) and at where the fuck I am going when I start the car again (up a red road, then a yellow road across to join another red road, and then, I know, a few miles up a road not even marked on this). Not that I need to look: I know the way, I ought to by now. I just thought looking at the map would help me to think, plan what the fuck I am going to do when I get there.

244

But there's no detail on this map, it's designed for motorway driving. It's just coloured roads on white. There's no sense of landscape, or ground relief: those graduated brown mountains and green wooded valleys I am going to and which, on proper walkers' maps like those still in the glove compartment of my useless garaged T-Bird, are as real as in actuality. Realer even, in some ways. Because maps are imagined land, and land is only land. You can spend hours over a map, it's better than a good book, better than even going to the place. It's like when I was a kid, the trembling, inletted line I used to draw, coming back upon itself until it met. And that was the Island. And then I'd draw trembling lines of rivers radiating from its heartland to the coast, and an *X* of crossed bones where the gold was. And then I'd get matches and burn the paper just enough at the edges so it looked like old 'vellum' or 'parchment', and roll it up into a scroll. (The art was in getting the pencil to waver in the right way, controlled but not too conscious, so the outline looked authentic. You know, irregular but somehow inevitable. Like Greenland is.) I used to love drawing that island, again and again, and it was always different, with different bays and promontories and rivers, I never could decide. But I think I actually thought it existed somewhere, because I'd drawn it, and I wanted to live there. It was my own island, although it never had a name. Now I'd name it after myself. *Boyle Island.* And when you think about it, the whole world must have been like that once, for people like Christopher Columbus and Sir Walter Raleigh. You look at old maps and they're nothing like the world is really, it's all imagination, all imagined land, they didn't know what lay out in the ocean to the west so they'd just draw an island where they felt like having one, and trying to find that island was the only thing that made them put out from the shore, they didn't really know what was out there beyond the sunset, they didn't even know if

245

they might sail over the edge. But they'd invented an island, and they made the outline look as irregular and convincing as they could. It was more a figment of a fantasy than fact. But it was on the maps, and called America, and that was all they knew.

I wish I could do that. Do a John Stonehouse. Just lose this car over some cliff into the sea so it looked like I was in it, then set out in a little boat until I came to land, a place where no one knew me and no one would ever come to look for me. A place where I didn't always have to live my life in the driving mirror, always watching the road behind me.

But there's nowhere like that left in the world. Not now. Not for me. Sail west from here, and all I do is end up in Cork or Connemara, which is where my father started out, except going east he was, a kid of ten, in the Depression, that'd be progress for you: fifty years later and back with the Spud Eaters. Though I suppose that's one thing Sir Walter Raleigh did for the world, even if he also gave us lung cancer: at least he saved the Irish from starvation. Because I've heard my Old Man say time and time again how if the spuds failed all you had was grass. The Old Man hated the place. The only thing my Old Man ever did for me, he used to say (meaning my grandfather), was get me out of fucking Ireland. But that was something, he'd say. He got me off of the old sod. I'll give the old sod that. That much at least. My father hated his Old Man too, he was a rough, hard old bugger, I think, Grampa Boyle, all he did all his life was work in a gang digging trenches for the drains on building sites. They was rough lads, those boys, my Old Man said. When they got too drunk after work to walk home to their lodging they'd just go back to the site and sleep in the cement shed. All they'd have for breakfast of a morning was a piss and half a cigarette. But they'd dig all day on that. All they seemed to live on was the beer, he said, and a half a pound of bacon

246

on a Friday, which they'd fry up on their shovels, they was that clean.

So that's the way it is, and that's the stock I come from. A long line of manual micks and NFA's, No Fixed Abodes. Set sail for Boyle Island and you land up in the Emerald Isle, *rough* and *rugheaded* he called them, the Irish, in that Shakespeare play we did in school, and he was right. Rough rugheaded bastards with fine eyes, and fuck-all else.

And I don't care what my Old Man said about my grandfather, because he might have got us out of Ireland, but he stopped too fucking soon, or rather turned the wrong way in the first place. Because if I'd been born in Worcester, Massachusetts or Newport, Rhode Island instead of Cardiff, Glamorgan I might have had a chance, I might have been somebody. Like Mark Frechette, that kid in *Zabriskie Point*, all he was was a carpenter until Michelangelo Antonioni happens to see him walking home one night from work, and that was it. He'd got the part, a part he didn't even try for. He could go out and throw his tools into the river now. He never needed them again. He was a star. Christ, just think of the luck some people get. I'd be out in L.A. now with some lovely piece. Instead of sitting in a hot car I don't even know if they're out looking for yet and waiting for these police escorts to clear.

The police are out there thicker on the ground than dogshit at the moment. Okay, they're thinking about a couple of hundred miners pushing and shoving at a steelworks gate, not private citizens in sports cars. But the sight of them's enough to make me nervous. And I might be looking at this roadmap on my knee, but I don't know if it's any more use than those treasure maps I used to draw. I'm starting to think I might need more than a road atlas and a survival knife with a compass in the handle now.

And I can't even bear to think about my gun, my beautiful blue two-two with my name cut in the hardwood stock. *STU* I carved originally, but then I altered it and put inverted commas too, so it read:

'STOO'.

But like I say, I don't want to think about that. It's in the flat, with the ammo, and all the other stuff which would have really come in useful for the first time now: the crossbow and the flak jacket and the replica Mauser and all the other gear I've collected one piece at a time over the last few years. I can't believe my own fucking stupidity: why the fuck didn't I keep some of that stuff hidden in the garage or the car for just this kind of emergency? All I've got with me now is what I could find in the lockup that looked as if it might be of some use. Like the old hatchet that would barely split a stick for firewood. Oh, and I've got that big kitchen knife, French, with a riveted black handle (made by Sabatier). I took it from Rusty's cutlery drawer. You can always use a 7-inch blade.

I can still see the look on her face when she saw me take it out and turn towards her with it in my hand.

It's strange the way you imagine beforehand how being locked indoors for five days with a girl like Rusty will turn out. As if, if things go well, you'll never be off her, or she off you, it'll be a teenage honeymoon, you'll end up spending all your day in bed.

Which was what I couldn't stop thinking all that day and night I spent alone in the flat before she got back. I was burning for her like a green log, and she wasn't even there yet.

It was enough just touching her things. Her furniture. Her cups and saucers. Or looking at her bed. Her shower curtain. Her bath mat. Her mirror. Her toilet seat.

It was enough just to open her drawers and her wardrobe, take out her clothes, smell them, feel the textures, plan what I wanted her to wear out of it all for me.

I didn't want to rummage. (I want to make that clear.)
I didn't want to find out her secrets or take out bits of
clothing to, you know, rub myself up with. I didn't want
to come in her lacy little panties. Though I'd been through
that before from time to time, in other flats. I'd even been
into that before once with my wife, it was that time when
I was wondering if she and that Leo were. Or whether
she was anyway with somebody. Some other guy. (I didn't
even know who he might be. I just had this feeling. This
suspicion. Though I didn't want to believe it really, any
more than I did with Raoul.) (I wanted to *imagine* it all
rather than *prove* it. Which was my mistake.)

But with Rusty I wanted to start off with a clean sheet.
(A clean pair of sheets.) I didn't care what she'd done
for a week out in Spain, or who she'd known before.
To me everything in her flat was sacrosanct (the way
everything in a church is Holy) because anything there
was something she'd worn or drunk from or stood on or
slept in or sat on. And I wanted to start from that. I
didn't want to *spoil* things for myself. Not when every
fold in the bedcover, or the way the bath-towel had been
flung over the rail, was sexual, to me.)

And so that first night, after I'd got into the place,
it was enough to lie naked in that air she had been in,
moved in. Lie naked on her wide bed (*why* so wide for a
single girl?), and breathe it in and feel it on my body and
feel myself stiffen into it, that same air she'd breathed
in and exhaled again for me to breathe that night. The
same air almost to the molecule, you could say, because
she'd closed and fastened all the windows before she
went away (though in case of burglars probably, which is
ironic, as they say, when you think of how I came in with
a duplicate of her own key through the front door). And
that was why I didn't mind not opening a window too,
not only in case it might be noticed by some nosy bastard
of a neighbour or a caretaker, who knew she was away.
But so I wouldn't dilute that essence, that air I could

feel my size and nakedness displacing, like getting into water still warm after *her* bath. Because there was that faint scent of something her flat had for me as soon as I went into it. It was warm and a bit stuffy from the sun through the big windows (she hadn't drawn the curtains before she left). But then there was something other than the smell of heat or warm carpet, something unique to her and the space she lives in: a thing every flat and every house has and every bedroom even, though most people don't realise this because they don't notice atmospheres or they get used to them too quickly or they can't smell shit from clay in the first place. I suppose most people's sense of smell has atrophied until it's about as much use as that stump at the bottom of the human spine that used to be a monkey's tail. Me, though, I've got a nose like a fox, or maybe it just gets heightened at moments like that, going into a girl's flat or an unfamiliar bedroom in the dark, like that time in Palace Road, at Buffy's. And I knew her parents would be out till eleven, at the earliest. I'd seen them drive away. They always went out on Saturday night. I'd been watching for weeks. I knew the whole pattern to a T. Sometimes she'd go out too and I'd follow her to the bus and the bus into the centre of town and she'd meet friends, a mixed group usually, and they'd go into a pub, one of those noisy poser's pubs where they must reverse the usual legal rule or something because everybody there looks under-age. But other times this boyfriend would come round (I suppose he was her boyfriend, he was the right age, perhaps a year or two older than her, and good-looking enough). In some ways I liked it when he did, because then I could stand out there in the big dark garden between those two cypress or whatever trees they were, staring at a lighted curtained downstairs window and wondering what they were doing to each other inside, snogging on the sofa or touching each other up again and again inside their clothes for hours (I thought of the stickiness and wetness of it, all that tireless toying, her being a good girl, a well-brought-up girl, and stopping him again and again at the middle finger but letting him have as much tit as he wanted, and then finally pulling him off into his trousers, while I did the same out by the trees). But other times I saw them fucking in there, and with the matter-of-factness of those who have been doing so for years, and then I didn't like her suddenly because I knew that her schoolgirl look of innocence just ripe and ready for the picking was a come-on that went with the school uniform and white ankle-socks, and that all she was really was jailbait. (Because I sometimes think the Catholic Church is right, at least about women: that sin is in them from the day of birth.)

But that particular Saturday night I knew by ten o'clock that she wouldn't be going out now and that he wouldn't be coming either, not that late.

And then at ten-past ten she started running the water for a bath. And then I wished I wasn't there, because I was torn again, because tonight the opportunity was there and it scared me.

I'd moved right up against the wall of the bungalow. Now I was standing right next to that lighted pebbleglass bathroom window she hadn't even drawn the curtains for because she knew no one could see in, and I was listening to the sound of the bathwater running, then a radio, and then the bathwater stopped running and there was the noise of the tank refilling instead and the radio (I couldn't make out what the voices were saying) and that sound of the water, which was her in the bath. And I could almost see her there, lying back and soaping all the places of her body, armpits, thighs, the crack in her arse, the space between her glistening pink-tipped tits. I stood there listening to the slip and splash as she washed herself, making herself clean and young and fragrant while I was out there thinking what you might call dirty thoughts, and I mean dirty, because, okay, she might be

251

in the Upper Sixth and have a boyfriend, she might know about putting her tongue in the boy's mouth when she kissed him, she might know a lot more things than that. But there were things she didn't even dream about yet, had never thought about doing or thought that anyone would want to do to her or have her do to him. What the hell do you know about the world when you're eighteen, and still in school? You don't know shit.

And then she must have pulled the plug because the water coughed once and started spurting into the drain outside the window, just by my feet, startling me for a moment. And by now I'd been standing there and imagining what she was doing on the far side of the window for so long I almost felt like getting down on my knees by the drain and lapping at that steamy soapy water she had lain in, for a taste of her.

And when I tried the door to the conservatory at the back, I found it was unlocked, like I'd somehow known it would be, and the next door, into the kitchen, was too. In fact the only door in the whole damn house that was locked, I realised, was probably the door to the bathroom itself, because I knew that although she might not have thought to draw the curtains across at the window she would have slipped the bolt to before she got into the bath (I always do).

And then everything was like in a dream, a dream I hadn't planned on having, because I'd only come there that night to watch: the doors opening silently under my hand like they were melting aside, until I got to her room, Buffy's room, the room she would come back to from the bathroom, with her hair wet and her body clean, I knew it was her room because it smelt like she would, clean and young and perfumed faintly with whatever soaps or oils or powders she would put on after a bath, I could smell her in that room as clear as I could see the luminous green numbers of the digital alarm clock on her bedside table, she wouldn't hear that go off tomorrow

morning. And I got upset later to think of the alarm
tone buzzing and buzzing at seven or seven-thirty the
next morning, time for her to get up and get ready for
school (though in actual fact it was a Sunday, no school
anyway). But trying to wake her at least, buzzing and
buzzing until somebody else came in to stop it, and it
was the thought of that machine trying to be faithful to
the hand that had set it that upset me and I broke down
and cried, because she was the first, though it might
have been a month or two months afterwards, it was
the same when my mother died, it's as if a thing like
that takes time to sink in, hit you. But I wasn't thinking
any of this as I stood there in her room in the dark and
breathed it in, the odour of her and of the dark itself,
the bedroom dark in which she had discovered her own
clitoris and how to stroke herself and make her nipples
stiffen lying there, what I hate is how a man can't always
make himself go stiff by wanting to, I don't know what
it is, why it happens sometimes, always at the worst
times, times when you'd give anything to be hard. But
sometimes too things are different in the flesh than in
your head. It's like things shift somehow, and it dies on
you. Or things get too real, like two sweat-stains on the
T-shirt when their arms go up. Or sometimes when a girl
throws back her head and laughs, or even an actress on
television, and Buffy did that too, except that it was a
grimace, a kind of a frown, throwing her head back on
the pillow, I called her Buffy because she looked like
Buffy St Marie the folk singer, I never use their own
names, I never like their own names (her name in the
papers was a stranger's). But they do, they throw their
head back in just that way and laugh, those women on
TV, and suddenly you can see the crowns of all their
upper teeth and sometimes you can see the black or silver
glint of fillings. And Buffy had one at the back there,
and you think, a girl of eighteen like this, with all that
beautiful thick shining hair, and she's got silver in her

mouth. And you know that outside and inside can be
different things. *Never look a gift horse in the mouth,*
my Old Man used to say, but the inside of a woman's
mouth tells you a lot, like that slag with the terrible
teeth I fucked in the Castle Grounds after that party
and two weeks later found this green leakage, Gonorrhea
the doctor at the clinic said. And I thought, Oh my Christ,
that bitch. That filthy pus-bag. She gave it me, then made
me give it to my wife. And now I'll have to fucking tell
her. And that's what I saw in Buffy when she threw
her head back as my hand went in. Young she might
have been, but pure she wasn't. I knew the worm was
in her. And then was when it died on me, just when I
had her ready in a big X on the bed. And that was why
I gave her the bottle, I thought of that boyfriend of hers
boasting to his mates about how many times, you can go
on and on like that when you're eighteen, nineteen, it's
hard at will or to a single touch, a kid like that, I could
break his back, I could pick him and hug him to death,
Buffy, I said, Here you go. Try this instead, How's this for
size? Because nobody gets out of it laughing, not with me,
there's a few who've found that out. Though sometimes
when they close their eyes and throw their heads back
on the pillow that way, a grimace and a laugh look just
the same.

So I said, Is it too tight?

She watched me, eyes aswarm with glitters. (God, she
had eyes like a tiger.)

Like I say, I took it as a nod.

I'll loosen it a bit, I said.

I got up from the chair and went across to the bed as
she sat up. She held herself half-turned away, lifting her
wrists a little higher up her back to help me. I liked the
way she did that, and the way her head was bowed as
she waited. I could see every tiny hair on the back of her
neck, and under the hemmed neck of her yellow T-shirt

the rest of her would be the same colour of suntan her neck was. And I suddenly wanted her, there and then and just like that, the way she was, it's always some little thing turns you on, not just the ropes, but that thin gold neck-chain she was wearing, and the way I could see her leg doubled on the bed and, between the white ribbed top of her sports sock and the worn cuff of those tight jeans, a glossy brown shin, gorgeous as a tennis-player's.

And when I think of it now, I'd have liked to start there, kissing her there, just where the elasticated top of her sock was printed on her skin, the white sock almost incandescent in my memory now against the dark of her skin. Kissing her there, licking her there, licking all around her leg above the circle of that sock. Then take that big kitchen knife and make a nick, a little cut, in the cuff of each leg of her jeans. And start tearing or slitting the cloth slowly upwards, to the knee and higher, always just ahead of where my mouth, my tongue, has reached, my hot pink rough tongue, licking every suntanned inch, every tiny brown mole of those spreadeagling legs, the way a dog will clean a plate, licking my way upwards slowly till she can't bear to wait for me and I can lick no further and the muscle underneath my tongue is aching. That's what I'd do to her now, I would, if she was here, I'm throbbing like a gearstick for her now.

But sometimes it can take as little a thing to put you off as turn you on.

I bent my head, I couldn't help doing it, and kissed the side of her bare brown neck, just where her neck-chain crossed the artery you have there, or perhaps it's a tendon, it stiffened as I touched it with my mouth.

One of the knots to the headboard was too tight to undo, I kept fiddling with the damn thing but I couldn't unpick it with my fingers.

I need to use the bathroom, she said. Badly.

I bet you say that to all the boys, I said.

I kissed her again on the neck-chain.

It's urgent, she said.

My period is starting, she said.

What? I said.

What? I said.

My period, she said. You know what a period is, don't you?

That was when I stopped fiddling with that knot with my fingers and went and opened the drawer by the sink and found the knife.

A fly crawls across the fly-smudged windscreen. Then another. Then another. They're on the bonnet too. And when I look down at the ground I can see others crawling on the potholed asphalted pavement and the kerbstones, climbing the scraggy blades of the yellow grass that grows in their cracks, it's been so long now since it rained.

But they're not flies. Not house-flies, anyway. 'Flying ants', we used to call them (though they don't look anything like ants). I remember them from when I was a kid, there would always be one day in summer when, somewhere on the way home from school, there'd be a local plague of them, crawling, swarming (and always on a day like this, a warm grey day). I used to wonder what happened to them afterwards, because you never saw them the next day, it was as if they were all born on the same birthday and the day after they were gone for ever, or at least until the same day next year (not the same date, just the same day, the same warmth and greyness). It was the same with the black-and-gold caterpillars you'd find another day, on those ragwort plants, I know it's called ragwort because I brought one to school once for Nature Class and she told me, a green plant with yellow flowers like little dandelion flowers, and the yellow of the caterpillars was the same yellow too, for camouflage I suppose, because Nature is very clever. (They must have all become butterflies or moths in time, though I don't know what kind.)

I look across the dry school field to the school buildings, modern, flat-roofed, brown brick, factory-style. But it's the sight of the red dust of those foot-worn paths in the grass and, on the football pitch, the stiff, worn reddish hollows between the goalposts that makes me cry. It's the thought of all the children's feet it takes to wear a path or a patch like that, little feet in shoes their mother probably polished for them and put on them and probably even tied the laces too, like my mother did when I first went to big school, it all comes back to me in hot tears, it's like a grief for myself and everyone I went to school with then, and for all those flying ants, and the caterpillars I stopped to look at on the way home after school, on their ragwort plants, who turned into some kind of butterfly and died, but who are still there every year, on a special day, one of those days when you get that sense of *déjà vu* they call it, because it's as if you've lived through it before, the temperature, the kind of light (a warm grey day like this one, even that cloud unshadowing the school field suddenly, just as it is now, and now unshadowing the buildings too), and you know that everything has been before and will be again, the shadow fleeing across the world, everything going on the same way, nothing changing, nothing being lost, even the tears, the same hot tears, the same ache in the throat I had when I cried as a child, but everything being born and dying, like these flying ants that crawl across my windscreen, Rusty's windscreen, all these and now another one, and now another one, they're crawling everywhere today, and nowhere tomorrow, they'll be under the ground, or in the sky (this luminous grey cloudy sky) and Rusty too, and Buffy, except that they'll all come back, they'll all come back. Not next year, but in another year, or in another life, we'll all come back. They'll come and I'll

257

come. Rusty will come, and Buffy, and next time, next time we'll meet, we'll meet by purest chance, our eyes will meet and it will stay like that, that glance will be enough to light our lives. Next time our eyes will meet for ever, and they'll love me.

Thirteen

Up here I'm a long way higher than I was last time, or the time before that. I'm almost at the ridge. Just now there was a buzzard floating out over those screes and gullies and I was looking across at it, above it. It's a long haul all the way up here. But I'm safer, this high up. Well away from Sunday ramblers. Only a serious walker would come this high. Nothing up here but those scruffy sheep, if sheep is what they are. (The way they go up these cliffs and rocks, they're like those ibex on *The Living World*. You see them tiptoe across the ledges like that, you'd never believe a dull thing like a sheep could be so dainty.)

The one problem is: I don't have the binoculars this time. What I could do with is that buzzard's eyes.

I sit for a minute, sweating, looking down on a tiny, slow car on that long hill doubling back on itself opposite, across the valley, towards that drab mining village. I'm high enough to see it from here, the black railyard and two rows of terraced houses at the foot of those black dunes. Them you can't miss, even with the naked eye. They're what you might call a local landmark. That's history, I suppose. Egypt's got the pyramids, Glamorgan's got mountains of slag. Like they say, breathtaking by moonlight.

Further around, on the green skirt of this mountain I'm sat on, I can see their cottage, all the way down there, so small it took me a second or two to pick it out by eye. Last time I came I remember I could see the kids' toys on the grass, through the binos, I could almost have told you what the registration number of that blue Volvo estate was. I could see my wife clear and close enough to count the stitches on the arse of her jeans.

But the strange thing is that although I was much closer to their cottage then, and closer to the other houses down there, I felt as if I was invisible. I had everything held slightly quivering in the circle of my binos, and it never even crossed my mind I might be seen as well.

But now, even though I'm all the way up here, and the cottage is so small I almost have to strain to make it out, I feel conspicuous. I feel watched. And huge. So huge that if I stood up just far enough for my head and shoulders to be above the outline of the ridge behind me, I'd loom so big down there I'd cast a shadow right across the valley like a cloud, everyone down there would turn their heads, look up, and I'd be silhouetted black, like the giant in the picture book.

And not only that. They'd know who I was as well, and that I was a wanted man. Because everything in your life is different when you're on the run and you can't afford a first mistake. So you have to be shyer than a rat, of everyone and every thing. Which is why (and this is crazy, I know, but I'm still doing it) I'm crouched peering down over this rock seven-eighths of the way up a mountain as if it was a windowsill and there was someone in the room who I didn't want to see me. I'm afraid even to open a can of pop in case a sheep hears the hiss and goes down to report it. Like when I heard that sheep cough just now and it almost stopped my heart, it was like someone coughing in their own bedroom. I never knew a sheep could cough like that, or clear its throat you'd almost have to say. You would have sworn it was a man.

I scan the ridge above me again. I've got to keep climbing, I know. Where I'm sitting now might be grassy and flat and sheltered and protected between two big rocks, the ideal place to camp. But only when I'm at the top will I feel there's not someone above me, watching me as

I watch down into the valley. I have to load up again and keep going, lugging this little one-man tent I bought in Neath and the Calor-gas ring and the canister for it and the spare one and the tinned food and the new enamelled plate and mug and the other camping stuff. And then, once I've finally unslung that, and pitched the tent, I have to come back down to this point again for the armfuls of bracken spears and fronds I pulled up lower down the slope for camouflage because I could see they didn't grow this high. All that grows up there is this springy short grass and the greyish lichens on the rocks.

When you think of it, it's crazy even coming here. Putting up a tent on a bare mountain, when down there is a cottage that's a damn sight better appointed for a long-term quiet retreat than any fucking one-man tent is, and a woman who's the only person left who might still help me.

Which I suppose is why I came here. Because I didn't know where else to go. I turned here without thinking, without having to think, like the needle of the new compass I've got round my neck on a cord keeps turned to north. When you're on the run, the world is too big a place for you to hide in. You have to go somewhere you know, even if it's only to a piece of mountainside above a house in Powys.

Of course, if they ever send a helicopter over I'll be spotted in a minute. And from that point of view, at least, I'd have been safer hiding out lower down, in the woods, like Marty Sheen and Sissie Spacek. Or like all those Vietnam veterans living in the forests in Oregon or Washington State, I saw a documentary about them on TV once, they were weird characters, it was like they couldn't cope with everything they'd seen and done out in Vietnam, the Army had turned them into psychos and now they couldn't live in the real world, or the real world wouldn't let them, like with Rambo in *First Blood*. (It was a pity about that muppet-mind Stallone, that could have been a good film but for him.)

But me, I'd never feel safe in a wood. Any wood. Too many eyes. Too many places for things to hide in and jump out at you from. Too many sudden movements, even if it's only caused by the wind, I'm always a little uneasy in a wood, even by daylight, let alone to camp there in the dark. It probably all goes back to that scene in *Bambi* or *Snow White*, where at night all the branches become arms, the twigs turn into knobbly, clutching fingers, and all the forest animals come out, as fierce, glowing eyes, those yellow eyes are all you see of them. It scared me as a kid, that scene. And it's like that thing the priest said to us once in school: You are born in a clear field, but you die in a dark wood. He said it was a Russian proverb, and the Russians didn't believe in God or Jesus Christ or Our Holy Mother Mary, but he was telling it to us now because it explained so perfectly why we should go to confession regularly, because the dark wood was like the unabsolved soul, and, although it was a Russian saying, he would go as far as to say that if only Russians did the same, and God knows in their Godlessness they should have had good reason to, even they would understand that proverb better, because it wasn't just simple peasant wisdom. It was a parable, like Jesus's. And what was a parable? You, boy. That's right. *An Earthly Story with a Heavenly Meaning*. And Graham Ford got smacked on the ear that other time because he got it wrong, he said *Earthy Story with a Heavenly Meaning*, and old Spiers smacked him hard with a book and said, *Earthy? Earthy?*, perhaps this would make him realise that what his ear was for was listening, and to listen better next time. And we all laughed, except of course for Fordie. But we all hated that old bastard with his jokes and his sayings and the way he would suddenly hit you without warning, coming up behind you, like he hit me that once when he said I'd been talking and I hadn't and I said, *Sir, I wasn't*, tears in my eyes almost because it stung and because I hadn't been, and he said not to try to lie to him, not to ever try to lie to him, because God knows everything about you, and so do I, He knows it even before you do. Not just your inner thoughts but even things you haven't thunk yet, that was how he always put it, old Spiers, that was his little joke. Even things you haven't thunk yet. He always put on a kind of pugnacious comical face when he made a joke, and looked at every one of the boys in turn to make sure you'd got it, and you'd sit in your desk and laugh when he looked at you. But I never believed him, I never believed a thing he said, even about God, the old bastard, because his coat was frayed and his shoes were always worn lopsided at the heel and his breath stank, he'd put his face towards you and you'd smell the lies on his breath, because no one with a blast of garlic breath like that could ever be telling you the truth, I knew that much.

But that was what he said that time about the sinful soul, and how sinful meant what it said, it meant sin-full, absolutely full up to the brim with sin:

> You are born in a clear field,
> but you die in a dark wood.

And that scared me too. Like that bit in the cartoon film did. Not what he was saying about confession. (He was always going on about confession, the old bastard. He must have had a guilty conscience about something.) But the saying itself, Christ, I thought. That's what it must be like. That's how it's going to be. And I knew that one day I would have to die too. Like that. In that dark wood of the soul. No, not of the soul. Fuck the soul. I don't believe in the soul. In that dark wood of fear, of simple fear, and of knowledge that that was what you were going to do now: die.

It was as if it only then hit me, for the first time. That even I was going to die. I must have been about fourteen.

And I don't like thinking about it even now, that dark

wood. The clear field I can imagine. And I like to think of that, it's a summery meadow, full of long seeded grass and flowers (they might be poppies or cornflowers, I don't really know what kinds of flowers they are, but they're all growing there, so many of them, like sometimes you see daisies starry on a lawn). And that's how I always wanted Mandy's childhood to be, and Darryl's of course, but Mandy's most of all because, I don't know, she was always my favourite, she was always Daddy's Girl. I wanted her to be playing in that meadow, in that clear field, and Carol and I were loving parents looking on, proudly watching her. Then she sees us and gets up from the grass and comes running towards us, she's smiling, and it's all in slow motion. (And I know that probably sounds pretty corny, I mean that's how they always shoot a scene like that in films. Only, when you think about it, all the things most people ever want are pretty corny too. If we only could we'd like to live the lives of the people in some TV advert rather than our own, and who can blame us? Because nothing in our life ever works out how we want it to. And there's nothing surer than that it never will. Even when you're a kid, out in the middle of that clear, grassy field, the wood starts growing inwards. It's growing from the edges while you're sat there playing.)

I'm about to shoulder my load and start climbing again when I catch a movement down there, outside the cottage, a figure, I can't see who at this distance.

Except I know it is my wife.

I can't see what she's doing, only that she's not moving, just standing there outside the door. She doesn't seem to be doing anything. She might be standing on that back step wondering whether to cut the lawn or not today.

Except I know she is staring straight back up the mountain at me.

She can't see me squatted here, pick me out, a single figure, off a huge rough mountainside of trees rising to bracken rising to outcropped rock. Up here I'm past spotting, let alone recognition.

Except I know she is looking at me. That she knows I might be out here somewhere. That I might even actually be looking at her now, this very instant.

Because I don't know how much she knows about me yet, about what I've done. But it occurs to me that of course the police will already have traced her, that they'll have been to see her, just on the off-chance of me being there, or in case she may at least have heard from me, a hurried phone call from a desperate man on the run (made no doubt with a single coin before the pips went). Let's face it, the police don't care which way they get their information or who from, to them the world is just a rat's nest anyway. I suppose the way they see it is, even if a wife can't legally testify in court against her husband doesn't mean to say that she can't be the one to turn him in.

Except I know she won't turn me in.

I know that she wants to get in touch with me instead, and that that's what she's doing now, down there, standing outside the doorway of that cottage. She's trying to *commune* with me, for Christ's sake, like with the Beast of the Mountain, or the Poor Giant who nobody loves and everybody is afraid of (everybody except the miller's daughter, the miller's black-eyed daughter). (The miller always had a lovely daughter in those stories. In the pictures in Mandy's book she was blonde, blonde as the straw she span into gold. But she pitied the giant because he loved her, and because that was how her heart was. She pitied the poor beast on the mountain, and the miners in the mine.)

And my heart comes into my throat to think what we have come to in our marriage, me hiding up here on the bare hillside like a wild thing and her living down there with another man, perhaps already pregnant with his child, if not with someone else's.

Though what does it matter now, whose child it is? I don't even know if my own children are my own. Who ever did in the whole history of the world? (That ginger or auburn light in Darryl's hair. Years I noticed it and wondered, Whose?) All you can ever guarantee is who the mother is.

And perhaps she's already knitting for it, like she did with Mandy, sitting there, full of her own secret. I can remember that, how still and calm and secretive she became, as if she knew something I didn't, and she did of course, feeling it inside her. And I now know too that was where I started losing her. Because it didn't matter to her (any more than it does to any woman) *whose* child or foetus it was once it was there. And it doesn't matter to her now. Because now it's *hers anyway*. It's her woman's secret, and that secret is sufficient to itself, it's all that occupies her now. She barely thinks of the sexual father to it or of the other man who will accept it as his own and bring it up in good faith that it is. She barely thinks of that man who is her second husband now. Just like she barely thinks even to come to the back step to stare up the mountain where the man who was her first husband is hiding like a hunted animal, and for all she knows the dogs and beaters already in the bracken lower down.

And I think of all I've done in hatred out of loss of her.

I get to my feet. It's a kind of defiance. I have to stand up, disclose myself to her, break the skyline of this ridge behind me and become that unmistakable, bulking silhouette that will cast the valley dark. I am what I am. I'm up here like the yeti, or the last live bear. I stand there, arms outstretched, feeling as exposed as for a sniper's bullet, and I scream her name as loud as my throat will.

But of course she betrays me in this. (As in everything else.) While I'm still screaming, and before it can even carry the distance down the mountain to her (if carry that far it even could), she turns away and goes inside.

At least you didn't come home from Spain pregnant, I said.

(She must have been in that bathroom a good hour. Which is a long time in a bathroom when you're not even taking a shower or a bath (which she wasn't, because I would have heard the water running longer).

I'd have thought she'd be glad of a bath after travelling all day. But perhaps she didn't trust me not to come in on her when she'd taken her clothes off. (I don't know what kind of a shit she thought I was.)

But I played fair, and after I locked her in I went and made a pot of coffee and put two cups out and poured myself one. Then I went and fetched two glasses and the bottle of Southern Comfort I'd seen in the kitchen cupboard. (I thought she could probably do with a shot of that and I didn't think she'd mind me having one as well, keeping her company in it, as they say.)

So I sat down again and smoked a couple more cigarettes and drank two Southern Comforts neat and a couple of cups of coffee (cold from the pot the second was) and just kind of waited for her to come out and rejoin me.

Like I say, I'd locked her in the bathroom from the outside, so she'd feel safe in there. I wasn't worried about her being in there on her own, even for that length of time, because earlier I'd gone through everything in there with a fine tooth-comb. It was one of those small, internal bathrooms, about the size of a toilet on a train. You know the kind, where the air extractor comes on when you pull the light cord. No windows even for light or ventilation, let alone to open and scream for help from or break out of or smash a jagged shard of glass from to plunge in your assailant's back as he embraces you. (I can't remember what film that was in, but it always struck me as pretty

267

far-fetched that an ordinary sliver of window glass would do that, let alone kill the man stone dead.)

(More likely, I'd have thought, to snap in two or cut your fucking hand to ribbons first.)

I'd cleared the medicine cabinet of any glass bottles too, though, not to mention things like her razor and blades. (There were two razors in the cabinet, actually. I was going to ask her about that some time. I mean, one razor in a girl's bathroom is one thing, obviously they have to shave their legs and underarms and so on, sometimes they even shave their bush so it doesn't show outside a swimsuit, my wife used to do that every summer. But two?)

Anyway, I'd taken out everything I could see that might start giving her ideas. So I knew she was safe in there. But, like I say, she was a hell of a long time coming out again. And when she did try the knob, and then rap the door for me to unlock it for her again, she kind of hung back, like someone who'd rather stay inside and talk to you across the doorstep.

I have a slight problem, she said. Or not so slight, actually. I suppose you'd better know about it. Given the situation.

I looked at her.

It's my period, she said.

It's come on early, she said.

The point is, she said, I need more tampons. Or will do very soon.

I thought there were some in the bathroom, she said. But I seem to have run out.

I went and got the glass of Southern Comfort I'd poured her almost an hour ago and held it out to her.

Cheers, I said.

I thought you might feel like a drink, I said.

I smiled.

I'll join you in one, if I may.

She was just looking at the glass, which I was still

268

holding out. She was looking at it with a kind of frown, a look of irritation almost, like she hadn't understood or couldn't even think about a question like that.

And she turned her back on me. And went back into the bathroom and slammed the door.

And when I think about that now, I can see I made a big mistake in letting her get away with something like that. I mean, ignoring me like that. (Not to mention ignoring the drink I'd gone to the trouble of pouring for her, I'd even put a fucking icecube in it for her, although that had melted by then.)

In fact, looking back I can see how I handled the whole thing wrong from the outset. Because I lost the initiative there somehow. Lost the upper hand. Because, let's face it, the initiative lay in that look she gave me when she saw me open her drawer and turn towards her with that seven-inch kitchen knife, and for a second she didn't know if I was going to use it on her or the ropes.

And where I lost the initiative, and lost her too, was in wanting her to 'like' me, find me 'interesting', I shouldn't have cared about that. I should have just put her through it, like the others. Because you can't give them a choice, girls like her. They're all the same. They think the way they look is their privilege, they think it comes free, gratis and without charge. It's just their good luck and they can use it any way they want to, because the bitches grow up from the age of fifteen knowing they've got most men dangling on a hook before they even start. Even before they're out of school uniform and ankle-socks, they know it. Buffy was like that, I used to watch her coming out from school, a Big Girl now, a Prefect now, in the Upper Sixth, her last summer in grammar school, already thinking about 'university' probably, and all the boys she'd meet there and all the attention she'd get, but still a schoolgirl, with her books in that worn old leather music-satchel that was just scruffy enough to be chic instead of swottish, and that little uniform skirt she couldn't have worn much shorter without inciting a Public Disorder let alone infringing school rules, and those short white socks to show off her bare brown legs. It used to break my heart to see her legs. And that's what they want. They want you to eat your heart out for them. They want you so you can't take your eyes off their legs, but they never want to make the payoff with what's between them.

All they want to do is turn you on, and leave you drooling in your pants.

I told her this, just so she was under no illusions.

I've seen you, I said. You think you're great. Heart-throb Queen Of Canton High, Miss Jailbait, 1983. Miss Teenage Wet Dream. You and that friend of yours. The dark one with the big tits.

You both think you can play around at being sexy, I said, because you're still in school. Because you think that all you're dealing with is schoolboys.

But sex is not a game, I said. And I don't play.

And that was how I should have treated Rusty.

Because no woman ignores me like that and gets away with it. Not any more they don't. So that when she tried it I should have pulled her up short. Reminded her of who was in control.

In fact, I should have said right out what crossed my mind when she brought up the subject:

At least you won't have to worry about getting pregnant.

That was what I thought when she told me. And that was what I should have said. Because at that point it would have taken her down a peg or two. (In fact, it would have turned her inside out. It would have gutted her. Just the knowing what was coming.)

But instead I tried to make some feeble fucking joke out of it. I tried to be a wit. I even fucking said it twice.

What? she said.

I grinned. I said it again:

At least you know one thing. You didn't come home from Spain pregnant.)

She looked at me.

Though in any average year, I said, I suppose a good few do. After the old Holiday Romance.

And all that happened was that it happened again, would you believe it. That frown went across her face again, that look of irritation. (Not just to say she had more important things than jokes on her mind but, beyond that, as if, frankly, I was getting on her fucking nerves.)

She didn't answer me. And again she turned her back.

And again I made the same mistake, and let the whole thing pass.

And, with her, somehow, that was how it always was.

And that was what I meant about the racoon, and what made me think of it. Because, with Rusty, I never did get through to her somehow. Any more than Mandy could scratch that racoon up off the page and cuddle it. No matter what I said, it fell flat. And I couldn't seem to pull back from that position of wanting to be liked, of wanting her to realise she could enjoy my company.

(You meet people like that. No matter how hard you try, you never seem to hit it off with them. Probably *because* of how hard you're trying. They can tell you haven't got the Inner Certainty. And once they sense that, you've blown the chance. You'll never earn their respect now. And after that, the harder you try, the worse it gets. Okay, they'll tolerate you. Or patronise you. Yeah. But there's no way back once someone's got you slated for a poodle. You can tell from the way they treat you. You can see it in their eyes.

And the only way to change that look would be to kill them. Smash them on the head with a tyre-jack or suddenly slip a knife in their guts, all the people who think they've got something over you. Then you'd watch that shrinking light of astonishment their pupils make as they realise they're dying. And at that point they'd Know Different, they'd know they'd been wrong about you, that you weren't their poodle, or anybody else's. That you never had been. But by then, of course, all this instant enlightenment would be too late. For them, at least.)

But she turned away. Turned her back on me a second time. Like I'd let out a fart in a phone-box. (As if to show that even to *hear* a remark like that was beneath her.)

It was a half a minute later that she turned around and looked at me. Those dark eyes were working, thinking.

All this time I've been wondering two things, she said. Why you're in my flat. And where it is I've seen you before. But now I'm starting to wonder how the hell you know I've been to Spain.

She thought of something, and looked across the room towards the bag she'd been carrying when she came in. She ran over to it and looked at a label on the handles. She shook her head and looked at me again. For the first time now her eyes looked scared.

It's just a flight number, she said. This wouldn't have told you where I'd come from.

I gave her a kind of modest grin.

So how did you know? she said. How did you know I've just come back from Spain?

I shrugged.

I know a lot of things.

She watched me. I liked her being scared. I could see her breathing flutter. (I could almost feel her heartbeat from it.)

Like what? she said.

What do you know? she said.

About me, she said. What do you know about me?

I grinned and shrugged.

Who are you? she said.

And then she must have thrown some kind of wobbly because she came up to me and started screaming it.

Who are you? Who are you? Who are you?
I had to slap her hard to shut her up.

What wakes me must be the sun coming through the
tent walls among the shadows from the bracken laid
crossways on the top. But there's a moment when I can't
remember where I am, opening my eyes and staring up
at those shadows, like someone coming out of general
anaesthetic. It's as if the tent is in the leaf-shade of a
jungle, overhung by ferns and saw-toothed palms.

I was dreaming something, but the jungle displaces it
and it's already gone. I never remember what I dream.

I did the right thing last night, in not even opening that
bottle of whisky I'd carried all the way up. Because in the
end I slept like a baby. I must have needed sleep.

It's only seven-thirty by my watch, and it's already
getting hot and sweaty inside the tent. I lie here with
the stuffy smell of the fabric's newness and the reek of
the bracken leaves and the sappy smell of the broken
stems, it all takes me back to when I was a kid, I don't
know when it was, how old I was, but I remember hiding
in the standing bracken, in Leckwith woods it was, with
that peaty reek of fronds and spores and growth, like the
smell of the tomato plants in Uncle Charlie's greenhouse,
I used to love that smell too, I thought it was from those
little yellow flowers on the plants, but it wasn't, it was
the leaf, Uncle Charlie told me, and he broke a piece of
leaf off and held it to my nose for me to smell, rich, faint,
that scent, and the smell of this bracken harsher, rawer,
pungent is the word, because it's wild I suppose. It's
amazing the memory there is in a smell, you breathe it
in just as far as your sinuses and the years fall away from
you, you're a kid again with one nostril blocked with snot,
hiding in a forest of ferns. Because there's nothing like
full-grown bracken for hiding in, you can crawl between
the stems and be totally unseen, it's another world down
there, or like the world was when everything was humid

swamp and tree-ferns and giant dragonflies and lizards. I don't know how old I was that afternoon, but I can smell the bracken still, and the heat was dappled on my back through the fronds as I lay there, I'm lying on my belly and listening to someone, another boy, crashing and plunging through the ferns towards me, he doesn't know where I'm hiding, then he stops and it's quiet, I can't hear him any more. And we're both listening. Flies, and the sound of the bracken moving in the wind. And I know he's watching too, watching for a head of bracken to move where the stems grow too close for me to crawl between without touching them, or perhaps he's already seen it moving and is quietly circling around behind me, crawling on his belly too now, like an adder (the one thing you have to look out for in bracken is adders, they have diamonds on their back and they're poisonous, the one poisonous British snake, because grass-snakes and slow-worms aren't, and slow-worms aren't even snakes at all but legless lizards, come to that). And I'm lying there and listening to this other boy coming stealthily towards me, he's holding the fronds aside and stepping carefully, he's still not sure where I'm hiding, and there's a half-scared grin on his face and on mine. I'm lying hidden, and I can feel the splashed heat on my back, and I know no one can see me. But I can't see the boy who is searching for me either. And everything, anything is better than the waiting to be found, so that you want to break the tension by screaming out that you're there. Because the shock of suddenly *being* discovered will wring a worse scream out of you, a terror up from the roots of you, perhaps it's the old memory of being hunted that comes out in that child's fear of being found, caught, and turned to stone, even when it's only in a game under the bracken, but the terror of being startled by the boy who is looking for me so great that in the end I can bear it no longer and stand up, surfacing sudden as a bather in the chest-high bracken heads and screaming to terrify him out of his skin before his shout of discovery could do that to me.

And, lying there in the tent, I think of those chickens coming home to roost at last. Because it's as if I only played commandos and cowboys and Indians and hide and seek and all those games in the woods and the long grass and the ferns as a kind of training for this, for being hunted now. The way kittens go through all those games they play so they can learn to hunt and kill and stay alive.

And so this is it. It's my turn now. I'm not the hunter now. The eye, tooth, claw. Not any more. I'm the one being hunted. The trembling animal half-hidden in the grass-stalks, waiting with its eyes closed. And I know now it's not the owl's sudden, penetrating grip which kills you. It's the long-expected shock of it.

I sit up in the sleeping bag. The kitchen knife is stuck upright in the ground next to the pillow of my rolled jacket. It has three brass rivets in its handle. I pull it out of the earth and look at it and wonder if I'd ever be able to put it into my own guts. (If I'd *have* the guts.) Like that Jap writer. Whatsisname. Tried to take over the Imperial Japanese Army. Used to pose around on motor bikes, in loincloths, carrying a samurai sword. Perhaps that was what he did it with, not a knife. (Perhaps you have to do it with a sword or it doesn't count. The right tool for the job. They're maniacs for ritual, the Japs.)

I sit up higher and pull off my black T-shirt and take up a fold of the flesh at my belly with one hand and with the other bring the point of the knife to touch it. More than touch it: feel its sharpness, a pressure just before it breaks the skin.

And I wonder what Rusty would feel, when she heard about it. How I sat here alone on a mountainside with a knife I'd taken from her own drawer, just that and a rucksack and a gold chain round my neck that used to be round hers and that I'd asked her for luck. Because I told her I didn't want her to wear it for anyone else, not that way, not when it was the only thing she did wear. Because she looked so beautiful. And I knew she would. Wear it again, or just leave it on, no matter what she said. Even if she didn't mean or intend to. Because let's face it she didn't even know she'd been wearing it that time till I took it up off her neck in my fingers and said it was a nice one and asked her if I could have it, would she take it off for me. Any more than I was conscious of wearing it myself until this minute. It's something you just forget, like a gold sleeper in your ear.

I press the knifepoint a fraction further into the roll of flesh. But I realise I could never do it this way. Not with this knife. And not up here, alone in this tent, on this mountaintop. (Because if it was in a film, even though Rusty wasn't here with me, watching me, she'd *know*, she'd understand exactly what was going through my mind at the end. Because the camera would be watching, the film would cut from me to her and her to me and then, when I had died, straight back to her, and it would be like something accidentally crossed her eyes for just a second, some sad thought, perhaps it was just a dead sparrow in the gutter, a baby sparrow that had fallen out of a nest, or a cloud crossing the sun and the light dulling at the window for a moment. Just some sad, completely unconnected thing.

(But then, eventually, the detectives would come and tell her anyway.

This is all he was wearing, the one will say.

And he takes the chain from a little clear polythene bag like they use for collecting traces or samples in, and drops it on the table into a little pile of links.

And this is the knife. And these are the keys. We found the car in Neath.

He left this letter for you in the tent, the other one says.

But she ignores him and takes up the chain to its full

length, by the clasp. It sways, just clearing the tablecloth. Then she lets go, sees it collapse into a little gold worm-cast again. Only now she takes the letter. She looks at the detective as she does so. Her eyes are dark, ceaseless.

I know what you think, she says. You'll just have to go on thinking it.

You didn't know him, she says.

Don't ever ask me, she says. What you know you know.

He was a strange guy, she says. A strange, gentle guy.

And maybe there'll just be a catch in her voice, or her eyes will shine with tears.)

(Because in a film there's never a wasted gesture or a useless emotion. Everything's as clear to the characters, the people in the film, as to the people watching it. It has to be. There's never any misunderstanding at the end of a film, because when Shane rides off everybody has to have the same emotion as the little kid who's calling after him. Because a film is like God. It's a witnessing of everything. Nothing that exists is not witnessed. From the outside, from the inside. And nothing that is not witnessed exists. That's all there is. God is a movie camera. And his film is a truth no one can argue with.)

And so it must have been easier to do it the way that Jap writer did, with his cohorts around him and the press and TV cameras focused on him, ready to beam the whole thing round the world. (Anyway, he'd probably backed himself into a corner where he would have lost face if he hadn't, like the ancient Romans after a defeat.)

But if I did it up here no one would ever know what my last hours and minutes were like. Nobody would know how I felt. I'd just be like a mysterious corpse in a detective story. There'd just be a body, and a knife, and blood on a groundsheet.

(I saw the blood on the sheet when she pulled away, and it was on me too.

How was that for you? I said.

She looked back at me the way she had been all the

277

way through, she'd never turned her face away, never taken her eyes off mine, her pupils off my pupils almost. In that light her eyes looked almost black. Ceaseless.)

I take the knifepoint away from my belly, let go the fold of fat.

There's a tiny noise outside.

I change my grip on the knife, because (aside from committing hara-kiri by stabbing yourself) you should never hold a knife like that, as if it was a javelin and you were going to throw it. If you want to knife some other cunt you hold it in front of you, almost like you were shaking hands with it. It's harder to take it off you that way, and harder to block.

There's a second noise outside. And the smell of fern is sharp now, fear-sharp, and my heart is pounding.

I'm wide awake, and scared as I was last night in that hour or so I lay here listening before I fell asleep from sheer exhaustion. Scared not of the dark but of what it concealed, of what I couldn't see, and of all those tiny sounds and movements of the tent in the breeze or of outside I could hear, sounds like an army quietly taking up positions all around me.

On my knees I peer out between the poppers of the tent-flap.

Finally I quietly unbutton the poppers one by one.

I duck quickly outside, whirling with the knife.

The sheep plunges away in startlement. Two ravens take off. They're close enough that I can see the blue in them.

Unpopulated mountainside. Grass, wind, rock outcrop and, beyond it and the slope's brow, distance of mountain and valley and dark squarish stain of plantation conifers.

I throw the knife point-first into the ground (it sticks) and stand and piss, wind behind me, looking at it all. A free man still, on a sunny morning, standing pissing in the sunlight. (I suppose it's like that guy on the TV said, the one with terminal cancer. Every new day is An Achievement now.)

I light the Calor stove and put a saucepan of water on it, for tea. It's the last of yesterday's water. Later I'll have to get some from the stream lower down. (It's probably got anthrax in it. What the fuck.)

From up here you can see for miles, down, down across the precipices of the abandoned quarries, down across the valley, to other valleys, other mountains, all a long way away by foot, but close for eyes, for seeing, since seeing is always as the crow flies, or the raven, they're mostly ravens, this high up, I saw another pair of them yesterday doing just that. Flying. Flapping across the valley eastwards, high, high above it all. I heard the croak first, like a pig's grunt. Then I looked up and saw them. Flying above the piled green tapestry woods down there and the hidden river and the sloping sheepfields, over towards the poured black dunes and, beyond them, the tiers and excavations of the opencast site. And I watched them and thought, if I was a raven it'd be simple, that's all I'd have to do, just take off and course for miles on the wind or an aircurrent, with just the occasional flap of a ragged wing.

Except that I wouldn't go the way they were going, over into Glamorgan, back towards civilisation or whatever in the way of it has crept up into those shabby little derelict mining valleys.

Me, I'd go the other way. And I turn my face west again, now, into the wind, looking out across the undulating land: for the next fifteen or twenty miles just bald unpopulated hills and rock gullies dry in summer, waterfalls in winter. Because if you had the right equipment and enough supplies, you could probably hide out there for most of the year and never see a soul. Rustling the odd sheep when you needed to. (Let's face it, even without a rifle or a crossbow or, come to that, even a slingshot, you don't have to be Ernest Hemingway to bag a sheep.)

I went for a walk in that direction last night, just to check the lie of the land. (Because you always need a back door to leave by.) I must have walked for an hour, or more. And it was eerie, for a city boy, to be able to walk that far into nothing or next to nothing, just grass and shale and rock. Like turning your back on land and swimming out to sea, just keep those arms splashing and maybe you'll make it to America. So I just kept walking, and I didn't see another human being or even a trodden footpath unless it was a sheep's (those little criss-cross tracks are everywhere). But no sign that other people come here, or ever have, though I suppose whoever owns the sheep must, sometimes, or the odd walker or camper like myself. And, now I remember, I did actually find a rusted can and a ring of stones where a fire must have been lit, probably last summer or the summer before that. But besides that, zilch. Not a solitary thing. And, after that, I started climbing further and further away from the flat, getting off the level grass, the obvious walker's route. I climbed and scrambled up into the rocks and crags, I suppose I was looking for a last-ditch hiding place, if it ever came to that. And suddenly it was as if no one had ever done this climb, or been here, before. Gone up through just this little gap between the stones and put a hand upon these rocks I used to help me clamber up. And it was a strange feeling, looking at those rough grey rocks and thinking that perhaps no one before had ever gripped them with a hand or trod them with a boot.

I mean, even in what I'd call The Countryside you only have to look at a stone in a footpath or in the wall beside a stile, and that stone is shiny. It might be a real rustic footpath, a proper country stile. But that stone is glossy from where footsoles have trodden it or people have put their hands on it to help them over – what was that line from that poem we did in school, it was written by a priest, the teacher told us. A wonderful poet and a pious

Catholic too. In other words, A man who loved God and who loved the world as well, as we should all try to. *Where generations have trod, have trod, have trod*. Yes, that was it. And that's what the Countryside is to most people: a nature ramble through a managed park, with preordained paths and rails and pointing-finger signs and toilets. (Just like The Sea means driving to Penarth and parking on the promenade and looking out at it across a shingle beach.) Because, let's face it, in this country there's hardly any of what you'll call real Country left. The 'Wild'. (And, like I say, me, I'm a city boy.) But when I climbed up among those crags, with all those greyish lichens on them, I understood the saying *Old as the Hills*. I turned my face into the wind, and I felt it blow all my hair out backwards, and it was like it had always been blowing across those rocks and mountaintops. And I thought, this rock I've just climbed up, foot by foot and hand by hand, isn't on a street plan. It isn't even on one of those big-scale walker's guides, like a 'cairn' is or those tussocks they use to show 'boggy ground', and you think that once you get there you'd find actual tussocks in the grass. It isn't *known* like every kerb-stone in a city is (there can't be one that hasn't been stepped off or spat on or mounted by a tyre). It isn't even known like the view of trees across some farmer's forty-acre field, over the five-bar gate. Or like those cliffs rock-climbers scale, have found a way up, with every chance crack or knob of rock plotted for a handhold or toehold, and the route a white dotted line on a photo of the whole public rockface.

But this rock I'd just climbed was just a rock. Rocks. Blank on the maps and in everybody's mind and memory. A minor detail of an unknown space between explored features (roads, spot-heights, named streams). It's as if it didn't even exist until I climbed up here and my eye fell on it, this huge rock apex growing up out of the grass like a rotten molar or a volcanic mountain that rises suddenly

out of the sea and becomes a new island. Never had a
human foot on it, let alone been mapped and named.

If it was a new island, I could call this rock Boyle
Peak, I thought. (Yeah. Or the Cape of No Hope. Because
there's nowhere else to go now from here, nowhere but
downhill now, Boyle's Peak's the highest point I'll reach.)

But I looked down at the fissured, rough, grey outcrop
rock under my feet and thought, If this didn't exist for
anyone before, was never climbed to by anyone before,
then it's mine by rights at least, since I discovered it.

And from where I was it was already like a relief map
of some rocky badlands, or a photo taken from a U-2
spy-plane eight miles high, every crack a canyon, every
patch of moss a forest. And I lay down on it and put one
cheek on it and shut one eye and looked across it in a
perspective of close range, and it was just like when I'd
looked across those fifteen miles of mountains earlier.
And like when you were a kid, and you'd play for hours
on a flat, rough piece of ground like this, where all the
splits and bumps and runnels were gorges and hills and
defiles, a whole landscape foreshortened in miniature,
and all you'd need here is a couple of toy soldiers to
hide from each other or a jeep to race and skid over the
bumps and topple over at the edge. Because that's all you
do need when you're a kid, somewhere to play, and the
imagination to play on your own. And that's the world.
A couple of yards of beach or a tipped pile of builder's
sand is all the deserts on the face of the earth. Or it can
be peaks like this, with cliffs and caves and valleys, and
every trickle as the sand dries is an avalanche. That's
why kids love playing with sand: it can be any kind of
land you want.

Because probably even as a kid you must know that
people like you don't end up owning land, not real land,
like all of this mountain here, or all those thousands of
acres of some Scottish duke's, or that big piece of Utah
Robert Redford bought. Mostly you won't ever even own

the room you sleep in as an adult. And so you make believe. Like in *Paris, Texas*, where Harry Dean Stanton carries everywhere that old, creased Polaroid snap of those few yards of desert scrub he bought once. And perhaps that's what it is, that everybody wants to own something that's theirs, in a way that you can't with your wife, or even children, your own flesh and blood, not *own* them, not really, because they look at other men and leave you for them, or grow up. And so you perhaps start to think of land instead, something big enough at least to put a house or park a trailer on. As if you could own that any more than you can a bitch of a woman, in truth. Because let's face it, all you really end up even occupying is that section seven foot by two foot by six foot of municipal ground they take out at the end to drop you in.

So here you are, I thought. You're thirty-six years of age. You're not a kid any more. But this is what you ended up with. A piece of rock outcrop on a worthless piece of mountain even bracken won't grow on. Boyle Peak. And all you can do is sit on your arse on it and watch the horizon till they come for you, like that guy shipwrecked on the desert island in the cartoon, just a pile of sand with a single palm tree growing in it, Christ knows what he'll eat or drink or live on there, all he's got is that pile of sand, the palm tree and the ragged trousers he stands up in.

Plus, of course, the big-busted blonde. She's always there. She's got to be. His only co-survivor.

And as long as she gets washed ashore with him, he'll be content: content even to watch the passing liners disappear over the curve of the earth, then carry on chasing the blonde around the palm tree. Because that's all they ever do in those cartoons. She runs, he chases, like the figures going round a vase. And that's probably how it is for most men, when you think about it. That's all they ever do. They think they're chasing tail. But it's their own. And at least no one can say that of me. Whatever happens from now on. At least I mostly ran down what I hunted.

I must be crazy. I really must be. Slithering and scrambling down a rough mountainside at this time of night. With half a bottle of whisky in me, and the half that's left shoved in my pocket.

But I was going ape up there, the dusk falling around me, just watching that one lighted window far down in a misting valley. Turning things over and over in my mind, and round and round. (The worst thing always about being on your own is not being able to stop yourself thinking.) And then starting to feel the whisky.

And even though it's getting dark now, the moon is higher, and it's like a moon in dreams, so big and bright I feel like a werewolf picking a way down through the black bracken. And the sky so bright with clouds it's like in those old cowboy films, though they shoot those night scenes through blue glass, I read once, really it's three o'clock on a blazing hot afternoon (they need strong shadow for the contrast). It's the Sonora Desert, you can see the sweat on the Apaches' faces in the glistening blue filtered light (they'd have to be Apache, even if that's a tribe that never got within a thousand miles of the Sonora Desert, because they're the only Indians who raid by night, yes, I think that's right, at least that's what they tell you in films, though actually they probably invented that just so they could shoot that scene so often, the darkness, the shadow, the treacherous blue faces gleaming), and always, above the black gully they are creeping through, those high, piled, high-piled luminous silver cumulus, just like tonight, in a sky that shows as deepened blue, okay, but clear as day, clear as outer space, you can see everything in that transparent dark, a blind idiot could see it's really afternoon.

And it's as clear as that tonight. Day For Night Shooting, they call that in the trade. I picked that up from the French film I went to see with my wife that time, it was at the university film-club. *La Nuit Américaine*. American Night. But *Day for Night* is what it was called in English. I don't know why the fuck it *was* called that, now I look back on it, it didn't seem to have a lot to do with this film. (Not that I remember all that much about it as a film. In fact, what the title meant was probably the only thing that struck me from the whole fucking experience.) Anyway, it wouldn't have been my choice of movie in the first place, is what I'm saying, but Carol always insisted on going to see French films, even after she'd left university, so she could Keep Up Her French, keep her ear in, as she used to put it. Though I bet she used to read the subtitles just like me and all the other morons in the audience if the truth were told. A film like that was just a kind of snobbery for her, an insight into *le chic*. Because really she would have loved to be one of those thin, classy Françoise Hardy-style Parisian swingers. One of those chicks who, okay, they're wide open, but they do everything in life with style and flair: smoking, eating, drinking, fucking, all the physical pleasures of life but two. I.e., you can be elegant and chic about everything except your own actual piss and shit.

I suppose the trouble with my wife and me was we were trying to live in different movies.

And this is how it turns out at the end:

Me Crazy Horse. Creeping and stumbling down a mountain in blue late dusk and then stopping, waiting, having another drink of whisky while it darkens, in the peaty, hot smell of the bracken, it's been so hot today and the heat still coming back out of the earth, the bracken fronds black and glittery, as the dusk darkens to moonlight bright as day, at least it is out there, beyond the trees I'm standing in shadow under and watching their cottage from: the left-on light in the glass-roofed conservatory and an outspill of yellow from a lit window at the side.

Me a shadow moving again now, a shadow moving from

a shadow to another shadow, crossing the dry-stone rear wall of their garden and moving over blanched grass as a light goes on in an upstairs window of the house, and I freeze. Then run, crouching, the moon so bright on this side I can see every roughness and irregularity in the undressed stones under my hand as I gain the back wall of the house, directly under that lit upper rectangle. I'm panting, sweating, as I scale the length of the back wall to the corner, then around it, and along the side wall to the lit window on the ground floor. Like I say, the first Apache brave reaching the log stockade then peering in on the interior.

Some fucking interior. Something straight out of rural France, not even rural Powys. The triangle of Brie (cut from a big white wheel of it in the shop), and some of that yellow cheese with holes in, on a wooden platter on the table which is just the other side of the glass I'm looking through. And the bunch of dusty blue grapes in the dish and the stripped stalks from it on the two white hexagonal plates and the crusts of bread and the greenish pips they spat into their hands before they laid them on the plates' edge.

And me Crazy Horse. Me her husband, looking in at it, when all I had up there on the mountaintop today was sweaty corned beef left in the foot of the tin from yesterday, with fat and that shiny gristle of a vein in it, and the ants on it, I had to brush them off, the little bastards, they get in everywhere, and it's true what they say, dead true, they'll take over the world once we manage to blow ourselves to fuck or Kingdom Come. And that was all I had, that and a drink of water warm from the canteen and the last two cream crackers. Followed by my own right hand for R and R, as usual.

I move out from the house again, without concealment now, not bothering about that any more, across the pale lawn to enter the shadow of a tree that is stark as an inkblot. (Me, I'm the blackest, densest object in this landscape. I'm as black and dense as a planet compressed to no bigger than an orange, though it weighs the earth.)

From this angle I can look up at the first-floor window instead, it must be the bedroom. Their bedroom, I can look up at a section of the ceiling, since they haven't even bothered to close the curtains. And why should they, living in a place like this? All that's out here is empty mountain, a few rocks and trees. That's what living in the country does for you, you start to think you've bought privacy at last, and solitude, and even safety. You think the biggest thing that might be watching you out here's an owl.

I've got a headache. An exertion headache. A heat headache. Somewhere behind the eyes. (Or where they say the third eye is.) I take the bottle of whisky out of the haversack and unscrew the cap and throw the cap away.

I swig from the bottle and move out onto the pale grass again, into moonlight. I'm not hiding any longer. (Not that anyone can see me out here anyway, no more than they could when the light in that bedroom window went on and I dropped down by the dry-stone wall, then ran in a crouch. But in fact when you're inside a lit room at night all you can see at the window is your own reflection. There's more danger of being spotted from a dark window than a lit one.)

I watch that bedroom window past the swigged bottle. There's a cross of struts which quarters the section of the ceiling I can see. And I can feel myself coming out of myself. Which would be fine, except that I can still feel this headache. I can't float that off. It's like when you've been running too hard on a hot day as a kid, you're red in the face, sweating, your head throbs, you're ready to explode. It's because it's so hot tonight, it was the same last night, and I couldn't sleep, I just lay there in the tent listening to all the noises again, all the tiny noises all around you that you never hear by day. It's as bad now, worse, if I could listen, if I could hear it, if my head would only stop pulsing that blood into my ears I'd hear it all around me, as I heard it last night, as I heard it out in the darkness of Buffy's garden: the tiny creeping and stirring and ticking and rustling and seething, it's like lying listening to the rain at night, because it's everywhere, it's falling on every stone and leaf and blade of grass, and if I hold my breath, and try to concentrate I can almost catch it in between the surges of the blood in my head: the secret, predatory, insect-like crawling of growth and fornication.

My wife moves out behind the cross of struts in her bedroom window, dead centre, like she was in a telescopic gunsight. And I freeze again instinctively to watch. She looks up, stretches out her arms and closes the red curtains in a movement that in its first instant is a gesture of spreadeagled abandonment. I stare at a pink glow of the curtains, while she turns instead to the man inside. (I know he's up there and I know what they're both there for. Who goes to bed at ten o'clock to sleep?)

(She lifts her arms and crosses her wrists behind his neck. She's warm and wet, wide-open. She closes her eyes, her neck reaching into the kiss.)

Then (and I watch it happen) the light dims behind that glowing screen the curtains make. (Dims, not goes out.) As if the main light in the room has been switched off and a smaller light somewhere else is switched on. (A shaded bulb.) (Or a candle in a candlestick.) For the candle-lit half-lit atmosphere. The flattering romantic glow. The bedside touch.

Okay, I say quietly to that dimmed rectangle. Okay.

Fourteen

She keeps pulling at me to stop, so she can have a rest.

I know she's tired, so I give her a minute or two. Further down, everything's silent as the grave. Though you'd think there was a party in that house, with all those windows lit. (Up here, we'd still hear the music if there was.) They lit up one after the other, and quick, those windows, like the two of them were going through the rooms.

Then we go on again. Up. It's slow work, going at her pace, trying to hold her hand as if you're helping her not dragging her, I don't want her to feel she's being dragged. I know she doesn't want to come. (That's natural, what kid ever did walk up a hill with you without grumbling? But I don't ever want her to feel she's been forced. Abducted.)

In some places now it's up to my chest almost, since I lost the path.

Not much further, Mandy, I tell her.

Meaning only, Till we get through this bracken. (There's still a long way after that. And the ground gets rougher.) But it's over her head here, and I don't know what she makes of all this. I don't want her to get scared.

She's very quiet. In fact she hasn't said a word, all the way up here. It's like she's gone back to sleep. As if she's sleepwalking up here. (Except for the way she keeps pulling at me to stop or slow down.)

I'm out of breath myself, almost. I give us another minute or two. It's still quiet and bright as hell down there.

I don't know how Darryl got left. I thought he could keep up. I shouted a couple of times when I noticed he wasn't there, but he didn't answer. (Which probably means he didn't 'get left'. He might have just stole back. Or hid behind some trees and waited till we'd gone too far ahead. He might just have been scared.)

The bracken is black and glittery. I'd never have believed a night could be so bright, so clear. You could read the newspaper by it.

But I don't think about the newspaper. (Or that face in it.) Under this moon things pale and fall from me, the way they always do. It's a knack like invisibility. Because that's what memory is. Forgetting. If it wasn't you'd go crazy. I read about it, how the brain wipes itself every night, it has to do that, like a tape, or one of those magic boards you can get for kids. You write through the celluloid screen with a pointed stylus, then pull the board out by the tab and push it back, and the writing's disappeared. I remember I bought Mandy one once, in Woolworth's. (Though she probably used it the once, after you showed her how it worked, and then wanted something new, or anyway some chocolate. She never was what I suppose you'd call an enquiring child. Not really.)

Later on we had that magic board hanging up in the kitchen, some scheme of my wife's. She must have been clearing out the kids' toy-box and had this brainstorm and came up with the idea of using that board for a weekly shopping list. Every time we ran out of something or used the last of it, like tea or fishfingers or tins of beans, we were supposed to write it on that board to remind us of what needed replacing, instead of just throwing away the tin or the empty jar. Then you could wipe it clean ready for another week, once you'd done the shopping. Which sounded like a good idea, I suppose. (If not a first-rate fucking wheeze.) Except that nobody remembered to do it, or couldn't be fucking bothered to (including my wife). So all it ever did, that board, was hang there empty. All it ever reminded you of, in fact, was the well-run and efficient household we never had, let's face it, my wife was hardly what you'd call domestic, let alone houseproud. Not in those days anyway. (In fact so far as the state of the kitchen went she was a fucking slut.)

Probably if you could patent that idea now you'd make a fortune out of it. You know, put a magnetised button on the back and you could stick it on a fridge, or anywhere. Run adverts for The Magic Memo or The Shopping List You Never Lose. It's big business, now, selling people gadgets or appliances they don't need and hardly ever use, particularly in the kitchen. Yes, kitchenware must be a multimillion industry these days. You go into Habitat or David Morgan's any day and see the turkeys buying stylish little numbers to slice an onion or press a piece of garlic through or eat an avocado out of or just hang up from a hook under their shelves to look at and have seen. They'll buy anything if it'll make them feel Upmarket, like they're living for a split second like the people in the Sunday supps, the Robert fucking Carrier crowd, every poky semidetached with a microwave and a pedal bin transformed into the gleaming stainless kitchens at the *Quat' Saisons*. Hang on a sec, won't take a minute, just run you up a Caesar Salad or an Omelette Arnold Bennett or a Croque-Monsieur, monsieur.

And that, too, was the kind of thing I was thinking when I went quietly through the back porch and into their kitchen, and stood there for a minute or two. Like the unasked guest, it struck me (because I was outside myself again, like I was watching myself in a film, or directing it even). An unasked guest, who approaches through the garden and then stops short, hesitates to come into an empty room. (Only of course really I was listening, trying to work out where they were and how the house lay.)

And it was standing in that kitchen that really made

me think of things like that. Because it had just been renovated, and the walls hadn't been painted yet or distempered, and they were still that pinkish colour of bare plaster. And I could see the sweeps and ridge-marks of the float in it everywhere, and I actually stood there wondering what kind of local cowboy jobber had made that mess of it or if she'd had a go at it herself, or he had. Until it struck me it was deliberately rough, to give the idea of an old country kitchen, the Rustic Look, because I started to notice how everything in that kitchen was of a style, or at least of a period feel, down to the stone bottle and Kilner jars on the shelving, the brand-new copper-bottomed saucepans hanging underneath in diminishing size, and that chopping board, it must have been a good four inches thick and mortised at the corners like a butcher's block, a real professional's, with the bits of chopped parsley still moist on it and the big knife lying beside them, a knife with a black handle with three rivets in it.

And what I'm saying is that all of this kitchen too was just another colour plate from the Coffee-Table Book of French Farmhouse Cooking, beg your pardon, *Cuisine*. The same book I'd already seen another still-life from through the window at the side. More Rural fucking Chic.

Never a streak of chickenshit on the eggs in the blue-hooped basin on the stripped pine table. Never a print of cowshit on the quarry tile floor. Everything as neat and clean and elegant and phoney as a showroom, in that kitchen of my wife's now.

And as I stood in that kitchen and looked at these things, I understood, as clear as water and for the first time, that it wasn't sex or love or desperation or even money that made her come up here and live with another man and fuck up my life and my kids'.

It was for this. For some dream of this stone-floored kitchen.

And not just because we (she and me) couldn't have afforded things like this, or a place like this (not with me running the T-Bird too, that is). Not because it was out of my reach, my wages, or because there wouldn't have been any point in trying to fake Provence in a four-room rented flat above a butcher's shop in Grangetown anyway.

But because I'd always laughed at things like that. Like with those magazines she used to bring home sometimes, *Ideal Home* or *House and Garden*.

House and Garden? I said.

It was the first time she'd bought it, I think. I picked it up.

We haven't got a garden, I said.

Come to that, I said, and laughed. We haven't even got a house.

And I flicked through it, because I knew I wasn't supposed to find it. And I knew I'd embarrassed her somehow. I knew she was ashamed and felt ridiculous, like I would have if she'd found me with a wank book.

Can you believe this shit? I said.

And I threw that heavy, supple magazine on the table, slap. And I laughed at her again. Because I hate all that Home Counties kitsch, the dream properties, the striped lawn and the cedar trees and the fucking lions on the gate.

And I laughed at her out of malice too. The way I laugh at those things out of envy. (Why not? I admit it. I hate the people who have things like that.) (I'm not Tony Barbecue. I'm no 'Marxist'. There'll be no 're-education' for those bastards. All there'll be for them is a quicklime grave.) (My kind of Marxist is more like Pol Pot. Like he said: Owning a typewriter, even, is a sin.)

I laughed at her for wanting to look at photographs of what we didn't have. I was proving a point. What did these things have to do with us? With her? As far as I knew, in those days we were more into dope and drink than patio furniture and barbecues and exposed stone. We'd never given a fuck about anything as long as there was food in the fridge and the kids had clothes and shoes and there was enough left over to go out on when we felt like it.

And so I laughed at her because I suppose I wanted to keep things the way they were. Not seeing that she was changing her ideas even then. Because what I knew was that when you live the kind of life we were living then, from pay-packet to pay-packet, day to day, night-out to night-out, you've got to stick together. Because that's your world. All you've got is yourselves and other people like you, people who live the same way. Okay, so some of them are dopeheads and headbangers and alkies and just plain no-hopers. I mean in those days we're talking about a social milieu of the fucking patrons of The Marchioness of Bute. Let's face it, it's not exactly the Wine Bar or Bistro style (or some Chelseafied attempt at it). What we're talking about is Sub-Prole City Life.

And so what I understood in that kitchen, and earlier, when I had my nose pressed up against her window, was that I wasn't 'good enough' for her, if you like. Not any more. Not where her head was at. And I hadn't been for years. And now I never would be. Because at least she knows that what I am I am. That I won't change.

(And you'd think, wouldn't you, that any real woman would admire that in a man? Not Carol. Not my cock-taking cunt of a wife.)

I went to the chopping-board and picked up that big kitchen knife and opened a drawer to put it away in, out of sight. But the drawer was the cutlery drawer: the one you'd open first to look for it in if you were given the chance to. So I opened one of the wall cupboards and hid the knife in there, behind some crockery. Because I didn't need a second knife that big. But I didn't want someone else's hand chancing upon it either. (You never know. It always pays to take care of details in advance. And as far as knives are concerned, a stitch in time is better than fifty under surgery, ha fucking ha. Not to mention scars for life.)

No sooner had I closed the cupboard, than she came into the kitchen.

She came in slowly, vaguely. Her head was leaning on one side and she was concentrating on unhooking an ear-ring from its perforation.

In the few seconds before she saw me all I could do was stand and look at her. (Not a few seconds, not that much. It might have been only a single tick on the sweephand, less.)

She was wearing black trousers and a red blouse, off the shoulder, and boots, as if they'd been out that night or were going out. It was an outfit I hadn't seen before, any of it. And it might sound crazy, this, because by now, after all this time, she must have bought and worn a lot of clothes I'd never seen her wear before. But it was seeing her in those new clothes that was the thing that cut me open, made me understand how much I hated her.

She'd just got the ear-ring free. She was looking at me now. It fell to the floor.

Her face went blank. She didn't jump or look startled, like she might have for a complete stranger in her kitchen. Her face just went empty, like it had been wiped. She looked at me. You'd have said she hadn't quite remembered who I was yet. But, looking back, it wasn't that. What it was was that she couldn't quite remember why I shouldn't have been there. Then she did.

What the fuck do you think you're doing here? she said.

I looked at her. I wasn't tense or nervous any more. (It's always been the same, I'm on edge till they see me, realise I'm in the room, as if the most frightening thing is not knowing if they're going to scream or not. But then it's easy. You're on the train. Things just happen, as they have to.)

In my kitchen, she said.

Her voice went hoarse at the gall of it.

In my fucking *kitchen*, she said.

Just walking *in*, she said.

The one hoop in her ear shook with her face.

There was a voice from the rooms behind her.

Carol, he said.

Then, louder:

Carol.

Then closer:

I think you'd better come and see the news.

Then he was standing in the doorway.

Who the hell's this? he said.

Then he knew.

What do you want? he said.

I looked at him. I suppose it's a universal law of life that you can never understand what your wife sees in the man she's going down on.

No, she said. No. I don't believe this.

She put both hands to the sides of her face and stared at me, pulling her bottom eyelids down till I could see the pink.

I just don't believe this, she said.

Then she turned and kind of reeled past him into the hall. Not like she was going anywhere, but as if she just couldn't bear to be in the kitchen any more.

He turned squarer-on to me. I looked at him and put my hand onto the handle of the kitchen knife in my belt, more than anything just to show him I had it. (Even without the knife, I knew I could take him out with one hand in a pocket. If not both.)

Go ahead of me, I said.

Look, he said.

Just fucking do it, I said.

I followed him into the room where they'd been eating earlier. She was on the sofa. The television set was on. Its back was to the window, so I hadn't noticed it before. The news was on. There were police on horseback, long riot-truncheons drawn. Then they were charging into a huge crowd of men scattering across a sunlit field.

I went to the table and swigged out of their unfinished bottle of white wine. I took half the cheese in one bite. I looked at her swallowing. Then at the television. I put the other half of the cheese in my mouth. I looked at her. I'd seen her cry before. Like the man said, There's nothing new under the sun. You can't step in the same stream twice.

I think you'd be well advised to get out of here, he said.

You're not welcome here, he said.

Why can't you just leave me alone? she said.

Her crying turned into a strangled wail of frustration or rage, her mouth turned down at either side, like in those two Greek masks. Like the one that isn't laughing.

Police in pairs were marching men away, some didn't have shirts on, as if they'd been sunbathing.

I ate a piece of brown bread. I watched the television, chewing. Now my wife was staring at it too.

What's this? she said.

Orgreave, he said. Yorkshire.

One man was almost being carried. The nearside of his face was jagged with runnels of blood. They looked like the cracks in a cracked egg.

Llew is up there, she said.

Is he?

They all went up yesterday, she said. In a mini-bus. It was in a kind of slow, vague voice.

They both looked at the set.

A police horse in a stiff-legged prance breasted away a man with a camera. Men bleeding were pushed and pulled into the back of a black van.

Jesus Christ, she said.

She stared at the set.

What's happening to this country?

She got up and switched the television off.

I can't take all this happening at once, she said.

She stared at the dead screen for a minute with her face in her hands. Then she looked at me.

You know the police have been here, do you? she said.

It was at this point, out of the corner of my eye, that I saw him look aside. His head just half-turned once on its axis and looked at the tall cupboard in the corner and then it was looking back at me again. As quick as that. Like a fieldsman taking his eye off the game for a moment just to check that another fieldsman's in the right position.

A detective and a local sergeant, he said.

He cleared his throat.

The detective was from Cardiff, he said.

What's this wine? I said. Excellent wine. Top flight. A real high flyer. Airline wine.

She said: Meursault. Do you know the difference?

Which generations no doubt have trod, have trod, have trod, I said. But it tastes okay.

Wine buff of the year, she said.

I looked at her. I suddenly realised what her trouble really was. She was bored with things. Everything bored her.

Me Crazy Horse, I told her. Fly me.

They wanted to talk to Carol, he said. They wanted to know if she'd heard from you. Or if you'd been here.

Actually, she said, they wanted to know a lot of things.

Must be that parking ticket I never paid, I said. No wonder the country's in the state it is.

I nodded at the TV.

There's the cavalry putting in a full shift giving the miners a good pasting. All day, in the hot sun, handling those big horses. In full uniform, not to mention riot gear. Carrying those heavy sticks. While the whiz-kids on the plainclothes squad are spending public money to track down phantom parkers.

My wife looked at me.

I don't know what all this is about, she said. And I don't want to know. They didn't tell me. And I didn't ask.

She got up from the sofa and crossed the room.

They left this, she said.

It was a copy of the *Echo*, folded. I looked at the picture she pointed to on the front page.

All it says in the paper is Serious Charges, she said. Including Assault on the Police.

I couldn't get over the picture. I had to laugh.

Can't they do better than that? I said. Couldn't you have given them a decent photo?

All we want is for you to go, she said. Leave us alone. You can't stay here.

I saw how they do this on TV once, I said. It's like Mr Potato Head. They have all these different eyes and eyebrows and noses and mouths. And hair and hairlines. And ears. All on clear plastic sheets. So you choose the nearest type for each and then keep fitting one on top of the other. Build up the whole picture.

Hey, I said to my wife. Or like that other game the kids had. Where you have these sets of faces, bodies, legs? And you swop them around? So Mr Bull the Butcher in his boater ends up with Mr Pipe the Plumber's body and the legs of Miss Prim the Spinster.

I laughed.

Miss Prim the sexton's daughter. The sexton's man-crazed, sex-mad daughter. I told the sexton and the sexton tolled his bell. He pulled his clapper. Dangled his dong.

I looked at the picture again. I showed it to my wife.

Would you say this man was a criminal type? I said. Or not?

I pulled the face to suit. (The corpse's deadlit eyes. The puffy cheeks. Brain of Cromagnon Man.)

I went to the mirror. I looked at my face. Looked at the picture. Threw the paper down.

Call up my lawyers, I told my wife. Tell them this time we'll sue.

She was watching me. She wasn't laughing at the joke. Then she was looking down. He was already looking at his hands. I could see him breathing. Like he was trying to keep himself doing it. Steady and often.

John McVicar said it was only the police photofit that kept him at large for so long, I said. I see what he means.

I'd just sensed him look towards the cupboard in the corner again. (Not at it. Barely towards it. Barely a nervous flicker of the eyelids.)

But by now I understood.

It was like when I tried the porch door outside and it was already an inch ajar (the way I knew it would be. I didn't even have to risk a noise turning the knob).

(Because there are times when you seem to control everything, understand everything. You can slip through walls. See into cupboards.)

Hey, I said. You got any more to drink?

That was the last bottle, my wife said.

There's some brandy, he said.

(Only he didn't wait quite long enough before saying it. Like I said, my wife is smart. She knows better than to try that. Or ought to. But this guy is duller than a brick. He thinks he's going to get me slewed. And then I'll roll across and snore in the corner, like the rat in the cider cellar in that story Mandy had.)

She'll get it, I said. Relax.

I strolled out into the space between him and the corner where the cupboard was. His eyes blinked away from mine and looked at my wife as she brought the bottle. It was almost half full.

Join me? I said.

He shook his head.

All this for me? Hey, I said. You trying to get me slewed? You trying to take advantage of a poor girl?

I laughed. But that first swig of brandy was hot.

Did you get her slewed, by the way? I said. You know, the first time? After that game? When France beat Wales? On the old hallowed turf? When you met? In the Royal Hotel? Bumped into each other amid drunken thousands on the sticky carpet of the Sportsman's Bar?

His eyes wavered, then just sort of slid somewhere else. I looked at the bottle.

Rémy Martin. Is this your brand? I said. Your cognac? The one you honour and cherish above all others? Till death do you part? Of course, I'm not a connoisseur, me, I said. As you know.

I took another mouthful. It was as hot as heartburn. I looked at my wife. I knew from my voice I was losing it a bit. Sometimes it hits you suddenly like that with spirits.

So what did they want?

She looked at him. Looked at me.

They wanted to know if I'd seen you.

She looked at me. Looked at him. Looked at me.

I told them I hadn't seen you. But that you'd been here. Recently.

What do you mean, 'been here'?

On the mountain, she said. Spying on the place.

What you talking about? I said. 'On the mountain'?

She just shook her head.

Eh? I said. What you fucking talking about?

She threw her hands up.

How many people do you think are going to park a blue and white American car up that little road? How many American cars do you think there are round here? Come to that, she said, how many men with shoulder-length black hair and cowboy boots are going to be wandering over this mountain, and she jerked a thumb back at it, with a gun? You were seen, she said. You're hard to miss.

I grinned.

So who saw me? I said.

His cousin saw you, she said. He lives over the back. And you talked to some friends of ours, miners, on picket duty.

Did I? I said.

This is a small community, she said. Strangers get noticed. And people talk, In fact people do nothing but talk. Especially now, with this strike.

His cousin, eh?

I looked at him. Looked at her. Grinned.

His cousin, I said, and your boyfriend.

She looked at me. They both looked at me. Then looked at each other. Then looked at me again.

You're not going to start that again are you? she said. Me and my boyfriends?

Anyway, he said. The police were right about one thing.

You don't say.

He got up from the chair.

They reckoned you'd be back, he said.

Then it got a little ridic., not to say comic, with him moving out into the room real casual (like his legs were, you know, stiff from all that sitting), and me wandering just as casual (or even casualler) in the same direction. (Both of us acting like this was the way we both just happened to be drifting.) I just made sure I stayed between him and that cupboard door.

Oh, I said. So the police said that?

The one did, she said. He said you might come here again. He said you probably would. So you can see you can't stay here.

Damn, I said. Foiled again. They must have put it all together, I said. All the, you know, pieces. The whole fucking jigsaw. One of those wooden ones the kids used to have.

I laughed.

That's the only kind a policeman can do. Ones with ten pieces. *Big* pieces. Cut out of plywood. With a jig saw, I said. A 'jig saw'. That's why they call them that.

He said men on the run were actually very predictable, she said. Particularly if you knew something about them, background and so on. Their weak point was, they always thought they were being very devious and clever.

Tell that to the two in hospital, I told her.

And what infuriated me suddenly was how you can live your ordinary life and not know someone's tracking you, piecing you together. *Thinking* you. Because they might have been watching me for days or weeks. All the time I was building a dossier on Rusty, they might have been putting together a picture on me. (Though that pair might have knocked to sell me a ticket to the policemen's ball, for all the fucking difference it makes now.)

(And what does it matter. There are things you'll never know. Whether they're knitting you up or unravelling you. There always are. Like whether my wife ever fancied Patsy, in the old days, watching them that one night, laughing at that joke I didn't even think was funny. Or whether there were other men back then, men I never had even that kind of passing suspicion about, or never even knew, Jesus Christ, I must have been so dull and trusting in those days, as if just because a woman lets *you* fuck her no one else is as well.)

But like the man says: Be a hammer not a nail.

So that was when I got tired of playing games.

You just stay where you are, I told him.

I went backwards to that tall cupboard in the corner, opened it. I had the knife out, just in case. I was trying to keep an eye on him too, and I didn't see it at first. Then the golf clubs fell over and it was there, behind the bag.

My wife said you were a bit of a sportsman, I said.

Your wife? she said.

Just stay where you are. I told him.

I took it out and broke it. It wasn't loaded. I looked in the cupboard. There was a big square biscuit tin on an upper shelf, *Teatime Assortment*. I reached for it, threw it on the floor and squatted quickly to take the lid off. It was just full of household junk. But there was another tin behind it. I squatted to that one.

Look, Stewart, he said.

I stood up with the knife.

Stay there, I said. Or I'll gut you like a fish.

I looked into the tin. Then I looked at him and shook my head.

Jesus Christ, I said. Don't you know anything? There are kids in this house.

(I mean, for fuck's sake. What kind of Husband And Father doesn't know any more about guns than to leave the empty shotgun with the cartridges just handy on the shelf above it? I mean, hasn't he ever heard of a kid using a chair?)

My kids, I said. My kids.

His eyelids kind of fluttered.

I'm going to confiscate this, I said. To coin a phrase. You're not fit to be in charge of it.

I squatted again and took a couple of handfuls of the shells and put them into my side pockets. I didn't even slip a brace into the barrels. For him I didn't need a loaded gun.

Let alone fit to be in charge of two children, I said.

I looked at my wife.

Get my kids up, I told her. Wake them up and get them dressed. You want me to go. I'll go. But I'm taking them with me. I'm taking custody of them.

Look, she said.

Move, I said.

You slag, I said. You fucking poxy cunting stinking slag. *Move*.

Fifteen

And the sudden anger, rage comes back even now, half-way up a mountain, the hatred of that bitch, in her fancy country kitchen, with her linen napkins and her napkin rings, and her Cossack trousers and those boots she was wearing, wearing even in the house, because for him, wearing them for him. I bet he picked them out for her, I bet they went round all the shops to find him a pair just like that, with those belts and buckles fitted like a stirrup. I thought they were black until I saw them again in the light by the fireplace, but they were green, that kind of almost blackish green holly is. I suppose that makes them 'classy'? Okay, so they probably cost the earth. So fucking what? I bet they think it's worth it. I bet they get their mileage from those boots, even if she hardly puts them on outside the bedroom. What's money compared to gratification? What's anything in the fucking world, compared to that?

I stop in the black bracken, sweating, panting. I put the gun down for a second across a greyish rock, where I can see it in the moon. Rubbing my neck doesn't do any good any more.

Not just the green boots. The other clothes. All those new clothes I've never seen, never seen her in, drawers and drawers of them, hangers and hangers full, upstairs, in that bedroom, all the creases and crotches, and buttons and bows, and hooks and eyes, yeah, hooks and eyes, the terrible fucking hooks and eyes of Memory. Things with zips and drawstrings and gussets and stitches and straps. Close things and swirly things. Colours she chose for him, wears for him. Takes off for him. Filmy blouses like a silk handkerchief you can crumple in one hand. A whole drawer of pairs and pairs of silky pants.

Sit down, I tell Mandy.

I pick up the gun.

Have a rest.

As I plunge down through the bracken she starts whining.

Where you going? she is saying. Where you going?

Two minutes, I shout back. Something I forgot.

As I get lower the snivelling turns into a scream. But I can't stop for that. Not now. The Spartans left their kids out on the mountainside at *birth*. All fucking night. I can't stop for that.

Because I hate to think of how light they must think they've got off.

And let's face it, it wasn't me who looked to where the gun was. (He would have gone for it himself, and used it, if I'd given him the chance. If I hadn't been a bit too wised up for that.) And if he hadn't brought the gun into it, the whole thing might have turned out differently. Without the gun we would have had to keep up a pretence. A kind of politeness if you like. If he'd only acted like he accepted the situation, then everything would have been alright.

But once he started looked at that cupboard he was saying, Anything Goes. From Hereon fucking In.

So what made the situation serious was the way *he* acted. I missed seeing that at the time somehow. That was probably why I didn't even load the thing then. I didn't want the situation to look too *heavy*. (Can you imagine that? Him ready to go for a shotgun soon as I move a yard out of the way to let him. And me trying to keep things, I won't say friendly, but manageable, anyway. *Restrained*.) It was like that with Rusty. Sometimes I'm slow on things like that. And people probably think I'm weak. My fucking trouble is, I want to be too nice. I let people take advantage, make a monkey out of me.

Because I want people to like me. And it is. It's a weakness.

But all that's over now. There's just me and my daughter now. And it's her I feel sorry for, because she didn't ask for a situation like this. She didn't ask to have a mother like that, with her poodle of a husband. She didn't ask to have a Stand-In father. Kids never get a choice in things like that. And it's the kids who suffer.

I can hear my breath shake as I lumber across a patch of bare grass. My knee still hurts like a bastard from where I tripped and fell earlier. But it's nothing like my head pounding and the sweat on my shirt and even trousers sticking to me, a heat I can feel glistening on my face like I'm going to explode.

I take out the bottle of brandy and pull the cork and swig from it but there's barely a trickle left, if you had a second bottle you'd say it was empty. But when it's the only one you do what I do and hold it upturned until a last drop then another drop distil on the tip of my tongue, though I can't taste it now, it's not even warm in my mouth any more. Then I throw the bottle away from me and it's as if it curves away in the moonlight in a long slow arc over the glittering black bracken, I fall over, and it's seconds before I hear the smash, far away, on the scree like that other bottle I threw over the cliff yesterday.

I get up. And it's like a dream going over this dry-stone wall again, an old dream in the old black-and-white movie of the moonlight, if only my head would stop pulsing and the sweat, the sweat's running down me like a shower curtain now.

And the lights are on in every room, front and back, up and down, so even the garden is ablaze with waste electricity, it's on full behind the glowing screen the bedroom curtains make, the sharp black cross of struts. Not that they're up there now, they're through with that, the dim-lit bedroom glow, the shine on eyes, the hooks and

307

eyes, the straps and boots. The primping in the mirror and the pumping on the bed. They've done with that. They're through with that, once and for all. They're sitting downstairs with the lights on, sitting there holding their breath or even holding hands and waiting for the police they must have telephoned the minute after I went out a quarter of an hour ago.

I don't even look at the porch door. I know it's locked now, just as I knew it would be ajar before. I know they'll have closed all the windows and locked all the outside doors and probably blocked the fucking chimney too, all that would have been the second thing they thought of after putting down the phone.

But let's face it, doors are only wood and windows glass.

I take two cartridges out of my pocket. Break, load it, snap it. Two's company. Three's a crowd. But one's a perfect number. I won't need no third. I'd rather hole up in all this brilliance and wait for them to bring the TV crews in and more lights and take my T-shirt off and sit fat as a Buddha and use a kitchen-knife, a kitchen-knife honed thin on a stone step.

I stand at the window I was at before. Nothing has changed. Everything is flooding together like into a Black Hole where you meet your own self coming back. Me, I'm running faster than the Ely River, glittery and black, the incoming cunt smell, sea tide off the flats.

Inside, the bunch of grapes in the dish and the stalks and the hexagonal plates and the spat black pips and the baguette rounds and the wholemeal homemeal homemade slices and the bottle of wine empty now and the candle to dine by, the fucking candle for Christ's sake, they're big on atmosphere, this pair, and not in an old, snotted wine-bottle even like in some phoney wine-bar but in a proper candleholder, a heavy brass saucer, with a handle, like Wee Willie Winkie took to light his way to bed, here snuffed out, brief candle, between two used plates. But I don't need no candle burning in a window to find my way home tonight. Not in all this.

And now, far away down the valley I notice for the first time the two-note music. *Dah*-duh *dah*-duh. The only tune a police driver can whistle.

I stand outside and look in at the laid table and it's as if I can't believe it's real, or at least that it hasn't been arranged, it's framed in the window like a kind of still-life that would be too corny or old-hat for anyone to bother to paint any more or, like I say, a glossy photo in some expensive book of recipes of French Country-Style Cooking, every pip and pared cheese-rind on those plates positioned with care, even the way the label of the empty bottle is turned away from me so as not to give the wine a free plug since it's the food, man, it's a way of eating and a whole way of life you're selling here not just a brand, oh, and the napkins, yeah, the linen fucking napkins they used to dab their prissy mouths like someone in a film, even those stiff-looking folds making it look like they were flung next to the plates with force or arranged again by some ad-man art-school graduate to make it look as if they had been, flung to suggest the haste, the unseemly fucking haste, with which the romantic diners left the table to go elsewhere, like with the quarter-inch of unfinished wine in each stemmed glass, and all that's missing in fact is the still-smouldering cigarette that bears the lipstick traces, An Airline Ticket to Romantic Places, Oh, How the Ghost Of You Clings, These Foolish Things, I mean for Jesus Aitch Christ's sake it's like one of those corny tableaus or an old scene with a Moral title, *An Unexpectedly Early Night* or *Interrupted By Passion*.

Except that, looking for a last time at that delicately littered dining table through that ground-floor window just before I smash my way in through it with the fucking gun-butt, what I actually think is: *The Last Supper*.

A Selected List of Fiction Available from Mandarin

While every effort is made to keep prices low, it is sometimes necessary to increase prices at short notice. Mandarin Paperbacks reserves the right to show new retail prices on covers which may differ from those previously advertised in the text or elsewhere.

The prices shown below were correct at the time of going to press.

☐	7493 1352 8	**The Queen and I**	Sue Townsend	£4.99
☐	7493 0540 1	**The Liar**	Stephen Fry	£4.99
☐	7493 1132 0	**Arrivals and Departures**	Lesley Thomas	£4.99
☐	7493 0381 6	**Loves and Journeys of Revolving Jones**	Leslie Thomas	£4.99
☐	7493 0942 3	**Silence of the Lambs**	Thomas Harris	£4.99
☐	7493 0946 6	**The Godfather**	Mario Puzo	£4.99
☐	7493 1561 X	**Fear of Flying**	Erica Jong	£4.99
☐	7493 1221 1	**The Power of One**	Bryce Courtney	£4.99
☐	7493 0576 2	**Tandia**	Bryce Courtney	£5.99
☐	7493 0563 0	**Kill the Lights**	Simon Williams	£4.99
☐	7493 1319 6	**Air and Angels**	Susan Hill	£4.99
☐	7493 1477 X	**The Name of the Rose**	Umberto Eco	£4.99
☐	7493 0896 6	**The Stand-in**	Deborah Moggach	£4.99
☐	7493 0581 9	**Daddy's Girls**	Zoe Fairbairns	£4.99

All these books are available at your bookshop or newsagent, or can be ordered direct from the address below. Just tick the titles you want and fill in the form below.

Cash Sales Department, PO Box 5, Rushden, Northants NN10 6YX.
Fax: 0933 410321 : Phone 0933 410511.

Please send cheque, payable to 'Reed Book Services Ltd.', or postal order for purchase price quoted and allow the following for postage and packing:

£1.00 for the first book, 50p for the second; **FREE POSTAGE AND PACKING FOR THREE BOOKS OR MORE PER ORDER.**

NAME (Block letters) ....

ADDRESS ....

....

☐ I enclose my remittance for ....

☐ I wish to pay by Access/Visa Card Number ☐☐☐☐☐☐☐☐☐☐☐☐☐☐☐☐

Expiry Date ☐☐☐☐

Signature ....

Please quote our reference: MAND